Without You

A Pine Tree Bay Book

By

Gilly M. Rose

Copyright © 2020 Gilly M. Rose

The moral right of the author has been asserted.

All characters and events in this publication, other than those clearly in the public domain, are fictitious and any resemblance to real persons, living or dead, or real companies/business names, is purely coincidental.

All rights reserved. This book or any portion thereof
may not be reproduced or used in any manner whatsoever
without the express written permission of the publisher
except for the use of brief quotations in a book review.

First Published 2020 by Balcary Press

This second (edited) edition published 2021

www.gillymrose.com

ISBN9798573388656

Written in British English except where other versions/languages are necessary for authenticity of character and story.

For Michael, Mac & Angus.
The best support team a girl ever had.

CHAPTER ONE
12 Years Earlier...

Jem

London

The last time she ever saw him was two days before their wedding.

It was only remarkable with hindsight; Nick, leaping on to the underground train whilst Jem raced across the platform, the sliding doors that crashed together about two inches from her nose.

She remembered looking left and right along the length of the carriages, hoping to see those same doors slide open. But the train had simply shuddered, heaving itself into action, just as Nick turned to see that she hadn't made it.

From inside the carriage, he had burst out laughing. Making a face and a goofy, 'Oops' gesture, he'd mimed phoning her later. And Jem had stuck her tongue out and crossed her eyes, which made him laugh even harder. Perhaps he had turned away as the train moved off, pressed his fingers to the bridge of his nose… she would never be entirely sure.

Stranded on the platform, panting slightly from their mad scramble down the escalator – a smile still hovering about her lips – Jem stood oblivious to the fact that her entire future was disappearing into a tunnel. She took a step back, obeying the disembodied voice that instructed her to *mind the gap,* and watched her reflection flicker like a faulty lightbulb in the windows of the departing train.

In the years to follow, she would remember every detail of that moment. The deserted platform. The empty coffee cups skittering back and forth beneath the plastic seats. The abandoned copies of *The Metro* fluttering in the back-draft.

Mind the gap.
Mind the huge, gaping chasm where your future used to be.

But she didn't know the half of it then. It would be two more days before she found out the size of the gap she'd be having to mind. And it would be much longer than that before she found out what happened to Nick Townsend.

CHAPTER TWO
Present Day - 30th September

Matthew

London

'Any good?'

The attractive woman sitting across the aisle from Matthew Albright indicated the battered paperback.

'Still making my mind up.' Matthew gave the woman a friendly smile, before returning his gaze to the book. In truth, he couldn't have answered her with any honesty – he'd been staring at the same page for at least a week now. The number fifty-six bus rattled and bumped beneath him, splashing its way down Goswell Road; the pages of his novel curling in the collective fug of fifty or so damp commuters.

'So unusual to find someone reading an actual book these days.' The woman wasn't giving up.

'Mmm.' Matthew nodded and smiled. He kept his focus on the pages in front of him.

Undeterred, she leaned over and lowered her voice 'And it's doubly rare to find an attractive man doing so.'

Matthew decided he could do with the walk anyway.

'Have this one on me,' he smiled, standing up and handing her the novel, just as the doors of the bus sprang open at the Barbican. *Love in the Time of Cholera,* the woman wrinkled her nose.

Stepping down onto the wet pavement Matthew slung his leather satchel across his chest. The bag bounced annoyingly against his hip with every stride, but he'd been using it for years and refused to swap it for anything new.

Frowning slightly, he thought about the woman on the bus. It had happened a few times in the last month but he still wasn't anywhere near ready. The sight of the slim white band of skin on the third finger of his left hand still jarred… reminders of Lissa seemed to be everywhere.

After three years of telling himself that ninety percent was good enough, that some couples – if they were honest – didn't even have that, the matter had finally been taken out of his hands. She was good like that, Lissa; knew her worth. That's why he'd fallen in love with her in the first place. Well, almost.

It didn't help that it was all completely a mess of his own making and Lissa certainly hadn't deserved that. After the final heartbreaking analysis, on both sides, she'd summed it up better than he would ever have been able to. 'I thought we were in the midst of this heady romance,' she'd sniffed. 'I thought that – with the super quick marriage and everything – you were sweeping me off my feet. But in reality, you weren't rushing ahead so much as trying not to look down. In case you stopped yourself making the leap.'

Matthew hadn't been able to argue. He should never have asked her to marry him in the first place. But, in the twelve years since he'd given up on looking for 'it' – believing 'it' to have been and gone – Lissa was the only person who had even come close. And he might have fooled himself for a while, but he hadn't fooled her. Well not in the end anyway. Just three years on from their wedding, the divorce was final. This was what had been running around his brain for ten bus stops and two paragraphs of his novel.

As he approached Paternoster Square, the feeble autumn sunshine tried to break through the clouds, but still a light drizzle persisted. Matthew cursed the umbrella wielding commuters, coming towards him at all angles like something out of an arcade game. Passing the steps to St. Paul's, he slowed his pace, allowing his eyes to travel upward. This was where the trouble with Matthew's marriage had really started – even though he hadn't even known Lissa existed back then. That bright Saturday morning, twelve years ago when Matthew had paced up and down the cathedral steps, with the growing certainty that Nick Townsend, his best friend – *the groom* – was about to run out on his bride to be: Jem.

And he'd been right; Nick had failed to show, leaving Matthew torn between rage and relief.

He could picture it as clearly as if it had happened only yesterday; Nick's father, his MBE swinging proudly from his right lapel, stumbling around the cathedral gardens clutching a top hat, whilst his mother chain smoked Dunhills and checked her phone every few seconds. Until finally, the call that both parents had been dreading came through. Nick hadn't been delayed, there was no hold up, he simply wasn't coming. It was seismic. Then someone had to deliver the news to Jem…

Matthew's feet clanked along the metal surface of Millennium Bridge, jolting his mind back to the present. Why did she continue to plague his thoughts, even now? He shook his head. He couldn't think about this today. *Wouldn't* let himself be derailed, not today of all days.

Crossing the Thames he glimpsed the swollen river swirling beneath his feet – the usual stew of debris and diesel spill that floated aimlessly above the murk. Running a hand through his dark blonde hair it felt more than a little damp and he hoped it wouldn't curl into an unprofessional mop before he reached his destination.

Today Matthew was meeting with Gerry Monroe, the son of Canadian billionaire Frank Monroe, and he needed the interview to go well. The Monroes had a vast network of potential clients. If Gerry liked what he saw, Matthew's freelance assignments could be all set for some years to come.

Matthew had dressed carefully for the meeting and he *had* thought twice about the satchel. He knew Gerry by reputation, who didn't? The famous property tycoon was the sharp type, having a fondness for Armarni suits with a classic Oxford brogue. But whilst Matthew wanted the job badly, he had stubbornly picked up his old favourite on his way out the door. And well, it went perfectly with his herringbone jacket – added a rural twist and set the right tone for where the job was based.

Pine Tree Bay.

Matthew had to admit it sounded almost too idyllic; a coastal resort in South West Scotland that Frank Monroe had built back in the nineties as some kind of homage to his ancestors. But whilst the resort, like Frank, was proudly Scottish, the design was all New England charm. The whole town including shops, art galleries, restaurants, pubs and hotels had been built in a clapboard style. If the pictures were anything to go by, it looked like the perfect coastal escape. Matthew had to admit that that was part of the appeal – a few months of sea air, in nowheresville – it was just what he needed right now to clear his head.

By the time he reached the OXO Tower and rode the elevator to the top floor, the sun was streaming through the clouds. The doors opened smoothly revealing a bright restaurant foyer where he was greeted warmly by the maitre d'. As Matthew threaded his way through linen table cloths and gleaming cutlery, he didn't rush; savouring the spectacle of the panoramic London skyline which reigned majestically over the Embankment. He could do this.

Approaching the businessman's table, Matthew took a deep settling breath… then immediately wished he hadn't. Gerry's aftershave greeted him from ten paces out; a heady, cloying scent that might explain why his media coverage rarely included a companion. Matthew found himself leaning backwards as Gerry extended his hand.

'Matt, welcome. Thank you for coming to meet with us this morning.' The affable Canadian drawl was at odds with the man's reputation for steely corporate negotiations but still it grated on him. There was only one other person who had ever called him Matt... Matthew suppressed a cough and returned Gerry's vice-like grip as firmly as possible without turning the introduction into a pissing contest.

Telling Matthew to 'Sit,' Gerry clicked his fingers to get the attention of a nearby waitress. When she didn't respond Gerry raised his voice to a gruff bark, sending the young girl into a fluster. Matthew felt his hackles rise. He didn't sit down on Gerry's command, choosing instead to offer his hand to the man's assistant – a boyish looking chap with a weak chin who turned out to be called Marcus. The young man fumbled over his words and looked generally uncomfortable introducing himself without his boss's cue.

In his own time, Matthew sat down and took his notebook and pen from the faded leather satchel that Gerry Monroe was surveying with unveiled disdain. *Just the breakfast then...* Matthew thought; clearly he wouldn't be working for this man any time soon. Deciding to have some fun however, he leaned back in his chair and crossed one foot over his knee. 'Ok, Gerry,' he clicked the top of his pen with a flourish. 'So what's the deal with this Pine Tree Bay place then?'

From the corner of his eye, he watched as Marcus's jaw fell south into a long, silent gasp.

Jem

Pine Tree Bay Resort, South West Scotland

Good grief!

Madam Zelda's lop-sided wig was seriously throwing Jem for six. She was twitchy enough about having to go along with all this codswallop in the first place without throwing a comedy toupee into the mix.

Before you start looking into the future, 'Madam Zelda', how about starting with a mirror?

Jem covered her mouth to stem the snigger that was begging to break free. She thought of all the things she could be doing back at the cafe instead of sitting in some gaudy motorhome whilst Mystic Meg here peddled her 'psychic' gibberish. How on earth did people keep their faces straight?

The fortune teller was now fanning cards out across a velvet tablecloth. Jem tried to concentrate and block out the voice in her head that was asking, '*What on earth are you, of all people, doing here?*'

It was all Madeleine Beaver's fault; Jem had been strong armed into this fortune telling 'road test' by the chairwoman of the Pine Tree Bay events committee. Today was the last day of September and all vendors being hired for the upcoming Pumpkin Festival – set to run throughout the whole of October – had to be vetted.

Jem had drawn the short straw and got landed with this clairvoyance claptrap – Madeleine treated the hiring of festival vendors as if she were assembling a crack team of MI6 personnel. The officious woman had *insisted* that Jem was the ideal person to check out the fortune teller, being 'more sceptical than the rest of the committee put together.' It said a lot about Madeleine that she considered this to be a compliment.

Still, Jem wanted to play her part in ensuring the festival was a success. It was important to Pine Tree and there were lots of visitors booked in to accommodation all over their little town on the strength of it. And, as Madeleine had been quick to point out, the fortune teller's title suggested she could be running a totally different kind of outfit altogether…

Focus on the cards. Focus on the cards! Jem willed herself back to the task in hand.

'Now, select any ten cards that you are drawn to my dear,' Madam Zelda was saying.

Jem waited to be drawn to certain cards whilst the fortune teller looked on expectantly, but the sound of waves rolling onto the beach outside, together with the salty breeze that wafted in through the lace curtains had Jem longing to be outside. The only thing she was feeling drawn to was the door.

The fact of the matter was, Jem didn't *do* destiny. As she was fond of explaining to anyone who would listen – this fate business was all well and good but it would come and kick you up the arse as soon as look at you. And usually when you least expected it.

Yes she knew people just loved to imagine they were travelling along some preordained timeline, but that was just a load of romantic nonsense. Life was a series of random events – influenced to a greater or lesser degree by how much attention you paid. And Jem paid attention. The only person she trusted to steer her future was the one staring back at her when she cleaned her teeth in the morning. It was a wisdom that had served her very well these past twelve years. As to the years before that… Well, the less said about those the better.

No, she thought – choosing any old random cards and passing them over to Madam Zelda – there was no leaving anything to 'destiny' for Jemima Small. Her life was a very well organised pursuit. She had ticks in all the right boxes. Nice house, successful business, a very good social life with great friends and neighbours. And, of course, her beloved black Labrador, Bear. Everything she needed was right there in that neat list. Life was ordered. Well planned. There was zero risk of emotional upheaval. It. Was. All. Good. She smiled to herself, satisfied. Then immediately frowned. Why was Madam Zelda looking at her with that strange expression?

The fortune teller had carefully laid Jem's chosen selection of Tarot cards on the table, muttering and tutting to herself as each one was revealed.

At length, she sat back and shook her head gloomily. 'Well, this is a right to-do isn't it?' she said, in a Yorkshire accent so thick it could have wedged open a door.

'Is it?' Jem looked blankly at the cards having absolutely no clue as to what any of them meant.

'Let's just say that these cards tell me about your past as well as your future, and in your case I'm afraid dearie, it looks like history is about to repeat itself.'

'Oh really?' Jem tried to smile politely but it morphed into a frozen grimace. *As if she'd let that happen.*

Madam Zelda paused for a moment, considering where to begin. 'Now, let's start with this chappie in your past', she pointed an arthritic finger at a card with a knight on horseback. 'This is the Knight of Swords,' she said, slowly looking up at Jem. 'The knight on the white charger. Well, he's *the one,* in all the stories, isn't he hmmm?'

Christ what next? The Ladybird Book of Tarot? Jem snorted inwardly.

'But,' the fortune teller hesitated, with a theatrical sweep of the knobbly digit, 'this man is ambitious. He'll stop at nothing to get what he wants. And the way he's grouped here with The Fool, Three of Swords and The Tower.' She raised her eyes slowly. 'Suggests a reckless man who caused you a lot of heartbreak?'

Jem blinked hard to stop from rolling her eyes. *Oh come on! Like that didn't apply to half the thirty nine year old women in the country.*

With no response forthcoming, Madam Zelda returned to the reading. 'But there was another young man around at the time too. Here look,' the woman tapped another card with her shell-pink fingernail. 'The Knight of Pentacles.' The old woman was gazing at *this* knight as if he was her favourite grandson. 'Now, this card symbolises a very reliable young man with a strong sense of responsibility and commitment. He seems to have got caught up in all of this too…' she tailed off, watching Jem shift uncomfortably in her seat. 'Is any of this making sense lovey?'

Jem shrugged and raised her eyebrows in a non-committal gesture to indicate it possibly might.

Madam Zelda sat back with a heavy sigh. She studied Jem for a long moment – long enough to make the younger woman feel hot under the collar – before inclining her head toward the cards. 'You don't believe in any of this do you dear?'

Jem squirmed under the woman's scrutiny. 'I, er…wouldn't say that exactly. I've just always been a bit sceptical about this type of thing that's all.' She could hardly say she was only there to check the old girl wasn't running a knocking-shop could she?

'So what *are* you doing here then?' Madam Zelda looked bewildered. 'I mean, I'm happy to read the cards and take your money, but if you don't believe in any of this you're just paying for advice you're never going to take.' She shook her head sadly. 'And seeing what I do here in these cards, well, you of all people can't afford to ignore 'em.'

'Is it really that bad?' Jem felt a stirring of alarm. Even though she didn't actually believe in any of this rubbish, she wasn't up for hearing anything truly awful. You know… just in case.

'It's not a question of good or bad, it's…' Madam Zelda paused as if deciding whether to go on. 'Look love, let's forget these for a minute.' She waved her hand over the table. 'Can you keep a secret?'

'Of course,' said Jem, silently praying that the old woman wasn't about to confess to seeing dead people or dancing naked under a full moon.

'The truth is, this job can get bloody boring at times. People come in here for a bit of excitement. They want to walk out that door thinking their whole life's about to change, but I can only tell them what the cards tell me. Most people are going to go home and live the same life they've been living for the past twenty years because that's the life they *chose*, the life they planned for themselves.' She hesitated a moment. 'But *you*...you had a path all mapped out once – involving these two men – she pointed at the knight cards. But the rug got pulled from under you at the last minute.'

Jem chewed on her lip and swallowed hard not wanting to admit that this whole episode was starting to freak her out. 'And you can see all this in these cards?' she asked, nodding toward the table.

'I just read what they tell me love. And these here are saying you're in for a bit of a re-run I'm afraid. The past is about to knock on your door... Now, do you want to hear the rest or not?'

'Well,' Jem shrugged airily. 'As I have booked the full half hour...'

'Ok then, let's crack on.' The older woman resettled to her task before clapping her hands together in delight. 'Now, the first thing you need to know is that *everything* is about to change!'

'Look, you really don't need to make up anything exciting on my account,' Jem insisted. 'I'm the one customer who *is* totally fine hearing that everything's going to stay the same. The past is the past and I have things in perfect order,' she smiled smugly. 'I work pretty hard to keep them that way.'

'Well you'll have to forget all that.' Madam Zelda waved a blithe hand over Jem's protestations. 'Now see, over here in your future, the King of Swords and the King of Pentacles... See how these are the same as the knight cards your drew over there for your past?'

Jem peered at the table. She might as well humour the old bat.

'In Tarot, The *king* cards often represent the older, mature versions of the *knight* cards.' The fortune teller paused for a moment, giving the clear implication some space to land.

'You're not suggesting...?' Jem shook her head in disbelief.

'Well, yes dear. It looks like one, or perhaps both, of these men could be about to make a reappearance in your life.'

'I can assure you that is *never* going to happen,' Jem chuckled.

'Well, that's not what the cards say... Anyhow that's not the troublesome part–'

'It gets *worse*?'

'Oh yes much worse,' Madam Zelda confirmed breezily. 'See here, The Ten of Swords?' Jem looked closely at a picture of a man lying face down with ten knives sticking out of his back. 'There is someone, or something, that is going to be working against you.

'How reassuring.'

'Now it could be these two chappies we've just talked about. But it could also be someone or something else entirely.'

'And to think I was worried that this wouldn't be an exact science,'

Jem murmured, before asking more clearly, 'And what about this card?'

'Hmmm…. The Five of Pentacles.' Madam Zelda pursed her lips. 'This is another warning card. It's telling you to keep your eyes open. Otherwise you run the risk of turning your back on the very thing that represents the solution to your problem.'

'But I don't have any problems.'

Madam Zelda smiled vaguely. 'If you say so my dear.'

'And…er you say this is all going to happen when?'

Somewhere deep inside the motorhome an oven timer started to beep.

'Oooh that's my pot-roast ready, our time's up I'm afraid love. It's a shame because I was right enjoying this one.'

Jem looked around; the woman was speaking as if a dozen clients were waiting outside the door. 'Well, if you don't have anyone else to see, perhaps we could carry on for a few minutes?'

'Oh I *am* sorry lovey.' Madam Zelda tapped her watch then pointed heavenwards. 'The spirits only give me half an hour at a time.'

'But do the cards say everything is going to be all right in the end?'

Madam Zelda placed a gentle hand over Jem's. 'What it all boils down to, is that you're going to have a choice to make. You just need to make sure it's the right choice that's all.'

'But how will I know what the right one *is*?'

'Well now, I'm afraid, the cards aren't clear on that.'

The only response Jem could manage was to sit open mouthed.

Madame Zelda waited for Jem to finish her zombie impression, eventually clearing her throat and saying, 'Well, now that's all sorted, there's just the small matter of the payment?'

Sorted? Jem fumbled for her bag, feeling as if she was coming round from a bad dream. 'Is this the part where I cross your palm with silver?' she managed to joke weakly.

'I'd prefer plastic if you don't mind. Don't like to keep too much cash in the van.' Madam Zelda pulled a card device from under her long black robe.

Rifling her purse for a debit card Jem handed it to the woman and watched she pressed it against the machine. As the transaction went through and Madam Zelda rattled on about the marvellous high-speed broadband connection to be found here in Pine Tree Bay, Jem nodded distractedly.

Handing back the card, Madam Zelda gave Jem's hand another little squeeze. 'I shouldn't worry yourself my dear,' she said reassuringly. 'These things have a way of working themselves out in the end.' Which Jem found discomfortingly vague coming from someone who purported to see the future.

As she made her way out, Jem had the strangest sense that reality had tilted. When the motorhome door opened, it was not the beach of Pine Tree Bay that greeted her but the steps of St. Paul's Cathedral and Matthew… She shook her head and took a deep gulp of air then closed her eyes to steady herself.

The air she sucked in was fresh and briny and when she opened her eyes the vision was gone and she was back in the present but still the strange feeling persisted. She looked up and down the shoreline trying to reorient herself. For a clouded moment, the town that had been her home for the last ten years – seemed somehow different. It was as if she were a stranger when, in reality, her cafe and bookshop, Small House Book & Brew, sat waiting for her at one end of the harbour whilst her old granite home book-ended the town at the other.

A sense of the surreal had draped itself about her during the reading and repeating her mantra that it was all twaddle was not shifting it. Before she could fully regain her composure, the reason for all this discomfort came bustling along the road; Madeleine Beaver was advancing rapidly, brandishing the renowned 'festival clipboard' as if it were the winning ticket in tomorrow night's Euromillions draw.

'Jem! Just the person! You're next on my list,' she trilled, pen poised over clipboard. 'Now, are we a 'go' for Gelda?'

'What?' Jem frowned.

Madeleine raised her voice, 'Are-we-a-go-for-Gelda?' she annunciated, nodding her head in the direction of the motorhome.

'Zelda?'

'Who?'

'It's Madam *Zelda* not Gelda.'

'No it's not! It says here it's Gelda!' Madeleine inspected the clipboard.

Jem pointed to a poster in the window of the motorhome.

'Oh no that's so inconvenient!' Madeleine looked horrified. 'I've had five hundred flyers printed inviting people to have their fortunes told by Madam *Gelda*. Do you think she'd consider changing her name for the duration of the festival?'

Jem stood opened mouthed for the second time that morning. Sometimes she didn't even know where to begin with Madeleine.

'Well it's just a hunch, but given that she's been telling fortunes under the name of Madam Zelda for the last fifty years, has a website and all her licenses under that name, not to mention *this*!' Jem pointed again to the poster. 'I'd put good money on it being a *no*.'

Madeleine, completely missing Jem's sarcasm, moved towards the fortune teller's door. 'Well one can only ask I suppose.'

'Madeleine!' Jem leapt in front of the clipboard. 'You cannot possibly expect this lady to change her name for the duration of the festival. It's totally out of the question. We'll never be able to get her to come here again. It can't be more than twenty quid to get the flyers reprinted. I'll stump up the cash myself if necessary.'

'Oh all right then.' Madeleine capitulated in a sulky tone, hastily amending the name on her clipboard. Then, raising her immaculately coiffured head she squinted craftily. 'But clearly you think she's good then? If you're saying we might want her to come back here *again*?'

'Yes, she was very good,' Jem conceded. Despite the befuddled mess the old woman had left her in, she would rather hire her than try to explain any reservations to Madeleine Beaver. Then, detecting that she had piqued the nosey mare's interest more than she would ever care to, she shook her head and shrugged, 'I mean, you know, she's credible enough, for anyone who's into all that mumbo jumbo.'

'That's wonderful! All vendors are now checked. Gerry *will* be pleased!' Madeleine beamed with satisfaction.

'What's this got to do with Gerry Monroe?' Jem's face clouded at the name.

'Well surely you've heard he's coming here on Friday? For the town meeting? Has no-one told you he's stepping into his father's shoes whilst Frank recovers from his illness?'

'Of course.' Jem remembered all too well. 'I wouldn't have thought he'd bother himself with the festival though?'

'Now Jem, Gerry may be an extremely busy man with much greater concerns than our little town, but he will be pleased to to receive *my* full confirmation that all the vendors for the festival have been vetted and secured. His assistant Marcus is flying up to see me personally tonight to go through the whole plan,' she preened. 'You *see*, Gerry *is* interested in the smooth running of events, even if he does prefer the "hands-off" approach.'

'That's the last approach that man favours,' Jem muttered under her breath.

'Pardon me?' Madeleine's nose twitched and her eyes narrowed.

'I just mean… he's got bigger fish to fry surely? Running Frank's entire empire whilst he recovers?' For an uncomfortable moment Jem wilted under the heat of the busybody's laser stare; cursing herself for having gifted the old bag a morsel of gossip. Thankfully however, Madeleine was too busy to dally. Marking her list with an officious tick, she dismissed Jem and set off along the road.

'The Monroe's are never too busy for Pine Tree Bay,' she called over her shoulder as she hurried off to look for her next victim. But she had only gone a few yards before adding, 'And I shall be calling round later for that twenty pounds!'

Jem exhaled as she watched Madeleine go, her high heels receding into the distance at an officious trot. She would never get used to that woman as long as she lived.

CHAPTER THREE
1st October

Jem

By now, the locals who lived and worked in Pine Tree Bay Resort were used to the first impressions of newly arrived tourists; the way they all seemed to look around with the same bewildered admiration. 'But it's just so quaint! I wasn't expecting it to be so charming!'

It was the word 'resort' that caused all the confusion. Visitors expecting some kind of Las Vegas assault on their senses were charmed beyond belief as they strolled along the sea front and gazed out at the gentle surf then back toward the picturesque town, set as it was against a Pine Forest backdrop.

If they continued for a mile or so along the sea front – where the commercial properties gave way to the residential area of the town – the terrain started to rise, eventually transforming into steep cliffs that bordered the east side of the cove. All along this rise, houses that had stood for centuries clung precariously to the hillside as if they may lose their grip at any moment and tumble into the sea.

Nestled at the foot of this hill, was a tall commanding villa called Withershins, where, on the morning after her meeting with Madam Zelda, Jem gently raised her head from the pillow and pulled back the duvet. It was five thirty a.m. and though this was her usual getting-up time, today she felt decidedly groggy. Shuffling her feet around on the wooden floor and locating her sheepskin slippers, she padded down to her warm country kitchen to make her morning cuppa.

At the sound of her footsteps a heavy thumping sound came from in front of the Aga where her twelve year old Labrador, Bear, beat his fat otter tail against the wooden floor then rose from his bed to stretch his legs. Sticking his rear in the air he let out a noisy parp, surprising them both in equal measure. 'Hmmm… Good morning to you too Bear,' Jem muttered as the dog spun round to inspect his own handiwork.

Making her usual builder's-strength morning tea, she pottered through to the glass garden room – an addition in her late grandmother's day – and threw open the French windows. Cinching her robe tightly, she gasped at the sharp chill rushing in to greet her. Autumn was upon them and the garden was covered in the first hard frost of the year. Every shrub and tree seemed to glisten in the morning moonlight but there wasn't a breath of wind; all was silent and still as Bear slid past her, ambling out onto the crisp lawn, leaving a trail of dark paw prints in his wake.

The tide was out but a silvery sea shone in the distance and through tall plumes of pampas she glimpsed the abandoned pools it had left behind. As a child, Jem had been fascinated by rock-pools; those little worlds stranded in time. Later that morning, kids would come to the beach with fishing nets to prod and poke at the water, causing all the inhabitants to scurry under rocks and burrow in the sand, before the sea returned to claim them and start the process all over again. Tiny neighbourhoods, bound together, then torn apart by a force completely outside their control.

Taking a sip of the scalding tea, Jem's mind wandered to the email she'd received at the end of last week. Yesterday Madeleine had alluded to it too; on Friday morning Gerry Monroe would be arriving in Pine Tree Bay for a town meeting. The telltale line between Jem's eyes deepened as she thought back to the contents of the email; Frank Monroe, the owner of the Pine Tree Bay Resort, was currently unwell, and Gerry – his son – was taking over the management of the resort.

It was a move that was creating unease throughout their close-knit community; Pine Tree Bay was Frank's baby and whilst he had people all over the world looking after his other businesses, for almost thirty years he'd always undertook to oversee everything personally when it came to this small part of his empire. Frank Monroe considered the people of Pine Tree to be his family. This handing off of the baton – even to his own son – was uncharacteristic. It suggested he was more than a little under the weather and Jem was concerned for the health of the man who had only ever shown them all the greatest consideration and kindness.

But facts had to be faced; this illness was bad timing too, given the new winter schedule that the town's events committee were trying to line up. It was an important shift for the resort this year – trying out off-season events to encourage a year round stream of tourists. They could have done with a bit of Frank's charisma and warmth about the place. Warmth that sprang from a genuine love of the town; something his son had never quite managed to convince her of.

Jem had her own reasons to be wary of Gerry Monroe but, leaving that unpleasantness aside, he had never once displayed any of the genuine affection for the town that came naturally to his father. Jem's grandmother, Marcia, would have summed the man up as 'too shiny by half' – and she would have been right.

At the memory of her grandmother, a salty breeze blew in and tickled Jem's cheeks, ruffling her long dark curls and gently bringing her back to the present. Shaking her head she made the firm resolution not to worry about Gerry Monroe. It would be clear how the land lay once he arrived at the resort on Friday and there was no point in worrying about it until then.

Instead she hugged the warm mug of tea to her chest, and let her eyes travel out to the horizon. Breathing in the dawn air she savoured her early morning routine, watching Bear putter about in the shrubs and stretching out the stolen morning minutes for a just a little while longer.

Some days Jem still marvelled at finding herself there, in Scotland, in her grandmother's house. It had the look and feel of a life she had once envisaged for herself and yet…

But no. She refused to pull at that thread – even though it dangled so temptingly after everything that Madam Zelda had said yesterday – instead she sprang into action. Throwing the remainder of her tea onto the faded hydrangeas, Jem beckoned Bear in from the garden. 'Come on my big boy,' she called softly across the lawn, her heart breaking slightly as the moonlight caught his, now very silvery, muzzle. 'Time to get ready.'

After walking the mile and a half along to the other end of Pine Tree Bay – past all the cheerful shops and businesses that lined the shore front – Jem let herself into the Small House Book & Brew cafe with Bear close on her heels. She was startled to see her chef, Jamie, already at his work station in the kitchen, furiously rolling out a length of scone dough.

'Jesus Jamie!' She jumped, placing a hand to her chest. 'For a minute there, I thought someone had broken in for your cheese scone recipe.' Then, taking a closer look at him, she frowned. 'Shit, did they wrestle you for it or what?'

'Awh is it that bad?' Jamie tried to check his reflection in the glass door of the oven. 'Lorna threw me out.'

'What? Again?'

The young man evaded the question, rooting around in a drawer for a dough cutter.

'What was it this time?' Jem sighed, she was almost afraid to ask.

'Same as before. There was a lassie in The Smugglers–' Jamie started to tell the story but Jem cut him off.

'Oh Jamie not again! It's no wonder–'

'No, no.' He held his hands up in defence. 'It's not what you think. And it's not what Lorna thinks either. It's just like last time. The girl had been in the café, recognised me, we were chatting whilst I ordered a drink so I offered to buy her one too. Lorna came in and got the wrong idea.'

Or the right idea. Jem just managed to stop herself from saying it out loud. That was not to say that Jamie was the unfaithful type. To the best of Jem's knowledge he had never actually cheated on any of the girlfriends he'd had over the five years she'd known him. But he enjoyed not cheating with far too many of the female visitors to the town. The lad had a twinkle in his eye and a ready smile and looking as he did – a bit too much like his namesake in the Outlander television series – he was enjoying more of this type of attention than ever before.

Lorna was stunning and kind, and half the men of the town were in love with her, whatever their ages, but she had a way of handling the attention that signalled that she was 'off limits' without being unfriendly. Unfortunately Jamie hadn't mastered this art. If this was the end of the line for them then Lorna was unlikely to be single for long, and Jem could do without a heartbroken chef moping about the place.

'Have you had any sleep at all?'

'I crashed on your sofa.' Jamie motioned to the back of the shop where Jem's study was. 'I hope you don't mind?'

At least he has the decency to look embarrassed she thought to herself. 'It's ok for this once. I wouldn't see you on the street. But you have to get this sorted Jamie.'

Then leaving him to stew, she headed off towards the back of the shop, winding her way through bookcases, reading nooks and standard lamps before reaching her office.

Thanks to Jamie, the wood-burning stove had been on for hours and a toasty warmth greeted her. Consequently, Bear was already in situ having stretched himself full length to lie across the sofa. With his head rested comfortably on a knitted cushion, he let out a contented sigh as Jem came into the room, confident from years of being over indulged that he wouldn't be asked to move any time soon.

Throwing another log on the fire and booting up her laptop Jem walked over to the full-length picture window that faced onto the back garden. The dawn light was turning the frost-covered shrubs a delightful rose pink. She paused for a minute to soak up the fleeting beauty before the early morning mist that had been sitting out on the horizon, rolled in to turn everything grey.

As she stood at the window, she heard Jamie's footsteps outside her office. He appeared with a steaming cup of milky coffee, a slice of his delicious flapjack and a cheeky grin. 'Peace offering?'

'I'm not the one you need to make peace with, but thanks, I'm ready for something. Now bugger off! You're eating into my writing time and I have got to get this blog post out before the start of the festival today–'

As her eyes travelled to where Jamie had set the cup down, something on the desk caught her eye. An envelope with her name hand written on the front.

'What's this? Don't tell me you're handing your notice in?'

'What and give up the best job in town? Never! No that was on the mat when I let myself in last night.'

She turned the envelope over in her hands for a moment and then looked back towards him with a twinkle in her eye. 'Didn't I just tell you to bugger off?'

He chuckled and then, in his best Scottish brogue, 'All right woman I'm away fae here!'

*
* * *

Jamie headed out the door, closing it behind him, and was off down the corridor before realising he was still holding the flapjack. Muttering something under his breath about a scrambled head, he retraced his steps and was about to enter Jem's office when a sharp gasp stopped him in his tracks.

Through the half-glazed door he could see that Jem had opened the envelope and was staring intently at the postcard it contained; her hand shaking as she reached up to cover her mouth.

Perhaps now was not the time to be bothering the boss with flapjack. He turned silently and headed back toward the kitchen.

Kate

A little further back along the shore, Kate Parker pulled up outside Coastguard's cottage.

She switched off the ignition, sat for a moment and simply listened. In the early morning silence, the ticking and clicking of the cooling engine, together with the distant roar of the sea, was soothing. Especially after six noisy hours of motoring up the M6 and through the winding roads that had brought her to Pine Tree Bay. She stretched her arms, yawned and looked around her. She was in no rush to get her bearings. In no rush to do anything.

After the cacophony she had left behind in London and the roar of wheels on tarmac, the silence here felt heavy; weighted down by a creeping sea mist that hung out in the bay as if ready to engulf the town, *Brigadoon* style. This fanciful notion caused Kate to chuckle and the noise startled her – there hadn't been much to laugh about over the past couple of days.

She contemplated the little white house to her left. The two hundred year old, stone built cottage that was to be her temporary home. It looked cute enough with its low roof and whitewash render, not to mention the neat front lawn bordered by a picket fence. Shivering remnants of the summer garden clung on beneath a blanket of frost and the small timber porch was entwined with faded apricot roses whilst a clump of purple asters struggled valiantly on at their feet. In a nod to the cottage's maritime history, the fence had been strung with old fishing buoys in cheerful colours of pink and orange, held together with bits of faded blue rope.

To Kate's right, opposite the front of the house, a small grassy foreshore abruptly gave way to a rocky beach. Kate surveyed the advancing tide, partially hidden by that silent creeping sea mist which now seemed even closer. She knew she should rush to unpack and head into the cottage, especially after driving all through the night, but she needed a moment.

'What did you expect?' she asked her reflection in the rear-view mirror. *That you would drive four hundred miles and it would all go away?*

With a sigh she reached onto the backseat for her coat and handbag. 'Give it a chance Kate,' she muttered to herself. 'You've only just parked up for heaven's sake.'

Outside, a few lights glowed from one or two of the neighbouring houses and there were more dotted up along the hillside above. She took a deep gulp of the salty air and felt something inside ratchet down a notch. So these were to be her neighbours for the next six months? Not that she was planning on getting to know any of them. Once this mess was cleared up she would be back to her old life, no point in putting down any roots out here in the back of beyond.

The high-pitched cry of a seagull seemed to signal agreement. Making her way through the garden gate, the frost crunched beneath her feet. She fished under the doormat for the key. It was there thankfully, as she had been assured it would but goodness, the reckless lack of security from these trusting country types bewildered her.

In the hallway she removed her boots and was immediately delighted by the warmth emanating from the porcelain tiles beneath her feet. *Mmm nice touch;* the under-floor heating permeated her cashmere socks. Hardly surprising though, thought Kate, the luxurious extras bore all the hallmarks of her good friend Penny's excellent taste.

At the end of the hallway a stylish lamp glowed from its perch above a slim console table, warm and welcoming to the stranger who had travelled through the night. The whole effect was one of cosy elegance and Kate felt immediately welcome in this strange little house. Back in London, Penny had explained that the house was actually two smaller cottages knocked into one. Kate was relieved to see that her friend hadn't exaggerated its proportions.

To the left of the hallway she found a small wing containing a bathroom and two low ceilinged but good sized bedrooms; one of which was a master with en suite and the other a small double. Popping her suitcase into the master for later unpacking, Kate padded back into the central hallway and over to the right wing of the house.

Here the whole of the original cottage had been knocked into one large open plan space. A kitchen diner opened out into a snug lounge area which was housed in a small fully glazed extension with a wood burning stove. This room promised the most amazing sea views – once the mist had cleared – and Kate looked forward to morning coffees pondering this vista over the coming months.

Speaking of which… looking around she found the fridge and poked her head inside. Perfect; Penny's housekeeper had dutifully filled it with the list Kate had supplied. As she reached for the milk, her eyes alighted on the chilled bottle of Chablis nestled just inside the door. *Why not?* She grabbed it, scrabbling around in the drawer for a corkscrew. Sod the fact it was breakfast time – after the last few days the whole world was on its head anyway.

As the cool crisp liquid hit the back of her throat she sent up a silent thank you to Penny's housekeeper. It might be a far cry from the exquisite thirty quid bottle she usually ordered from her Marylebone vintner, but she wasn't planning to take tasting notes.

Despite the cosy warmth of the cottage, she found the prospect of a real fire irresistible and put a match to the stove. Then finally, she settled, glass in hand to watch the flames take hold. The snap and crackle of the fire was a gentle relief to the heavy silence and she had a moment of simple calm as she savoured the sharp taste of the wine on her tongue, the warmth of the sheepskin rug beneath her feet and the glow of the dancing flames before her eyes.

After the all night drive, her eyelids soon started to droop and she might have nodded off had the sound of her phone not startled her. Unwilling to move she checked her smart watch display to see who was calling. Tom, her boyfriend. *Again*. Could she even call him her 'boyfriend' when he was married to somebody else? She didn't know the protocol. Whatever he technically was, he was taking a hell of a risk calling.

It wasn't that she didn't want to hear from him but if the people looking into her, back at the firm, found out, it wouldn't look good for Tom. And it wouldn't be out of the question for them to requisition her personal phone records. Kate still had no idea how deep they were planning to go. Let's face it – *she had no idea* – period. Tom wasn't thinking straight and that couldn't be good news for either him or his family.

She chugged a large mouthful of wine and grimaced slightly as it went down. This thing with Tom had been past its sell-by date for months anyway, she'd just been too busy to finish it. Through desolate eyes Kate surveyed her cheerful surroundings. Well, she wasn't going to be too busy for anything now was she?

Jem

The day had not improved for Jem. Whilst she'd long ago decided that the concept of multi-tasking was a myth – lots of things done badly at the cost of one thing done well – sometimes it was necessary when you ran a bookshop that was *also* a cafe. But she really shouldn't have tried it today.

By six p.m. she'd managed to mess up a large book order, spill coffee on a lovely old lady who'd travelled all the way from New Jersey, and been rather too sharp with an officious gentleman who complained how 'shameful' it was that she had nothing on her shelves by Sir Walter Scott.

Frazzled was not the word.

After waving Jamie and her head waitress, Isla, off for the evening, Jem locked up the shop then walked into her study recalling the mental note she had made earlier to amend her stock list. The mountain of paperwork that stared reproachfully from her desk did little to ease her mood.

Bugger it all! Jem scowled and flopped on to the sofa where she was immediately joined by Bear who hopped up and snuggled himself into a Labrador-sized comma in the crook of her arm. She absentmindedly ruffled the fur beneath his collar and stroked his velvety ears as she stared into the dying embers of the stove.

Jem had the decidedly unsettling feeling that she was ending the day a different person to the one who started it. What she really wanted was to rewind the clock to the version of herself who had pulled back the duvet that morning, ready to start the day all over again.

But what would she do differently?

Her eyes went to the postcard, now propped up against her laptop. Well, number one on the do-over list would be to throw the envelope which had contained *that* straight into the fire. Unopened. Nobody that knew Jem would ever think of sending her a card with a painting of St. Paul's Cathedral on the front. Nobody that knew her *well* that was. Also, who on earth would send her a card with no note and no address? Just an envelope with her name handwritten on the front – the handwriting of which she didn't recognise.

She stood and reached for the postcard, ignoring the huffy snort that came from Bear, and sat back down to study it for the umpteenth time that day. Throughout her twenties she had spent a lot of hours in the company of paintings that were very similar to the one she was staring at now. So much so that, although she was no artist herself, she could describe how each effect had been created.

The very specific palette choices that were needed to produce the faded green patina of the cathedral dome, the size of the sable rigger that had been used to define the Corinthian columns in such fine detail, and even the artists choice to do this whilst leaving other areas of the composition as mere suggestion. To Jem these were all as revealing as the presence of a signature, of which there was none.

So, she had to ask herself, why was someone sending her anonymous examples of work that looked almost identical to Nick's? The same Nick who had run out on her, on the day of their wedding twelve years ago, and smashed her heart to pieces. And why now? Coming as it had, on the back of Madam Zelda's predictions yesterday, well, it was enough to put the willies up anyone wasn't it?

Jem rubbed her hand over tired eyes. In fact – if she really *had* been granted a do-over – she would extend it back to the previous day. Tell Madeleine Beaver that she could sod off and find someone else to try out her bloody fortune teller!

Jem's ring tone interrupted her thoughts and she checked the display, grateful to see the name of her best friend Helena, who ran the White Pebble Gallery further up the High Street. She pressed the green button and greeted her friend warmly.

'You all ready to set off?' Helena asked.

Jem thought for a moment and then groaned, 'Oh heck, I completely forgot!'

'We can take a rain check if you want?'

'What and risk the wrath of the Mad Beaver? She'll have us court-martialled.'

Helena laughed. 'I'm just locking up so I'll see you in ten. I'm bringing a bottle of wine that was left over from the exhibition at the weekend, so we can have a drink before we set off.'

'Ooh great idea – I could certainly do with one.'

'Bad day?'

'Wait till I tell you.' Jem's tone sounded ominous.

'Intriguing. In that case, see you in five.'

Jem hung up and threw another log on the fire before hunting out some wine glasses. She had completely forgotten that tonight was the town try-out of all the stalls that were being laid on for the Pumpkin Festival. Cute wooden cabins had been set up all along the shore front from which stall holders would be selling various Halloween themed, locally made goodies every weekend throughout October. Luckily for Pine Tree, there was a wealth of talented artisans dotted throughout Dumfries and Galloway who were only too happy to sell their goods at the festival.

Unnecessarily, Madeleine Beaver had arranged for a *try-out evening* and ordered the members of the events committee to provide feedback to the stall holders that would 'enhance visitor experience.' Jem had no intention of doing any such thing. But she was looking forward to meeting the many artists and makers hardy enough to commit every weekend in October to standing out in the freezing cold. She also hoped that she and Helena could be on hand to provide a gentle counter-balance to *the Beaver broadside*, knowing first hand that Madeleine's feedback could be brutal.

An alert bark from Bear told Jem that her friend was coming through the back gate and she unbolted the rear entrance of the cafe as Helena swept across the threshold brandishing a bottle of white wine.

'I come bearing Vouvray!' she exclaimed, folding Jem into a cloud of perfume and a warm embrace.

At the age of forty-nine, Helena Forrest was ten years older than Jem but no one who saw them together would think there was such a gap. Helena had a kind of timelessness about her that defied the ageing process. She was tall and willowy with thin wrists and ankles and a mane of untamed golden-red hair. She had a graceful way of moving that she attributed to many years of ballet when she was a young girl. Jem ushered her best friend in from the cold and through to the warm study where two empty glasses stood waiting on her desk.

'Oh thank goodness for the fire,' said Helena. 'It's brass monkeys out there darling.' Although she had been born and raised in the East End of London, Helena spoke with the husky, aristocratic tones of a Joanna Lumley soundalike. She had never lost the cockney vernacular however, and the combination was often hilarious – even if Helena did innocently protest that she wasn't intending any comedic effect.

Jem poured the wine whilst Bear greeted Helena with a mouthy hello and a lazy wag of his tail before collapsing in front of the fire as if he had just completed a ten mile run rather than a trot to the door and back.

'So, come on, what's up?' Helena asked, always one to get straight to the point.

'Oh, we'll get to it in a minute,' said Jem handing her a glass. 'You tell me about your day first.'

They settled on the sofa and Helena took a sip of Vouvray before letting out a sigh. 'Ok, my day. Busy, run off my plates with orders from Saturday's exhibition and a few walk-ins besides. Kerching! Very happy with that thank you. Now, that's out of the way – over to you.'

Jem laughed. 'Well here's to your buoyant sales figures.' She clinked her glass against Helena's and then walked over to her desk and picked up the postcard. 'I need to ask you about this,' she said, handing it to Helena. 'Did you by any chance drop it through my letterbox last night?'

Helena studied the card and shook her head. 'No, I've never seen it before. But I'd certainly like to see more by this artist.' She looked up at Jem. 'Have you any idea who it is?'

'I know someone whose work looks *a lot* like this.'

Helena immediately went back to studying the card, her brows knitted together. 'Surely you're not suggesting…?'

'I am. I think this painting is by Nick Townsend.'

Helena took a deep breath, opened her mouth to speak but clearly couldn't settle on which question to ask first.

'Exactly,' said Jem. 'Now, multiply that tenfold and you'll have some sense of where I've been at all day.'

'Oka-a-ay,' Helena said. 'So let's work through this. First of all, what makes you think this is Nick's work?'

'Well primarily, it's the colours. It's just so typical of a palette he would have used. And there's certain – I don't know – *flourishes* here and there that remind me of the stuff he did when we were together.' She paused a moment before saying, 'And then, of course, there's the subject matter.'

'Yes,' agreed Helena. 'I had noticed that. It would certainly be rather insensitive for anyone who knew your history to send this to you.'

'That's why I really knew right from the off it wasn't from you. I just had a vague hope that you were getting everyone interested in a new artist and simply picked the best example of their work to send out.'

'I'm sure there's an explanation along those lines Jem, I'm not the only gallery owner around here,' Helena said pragmatically. 'Look you haven't seen or heard from Nick in twelve years. And, after the way he left, well he'd have to be some kind of monster to choose *this* as a way to get in touch.' She put a gentle hand on Jem's arm. 'Would you even *want* it to be from him?'

It was a simple question. But there wasn't a simple answer so Jem said nothing and instead asked, 'Are there any of the other galleries planning this type of exhibition that you've heard about?'

'Can't say I have, but honestly, I've been so busy at the White Pebble that I'm a bit out of the loop with everyone. It's entirely possible.'

'Ugh…' Jem blew air through her cheeks and flopped back down onto the sofa. She turned to Helena. 'Am I totally overreacting?'

Helena looked at her friend squarely. 'Darling, after all that you went through, you've *totally* earned the right.'

Jem chuckled slightly, they needed a change of subject. 'You're never going to believe this but I had to go and check out Pine Tree Bay's answer to Mystic Meg yesterday too.'

'Oh yes I heard!' Helena rubbed her hands together gleefully. 'The fortune teller! What did she have to say? Did she see a tall dark handsome stranger in your future…. Or perhaps your *present*?'

'Worryingly, she seemed much more preoccupied with the tall handsome men from my past.' Jem laughed, deliberately ignoring her friend's inference.

'Come again?' said Helena.

'Our Madam Zelda seems convinced that I'm about to be visited by boyfriends of Halloween's past,' joked Jem. 'I'm sure these people must have a way of tapping in to clues we're inadvertently giving off, but even I have to admit, she had me going for a minute there yesterday.' Jem laughed nervously.

'What did she say exactly?'

'She said that two men from my past are about to make a reappearance. Oh and to look out for someone stabbing me in the back.' Jem's eyes were full of mirth but watching Helena's response, her expression turned to one of incredulity. 'Oh no Helena – please don't tell me you believe a word of this rubbish?'

'Well not usually, but with *this*,' she held up the postcard, 'following so soon after… You've got to admit it is a bit of a coincidence.'

'Yes and that's *all* it is,' said Jem draining her glass. Together with her earlier, private reservations, Helena's reaction was making her uneasy. She started to shift forward on the sofa. 'Now come on, let's get going-'

'Er, not so fast Ms Small, you're not getting out of it that easily.'

Jem knew where the conversation was headed and she was eager to avoid Helena's probing. Her friend meant well enough – they'd been through a lot together – but Helena had long made it clear that she didn't approve of Jem's practical approach to her love life. And right now, Jem couldn't face another lecture on the stupidity of keeping Finn McDeer, the town's outdoor pursuits expert, at arm's length.

Jem stood up and checked her watch. 'Good lord, look at the time!' She took the glass out of Helena's hand and handed her the full length camel coat that she'd arrived in. After struggling into her own oversized puffa jacket, she grabbed Bear's lead and the trio headed out of the front entrance into the dank autumn night air.

Thankfully there was no rain. The skies were clear and the waxing Hunter's moon sat low on the horizon, its orange glow reflected in the gentle ripples of the bay. A light, cool breeze tickled the two women's cheeks as they made their way along the shore front in the direction of the Pumpkin Festival stalls. The chilly night was welcome after the somewhat fuggy warmth of Jem's study, and both women savoured the fresh evening air after being cooped up in their respective businesses all day.

Drawing closer to the action, Jem was cheered by the scene of folk gathered around fire bowls to keep out the autumn chill, mingling convivially and warming their hands. After browsing a number of stalls and chatting to the vendors at each one, she and Helena came to a cabin that was set up as a hot chocolate station. It was clearly a hit if the amount of people wandering around with steaming mugs were anything to go by. After paying the stall holder they took their huge enamel cups – which were overflowing with piles of mini marshmallows – and made their way over to the warmth of the fire bowls. There they both mingled, saying hello to friends and neighbours who had gathered and who's children were all making a beeline for Bear.

A tap on Jem's shoulder whilst talking to one of the other cafe owners caused the woman to smile and melt away into the crowd and Jem turned around to see Finn. He was dressed in his usual attire of jeans and a closely fitted thermal jacket with a slouch beanie pulled down over his ears, Jem grinned up at him, glad he'd managed to get back from his trip to the Cairngorms in time for the festival try-out.

Finn regularly lead mini bushcraft and survival courses in the surrounding woods which proved popular with school trips as well as drawing a lucrative corporate team building crowd. He was also the closest thing that Jem had to a boyfriend. Jem didn't actually want a partner and, apparently, Finn didn't either, but they liked each other well enough and they liked sleeping with each other even more so. Theirs was an arrangement which suited them both; someone to go out on the town with every now and then – and someone to stay in with more regularly.

'You made it back then,' Jem said sounding pleased.

'You've got cocoa froth on your lip.' He smiled down at her affectionately. His thumb strayed hesitantly towards her mouth as if he were about to smooth it away but thought better of it at the last minute.

'Bloody hell how embarrassing!' Jem shrieked. 'I've been talking to hordes of people sporting a chocolate moustache!' She quickly wiped her mouth.

Finn smiled slowly and she recognised the look. 'I'm just on my way home actually.' He inclined his head back up toward the town. 'Just dropped in to make sure the *Mad Beaver* could tick me off her list.'

'Drop by later?' She raised her eyebrows then watched him bend down to give Bear a fuss. 'We'll be home by half nine.'

'Sounds great,' he grinned. 'Gives me a chance to shower and unpack. See you then.'

Jem watched him go, his strong legs carrying him effortlessly up the hill. She marvelled at how easy it was to invite a man into your bed for the night when there was nothing at stake.

*

From the opposite side of the fire bowl, Helena, who had been chatting away to friends and neighbours, watched the exchange. Was Jem so blinkered that she couldn't see what was happening there?

Helena liked Finn enormously, he was as solid and dependable as his broad shoulders suggested but he was heading for heartache. She just wished Jem could see what was good for her. But, Helena knew better than anyone that when it came to matters of the heart, Jem had a firm policy, dictated largely by her past.

It wasn't always easy. Watching someone you cared about cut themselves off from their chance at happiness. When Jem had come into Helena's life twelve years ago, Helena had been living all the way down in Devon. Jem had shown up in town with nothing but a suitcase and a puppy and Helena had immediately taken to her. Here was a young girl with a broken heart but a bright future, she had thought to herself. Jem was young, she would get over it – and part of Jem had – but another part hadn't.

When, after two years in Devon, Jem had told Helena she was moving to Scotland, to the house she had inherited from her grandmother, Helena had come along to help with the move. And, falling under the Dumfries and Galloway spell, she'd decided to break for the border herself. She had hoped the move would signal a fresh start for Jem, allow her to finally move on. But it hadn't happened and no amount of pushing on Helena's part could seem to change that.

Of course anyone hearing Jem's story – jilted on the day of her wedding – would understand. It would leave a scar sure enough. But something had happened *after* that day. Helena suspected it was the same thing that compelled Jem to hang around in Devon for two years before moving on. But Helena had never been able to get to the bottom of it; the past was somewhere that Jem never ventured. And whilst Helena had tried some gentle probing, she wasn't about to drag the girl to places it was painful to go.

Helena was resigned to looking on whilst her warm and caring friend shut off her emotions like some modern day Miss Havisham. But there was one thing for sure – men like Finn McDeer would not wait forever.

Wherever Nick Townsend was, she hoped he was paying for what he had done to that girl's life – for the things he had set in motion that day – and she hoped that Jem's fortune teller was wrong. Nick had disappeared without trace and Helena hoped he would stay that way. Where he had vanished to was anyone's guess and as to *why*… well only he would ever be able to answer that one.

Matthew

London

'Good evening Gerry.' Matthew was caught slightly off guard by the caller ID that flashed up on his mobile display. He hadn't expected to hear back from the interview until much later in the week. If at all.

'I hope I'm not disturbing your evening Matt, but I just wanted to let you know that we want you on board for the Pine Tree Bay project.'

Matthew was astonished. He had deliberately gone out of his way *not* to get the job. It made no sense. He needed to think quickly.

'Gerry, that *is* great news,' Matthew said smoothly. 'But can I be straight with you?'

'Of course.'

'Something dropped in my lap this morning that I'm really interested in pursuing. It's a role with an old firm that I've worked with previously. They've put a lot of work my way in the past and I'm hesitant to let them down.'

This wasn't actually too far from the truth – Matthew had looked up some old contacts on his way back from the Southbank the previous day. The old network was a well worn path and Matthew was fairly confident that some freelance work would come of it.

'Thing is Matt, after what I heard yesterday, I'm pretty keen for you to run this consultancy piece for us so whatever your old client is offering, Monroe Holdings will double it.'

Double it? Christ! That was going to be hard to refuse.

The trouble was, Matthew had conducted the interview in the style of an over confident, arrogant prick. The intention was for Gerry to be infuriated rather than impressed by him. It wasn't an act he could keep up for much longer than the hour it had taken for the interview.

'It's not about the money Gerry, honestly,' Matthew said now. 'This isn't a negotiation tactic. It's a case of professional integrity and not wanting to let my previous client down. If there's a chance for us to work together in the future at some point…' Matthew tailed off.

'Ok, I hear you and I respect that decision. But I wonder if you would just do me one favour?'

'I'll try,' Matthew said noncommittally.

'I'm travelling up to Pine Tree Bay for a meeting with the business owners on Friday morning. I wonder if prior to starting this new role you would come and cast your eye over our project? Take a quick look at the way things operate up there – just to give me your initial impression? After that, if you still want to pursue this role with your previous client we can part friends and look forward to working with each other at some point in the future.'

Gerry then dropped an extortionate rate that Matthew could invoice him for the two days work.

Matthew couldn't deny that the funds would come in handy, but something about the deal sounded too good to be true. Then he remembered – Lissa was planning to clear the last of her things out on Friday before the sale of the flat went through the following week. The timing seemed serendipitous.

What the hell, it was only two days. 'That sounds like something I can agree to Gerry.'

'I'm glad to hear you say that,' Gerry sounded relieved. 'Marcus will email you with all the details.'

Matthew put the phone down, and headed into the small kitchen of his first floor apartment . A siren blared from the direction of the main road then quickly faded, allowing the monotonous hum of the city to reclaim the airwaves around his building.

He grabbed a cold beer and lifted the magnetised bottle opener from the front of the fridge door – a kitsch souvenir from the first ever city break he took with Lissa. He thought back to that stifling hot day in Lisbon. Lissa, looking stunning in a white, knee length sundress and a wide brimmed hat, had wandered into a gift shop just along the street from their hotel, hunting for souvenirs. She had charmed the shopkeeper with her pigeon Portuguese and the guy had congratulated Matthew on his beautiful wife. Matthew had paid over the odds for the bottle opener and asked Lissa to marry him.

It had been a moment of ego, an impulse. And it had been grossly unfair. But surely he had been right to try?

He returned the bottle opener to the fridge door with a loud snap deciding he would leave it there for the new owner.

Raising his arm to lean against the window frame he looked out on the post-work drinkers mobbing the streets below. The music from a nearby jazz bar floated up and in through the single glazing of the Edwardian conversion. He wondered what his next home would look out onto, or the one after that, and in what possible way it could matter. His life seemed to stretch before him in an endless grey stream of clients, offices, apartments.... But what was the alternative? He had tried and it just didn't work.

A day at the coast would probably do him good. It *was* flattering to think that someone in Gerry Monroe's lofty position sought his professional opinion. But he'd been around long enough to know that, in business, if something seemed too good to be true, then it probably was.

Taking a sip of beer Matthew told himself to relax; he hadn't committed himself, he'd simply promised the guy a couple of days in

Scotland – for an amount that would cover at least three months rent on his next flat – then he'd never have to see the arrogant tosser again.

CHAPTER FOUR
3rd October

Jem

Scotland

'I don't ever remember having an October like this one,' Helena remarked three nights into the festival, as she and Jem once again strolled along the shore road. They were en route to their local, The Smugglers Arms. 'I mean, I'm not complaining because the business I'm doing is phenomenal, better than the summer even, but my body is screaming, "We normally get a rest at this point!" And I'm asking it to ramp up.'

'All the other business owners are coming into Small House saying the same thing,' agreed Jem. 'The American visitors have really gone for the Halloween vibe in a big way. I'm half expecting Michael Myers to rock up and tell us off for stealing his thunder.'

Helena giggled. 'Well let's hope not darling!' Then, seeing Madeleine Beaver advancing along the pavement she lowered her voice. 'Mind you, if Pine Tree were to become the setting of a slasher movie, no prizes for guessing who'd be bumped off first… Madeleine darling!' Helena gushed loudly. 'How on earth do you do it? The festival is a phenomenon!'

Jem – out of Madeleine's sightline – narrowed her eyes and made a vomiting gesture.

'Oh you know how it is for people like us Helena,' Madeleine simpered. '*We* are born for leadership. This sort of community event is the *raison d'être* for ladies of our upbringing.'

Helena nodded sympathetically. 'And with all your experience at Westminster…' (Madeleine, the wife on an MP, never tired of reminding the committee that she had parliamentary connections). 'I mean to say,' Helena continued, with a tinkly laugh that Jem had never heard before, 'this must all seem like the amateur league in comparison.'

'One always does what one can to help out, Helena.' Madeleine nodded graciously before swanning off down the street. 'Must dash. Lots to do!' She threw a royal wave over her shoulder as she sauntered off.

Jem poked Helena sharply in the ribs. 'Will you stop encouraging her? She already thinks she's the bloody Queen of Pine Tree Bay.'

Helena giggled. 'I'm sorry I can't help it. I just, sort of, go into *Madeleine mode* whenever I see her.'

'Well stop it. It's like watching a couple of yahs having a posh-off! Wait until she finds out you grew up in Canning Town and demotes you to the commoner ranks like the rest of us.'

'I already told her where I grew up.'

'Yes, but you pronounced it *Cannington* and told her it was Surrey borders.'

'Well it's not that far outside Surrey.'

'Give or take fifty miles.'

'Spoilsport.' Helena pretended to pout.

Jem huffed. 'Seriously, the busier this place becomes, the more omnipresent she is. I swear to God, at the festival try-out, I couldn't even nip to the loo without her following me to check that the toilet paper was fully stocked up.'

'Oh darling no! Were you tempted to write something naughty about her on the lavatory wall?' The two women giggled and Bear wagged his tail in solidarity. 'You have to admit she's whipped us all into shape though. This place looks amazing. It's a regular trick or treat paradise. Never mind Michael Myers, the kids all think they've been spirited onto the set of *Hocus Pocus*!'

The town *had* gone all out for the Pumpkin Festival. Street lamps festooned with glowing pumpkin lanterns and all the shop fronts draped with brightly illuminated cobwebs. Witches on broomsticks looked set to take flight from every rooftop, whilst colonies of bats dangled from the eaves. The Barnacle Hotel even had a montage of macabre figures and coffins arranged in a 'set' on the front lawn; something which the staff moaned endlessly about, being the ones expected to lug it all inside at the first sign of rain.

The weather was holding up its end of the bargain though; so far they'd been treated to cold crisp autumn days with the odd sea fog rolling in helpfully every now and then to add a bit of atmosphere. The nights were bloody chilly however, and Jem would be glad to get to into the pub to warm up. She quickened the pace.

'Someone's keen for her first glass of Pinot,' Helena struggled to keep up and even Bear was falling behind.

'I am. It's relentless at the cafe just now. And that's tricky with a heartbroken chef on my hands.'

'What?' Helena quickened her step so as not to miss a scrap of gossip.

'Lorna came into the café today to break things off with Jamie for good.'

'But I thought it was just a bit of harmless flirting on his part?'

'It *was*, according to Jamie. And to be fair I do think he's telling the truth – that nothing actually happened – but Lorna has had enough. With a bit of time to think she's come the conclusion that she doesn't trust him; says that it doesn't matter whether it's just banter with these girls, she's always waiting for the one time that something *does* happen.'

'Jamie's not going to meet another Lorna in a hurry.'

'I think that realisation hit around lunch time today.'

'I should think they were queueing around the block when she walked out.'

'I wouldn't have been surprised. I had a quick chat with her afterwards and she's headed off to her mum's for a few weeks to let the dust settle. I think she's worried Jamie might talk her around if she stays in town and she wants to be somewhere that can't happen. She's pretty cut up about it, but I don't think she'll change her mind.'

'And Jamie?'

'Worse than useless. I had to send him home at two o clock after he got into an argument with a customer about his cock-a-leekie soup!'

'Come again?'

'Oh don't ask,' Jem rolled her eyes. 'Something about prunes.'

'I'm ordering you a very, *very* large glass of wine,' Helena said insistently as they drew up outside the pub.

As always, The Smugglers shone like a beacon of friendliness from its handy location at the mid-point of the shoreline. Rab, the landlord, had really gone to town with the festival and if Captain Jack Sparrow himself happened to sail into Pine Tree Bay this Halloween, he and his shipmates would be very much at home amidst the ghoulish smuggling paraphernalia that Rab had crammed into every nook and cranny of the old inn.

As Helena pushed open the door she was momentarily startled by a ghoulish 'Mwah-Ha-Ha-Ha!' that rang out across the harbour. It was the sound effect from an old travelling fair that Rab had found on Ebay and was currently driving everyone in Pine Tree Bay half mad, going off at all intervals whenever anyone entered or exited the pub.

Whereas most people in the town were allowing the festivities to gently build up, leaving the actual costumes until the end of the month, Rab wasn't about to pass up the opportunity for thirty one days of fancy dress; he and his team were greeting customers in full Halloween costume. Rumour had it that he'd turned his upstairs lounge into a temporary dressing room, complete with mirrored light stations, and the whole team had to rendezvous a full hour before shift to 'get into character'. As most of the people in Pine Tree Bay ran to two or three different jobs, this was causing much consternation amongst the staff. In truth however, they all loved Rab's enthusiasm – it was what made The Smugglers a fun place to work – even if they'd never admit that to his face.

Bear raced to the bar ahead of the two women, placing his paws on the counter and waiting for one of the dog loving staff to pass him a gravy bone from the jar that sat beside the beer pumps. Helena followed quickly behind.

'Two of the largest Pinot Grigio you can fit into a glass please Rab.' She beamed at the pub's elaborately dressed owner.

Rab bowed theatrically as he popped a gravy bone in Bear's mouth then turned to pull two wine glasses from the shelf. 'Coming straight up m'lady.' He tugged his pirate bandana in mock deference. 'I take it you're both coming to the meeting tomorrow morning?'

'Absolutely!' they both said in unison then laughed at their own veracity.

'I'm not sure what's going on,' Rab said with a troubled look. 'There's a change in tone when Gerry's doing the talking. I've a bad feeling about it all.'

'Has anyone heard how Frank is?' Jem cut off any further speculation which would just give them all indigestion until they found out the real reason for Gerry's visit tomorrow.

'Finn tried to call him today,' said Rab. 'But Frank's line is diverted to Gerry's assistant – that Marcus gadgie, the wee shite.'

'I heard Frank's recuperating at his lake house,' said Helena. 'But we don't have the number there either. Anyway if he's as ill as Gerry suggests, we should probably leave him alone to get well.'

'But we should send some sort of gesture. A card from us all or some flowers, surely?' offered Jem.

'Ah Finn's been over all that with Gerry,' Rab waived the suggestion away. 'He just says to send it to the usual address for Frank and it will get to him. It all sounds very fishy to me.' Placing the wine on the counter he rang up the till.

'I agree, but what can we do about it?' Helena handed Rab a twenty.

'What can we do about what?' A tall figure loomed up behind Jem and Helena and they both turned to see Finn standing behind them.

'Ah, speak of the devil,' said Rab.

'The *horny* devil,' Helena murmured, earning her a swift kick on the ankle from Jem. Desperately regretting her decision to confide a little too much to her friend on their last girl's night in, Jem was relieved to see Finn stoop to give Bear a fuss and miss the comment.

'Finn,' Rab greeted his friend warmly, handing Helena her change. 'We're just speculating about the meeting tomorrow, have you heard anything?'

As well as being the town's outdoor pursuits expert, Finn was the head of the Pine Tree Bay Community Council. The trio waited expectantly for his answer, eager for any additional information his position in office might bring.

'The only thing I know for sure is that there's another guy attending the meeting with Gerry tomorrow,' said Finn. 'Gerry described him as a business consultant. Matt something or other. I'm as much in the dark as you lot about everything but there's no point in speculating until we hear what's what in the morning.'

'Oh you're as bad as Jem,' said Helena. 'Where's the fun in waiting to hear what he's got to say when we could pass a perfectly pleasant evening planning a hundred and one ways to take the egotistical prick down a peg or two?'

'Oh I'm sure he'll get his at some point. If he hasn't already.' Finn looked meaningfully at Jem who shook her head almost imperceptibly.

'Well, if it's a good bit of gossip you're after,' Rab changed the subject – much to Jem's relief – 'There's a new girl in town.'

'Oh good,' she murmured, 'Perhaps she'll take Jamie's mind off Lorna and I can get my chef back.'

'Jamie and Lorna have split up?' Rab's nose was up, scenting more fodder for his hoard of tittle-tattle.

'Oh I'll fill you in later,' said Jem, knowing that he would have the news from someone else before the night was out.

'Well I wouldn't have thought Jamie would be this new lassie's type,' said Rab. 'Mind you, I've been wrong on that score before.' His eyes flicked briefly between Finn and Jem. 'I would say she's in her mid thirties, maybe he'd be a bit young for her.'

'Well, maybe she can at least distract him for a couple of weeks until a new batch of young female tourists arrive.' Jem took a huge gulp of wine. 'Otherwise I don't know how I'm going to cope with him hanging about the cafe like a wet rag, moping over Lorna.'

'You're all heart Jem.' Helena looked at Finn over her wine glass and they both burst out laughing.

'*What?*' Jem pretended to be incredulous, having long denied her reputation as something of a task master in the cafe.

Meanwhile Rab continued to ramble on about the town's recent addition. 'She's here for more than a couple of weeks though this Kate.'

'Good God, are you still going on about this new girl?' Helena scowled at Rab. The uncharacteristic sharpness in her voice took both Jem and Finn by surprise.

'Well, I'm just filling you in that's all.' Rab leaned over the bar. 'Her name's Kate, she's from London and she's rented Coastguard's cottage for six months. She's a friend of Lady Penelope. On sabbatical from her job in corporate finance apparently. Taking some time out before returning south next April.'

Rab took his job as landlord very seriously believing it came with the duty of unofficial town crier. Rather than stand on the corner with a bell shouting the news however, he just passed it on to everyone that came into the pub. Satisfied that he had fulfilled his role, he left the trio to go and serve another group at the other side of the bar.

'Well thank goodness he's remembered he has customers,' said Helena sniffily as Rab headed off. 'Kate this and Kate that! What do we care about *Kate*?'

Finn exchanged a look with Jem that said he was wondering what on earth had rattled Helena's cage, before nipping off to find them a table. Much to Bear's delight, Finn bagged seats next to the blazing fire where the four legged member of the group promptly stretched out to bake his old bones.

Friends and acquaintances from around the area drifted in and out of the pub stopping to have a word with either one or all of them throughout the course of the evening, and Jem couldn't help but notice that the festival seemed to have put everyone in convivial spirits, even if they were all slightly on edge about the meeting that was planned for the next day.

As the clock struck ten, Jem drained her third glass of wine and raised herself, a tad unsteadily, to her feet, 'Time for me and Bear to hit the road I'm afraid folks. She put her hand to her head. 'Think that last one was my limit.'

'Right I'll walk you back,' said Finn, reaching for his coat.

'You've got half your drink left Finn, I'll be fine. Anyway, you're the other side of town so you keep Helena company and make sure *she* gets home ok. She can't take her drink like she used to.' Jem giggled.

Helena rolled her eyes. 'Look who's talking.'

Finn smiled at Jem but didn't argue. She was glad he knew her well enough to pick up on her signal – she wasn't looking for company tonight.

Kate

By Thursday evening Kate suspected she might be going slowly mad.

This place was going to kill her. She was two days into a six-month rental and she was living in some kind of Halloween themed nightmare. There were lanterns, ghouls and cobwebs around every corner. You couldn't walk fifty yards without tripping over a pumpkin and the landlord of the only decent pub in town thought that dressing up as a pirate zombie every night qualified him for the Royal Shakespeare Company.

She had never been unemployed for more than a week throughout her whole adult life and the tedium of the empty days was already driving her to distraction. She had tried to keep herself busy and introduce a modicum of discipline into her temporary life, but even with an early morning jog and an evening stroll, there were still all the hours in between with just the voice inside her head for company.

She was going to have to do the one thing she had been putting off. She picked up her mobile and moved to sit in the part of the room closest to the sea – in order to get the meagre two bars of signal available – then dialled her sister's number.

Suse answered on the second ring. 'About fucking time. Where the *hell* are you?'

'Nice greeting.'

'Well what do you expect?' her sister practically screeched down the line. 'I've been leaving messages for days!'

'I texted you that I was ok didn't I?'

'For all I knew some serial killer could have had you *and* your phone!'

'Suse, you seriously need to stop listening to all those crime podcasts,' Kate sighed.

'You haven't answered my question. Where are you?'

'Scotland.'

'What in God's name are you doing in Scotland?'

'Hiding.' Kate felt a bubble in her throat.

'Paula said you'd been suspended.'

'Suse? Why on earth are you giving me such a hard time if you've already spoken to my assistant?'

'I only spoke to her an hour ago. I've been worried sick since you didn't answer my messages on Tuesday. I've been ringing everyone to find out where you are–'

'Who's *everyone*?' Kate's heart sank. This was the last thing she needed. 'You know what? Don't answer that. I'm feeling sick enough about this as it is without worrying about the rumour mill you've just set into motion. This whole rotten thing is going to ruin my reputation and my career.'

'Look,' Suse said matter of factly, 'Paula didn't go into detail so you're still going to need to tell me what's happened.' Her rhino-hide sister didn't sound the least bit chastised.

'I honestly don't know.' Kate took a deep, steadying breath, 'I went into work on Monday morning as usual but my pass wouldn't let me into the building. So naturally, I went to security to ask them to reset it but instead they took me to a meeting room. Then the chairman came down and told me I'd been suspended.' Kate swallowed. 'For six months, pending the investigation of some *irregularities*.'

'But you're a senior director Kate. Surely the company can't just suspend you without any details.'

'They can and they have. And let's face it – if I *were* involved in something dodgy I'd be hastily covering my tracks right now. In their shoes I'd do what they're doing – tell me nothing then watch very carefully for my next move.'

'Well, what *have* you been involved in?'

'Gee, thanks for the vote of confidence Suse.'

'No I don't mean it like *that*. I mean what projects have you been working on lately?'

'You know it's all confidential! They could sack me just for telling you. I've been racking my brains and I have absolutely no idea what's behind this. It's driving me insane, I just keep going over and over exactly what they said to me and I can't come up with any clue as to what it could be about? I can tell you this though, if the investigation is going to take six months, it's not something trivial.'

'Who's "they"?'

'What?'

'You said you keep going over and over what "they" said, but earlier you mentioned that it was just the chairman who came down to see you.'

Bloody Suse, she should be a detective. Kate let out a huge sigh. 'Tom was with the chairman when he came down.'

'Tom? Tom Farrer? *Your* Tom?'

'Well he's not *my* Tom is he? Not according to the company. Nobody there knows about us. Which is how I intend it to stay.'

'Well of all the bloody rotten–'

'Suse, there's nothing he could have done. If he'd refused to come to the meeting room it would have looked odd. He's my boss; it's natural that he would have to be there when one of his senior staff gets suspended.'

'He could at least have the decency to call you.'

'He's tried. Lots. I'm not taking his calls. I don't want to drag him into this. If they find out he's even tried to contact me outside of the official channels it'll compromise him. I just don't want that.' Her voice shook slightly and she worried at her temple. 'Of course, I don't want any of this, but I'm stuck in limbo until they decide to tell me more.'

'Ok well, look, what's your address there? I need to make some arrangements, but I can be with you by Saturday.'

'No Suse, that's not necessary, I'm...'

'I am not leaving you there *alone*. Driving yourself mad going over and over all this. Where exactly are you anyway?'

'I've rented a cottage from my old colleague, Penny. It's on the south west coast, overlooking the sea.' As she said this, Kate looked around the room. Her surroundings were one of the few things she was taking comfort in at the moment. 'It's quite lovely actually.'

'What's the town?'

'Well it's an incredibly parochial little community as these back-woods places always are, but it's pretty enough. It's an old fishing port that some Canadian tycoon has turned into a kind of Caledonian Newport.' Kate laughed. 'It's very charming though. And, from what I can see, it's thriving.' Despite her earlier grumbling, she suddenly realised she was quite taken with Pine Tree Bay.

'Yes, yes, it all sounds lovely. But what's the name? What's your address there?' Suse was practically clucking.

Kate walked away from the bay window and watched as the bars of signal fell away from her mobile display. 'I'm sorry you're breaking up.'

'Kate? Kate?'

'Call you later Suse when I have signal. Bye.' She hastily turned off the phone and put it on the coffee table.

Much as she loved her sister, the last thing Kate needed was for her to turn up at the cottage, with force field in tow. Suse would no doubt breeze in with enough food for an army and start re-arranging all the cupboards before questioning Kate with forensic scrutiny. Then she would make friends with all the locals, dragging Kate to some community bake-off event or whatever town bonding activity she had unearthed, before swanning off and leaving her with a surfeit of food she didn't need and friends she didn't want.

Kate hastily pulled on boots and a coat and headed out into the chilly night. A walk along the sea front would clear her head. She set off in the direction of the town, the bright lights of the festival drawing her toward them like a beacon.

In the past few days she had noticed this tendency in herself to keep shifting her environment in order to escape her thoughts. But it wasn't working – her worries just followed her everywhere. The only place she had found a tiny window of solace was that lovely book shop and café which sat at the far end of the sea front: Small House Book & Brew.

There she had, briefly, been able to lose herself; wandering around the oak bookshelves, imagining that she *was* the person that she'd been describing to anyone who asked.

Just a woman on sabbatical who had taken six months out of life, to hole up in a cottage and read all the books she had meant to get round to over the last twenty years. Not the Head of Corporate Investments at Allocott Finance, who appeared to be facing some pretty serious allegations.

Why couldn't she be that other woman? She had just to set her mind to it, surely? Kate knew she hadn't done anything wrong, so wasn't this just a case of letting the investigation play out? Returning to work once the misunderstanding was cleared up? And then she was back to wondering just exactly what that misunderstanding was.

It would have helped Kate's circular thinking if she had *some* small inkling of why her employers had suspended her. But she didn't. So she could only work with what she knew.

The bracing wind stung her cheeks and she pulled the fur-lined hood of her parka tight around her face. As her footsteps drummed a monotonously soothing beat, she started to feel calmer, allowing the rational side of her brain to kick in. Once again, she considered the facts.

Her role at Allocott was one of strategy, leadership and oversight. She didn't get involved in the actual deals any longer – that was the job of her team. If something *was* amiss with a deal then of course, ultimately the buck stopped with her, but the member of staff responsible for it would have to be suspended too. Paula, Kate's assistant, had confirmed that Kate was the only one to be investigated, so, whatever they were looking into didn't involve anyone else.

So, if this wasn't about a specific client, then it must be related to some general misdemeanour. But she had been suspended for six months, which meant there was a lengthy investigation underway. This suggested copious amounts of documentation or a complicated structure of records that needed to be investigated. It could also signify that outside authorities were involved. This all pointed to one thing – a breach of regulations. But Kate had been racking her brains for anything of this nature and she could come up with absolutely nothing.

Before she could speculate any further, Kate was forced to tune back into a her surroundings by the black Labrador lumbering towards her as if his main goal in life was to deposit slobber all over her expensive Canada Goose parka. Thankfully, his owner called him back before he could get too near. Kate looked more closely and recognised the manager of the bookshop and café that she was so taken with.

As they drew level, Kate smiled and stooped to stroke the cute dog, being careful to keep his muzzle directed away from her expensive coat.

She was not usually a doggy person but even she had to admit that this old chap with his smiling silvery chops and shining black eyes was quite charming.

'Oh now aren't you gorgeous?' Having often observed over the years that a good way to ingratiate yourself with someone was to delight in their pet, she put the tactic to good use with the owner of what she suspected might become her favourite Pine Tree haunt.

'Be warned,' Jem grinned, drawing level with Kate. 'He'll have you standing there all night doing that if you're not careful.'

'Oh, I don't think either of us would mind,' Kate murmured. As she buried her hand in the folds beneath the dog's collar, she suddenly felt calmer than she had in days. 'You're the lady who owns the bookshop aren't you?' Straightening up she put her hand out. 'I'm Kate Parker. I'm renting Coastguard's Cottage for the next six months.'

'Oh well in that case we're neighbours.' Jem shook Kate's hand warmly; even if the greeting was a bit formal for these parts it didn't hurt to be nice to potential customers. 'I'm Jem Small, I live in the granite villa just a way down from you, the one called *Withershins*.'

'I know the one you mean, wow that's a beautiful house.'

'Yes it belonged to my grandmother, it's been in our family for generations.'

'*Withershins* is an unusual name. I've never heard it before.'

'Yes it's a strange old Celtic term. It sort of means 'against the expected way of things' or time running backwards. My grandmother always wanted to change it because it's meant to represent bad luck but I've never believed in all that. I've always loved the mysterious sound of it.'

'I've only been here a few days and I've noticed quite a few old customs like that,' said Kate. I love the combination of the old and the new here. It's been very tastefully done.' She tactfully avoided adding that the town currently looked like somewhere The Addams Family might take their vacation.

'You've arrived at an interesting time,' Jem said, reading her mind. 'This is our first ever Pumpkin Festival and our events co-ordinator has been somewhat, *enthusiastic* with the decorations.'

'Ah right,' Kate chuckled. 'That explains it.'

'But if you're planning to be here for six months you might be interested in the town meeting tomorrow morning at The Smugglers. Everyone is welcome. Gerry Monroe is going to be making some kind of announcement.' Jem grimaced slightly.

'Thanks I may just do that.' It was the first interesting thing Kate had heard since arriving in Pine Tree Bay. She would certainly like to see the great business tycoon in action. But she said none of this, instead asking,

'Am I right in thinking that you're the owner of the café and bookshop down the other end of the bay?'

'Yes, that's right. Well co-owner with Bear here obviously. He has first dibs on all the sofa's and wood burning stoves at any time.'

'I noticed,' Kate said, smiling at Bear. 'It's a real haven though. I'm… sort of taking a sabbatical and just to be able to disappear into one of your reading nooks with a latte, a good book and one of your amazing scones is exactly what I need right now.'

'Well I look forward to you becoming a regular.' Kate noticed Jem open her mouth as if to ask more but thankfully she had the good sense not to pounce on a first meeting. It was something that ghastly Beaver woman who wandered about with the clipboard could learn. She had collared Kate over coffee that morning and turned a perfectly lovely hour into something resembling an interrogation from the secret police.

But to Jem, Kate simply said, 'Me too. Lovely to meet you. I'd best let you get this old boy home.'

She continued on, her heart feeling a little lighter. In all her time living in London she had never once stopped on the street just to pass the time with a neighbour. Turning at the entrance to The Barnacle Hotel, ready to retrace her steps, Kate noticed a tall, attractive, fair haired man climbing out of a cab. Hmmm, perhaps Suse had a point; mingling with the folk around town might not be so bad after all, especially if they were all as handsome as that.

Scotland   *Matthew*

Matthew Albright, dressed in dark moleskin jeans, a grey tweed jacket and a thick woollen scarf, grabbed his overnight bag from the backseat of the cab and headed toward The Barnacle Hotel. He stopped for a moment to take in his surroundings. Maybe a walk along the shoreline before checking in might freshen him up a bit.

Before the thought could take hold a young woman in uniform was at his side. Grabbing his bag and introducing herself as 'Isla' she bundled him into the hotel jabbering, 'You're our last check-in of the evening Mr Albright and I clock-off in five, so if we could just get you settled in I can go home and you can get yourself all tucked up in bed at a reasonable hour ready for your meeting at The Smugglers tomorrow morning.' She bustled him to the front desk and thrust a form and a pen under his nose. 'Now, if you could just fill this in and I'll get your key ready for you.'

Matthew hastily completed the form, wondering what horrors might befall him should he be the cause of any unplanned overtime. The eagle eyed receptionist couldn't be in that much of a hurry though – she was scanning every word he wrote.

It was always the same when he arrived for a new job – the curiosity was palpable – but it didn't normally extend to the hotel staff. Mind you, this Isla seemed to know everything about him before he'd even got out of the cab. Handing over the forms he refused the offer of a morning paper, no he didn't need to be shown the breakfast area or to his room, if she would just give him the key together with directions that would be fine.

'All part of the service!' Isla flounced around to his side of the counter and asked him to follow her. It had been a long day – the flight from City Airport had been delayed – and perhaps he was being a little curt but he just wanted to get to his room. And was there no end to the girl's jabbering? Isla never came up for air as she led him through a warren of corridors which he was sure he'd never find his way out of tomorrow morning.

She was asking him if he'd worked for Gerry long but he was concentrating so hard on keeping a mental note of the layout that he didn't have chance to put her straight before she launched into telling him all about herself. Matthew was silently wishing he'd had the foresight to bring a trail of breadcrumbs when the girl suddenly mentioned a name that caught his attention.

'Sorry? What was that?' he asked.

'Yes, just an evening job this. Like I was saying, I work at Small House Book and Brew in the daytime – it's a cafe and bookshop down the other end of the harbour.'

'And who did you say the owner was there?'

'Jem. Jem Small.'

It was ridiculous. After twelve years her name could still cause his pulse to quicken.

Matthew suddenly perked up. 'And this is just at the other end of the harbour you say? Has it been there long?'

'Well, it was renovated at the same time as the rest of the resort. Part of Frank Monroe's big vision you know? It wasn't as popular as it is now mind, not before Jem came, she's really put it on the map. I remember growing up here and that place was always forgotten down there – just slightly out of the town. But Jem knows what she's doing. She's turned that in to a selling point. Sort of a traveller's rest thing going on. And-'

Christ, at this rate he'd be here all night. 'Sounds like a great person to have running the place. And Jem is like you, a local to the town is she?' he asked, breaking into her monologue.

'No, Jem came to live in Pine Tree ten years ago. Don't tell anyone I said this but she was like a breath of fresh air around here when she first arrived. Brought a lot of good ideas to this town. Anyway, I can't stay here all night gossiping. And you best get some rest before you're up in front of the town with Gerry Monroe tomorrow morning.'

Bidding Isla a goodnight, Matthew hurried into the room. He pulled the laptop from his bag.

Frustratingly it took a minute or two to get on to the hotel wifi and he noticed his hands were shaking slightly as he entered his email details and agreed to whatever terms and conditions they wanted him to sign up to.

Finally, after typing his criteria into the search bar and scanning the results, he felt something that he hadn't felt in a long time; he actually felt… *something*.

Jem

A mile back along the shore Jem was shouldering her heavy front door and she and Bear stepped into the warm hallway. She really needed to get a joiner to look at it soon; the damp was causing it to stick terribly and with winter coming it was only going to get worse. Finn had offered to look at the door for her on a number of occasions; he was handy around the house and she could have set him going with a whole host of projects. Which was all the more reason to get the joiner out soon. The last thing she needed was to allow herself to become reliant on Finn for free help around the place.

His hurt expression when she'd refused his offer of company had lingered with her a little on the walk home but running into the new girl had distracted her from brooding too deeply. Kate seemed nice enough. She'd brought the city with her – that much was clear – but a few months in Pine Tree Bay would sort that out.

Bear trotted through to the kitchen for a good drink and flopped down on his bed in front of the stove. Jem followed. She set the kettle to boil on the Aga. Bugger the de-caff; tonight she was in need of a good, strong brew.

She switched the radio on for some company and the velvet voice of Trevor Nelson floated around her large kitchen. As she pottered about making the tea and searching for biscuits she realised she was slightly drunk and chastised herself for the hangover she would have tomorrow, of all days, when she needed to be sharp for whatever news Gerry Monroe was bringing their way.

Scrabbling around for a packet of custard creams that she was sure she had hidden somewhere at the back of her larder, she angled her body sideways to reach the back of the overstuffed cupboard.

As she did so, she heard something slip to the floor. Bending down she smiled at the image staring back at her. It was a six by eight photograph that she had pinned to the inside of the larder when she first moved into her grandmother's house almost ten years ago.

Her twenty three year old self smiled back at her from a beach in Devon. She remembered pinning it there to remind herself what her body was capable of if she didn't gorge on biscuits! At least that was what she had told herself at the time. Maybe it had been there so long that she'd stopped noticing it… Instead of pinning it back on to the cupboard door, she took it over the the table.

It had been taken on a perfect summer's day. Three wetsuit clad twenty somethings with their arms slung around each other's shoulders grinned out at her. She hardly recognised herself. The carefree, effortlessly thin girl with a smattering of freckles across her nose, standing in the centre of two handsome young men. Nick on one side and his best friend Matthew on the other.

It had been a red letter day. She, Matthew and Nick, kiteboarding down on the Devon coast at Woolacombe in the blazing sunshine. Jem, new to the sport at the time had caught her first proper ride and they'd all whooped for joy that she'd finally nailed it.

Someone, she couldn't remember who, had captured the high they were on at the time and here it was; a single shining moment like a butterfly caught in amber relegated to the inside of a cupboard door. That day Nick had jokingly christened them *The Three Must Kite-eers* – and she and Matthew had rolled their eyes at the unbelievably lame title. They *had* been pretty much inseparable from that day onwards though.

Where had they gone? Those three? They had each ceased to exist from the moment that picture was taken, as everyone inevitably does.

After that shot, she remembered they'd joined the other surfers and boarders in front of the beach fire and Jem had watched Matthew melt away from the crowd with one of the pretty surf-babes - his usual MO. She and Nick had settled into the evening, chatting with the crowd over beers.

As the memories flooded back, her eyes lingered on the man standing on the right of the picture as she absentmindedly ruffled the fur beneath Bear's collar.

'Where is he now eh boy?' she murmured.

Bear rested his head on her lap and looked at her with mournful eyes as she continued to study the old photograph.

Where did you go? And why didn't you come for me?

Then she jumped at the sharp, insistent knock that was rattling her front door.

Jem

It was late. Who on earth could be calling round at this time? Jem sighed wondering if Finn had failed to take the hint after all. Opening the door however, the person she saw caused her jaw to fall open in astonishment.

'Madam Zelda?' Jem's eyes widened.

'Call me Beryl love,' the clairvoyant said, as if there was nothing remotely strange about calling round on someone you hardly knew, just before midnight. 'Ooh is that the kettle I can hear whistling? I could do with a brew. I'm spitting feathers after that walk along the shore road. These pins don't go as fast as they used to. Kitchen this way is it?' She bustled past Jem and made her way along the hallway.

'Please, come in,' Jem muttered dryly under her breath as she closed the door and followed the dumpy woman into the kitchen.

Depositing a large velvet bag on the table and collapsing into one of the painted wooden chairs, Beryl let out a heavy sigh. 'This festival of yours is going to be the death of me! Just the two sugars for me dear,' she sniffed.

Jem removed the singing kettle from the stove and took two mugs down from the dresser. Just as she was about to place a teabag in each one, Beryl held her hand up. 'No teabags for me. Can't stand the things. Now I see you have a lovely teapot on the second shelf up there.' She pointed to the Clarice Cliff heirloom which had belonged to Jem's grandmother then proceeded to rummage about in her big velvet bag. 'Here, you can use this.' Beryl pulled a brightly decorated box from the bag and thrust it at Jem. 'I can guarantee you've never tasted anything like it.'

Jem, feeling increasingly wrong footed, finally found her voice. 'But I er… don't have a tea strainer.'

'Problem solved!' The fortune teller produced a silver strainer from the velvet bag. It was a bit like having tea with Hermione Grainger.

'The thing is Zelda…'

'Do call me Beryl lovey. Beryl Clutterbuck. I did try reading under my real name for a while but it was difficult to drum up any trade. The minute I changed to Madam Zelda, I was flying. For all folk's talk about keeping it real these days – they still prefer a bit of the old codology when it comes to the mystical arts.'

'Yes I'm sure they do,' murmured Jem, placing the teapot on the table together with a jug of milk and a bowel of sugar. 'The thing is Beryl, with the meeting tomorrow, I was really after an early-'

But Beryl's beady eye had already flickered to the photograph that Jem had left on the table before running to answer the door. 'Taking a little trip down memory lane were we?' she asked, peering at the image.

'Yes,' Jem flushed. 'Believe it or not that photo has been pinned to my pantry door for the last ten years. I'd forgotten it was there. It fell onto the floor when I was looking for some Custard Creams.'

Beryl's eyes lit up. 'Custard Creams you say?'

Jem laughed, there was something about Beryl that you couldn't fail to warm to, however hard you might try. 'Yes I think I've got some here somewhere.' She went to have another look for the biscuits. Whilst she was rooting at the back of the cupboard Beryl suddenly piped up.

'I know you're struggling to believe in all this but I received a message for you tonight.'

'A message?' Jem asked, her head still in the cupboard.

'Well, I've been getting it for the past few days to tell the truth… it's only happened once before…'

'Got them!' Jem finally put her hands on the biscuits and brought them to the table then frowned at the older woman. 'What's only happened once before?'

Beryl poured them both a cup of her special tea. 'Milk love?'

Jem nodded. Beryl poured the milk then spooned two large heaps of sugar into her own cup whilst Jem covered hers with her hand to indicate none. 'Go on,' she nudged the older woman to explain.

'Well, it's a long time ago now but I once did a reading for a friend. A close friend. It was a reading a bit like yours. It had a warning element to it.' Beryl's face turned serious and Jem started to feel a prickle of anxiety at what might be coming next.

'My friend didn't take it too seriously, and he said as much, whilst the cards were out on the table.' Beryl raised her eyes slowly to meet Jem's. 'And the very next day, the first reading I did – for a completely different client I might add – threw up the exact same cards as the night before.'

'You mean the reading you'd done for your friend?'

Beryl nodded.

'Perhaps it was just the way they went back into the pack?' Jem shrugged.

'Not possible the way I do it.' Beryl shook her head sadly. 'No, it's the Tarot's way of telling me that a reading must not be ignored. That the message it contains is vitally important. I don't know that it happens to other readers but that's the way it works for me. I've been working with those cards for over fifty years. We're like old friends.'

'But what has all this got to do with me?' Jem asked.

Beryl swallowed a large gulp of tea. Placed her cup steadily back on its saucer. 'It's happened again. With the reading I did for you.'

'You mean the same cards you read for me came up again the next day?' Jem pulled the cardigan she was wearing tight around her chest as if feeling a sudden chill.

'And the next day, and the day after that,' Beryl nodded. 'I had to come see you otherwise those cards won't let it lie.'

Jem took a moment before asking. 'What happened to your friend? The one you said this happened with before?'

'Well, that one ended up in a spot of bother I'm afraid dear.' Beryl screwed her face up briefly then, seeing Jem's look of alarm, 'Oh it's all over now... It was all over a long time ago to tell the truth. But... Well, if we'd listened it might not have turned out the way it did.'

'So, what next? For me I mean?'

'Well, *I've* done my part, so hopefully now that sorts things out.' She placed her hand calmly on the table between them. 'Let's just have a natter whilst we drink our tea shall we?'

Jem said nothing. Was she actually hearing this right? The woman had invited herself in, scared the bejesus out of her and now she expected a cosy chinwag as if nothing had happened?

Beryl sipped her tea and tapped the photograph. 'Now, I wonder how much of a coincidence it is that the cards sent me on the night you were taking this little saunter into the past eh?'

Jem blinked hard refusing to be drawn but Beryl carried on regardless. 'So, which one's the Knight of Swords and which is the Knight of Pentacles then?'

Jem rolled her eyes. 'How do you know it's either of them?'

'Suit yourself.' Beryl smiled mysteriously and went back to studying the photo. 'The dark one's a dish isn't he? Mind you, I wouldn't kick the other one out of bed either.'

Jem half choked on her mouthful of tea. 'Beryl!' she spluttered.

'What?' Beryl asked innocently. 'I'm seventy five love, I'm not dead! So come on then who are they? You certainly look happy enough – standing here between both of them.'

Clearly Beryl was never going to shut up unless Jem gave her something. 'The one on the left is Nick. He was my boyfriend at the time.'

'So am I right in guessing he *wasn't* the reliable one?'

Jem pursed her lips feeling an invisible thread pulling her back to the day that she first met Nick Townsend. 'When we first got together, he was the most reliable man I'd ever met.'

Nick Townsend *was* a man you could rely on. From the very first day Jem met him, he demonstrated the quality that parents all around the world were longing for their daughters to find; a solid dependability. And, on a rainy day in June, fresh out of university with a first in English, it was the quality that Jem was looking for in a boyfriend.

After sprinting along London Bridge – trying to make it to an interview that she was, literally, running late for – Jem had hurtled down the Nancy Steps into Montague Close and managed to somehow dive head first into the stone stairwell; knocking herself unconscious in the process. She would never know how long she lay there before coming round but when she did, she woke to find an impossibly good-looking man crouched beside her, speaking in soothing tones whilst his friend urgently called for an ambulance.

With a nasty gash to the head and blood trickling down her face, she tried her best to sit up but her dark haired, dark eyed rescuer had insisted that she didn't move. Instead, she gratefully let him cradle her head in his lap and blanket her with his jacket. And, whilst his friend gave all the details to the ambulance service, the man did his best to keep her spirits up.

'It seems strange saying this, given that your head is currently laying in my crotch, but I'm afraid we haven't been introduced. Hi, I'm Nick Townsend.' He spoke in a cut glass accent and held his hand out. Accompanied with a boyish grin, the cheeky introduction completely disarmed Jem.

She laughed. Then immediately wished she hadn't. 'Ouch!' she grimaced. 'You need to stop being funny. I'm Jem, pleased to meet you.'

'That's Matthew.' Nick indicated his friend who was still on the phone to the emergency services. Matthew smiled over, warmly, and when for a fleeting moment their eyes locked together, Jem felt a strange flicker of recognition. But that was impossible; she knew without a doubt she'd never met either of these guys before. Nick's voice had cut though her thoughts – explaining how he and Matthew had been heading back to the office when they found Jem unconscious on the stairs – and the moment was gone.

The paramedics were slow in making their way though the London traffic. Nick handled all the impatient commuters, angry at finding their path blocked by a wounded stranger. He kept up the charm offensive and made her laugh. A wincing Jem tried to make him stop; if only there wasn't a sledgehammer driving its way through her skull, she'd be enjoying herself.

The ambulance finally arrived and Nick insisted on accompanying her to the hospital. Even (mortifyingly) holding her hair back when she started to be violently sick. It was just Jem's luck; she was giving a live performance of *The Exorcist* for the best looking man she'd ever met. If the head injury didn't finish her off, she might just die with embarrassment.

When they arrived at Accident and Emergency, things didn't happen fast enough for Nick. He badgered the hospital staff to move her up the triage queue; fabricating stories about her babbling incoherently, throwing in terms like 'brain damage' and generally expediting things. After she was finally admitted, with a diagnosis of concussion, Jem thanked him for his help and waved him off, disheartened that he hadn't asked for her number and pretty certain she would never see him again.

She'd been surprised therefore, to wake after a snooze the following afternoon to find him sitting at her bedside brandishing a bottle of Lucozade and a bunch of grapes.

'Ta Da! I have *always* wanted to do this!' Nick beamed as she opened her eyes.

'Is this the new thing?' She yawned, sitting up in bed. 'This is the second time in two days I've woken up to find you by my side.'

'Yes but I'm gradually weaning myself off. Look,' he said innocently indicating his empty lap. 'No crotch in your face this time.'

Jem had burst out laughing. 'What kind of twelve step program is this?'

'I'm not sure but my therapist insists that you work with me on it.'

'For how long?'

'For as long as it takes I'm afraid,' he nodded gravely and set her off giggling again.

When the day came for her to leave hospital he was, of course, there to take her home. 'I'll get us a cab,' he said taking charge, his hand already in the air as they emerged onto the busy London street outside St. Thomas' Hospital. 'What's your address?'

'Not so fast Superman.' She was referring to his tendency to swoop in and sort everything as much as the fact that he had one hand in stuck in the air. 'I need some decent food and you are taking me for a slap up lunch.'

'Hmm... that is not actually a bad idea Lois,' he played along with the theme. 'And where would madam like to dine this lunch time?'

'Somewhere warm, cosy and out of the way that doesn't serve hospital food.'

'I know just the place.'

He took her to the alarmingly named Boot and Flogger, which was nestled down a side road just off Southwark Street and which, she had to admit, did fulfil the brief she'd given him to almost spooky perfection.

The dark, intimate surroundings led them to linger long after all the office diners had scurried back to their desks. They spent the afternoon working their way through two huge bowls of pasta and and a smooth Merlot, growing increasingly excited at all the many things there were to know about each other.

Jem told Nick about her grandmother, Marcia – whom she adored – and her mother; the latter being a much more complicated relationship. Try as she might to pass off the abbreviated version of her background,

Nick was having none of it. So Jem found herself confiding things that she rarely shared with anyone. How her mother, Sheila, had been a heavy drinker, even before Jem's father had died, and how once he was gone, the drinking had taken hold to an impenetrable degree. She glossed over the fact that, at twelve years old, with barely enough chance to grieve her father's passing she'd had to step into the role of carer, watching her mother grow steadily more incoherent and aggressive.

Jem didn't dwell on the four disastrous years that followed – it was all far too *Angela's Ashes* for a first date. But she did tell Nick how her grandmother had arrived on the morning of her sixteenth birthday, the age she was legally allowed to leave home, to take her to London. That had been when Jem's life really began.

Nick had listened to her story with a kind of horrified awe. His own childhood couldn't have been more different. A public school upbringing as the son of a diplomat based at various – exotic sounding but in fact incredibly boring – locations around the world. Embarrassed that his earlier complaints of being foisted off on a series of cousins in between school terms now sounded horribly privileged. In comparison to Jem's early life his had suddenly taken on the rosy tint of some *Famous Five* idyll. Surely she must think him an absolute heel.

Jem had laughed at his public school turn of phrase, amused by his stories as she sipped her wine. She was finding out so much about him and she liked what she heard; that he was an artist who loved to kiteboard, that the city job was just a means of securing his dream to retire young and sell paintings from his house on the coast. Captivated and half in love with him already, the long afternoon had stretched into evening and Jem confessed her own small dream of some day running a book shop.

Somewhere along the way their hands had become entwined and, with old scars and new dreams all laid out on the table, Nick had leaned in to kiss her. As first kisses went, it was up there. She closed her eyes knowing that the scent of sandalwood on his jaw and the taste of red wine on his lips would forever remind her of falling in love.

When they drew apart he held her gaze for a long moment. Affecting the tone of a character straight out of a Jane Austen novel he said, 'Miss Jemima Small, from the first moment I saw you spread-eagle and unconscious on the stone steps at London Bridge, I just knew you were going to be remarkable.'

Two bottles of wine in, they both thought this was the most hilarious thing they'd ever heard.

'Sounds like you fell in love with him right there and then?' Beryl's voice sounded very far away.

Jem looked around her kitchen in something of a daze. Had she really just said all that? Out loud? To Beryl? She hadn't even divulged things to Helena in this much detail. She looked suspiciously at the tea she'd been drinking then frowned. 'Are you sure you're not plying me with some kind of truth potion?'

Beryl, who had refilled the kettle and popped it back on the stove laughed. 'Don't be daft love. There's nothing like a cup of tea to loosen the tongue is there? So go on then. What happened after that?'

'Well,' Jem said dreamily, 'from that day – the day that I left the hospital – we were basically joined at the hip…'

Nick and Jem soon became an item and their friends quickly learned that if you were inviting one of them to something, you would naturally be getting the other. No one seemed to mind much, except perhaps, Nick's best friend Matthew. Jem understood that Matthew, whom Nick had done practically everything with up until Jem's arrival, must feel somewhat abandoned and she worked hard to befriend him.

This was how, over the course of the next few years, the three of them fell into the habit of going everywhere as a team. Jem came to value Matthew's friendship just as much as she valued Nick's love and she sensed the feeling was mutual. Over time, she even came to feel somewhat protective of their little trio. And, though she sometimes found herself thinking it might be good if Matthew found a long term girlfriend, so that some kind of permanent foursome could be established, she also worried that if that were to happen it might spoil what they had. Jem knew it was an unreasonable line of thinking. She tried not to dwell on it too much.

But, on the glorious day of the photograph – some time after they had all grinned out at the camera like a trio of kiteboarding loons – she watched Matthew steal away with the pretty surf babe then quizzed Nick about it.

'Why do you think he never settles with anyone?' Jem asked. They were on the beach at Woolacombe, watching the water shimmer in the golden pool of the setting sun.

'Who, Matthew?' Nick asked.

'Yeah, I can't understand it. I mean, he's warm and thoughtful – someone you'd think has, you know – *stickability*. Look how he is here, with all the kiteboarders. He's always helping people with their kit and walking them through whatever trick they've been half drowning themselves trying to learn.'

'You mean he's always helping *you*,' Nick said with a playful grin.

'Though, I have to admit, you do rather need help.'

She went to swipe him and he dodged it.

'It's not just me!' she said indignantly.

'It's *mostly* you.'

'Well I am only a novice to be fair.' Jem pretended to be grumpy.

Nick drew her into an affectionate cuddle before returning to the subject of Matthew. 'I don't know what it is to be honest. Up until you and I got together I had him pegged as a serial monogamist. He only had two or three long term girlfriends at university.' Nick stared into the distance. 'Maybe that's why he's like he is now. Maybe he wants to play the field a bit before settling down.'

'Don't you talk about this stuff with him?'

'Nah,' Nick shrugged. 'We used to, at uni, but these day's he's a bit cagey about his love life.'

Jem began scooping up sand and letting it fall through her fingers. 'I don't get how someone who's that, you know, reliable, can be so flighty when it comes to women?'

'Didn't we already establish that he's not 'flighty', as you call it, with all women.'

'Well, with all the ones *I've* known him to be with.'

'But not with *you*.' Nick held her gaze for a moment and a slight edge crept into his voice. Suddenly he jumped up, shook the sand from his shorts and said with a wicked grin. 'Come on *novice*, I have a few new moves to teach you back at base!' He waggled his eyebrows suggestively.

She burst out laughing and rolled her eyes. But she never needed asking twice.

Jem steered clear of quizzing Nick about Matthew after that. She wasn't sure why but the conversation had left her feeling uncomfortable. Like Nick often said; life was good and there was no need to question everything.

'The only fly in the ointment at the time, was my grandmother, Marcia,' Jem heard herself saying to Beryl as the singing kettle brought her back to the present.

'What, she didn't like him? Your Nick I mean?' Beryl poured hot water into the teapot so that they could replenish their cups.

'It wasn't that she didn't like him,' said Jem. 'She was always nice to him. She was happy for me. But I couldn't get her to open up about her feelings where Nick was concerned. I always thought she was holding back.' Jem bit her lip. 'And then, just six months before Nick and I were due to be married, she got diagnosed with pancreatic cancer…'

Jem was beside herself. How could she be losing the person who's unconditional love had once been her only lifeline, who's friendship she had come to depend on and who's wisdom had become her compass?

Jem spent the following months constantly at her grandmother's side. Marcia wouldn't allow any maudlin scenes; against doctor's orders they drank and ate what they liked, had parties with Marcia's eclectic and varied bunch of friends, listened to loud music, danced in the kitchen; Marcia even insisted on going horse riding – something Jem had not even realised her grandmother could do. Marcia wanted Jem to remember those last months as a happy time and, ultimately, she got her wish. Nick understood and gave Jem and Marcia the space they needed. Jem was grateful he wasn't the clingy type; didn't make her feel as though she was abandoning him in the lead up to their wedding.

One evening, after a particularly raucous group of Marcia's friends had finally taken the many hints that Jem was dropping and pushed off, she and her grandmother sat in the quiet kitchen, catching their breath.

Jem had started to clean up, but Marcia told her, rather irritably, to leave it all until the morning and pour them both a brandy. Jem did so and they moved through into the living room, sinking into Marcia's battered chintz sofa, where they could sip their cognac and put the world to rights.

It's now or never, Jem thought to herself and she finally summoned up the courage to ask Marcia what she really thought of Nick.

'You know as well as I do that it doesn't matter a jot what *I* think about him,' Marcia said gruffly. 'It only matters what *you* think. I hope I've taught you that much at least.' She stared into her glass as she spoke.

'Well, that's true I suppose,' Jem said hesitantly. 'But it's one thing not to know *if* I have your approval and another thing entirely to know you could never give it.

Marcia looked at Jem and sighed. 'It's not that I don't approve of Nick,' she said at length. 'I don't know that I would think anyone was good enough for you.'

They sat in silence for a while and Jem supposed she would have to be satisfied with that, when Marcia suddenly piped up. 'You know, once things have run their course, there will need to be some strong young men to help me into the church. Of course I'm sure that Nick will step up…'

'Of course,' Jem whispered, hardly able to imagine such a thing, let alone speak of it.

'And perhaps you could ask Matthew too?' Marcia fixed Jem with a piercing stare.

Jem promised. Under the scrutiny of that gaze, she wouldn't have dared do anything else.

And so, when that awful day dawned, just weeks later, Jem had done exactly that. Nick and Matthew had looked so dignified and sombre as they joined the other pall bearers in doing this last thing for Marcia. Jem had been moved to see that Matthew's face was wet with tears as his eyes sought hers when the men reached the front of the church. And, of course, Nick continued to be her rock not only that day but throughout each of the difficult weeks that followed.

'Just one more for the road I think.' Beryl was topping up their cups with the last remnants of the second teapot which now sat on the coffee table in front of Jem's sofa. 'I see what you mean about your fellah being the reliable sort. Why do you think Marcia was so insistent on this Matthew being so involved in her final arrangements though?'

Jem looked around with a slightly dazed expression. When had they moved into the lounge? Every time Beryl remarked on her story it was as if she were breaking into a dream that Jem was having. Perhaps those three glasses of wine in the pub had been larger than usual? She really was feeling quite woozy and she had *never* talked so openly about her past to anyone before. Her brow furrowed as she pondered Beryl's question. 'I've never thought about it to be honest.'

Beryl picked up the photograph again and took a closer at the lighter haired of the two men. 'Do you think Marcia was trying to tell you something? You *had* just asked her what she thought about Nick after all?'

'You mean… when I asked about Nick, Marcia diverted my attention to Matthew?'

'Oh don't mind me love.' Beryl waved her hand and batted her eyelids. 'I'm just thinking out loud. Obviously she must have *loved* your Nick. What with him being so dependable and all?'

'Well that's kind of the problem…'

When Jem arrived at St Paul's Cathedral on a spectacularly sunny November morning, it had never for one moment crossed her mind that Nick wouldn't be there. She knew it unquestionably; just as she knew that if she opened her mouth there would be air to breathe. Today they would be married and tomorrow they would start their married lives; together with the little black Labrador puppy that Nick had brought home on their last evening together three nights ago.

And so, as she drew up in the wedding car, wishing beyond any other thing that Marcia was there to give her away, there was no question in her mind that there would be someone to give her away *to*. But it had been apparent from the moment the engine slowed that everything about the scene was wrong.

As the driver prepared to set her down, she immediately noticed that those who should be waiting expectantly inside the chapel were standing outside, wearing frowns instead of smiles, clutching phones instead of confetti. Momentarily she was annoyed that people should be spoiling the order of things. She hadn't wanted anyone to see her dress until she walked down the aisle.

And then realisation dawned.

It was the sight of the reverend, outside the vestry. The man who, only last week, had smiled beatifically at both she and Nick during their rehearsal, now stood grim faced outside the church with Nick's parents. All morning she had pictured him, greeting her at the bottom of the aisle with his calm, mellifluous voice, crooning, 'Dearly beloved…' But instead here he was, cassock flapping in the wind, irritably smoothing his combover whilst firing questions at Nick's dad.

Nick's parents, whom she had met just a handful of times wore expressions of what Jem could only describe as embarrassment. Nick's mother, Nancy was dragging on a cigarette as if it were life support and his father, the MBE, the reason Nick and Jem were able to marry at St Paul's Cathedral, was staggering around like he'd been hit by a car.

And, as if all this wasn't confirmation enough, the expression on Matthew's face sealed it. As Jem's car drew to a standstill his deep blue eyes, filled with concern, locked with hers; reminding her of the first day they had all met, when Nick had been by her side and Matthew had been calling the ambulance. Only this time there was no reassuring smile.

Matthew walked slowly toward the car, all the while maintaining eye contact. She knew what he was telling her. He was willing her to be strong; communicating silently that she needed to prepare herself. He spoke briefly to the driver, then opened the door and climbed in. She faced him clear eyed and raised her chin slightly, ready to take what he had to say, but he didn't speak. He clenched his jaw and she saw everything in his expression, he shook his head almost imperceptibly and Jem turned to see that the car was moving and St Paul's was disappearing far, far behind her.

*

In the lounge of Withershins, Beryl pulled a woollen blanket from the back of the sofa and lay it across Jem's sleeping form. She brushed a stray curl from the younger woman's cheek then walked into the kitchen to check on Bear. Seeing that the Labrador was snoring happily on his bed in front of the Aga, she packed the box of tea and the silver strainer into the purple bag and made her way back out into the hallway. She paused for a moment half way along the hall, in front of a picture of a grey haired vibrant looking woman with a necklace bearing the initial 'M'.

Placing a hand against the picture frame she spoke softly, 'Nice to know who I'm working with. Your girl will get a good night's sleep now she's got that lot off her chest.'

And then she quietly let herself out of the front door.

CHAPTER FIVE
4th October

Kate

The next morning The Smugglers was heaving and Kate arrived just as proceedings were getting underway.

This was so *not* her scene. Suse would probably wet herself when Kate told her she'd engaged in something as community spirited as a town meeting. She felt slightly conspicuous, having no reason to be at the gathering other than sheer nosiness, but no-one seemed to notice the newcomer in their midst. And anyway she wasn't about to pass up the opportunity of seeing business tycoon Gerry Monroe in action. It was the corporate woman's equivalent of an Ed Sheeran concert.

How ironic it was that here in nowheresville she found herself with the opportunity to get up close and personal with such a global corporate player. She was hoping to have the opportunity to meet the man himself at the end, but for now she hovered at the back until another late-comer, who introduced himself in whispered tones as Jamie, brought them both a chair from the other side of the room.

She had just taken her seat when the tall slick looking Gerry Monroe took the floor. Hmmm, Mr Monroe was not a tall man but one with undeniable presence. She felt a current of electricity pulse through the crowd when he entered the room – but not in a good way. He was undoubtedly attractive but something was off. Something that didn't come across in the proliferation of media coverage that followed him around the world. She supposed if she were that way inclined she might describe him as having a 'dark aura', but she wasn't, so she would just have to sum it up by saying he looked like a bit of a git.

She imagined this innate ability to unnerve an audience was extremely effective in discouraging challenge and criticism. No wonder he had a reputation for getting what he wanted. The man oozed power and influence and a not a small amount of menace. It would intimidate even the strongest of characters.

In a surprisingly warm Canadian accent, Gerry started off by taking a few minutes to thank the town for their get well wishes, promising that he would be sure to pass these on to his father. He clearly took umbrage when someone in the crowd muttered that they would much rather pass on the wishes themselves, but unable to determine who had actually delivered the heckle, he had no choice but to move on.

Unable to resist, Kate leaned over to Jamie and whispered, 'Now I'm sure you'll all be wondering why I've called this meeting.' Just as Gerry Monroe cleared his throat and in an authoritative tone launched into his prepared speech.

'Now, I'm sure you will all be wondering why I have gathered you here today.'

Jamie sputtered with laughter but managed to turn it into a cough and held his hand up in apology as Gerry Monroe fixed him with a steely black-eyed glare. Kate, having never before experienced the joy of being the bad girl at the back of the class, basked in the glow of her new friend's admiration.

At the front, Gerry continued his speech. 'I'll come straight to the point and I won't insult your intelligence by trying to sugar coat things.'

In Kate's experience when people were at pains to point out that they weren't trying to insult your intelligence, it meant you should definitely prepare to be hoodwinked. She pricked her ears for what was coming next.

'You will all remember last year, the sad and sudden death of Peter Bartlett who had, up until that point, looked after the commercial business reporting for Pine Tree Bay resort.'

A murmur of respectful acknowledgement went around the audience before Gerry continued.

'At the time you will also remember that my father asked me to find an accountant to step into Peter's shoes until another suitable local candidate could be found to take over the reins.' Kate noted the crowd were silent at this point as they waited for the other shoe to drop.

'When my team took over,' Gerry continued, 'they conducted a thorough review of the accounts to date and unfortunately, I'm sorry to have to tell you all, some *anomalies* were found.'

The crowd immediately started to fire questions at Gerry.

'Are you implying that Pete Bartlett was on the fiddle?' This was from the red faced, pirate impersonating, bar owner who Kate had met a few nights ago. Based on what she'd seen to date, Kate suspected this man could gossip with the best of them, but he certainly wasn't about to let Gerry Monroe run a dead guy down in public.

'Pete was as honest as the day is long!' shouted a woman at the front.

Gerry Monroe raised his hands like the Messiah settling his flock. *He's enjoying this,* thought Kate.

'All I am saying,' Gerry continued smoothly, 'is that, whilst we do not understand how it has happened yet, all indications are that the commercial traffic, and more importantly, *the profits*, from the business units in this town have been under-reported for the last five years.' He paused to let his words sink in. 'And as a result, the leases that you, as business owners, have been paying to my father's company may be seriously under valued.'

Everyone started to speak at once. If Gerry was thinking of increasing the leases it was going to affect all their livelihoods. Perhaps even put some people out of business.

'Mr Monroe!' Jem's voice rang out firmly above the agitated crowd as she rose to her feet. Suddenly the room became very silent. Clearly, thought Kate, Ms Small was a force to be reckoned with around these parts. 'As you well know, most of the business owners here,' she gestured around the crowd, 'are sole traders who run their own profit and loss accounts. Under the terms of our leases we are under no obligation to report our profits to you but we have always provided the figures, via Pete, as a favour to your father.' People in the crowd were nodding at Jem's summary of the situation. 'So I, for one, would like to be very clear on exactly what it is that you are suggesting here today. Are you accusing the people here of under-reporting their profits to Pete Bartlett? Or, are you accusing Pete of under-reporting those figures to Frank?'

The room was silent as everyone waited to hear Gerry's response. If it weren't for the fact that Jem was still holding the cup and saucer she'd picked up on arrival, she would look very commanding indeed, thought Kate.

Gerry Monroe cleared his throat and Kate's practiced eye saw a barely perceptible shift in the man; there was something about Jem Small that made him uneasy. This was getting more interesting by the minute. 'That is what I am proposing we find out Ms Small. My people-'

'Before you tell us about your 'people' Gerry, would you first mind explaining to everyone here, your basis for suspecting that Pete Bartlett's figures were incorrect in the first place?'

'Since taking over the reports,' he answered airily, 'my team have monitored customer traffic *and* a sample of sales revenues compared to the previous five years-'

'So what you're saying is that you've been spying on us.'

'That's hardly my father's style Ms Small. I would have thought you of all people-'

'Gerald!' Jem cut him off sharply once more. Kate noticed that he did not seem pleased at all with this formal version of his name. It *was* rather like a mother admonishing her child thought Kate, amused at the mental image of the business tycoon in short trousers and a school cap. Presumably this was the precise effect that Jem was going for. Kudos for the tactic. It took some guts with a guy as intimidating as Gerry Monroe.

'Firstly,' Jem continued, 'as you very well know, we have doubled our marketing budget over the past two years. The first year of marketing brought increased visitors for *this* year, and this year's spend will hopefully bring even more visitors in for the next. As someone in your position is well aware, there is a lead-time associated with marketing and so of course there are going to be differences in the year on year sales revenues you've compared. Secondly-'

However, before anyone could hear what Jem's second point was, three things happened in quick succession.

Firstly, the door to The Smugglers swung open setting off Rab's Halloween sound effect which secondly, caused everyone to gasp and jump out of their seats then giggle at their own ridiculousness as a stranger walked through the door. Thirdly, as Jem turned irritably to see who was interrupting her in full flow, she inhaled deeply and lost her grip on the cup and saucer she was clutching which clattered noisily to the floor and smashed into pieces.

Intriguingly, as Gerry Monroe watched all this unfold, the faintest of smiles played across his lips and indeed it might, thought Kate, as the whole thing *would* have been quite comical had it not been for the startled look on Jem's face. Whatever had just played out had dramatically changed the power dynamic within the room and Kate was not entirely sure that the timing was coincidental.

Gerry Monroe smoothly reclaimed the floor, 'Ah Matt, thank you for joining us, great timing as always. Ladies and gentlemen this is Matt Albright.'

Kate turned to see the dishy guy who had exited the cab outside The Barnacle the previous night. Matt Albright, who was frowning and checking his watch, was obviously more than a little puzzled that the meeting was already underway. Clearly a professional however, he covered it well. Once introduced he started nodding and smiling affably, as he said 'Good Morning' to everyone.

Whilst Gerry Monroe rattled on about how 'Matt' was going to be his 'eyes and ears on the ground in Pine Tree Bay for the next few months' and the crowd were distracted by the newcomer, Kate watched Jem very carefully. All notions of roasting Gerry Monroe seemed to have been forgotten as she crouched silently and, with shaking hands, collected the broken pieces of china from the floor. And when Jem ducked through a door immediately to the side of her chair, Kate silently edged her way around the back of the room to follow her.

The kitchen was empty – apart from Jem – who stood stock still, her hands gripping the counter, the broken pieces of the cup and saucer she had been holding sat on the work top in front of her. The first thing that struck Kate was how pale Jem looked. All the blood that had drained from her face when Matt Albright walked into the pub had yet to return.

Kate gave a little cough to announce her presence and Jem shifted slightly then looked at Kate as if she was trying desperately to pull herself together. She was frowning but the penny quickly dropped and she shook her head slightly. 'Oh, Kate, hi. You decided to come then?'

'Jem, I know we don't know each other very… Let's be honest, we don't know each other at all so, I hope you don't mind me asking but… are you ok?'

Jem

Get a grip. Get. A. Bloody. Grip!

Finally finding her voice Jem stammered, 'Yes I... I was just startled by Rab's daft sound effect thing. I lost my grip on the cup and saucer.'

'I think it gave everyone a fright to be honest.' Kate laughed, then said more gently, 'Is that all it was then? Because, frankly, you look as if you've just seen a ghost.'

'Yes that's all it was. How stupid. I was enjoying giving Gerry Monroe a good grilling too.' Jem spoke too quickly, her laugh a touch too brittle. Even to her own ears she sounded nervous. She just needed a minute. To gather herself. Before she had to go back out there.

'So, who's Matt Albright then?' Kate asked.

'Matthew-' Jem said it before she could catch herself. She bowed her head and took a deep breath. 'Was it that obvious?'

'Well, only to me I think, I'm pretty sure everyone else was distracted by the *Thriller* soundtrack.' Kate grinned.

Jem glanced towards the door behind which Matthew's friendly, confident voice, a voice she hadn't heard for nearly twelve years and one she'd thought she'd never hear again, was now addressing the town, *her* town.

Finally, she spoke, 'I knew him as *Matthew* Albright. He doesn't like his name being shortened to Matt. Well, there was only person who could ever get away with it back when I knew him. It's no big secret really, I was supposed to get married but...' she shook her head irritably and wrung her hands, 'I don't know why I feel embarrassed saying this, it's not like *I* did anything wrong, but the man I was supposed to marry never showed up.'

'I see.'

'Matthew was my fiancé's best man. Matthew was the one who met me at the church to tell me that Nick wasn't coming. He took me home, helped me sort my head out in the month's afterwards. But we... we lost touch and it's just a bit of a shock him turning up here out of the blue that's all. Sort of... brings it all back you know?'

Jem hadn't revealed much but the rate she seemed to be divulging her business to all and sundry these days was causing her to question her own, hitherto, good sense. She wouldn't be sharing the rest however. She wasn't about to tell Kate that Matthew had been the only thing that got her through the months following the wedding. That, in those first few terrible weeks, when she was little more than a hollowed out shell, he made sure she got up every day. Made sure she ate, dressed, called her from work every morning to check she'd been out for a walk then came straight to the flat every evening to cook her a decent meal.

Between Matthew's care and Bear's dependency, Jem had made it through those black months. Predictably, Matthew had done the right thing, stepped in and cleared up the devastation his best friend had left behind. Fulfilled his responsibilities as best man, best *friend*, to both of them, even though there had been no *actual* wedding.

Kate spoke hesitantly, sounding a touch confused, 'Well, I can see that would be a shock. Sounds like Matthew is one of the good guys at least?'

'Yeah, I suppose...But that's the trouble with the good guys isn't it? You never know if they're helping you because they *should* or because it's what they want?'

When Jem looked up, Kate was staring at her with a puzzled expression.

'Anyway I sort of, left that part of my life behind me when I came here,' Jem said more robustly. 'Seeing Matthew, well, it's a reminder of a tough time that's all.'

'Of course,' said Kate, her expression now turning to one of concern.

Jem hated that look. She couldn't bear to think that anyone was feeling sorry for her. For months after Nick had bolted *that look* had been everywhere. On the faces of friends, colleagues, neighbours, ...Matthew. It was one of the reasons she had to get away from London. It was also the reason she now regretted confiding in Kate. That look was the reason she avoided telling people about what happened. Being jilted was something that, inexplicably, changed you forever in someone's eyes.

She gave herself a mental shake, squared her shoulders. 'Look Kate, could I ask that you keep what I've just told you to yourself?'

'Of course, you have my word.' Kate said. Then, clearly trying to lighten the mood, she added, 'It helps that I don't actually know anyone around here to tell anything to.'

'Thank you.' Jem smiled, relieved they were back on to a breezier footing. 'Well,' she said with a brightness she didn't feel. 'I suppose we best get back out there and find out what the hell Gerry Monroe's up to.' She started towards the door.

'Just before we do.' Kate placed a stalling hand on Jem's arm. 'I hope you don't mind me asking but... your wedding? The groom? What happened to him?

Jem wished she had never started down this path. She didn't even know this woman. But she had shared the confidence so she answered honestly all the same. 'The truth? I haven't got the faintest idea.'

Nick

Andalucía, Spain

> *"...In recent years a new and exciting artist has been steadily garnering more than a little recognition amongst the serious collectors of Italy and South America. Triggered by an initial flurry of investments from some of the more heavyweight enthusiasts just over five years ago, a new darling of the modern oil painting world has emerged. A painter who, until relatively recently, was a complete unknown.*
>
> *Nothing particularly out of the ordinary about that, you might think, in a world where art moves in and out of fashion and collectors' tastes have all the constancy of an Off-The-Nore wind, until we mention that the artist in question insists on complete anonymity. Whether this is from choice, necessity, or the result of a shrewd marketing ruse, is unclear, but one thing is certain; it is a move which has some of the wealthiest collectors of the art world speculating in their droves.*
>
> *The cloak and dagger approach is clearly paying off. The prolific artist, who has, somewhat fortuitously, acquired the moniker of 'The Ghost' amongst buyers, has sold in excess of forty paintings in the last five years. Although many of the sales are private, the oil and acrylic on canvas 'Deja-Blue' which is part of the painter's emotionally charged Surf Girl series, recently sold at auction for a price in excess of $60,000.00..."*
>
> *P Chalcott, Marshall Arts Magazine*

Nick Townsend closed down the on-line article and smiled to himself. His agent was going to love this. Perry had been endlessly excited by the anonymous artist angle from the moment he'd first dreamt it up. And Nick had to admit, his agent *had* struck gold. Perry had earned every cent of his commission, twice over, just for coming up with the idea.

The art world loved a gimmick and this one had created a demand for Nick's work, no question, but, more importantly, it had allowed him to get his paintings out there in the first place. When Nick had first arrived in Spain twelve years ago he'd despaired of ever being able to make real money from his work. How could he when it was impossible for his face to become known? Perry's idea had solved that problem and made them all a good slug of cash into the bargain.

Nick poured himself another coffee and stared out at the amazing vista before him. His large modern house was situated on a remote Andalucian hillside, with floor to ceiling windows that looked out on to a wide valley of olive groves sweeping down to the sea below. The villa and the many acres of surrounding land had been bought for a song when he and Zara first arrived and since then they had extended it massively. It had been, and still was, ideal for the privacy and anonymity they required.

As he sipped the sweet Sumatran blend that Zara insisted they shipped in each month, he thought back to the day twelve years ago when he and Perry had first met. He'd only been in Spain for a few weeks and, jumpy as a cat, he'd panicked thinking Perry was some kind of private investigator. It was amusing to think back on how nervous he'd been at the start.

Running out on the wedding and arriving at the Spanish villa twelve years ago, were all still, to a large extent, a blur in Nick's mind. He remembered the sensations of that time – the fear, the shame, the hatred, the all consuming desire – more than he remembered the actual events. It was as if he had accidentally stumbled off the path of his own life into the fast flowing river of someone else's. Zara was the current, dragging him ever further from the future he'd planned with Jem, yet at the same time, enabling his one big dream. Such had been his state of mind back then, the day he first met Perry Charles.

After weeks of living in fear, too scared to leave the villa, Nick had found himself feeling desperate. Very close to losing his mind altogether, he'd grabbed his car keys and charged out of the house. Not really sure where he was headed, he had pointed the car in the direction of the coast. It was winter; there wasn't going to be much in the way of available cafe or bar culture down in the resorts but that was exactly what he needed. As the miles between himself and the villa grew, he'd noticed his chaotic thoughts starting to slow, allowing him to arrange them in some sort of order.

Five weeks after running out on his wedding to Jem Small, Nick was still consumed by the enormity of what he'd done. And the heartbreak of what he'd lost. What he needed above all that morning was to get away from Zara for a few hours. The woman seemed to have no concept of this new existence they had entered. The line they had crossed. Yes, Nick had played his part in ending up in this impossible position but his part had been one of weakness, disloyalty and betrayal. It was Zara's actions that had turned them both into criminals. The one saving grace for now, at least, was that no-one else seemed to have cottoned on to that.

Still, as he dodged the rutted potholes, Nick was nervous. Not just about being on the run, but about all kinds of things; venturing out in a country where he could hardly speak the language, the weight of a new existence where he would forever have one eye on the door, and the endless days that stretched before him with only Zara for company. And, reflecting on the past five weeks, he suspected it was the final item on that list that filled him with the most terror.

Nick had honestly thought that once they arrived in Spain, he and Zara would talk. Properly. Reflect on all that had led them there. That she might just explain what on God's earth she had been thinking, dragging him into this. He'd hoped they could establish some kind of intimacy, *outside* the bedroom, but she would not be drawn. She just seemed happy to languish by the pool, pretending they were on some carefree, extended holiday.

Nick felt anything but carefree.

He could imagine what they were all saying back in London. That he'd run out on Jem. Couldn't handle the responsibility of marriage. Scarpered. *Escaped*. They would never ever know how wrong they were. Well, if he was lucky.

He'd always known it was unhealthy; the extent to which he wanted Zara, desired her physically. He couldn't explain it but she'd always made the blood run that bit quicker through his veins. It had been that way ever since he'd first set eyes on her at university. Matt had warned him constantly; she was trouble. Sensible Matt.

Right through his uni years, even during the 'off' periods, when Nick had assured Matt that he was done with Zara, he had always seemed to know where she was. His body answering some instinctive need to be in her orbit. Then, she'd finally made her choice – someone else. And Nick had managed to pull away; spin off into a world that wasn't at the mercy of her gravitational force. And whilst with Jem, things had never quite matched the excitement that had gone before, it had been so much better, less crazy. And he'd been happy, fulfilled, in control.

Until Zara had reappeared six months before the wedding and turned everything upside down. It was supposed to be an ego boost. He wasn't intending to sleep with her. Jem was spending most of her time with her grandmother so his evenings were free. He'd known he was playing with fire but he could handle it. He was eager to show Zara how far he'd moved on. And at first he really thought he had – that the tables had turned – she was making her play and he was flattered. Let *her* hunger for him for a change. But instead he'd ended up screwing her. And boy had she screwed him back.

Those first few weeks in Spain he'd had to ask himself – did he even *like* her? But even as he was asking he still couldn't get enough of her. Night after night, mornings, afternoon – it never diminished. Self destruction had never been his thing; drink, drugs, he could take or leave them, but this was something else. The physical attraction was destructive. It gave her some kind of hold over him. And *she* was addicted to *that*. He knew that much; Zara might truly think she was in love with Nick but what she was really in love with was the effect she had on him.

It was fucked up. They were both fucked up.

With this running around his head Nick had accelerated; increasing the miles between himself and the villa he had headed toward the coast. He noticed signs from the main highway for a small resort popular with Spanish tourists. It was somewhere he'd been with Jem a few years previous and though he had no desire to be reminded of better times, he yearned for something that was, even remotely, familiar. He parked the car and wandered through the small town finding it mostly closed up for the winter season.

Nick had been meandering around a small art gallery that was tucked away down a back street when he first bumped into Perry. They had exchanged a few pleasantries about one or two of the paintings. Perry was from the US and had that friendly, easy charm that, up until a few weeks ago, Nick would have attributed to himself.

To his great suspicion however, Perry had later walked into the same chiringuito that Nick had stopped to take lunch at. Noticing Nick, Perry made a beeline for his table. Nick's heart had beat a little faster as he saw the man striding toward him. It had taken great effort just to stay calm, forcing his body to move slowly, casually.

'Hi again,' Perry greeted him. 'Is it ok if I join you? Those *gambas* sure look good.'

'Of course,' said Nick, mimicking Perry's easy charm as best he could. 'Take a seat.'

'My Spanish is not so hot,' said Perry. 'I can get by enough to buy art over here but it's kind of a relief to meet someone I can speak English with for a change. I'm Perry, Perry Charles.' He held out his hand.

Nick shook it. 'Carl Ramos, pleased to meet you?' No matter that he had practiced it a thousand times with Zara, it still felt strange on his tongue.

'You're Spanish? With your accent I thought...'

'My father was Spanish,' said Nick quickly. 'We moved to Britain when I was very young and I was brought up and schooled there – hence the very English accent.' *Stop talking so much.* 'Anyway what brings you here Perry? I assume you're from the US?'

'Correct. I'm an art agent,' said Perry. 'I specialise in Spanish and South American painters. European art sells very well in the States so I make a trip out here every Fall and try to pick up some new artists for shows in the US. I'm guessing from the conversation we had back there in the gallery you're a painter yourself Carl?'

'I paint,' Nick said dismissively. 'It's more of a hobby though, nothing commercial.' He had a feeling he was on the brink of something, the conversation was going down a road he wouldn't easily be able to back out of and he needed to close it down. Already the guy knew his 'name', that he had a British background, that he was a painter. Zara was right, it was too risky to be where other people were just yet.

Nick thought back to all the films he had ever seen where a private detective rooted out the criminal and didn't it always start like this? Some guy all easy charm and innocence turning up a little too frequently. It put him on his guard.

As if sensing Nick's discomfort, Perry suddenly looked at his watch. 'Shoot, I completely forgot I have a call to make to a gallery in the States. I need to catch them first thing before they open and with the time difference… Look take my card.' He fished one out of his wallet and handed it to Nick. 'I'd love to see your paintings some time, if you would be so good as to show them to me. I'm always on the lookout for new talent.'

Nick had thanked him and watched him walk out of the restaurant, before hastily paying his bill and running back to the safety of the hills.

Remembering that day now, twelve years on, Nick was amused at himself. He'd been a nervous wreck back then and imagining Perry as some kind of private detective was hilarious. Remembering the seductive power that Zara had once wielded was not quite so much fun.

His phone rang and he looked at the caller ID. *Hablar del diablo.*

'Perry hi.' Nick said in greeting.

'And how is *The Ghost* this morning?' Perry's gravelly laugh almost deafened him. 'I hope you're in the studio making money for me Nick?'

Perry and Nick had become sufficiently close over the years for Nick to share his real name, though he had never shared the story that came with it.

'Of course,' Nick lied. 'Hey, I just read the piece in *Marshall Arts*. Laying it on a bit thick weren't you?'

'I've got my cut to think of!' Perry's laughter blasted his ear again. 'And if you could find it in your heart to part with the last painting in your *Surf Girl* series then, hell, we'd both be in the money.'

Nick chuckled, not this again. 'Some things are not for sale Perry.'

'Nick, I'm an agent. Everything is for sale at the right price.'

'Well not that one.'

'Worth another try,' Perry muttered down the line. 'Anyway listen up. It's not entirely a social call. I've had a request for a commission.'

Nick sighed, 'Perry, you know I-'

'No, I know you don't take specific commissions, I know. But I wouldn't be doing my job as your agent if I didn't run this one past you. It comes from a real player Nick. Have you heard of Frank Monroe?'

'Hasn't everyone?'

'Exactly. Well his people have been in touch. Specifically, his *son* has been in touch. He's a real heavyweight. He's prepared to pay you one hundred and fifty thousand for a commission. And that's one hell of a deal at the current exchange rate.'

Nick sensed that Perry was holding his breath. If Nick accepted the commission, Perry's cut on that one piece would match the whole year's earnings for his work to date.

He wasn't actually considering it, but he'd be lying if he said it wasn't a massive buzz. His work was attracting the attention of the really big players. Wasn't this what most artist aspired to? If they were honest?

Perry read him well, as usual. 'Your silence says it all! It's fucking awesome isn't it? But I'm presuming it's the usual *no?*'

Nick finally spoke, 'You presume right.'

Perry laughed. 'Thought so, but listen, this is the fun part, they had a condition. Get this – if you agreed to the commission, you had to personally unveil the work in one month's time.'

'Good God really? So they can't have been serious then?'

'They said they wanted you to deliver it in person to… hang on I wrote it down here somewhere… here it is, The White Pebble Gallery at Pine Tree Bay Resort in Scotland.'

'Scotland? I thought Frank Monroe was Canadian?'

'Yeah, he is. But apparently he built a town on the Coast of Scotland back in the nineties. Something to do with his roots.'

'But the guy clearly has no clue about the way I operate?'

'It's all dollar signs at that level. They probably want publicity for the resort. It would have been a real coup to have your work, and *you*, unveiled at the same time! Anyway I just wanted to run it by you, for the fun of it if nothing else.' More barking laughter followed. 'Catch you later.'

After Perry hung up, Nick typed the name of the gallery into his phone. Whilst he wasn't the same paranoid wreck who arrived in Spain twelve years ago, this was an unusual request. A telltale prickle across his shoulders told him he might want to pay attention.

But, before he could press search, he was accosted by a ten year old whirlwind of arms, legs and hair that ran into the kitchen and flung herself onto his knee. 'Daddy, you promised we could go to the beach today before it gets too cold!'

Nick swept his daughter up into a big bear hug. 'And here I am waiting for you! Where's all your beach gear?'

'Mama's just getting it ready.'

'Your bucket and spade?'

'Dad! Don't be ridiculous! I'm way too old for that now. I'm taking my headphones. I'll just chill and listen to some tunes.'

Nick grinned, knowing that once they got down there his daughter would most likely be racing him into the waves and begging him to buy yet another boogie board.

He stood up and swung her around making her convulse with laughter. 'Well, it would appear that whilst the bucket and spade are out, we are not too grown-up for spinning are we?' Sophia screamed louder as he twirled faster. She was still his little girl.

'Right!' He stopped spinning and deposited her on the ground. 'Go fetch your things from your room and let's get to the beach!'

His daughter ran off down the hallway, dizzily bouncing off the walls, the sound of her giggles echoing around the vast room. Smiling, Nick picked up his phone to run his earlier search. He used his thumb to scroll down the images until he came to a picture of the author for the Pine Tree Bay blog. And the woman staring out at him from the small screen caused his own head to spin.

Matthew
Scotland

In The Smugglers, Matthew scoured the bar room for the umpteenth time. He shook hands with people. He smiled. He said how pleased he was to meet everyone. He was vaguely aware that Gerry repeatedly introduced him as someone who was going to be in town for the next few months. Matthew didn't bother to correct him. He was on autopilot, his eyes continually scanning the crowd.

And then he spotted her. Coming through a swing door on the opposite side of the bar. A jolt of adrenaline surged through his body. Was he excited or annoyed that she could still have that effect on him? Some strange mixture of both perhaps.

He continued to greet different business owners warmly, telling them what a beautiful town Pine Tree Bay was, how great it looked all dressed up for Halloween – how he was really a Matthew not a Matt. But it was all just preamble to the main event. He kept her in his eye-line the whole time. Aware of where she was in the room without actually catching her eye, as he manoeuvred his way around to her vicinity.

All the while his internal monologue ran interference. Would she approach him? She must have seen him arrive. Would *she* come seek *him* out? He was over thinking things. *Just greet her like any old friend you idiot.* What exactly was he expecting was going to happen anyway? She was more than likely married or at the very least in a relationship.

And then she was in the next group of people. He glanced over, watched her tuck a strand of hair behind her left ear in a gesture so achingly familiar it made his heart quicken. She wasn't wearing a ring. Gerry was about to steer Matthew in her direction. He took a deep breath, prepared himself.

And then a loud woman brandishing a clipboard loomed in front of his face. 'Mr Albright, may I call you Matt?'

'Actually I prefer-'

'*I* am Madeleine Beaver. On behalf of the people of Pine Tree Bay,' the woman gave a magisterial sweep of her clipboard, 'it is my great pleasure to welcome you to *our* town. Gerry here tells us that you are going to be his "eyes and ears on the ground" and we are all here to assist in any way we can. If you have *any* difficulty in obtaining *any* of the information you need from *anyone*, please just come to see me, *I*…'

The wittering woman continued her imperial welcome but Matthew's gaze travelled slowly to the person on her left. Their eyes met and there was a moment of silent recognition. Then Jem smiled playfully, rolling her eyes and inclining her head toward Madeleine Beaver. Matthew, suppressing a laugh pounced on the opportunity to cut the intolerable woman short.

'Jemima Small! It *is* you, I can hardly believe it!' He faked the surprise.

'Hello Matthew.' Jem smiled warmly, calmly, disappointingly *unfazed* to Matthew's mind, whilst Madeleine Beaver, now thoroughly put out at being interrupted in the midst of her grand speech, was studying them both with the air of a hound picking up a juicy scent. 'So you two know each other *already*?' Her shrewd brown eyes shifted from one to other.

'Yes Madeleine,' said Jem evenly. 'Matthew and I actually go way back. We knew each other when I lived in London.'

Matthew nodded and his voice was steady despite his emotion. 'I saw your name in the documentation that Gerry asked me to look over,' he improvised, 'and I thought it was just a coincidence. But here you are!' And then he somewhat clumsily held his hand out to shake hers – as he had been doing all morning – but she said, 'Oh for God's sake come here Matthew!' And hugged him like the old friend he was.

The ease with which she instigated the embrace wrong footed him. It suggested a lack of self consciousness on her part and, though he hated to admit it, he wanted her to appear a little more shaken at his turning up out of the blue. When he considered his own jumbled mass of emotions at just being in the same room with her, he felt slightly ridiculous in comparison.

'How on earth are you?' He sensed he was doing a really bad job of concealing his delight. He was still holding her shoulders after the hug, drinking the sight of her in.

'I'm really well thanks,' she nodded. 'And yourself?' Her eyes flicked left and right signalling that she was conscious of the people around them.

'Well, I have to say, I'm all the better for bumping into you.'

He dropped his hands but gave her a meaningful look, trying to convey just how pleased he was to see her again, which meant he was completely blind sided when she said, 'So Matthew, tell us, are you here to put us all out of business? Because I warn you, we won't take it lying down.'

Her tone, whilst not deadly serious, had clearly been meant to put him on his guard, and he was just about to say that in all honesty, he was still working out what he *was* there to do, when thirty kilos of black fur almost knocked him to the ground.

'Hello you!' Matthew made a big fuss of the Labrador then looked toward to Jem, 'Is this…this can't be… *Bear*?' Bear stood on his hind legs, trying his best to lick Matthew's face whilst wagging his tail as fast as it would go.

Jem nodded.

'I missed you too boy.' Matthew laughed and spluttered, scratching beneath Bear's collar and fending off slobbery kisses. His eyes felt ridiculously moist at seeing the puppy who had been like his own for a few months now very grown up and grey around the chops.

Jem swallowed hard. 'I never did manage to stop him from jumping up. Mind you I haven't seen him greet anyone like that in a long while now. I think he might remember you.'

'Well let's see.' Matthew asked Bear to sit and shake hands and the Labrador dutifully obliged. Matthew looked back at Jem his eyes shining with triumph. 'He does remember!' Silently thanking Bear for breaking the ice between them Matthew then steered her to a quiet corner. 'Look, can you hang around for a bit? Can I talk to you before I leave? I'm heading back to London this afternoon and I'd love it if we could catch up before I go.'

But Jem didn't hesitate. 'I'm sorry,' she shook her head, 'I'm completely snowed under this afternoon what with the festival and everything. Plus I run a busy cafe and book shop down at the end of the bay.' He noticed that she wouldn't quite meet his eye.

'Yeah?' He couldn't help the edge that crept into his voice. 'Sounds really busy.' *Was she really not going to give him just half an hour?*

'It is.' She looked at her watch. 'In fact I should have been back there ages ago so I've got to run.' She started to fish Bear's lead out of her bag. 'I'm sure we'll run into each other though, if you're going to be around.'

'Actually, I'm not-'

But she didn't give him chance to finish before suddenly looking up from the bag, saying, 'I have to ask. Have you ever heard anything Matthew? About what happened, or where he is?'

So he'd been right all along, it was still Nick. Matthew shook his head but said nothing. He was damned if he'd show her how crushing that question was.

She nodded curtly. 'Understood.'

Jem hitched the bag on to her shoulder, looked as if she was about to leave, but she stopped and changed tack. Then in a cool, clear voice she said, 'Look, before I go I just want to say something. I meant it earlier. If Gerry Monroe has hired you to mess with us, we won't take it lying down. If he thinks he can swan in here, slag off Pete Bartlett and use *our* hard work to line *his* pockets, he's going to have a fight on his hands.' She paused, raising her chin. 'And if you're here to do his dirty work, well that goes for you too.'

Matthew didn't know what to say for a moment. He had been so keyed up about seeing her again. All they had once been to each other and this was what she was focussing on? 'I don't doubt that for a minute,' he answered cooly. 'But I'm just wondering what happened in the last twelve years to make you so uptight and paranoid?'

Her nostrils flared. 'How long have you known Gerry Monroe, Matthew? Five minutes? Wait until you've known him for as long as we have *then* rethink that question. He's already talking about undervalued leases on all our businesses, which probably means he's got something far worse than increasing them in mind for us.'

In all the many times that Matthew had envisaged them meeting up again, he had never imagined they would be arguing about property leases. He felt a complete and utter fool for his earlier excitement.

'You're right,' he snapped. 'I don't know Gerry very well, but I know what *I* stand for. And whats more, so do you.' Matthew searched Jem's face for even a flicker of the closeness they had once shared. Taking a deep breath he willed himself to calm down. His voice became softer, 'Jem, do you really think I'd be involved in some underhand plan? Especially one that I now know would so closely affect you?'

She didn't answer. How could she *not* answer? After everything?

He ran his hand over his jaw. 'Look, in my line of work, of course I deliver bad news, that's part of the job, but the way I operate it's never a surprise to anyone. The people I work with are aware what's coming down the line. I'm known for being above board.' Why was he having to defend himself to *her* of all people? Taking a step back he folded his arms. 'Christ, even if you've forgotten everything else about me, I thought you'd at least remember that.'

She refused to be drawn on the past. 'People change.'

'Well, as you won't even grace me with half an hour of your time, I don't have much chance to prove otherwise do I?'

'You took a job with Gerry Monroe.' Jem smiled tightly as she belted her coat. 'I'd say that proves your judgement is off.'

'I haven't actually accepted the job *yet*.'

'Well, if you want my advice, Matthew, don't.'

'Let me get this straight. You're telling me *not* to take the job here?'

Jem called Bear, fastened his lead and then turned toward the door. 'It really has been good to see you again Matthew. But, I don't want to find myself in a row with you over whatever it is that Gerry's got planned. I mean it in the best sense when I say that I hope we *don't* see you here again any time soon.' She kissed him; a brief, dry peck on the cheek. 'Goodbye Matthew.'

Then she was gone. Leaving him to stand and wonder what he'd wasted half a lifetime wishing for.

*

As the door to The Smugglers closed behind her, Jem let out a huge sigh of relief. It was over. She had faced him and she'd got through it.

Ok so she'd been a bit manic. Well maybe, on reflection, a lot manic. *Shit!* Had she actually been ranting on at him about property leases? She'd promised herself back in the kitchen that she'd be cool and nonchalant, then… Oh God, where had all that anger come from? And why had she had to ask about Nick?

Ok ok, so she'd been all over the place, but the point was, Matthew was leaving with the clear message that there wouldn't be a warm welcome for him if he took Gerry's offer and came to work in Pine Tree Bay. Not from Jem at any rate – Madeleine Beaver would probably hang out the bunting! She couldn't face Matthew here, not with all that he would bring. And he would only be coming to do Gerry Monroe's dirty work – how awful would that be?

She hitched her bag on her shoulder and looked around the blustery shore front. Her eyes came to rest on Beryl's motorhome. Drawing her collar up against a sudden blast of icy wind, she thought about the fortune teller's warnings, then gave her head an involuntary shake.

No! Whatever mysterious spell had conjured Matthew Albright here could bloody well send him back to where he came from. If that man was to become a regular around Pine Tree Bay her hard won equilibrium would be in tatters and she wouldn't risk that – it was the most valuable thing she owned.

She refused to go back. Been there done that. This heavy feeling in the pit of her stomach would pass. She was right to send Matthew packing and whilst she might have come across as a bit of a frosty faced cow, it had been necessary. She doubted very much he'd be accepting any job that brought him back to this town.

Regardless of what Beryl might have insisted fate was not going to weave its spell around her now; not here in her safe haven. Not if she had anything to do with it.

CHAPTER SIX
31st October

Jem

Scotland

Three weeks later the locals of Pine Tree Bay were exhausted. The thirty first of October had arrived and it was the culmination of the Pumpkin Festival; Halloween was finally here.

Visitor numbers were at an all time high and now the rest of the residents and business owners had finally caught up with the shops along the sea front. The whole of Pine Tree Bay was decked out in glowing pumpkins, spiders, ghosts and ghouls. Cobweb wreathed skeletons dangled from the trees and broomstick riding witches adorned every roof. The whole community had entered into the spirit and draped the town in whatever Halloween decorations they could cobble together using bits and bobs found in their attics and sheds. Jem questioned whether they hadn't all gone a little bonkers.

On the morning of the 31st, having decided to clear her head before the day's Halloween madness, she had scrambled into her running gear and taken Bear to hit the forest trails which sat up above Pine Tree. At his advanced age it was a miracle that Bear could keep up with her – but then again – her days of cluttering up Strava with seven minute milers were well behind her too.

The running bug had eluded Jem these last few years, which had obviously contributed to her slow down and though she hated to admit it, she just hadn't felt the same need to pound out the miles once life had become more settled and happy; a good hill walk would do her these days. Over the last two weeks however she had clocked up more running sessions than the whole of the last six months put together and now she sat on a tree stump at the top of the forest ridge, brooding over the conversation she'd had that morning with her head waitress, Isla.

Just as Jem had pulled the trainers from her kit bag, Isla had breezed in to her study. 'You've been hitting the trails a lot lately. Getting in shape for something are we?'

'Nothing in particular,' Jem muttered, frowning as a crust of dried mud fell from the sole of her running shoe and onto the wooden floor.

'Or some*one* perhaps?' Isla arched an eyebrow, commanding Jem's full attention.

'And who might that be?' Jem could out-arch anyone but Isla was not a bit fazed.

'Well now, let me see.' She held out her hand to count on her fingers. 'Could it be Pine Tree's very own answer to Bear Grylls? Unlikely, as he's been getting a load of you with your kit off for quite a while now so clearly he likes what he sees already.' Jem gasped but Isla carried on regardless. 'Or, could it be Mr big-shot Gerry Monroe? *Very, very* unlikely.' Isla shivered as if she had a sour taste in her mouth.

Jem made a disgusted face then laughed despite the fact that Isla was sailing very close to the wind.

'So that just leaves option number three; the tall handsome blonde with brains who rode in on his surf board three weeks ago and put that slightly edgy look in your eye?'

'Surf board?'

'He told me he's a kiteboarder,' Isla said knowledgeably.

'Well, yes, but you made him sound like one of the beach boys.'

'Aha! So you admit it's him then?'

Jem held her hands up in exasperation. 'Look. Me going out for a run has got absolutely nothing to do with anyone but me and this gorgeous boy here.' She reached over to scratch Bear under his chin then abruptly turned to back to Isla. 'And why would I be getting myself in shape for someone who popped back into my life for all of five minutes and is now long gone anyway?'

Isla couldn't contain her glee. 'Because he's 'popped back' again. And this time for a lot longer than five minutes.'

So this is really happening then. Jem didn't make eye contact with Isla, afraid she might give herself away and bent to pull on her trainers.

'He checked into The Barnacle last night,' Isla rambled on. 'Said he's going to look to rent somewhere for the duration of his contract.' The waitress inspected her nails innocently. 'I told him your annexe was free.'

'Isla...?' Jem shot upright with panic.

'What?' Isla gasped all wide-eyed. 'You said yourself if we had any enquiries at the hotel about longer term lets we could mention your place? I wouldn't have been doing my job properly if I hadn't mentioned it to him now would I?'

Jem could have cheerfully throttled the girl – now she really did need this run.

But Isla wasn't finished. 'And he's coming here to work this morning. I told him about the free wifi and our policy of keeping everyone fed throughout the day and he thought it sounded much better than working in his hotel room.' Isla ignored Jem's soaring eyebrows. 'Anyway from tomorrow, once the festival is finished, he needs to start visiting all the businesses in Pine Tree Bay, so I told him that this was as good as place as any to meet a few of the community ahead of that.' Isla smiled, thrilled at her own industrious efficiency, and then delivered the final nail in the coffin. 'He said he'll catch up with you about renting the annexe at the same time.'

Jem didn't wait to hear anymore. With a terse, 'Come on boy,' she and Bear headed out of the back door and up into the forest to work out a plausible reason why her garden flat would not be available when Matthew asked about it later.

The forest trails were Jem's refuge. This morning, she and Bear had climbed them at a jog, crunching through a carpet of needles, fallen from the trees that gave the town its name. Resting here, on the highest ridge, she drew deeply on the restorative effect that this view always had on her. A blaze of burnished autumn colours from the deciduous woodland that edged the trails and, at this time of year, snaked in a riot of rust and yellow all the way down to the silver blue bay below.

Jem needed to give herself a good talking to. Matthew's presence in Pine Tree, unsettling as it was, simply shouldn't cause this much anxiety. Of course it was a shock to see someone from such a pivotal and devastating moment in your past but her reaction to that first appearance had felt too extreme. The more she thought about it, the more she realised that it wasn't so much the events that were unfolding, so much as the shift in her ordered life that they signalled.

She was thirty nine years old. If life had taught her anything it was that relationships were difficult to put your faith in. She wasn't sorry for herself, she didn't think she was indelibly scarred and closed off, but she was a pragmatist; and the fact remained that, of all the big loves in her life, there was only one that had endured and that was her beloved Bear. And even that couldn't go on forever… Her father, mother, grandmother and Nick were all gone for one reason or another and of all of these, only her grandmother had left the real legacy of love and wisdom, and yes, it had to be said, some financial security, to enable her to make a life.

And, she thought as she continued to gaze down upon her town, it really was a great life. She loved living in this wonderful close-knit community of special people. There were many close friends she could rely on for company and support, she had a solid roof over her head and a business she was proud of. She had managed her way through the difficult times and come out the other side, happy and moderately successful. Why did it feel like this was all suddenly under threat? That something or someone was insistent on pulling her back to the past when she just wanted to leave it where it was.

That was why Matthew's arrival was unsettling. He was unfinished business yes, but he was business she did not *want* to finish. That was why she left London in the first place. He represented what she had lost. Whenever he looked at her he saw the jilted girl, all set for one life and now having to settle for another. That wasn't who she was anymore. That wasn't the way that people here in the town saw her; the mirror that *they* reflected back was the one she wanted to look into.

And then there was what had happened before she left London. There was no one more shocked than Jem when she had found herself falling for Matthew in the months after Nick disappeared. But he'd been so easy to fall for. So kind, so gentle, putting her back together piece by piece, until that evening when, after months of a slow burning chemistry between them, it had finally happened.

When she had reached for him and he, responding tentatively at first, had returned her kiss with an intensity that was completely unexpected yet, at the same time, so *right*. The way they'd gradually built toward something that was well, to be frank, off the charts. Afterwards, she'd been startled to realise how different it had been compared to anything she'd shared with Nick.

Ironically though, it was the night spent with Matthew that had suddenly brought it to mind – the fact that she hadn't had a period since before the wedding. She knew it had to be the worry of the last four months but she also knew the sensible thing was to take a test and so she'd taken a walk to the chemist on Upper Street. All the way home, as London pulsed in the bright sunshine of an early Spring day, she told herself it would be negative. She had no other symptoms. She had *lost* weight not gained it. It was impossible that she was going to have a baby. Life was just starting to look like it could be bearable again; surely fate wouldn't be cruel enough to throw her yet another curve ball. Half an hour later, two blue lines confirmed otherwise.

Of course she was pregnant and *of course* it was Nick's baby. The previous night she'd seen the glimpse of some potential happiness just around the corner, so wasn't it typical of the way her luck was running that this would happen. But there was also a sense of excitement. A sense of new beginnings. She was going to be a mother!

Jem couldn't bear to think of telling Matthew. She already knew how he would react. Fuelled by his sense of obligation she knew right away what he would offer to do. She couldn't afford to let her feelings grow any deeper towards someone who's sense of honour might lead him down a path he'd never intended. It was just easier to take off. After a call to one of the kiteboarding crowd in Devon, she'd handed in her notice at work, packed up what little could be crammed into her Mini, and escaped to the small fishing village of Appledore.

Before leaving London she had posted a letter through Matthew's door. She didn't tell him about the baby. If he really wanted to, he would be able to find her and if he came, he would be coming for *her* not from some sense of responsibility.

She slept on a friend's sofa for a couple days then rented a cottage. Whilst staying there, she met Helena and they had immediately become close friends. And thank God for that because she'd been in real need of a friend two months later when the pregnancy she had become so thrilled about, came to a slow, painful and devastating end.

Then, out of the blue, Mrs MacBride, the lady who had been renting her grandmother's house for the last thirty years in Pine Tree Bay – the house that Jem had inherited on Marcia's passing – decided she needed to downsize. Jem travelled to Scotland to investigate and Helena offered to come on the trip with her. It was on this trip that the plan was hatched between them to move permanently to Pine Tree Bay; Jem to set up a book shop and Helena to open a gallery. A year later they had both arrived and ten years later here they remained.

Truth was, Matthew never *had* come looking for Jem in Appledore.

A reply to the letter she had written to him when she left London found its way to her via a redirected mail service. It was all as she expected; Matthew understood. He would respect her wishes. He wished her well. He had carefully avoided mentioning that final evening they had spent together.

Reading between the lines Jem detected his grateful relief. She had released him from the messy situation that Nick had thrown him into and he was taking this welcome opportunity to disentangle himself. She had been right to give him the option to back out – to resume the bachelor lifestyle he had been so enjoying before having to bear the weight of Nick's decision.

But Matthew *had* at least confirmed one thing in his letter; that he'd heard from Nick's parents. Nick had called them to confirm he was ok. There was no explanation about what he'd done, no mention of Jem other than that he was sorry for the pain he must have caused. He was out of the country and he had no plans to return. Jem had felt a fierce rage at Nick's casual dismissal of her. Any last hopes of a genuinely understandable reason for his disappearance faded and she was left with nothing but anger toward him.

And despite the fact that Withershins was ready just weeks after receiving Matthew's letter, it was a whole year before Jem finally made the move north. There was always a reason to stay a few months longer. And in that time, Matthew never came.

The wedding, Nick, Matthew, the loss of her precious child – they had all been left behind in a box she had no intention of ever opening again. It wasn't a case of hiding things away, just a matter of leaving old baggage behind. But now that baggage had found her – like a long lost suitcase full of outdated clothes that clashed with all the new stuff in her wardrobe.

Jem, could feel her muscles starting to tighten. How long had she been sitting there? She'd paused her run without stretching and now she was ceasing up. A squall had blown in, seemingly from nowhere in this relatively sunny day, so she zipped up her running jacket and tucked her ponytail into the hood then pulled the drawstring tight around her face.

She'd spent too long ruminating on the ridge – time to get back to the cafe. The past was the past and she needed to leave it there.

She started the twenty minute descent back down the trail, Bear trotting alongside her. Whether she liked it or not, Matthew was back in her life. It wasn't what she wanted but that was how it was. Now, she needed to swallow her feelings and focus on the *real* problem that Matthew represented *today*, everything else was water under the bridge. A previous life.

The town was potentially under threat, with a rise in lease prices many businesses would find it difficult to make a profit and people weren't going to work their fingers to the bone just to break even. And that could be the least of their worries knowing Gerry Monroe. Jem was determined that Pine Tree Bay would not become a series of boarded up buildings like so many of the other towns across the country. She could think of no reason why Frank Monroe suddenly seemed to be willing to risk this possibility either.

The talk in the town was sour. People grumbling that they should have known better than to put their trust in these cut throat business types but Jem didn't want to believe that Frank was behind this. It just wasn't his style. Gerry was up to something and there was only one way to find out what that was. At least in this respect, her previous closeness to Matthew could be of use. She would head back to the cafe, smarten herself up and above all *keep her composure*, as she sat down to coffee with Gerry's new right hand man.

Matthew

Small House Book & Brew was certainly in the Halloween mood. A huge cauldron had been set up outside and a green faced Isla, dressed as the Wicked Witch of the West, complete with red and white stripy socks, was reluctantly having to top it up at regular intervals to provide a constant flow of dry ice.

'As if I didn't have enough to bloody do!' she grumbled, stomping around the cauldron, as Matthew approached the cafe; his laptop secured under one arm and his battered satchel in the other.

The place looked busy and he suspected there would be small chance of securing a table but Isla led him inside to one of the reading nooks tucked away in the Self Help and Spirituality section at the back of the store. He wondered if she was being sarcastic but she assured him that it was a part of the shop where he was unlikely to be disturbed, 'Nobody round here goes in for all this shite!' She waved a dismissive hand over Deepak Chopra and pulled a notebook from her witches garb.

An amused Matthew gave Isla his order and then settled into the very comfortable booth and opened up his laptop. He didn't start work immediately, choosing instead to look around him and take it all in. Jem had done it – created a cosy, home from home for people who loved to buy books and coffee – like she had always promised she would.

Handcrafted bookcases painted in muted sage green, with overhanging gunmetal grey picture lights, provided the perfect back-drop for multi coloured book spines. But instead of being laid out in the usual regimented rows, the bookcases had been arranged in a series of quadrangles allowing each corner to house a cosy reading nook. The wooden seating was painted in the same sage colour and stuffed with colourful antique cushions of faded blues, reds and yellows. Worn leather arm chairs were dotted around the place, together with the old standard lamps that cast their muted light over side tables piled with books.

These cosy reading areas provided the perfect overflow to the main café – located at the brightly lit front of the shop, overlooking the sea – the ideal place to spend a rainy afternoon reading (or beavering away on a laptop in Matthew's case) with the low, up-beat hum of indie folk music playing in the background. The whole effect, Matthew thought to himself, was one of having popped in to visit a friend with a really well stocked library and a great eye for décor. A friend who could bake delicious cakes, breads, quiches and scones. It was clear from the busy hum that Jem was running a good business.

Would she be annoyed by his sudden arrival back in town, back in her life? She'd told him not to take the job after all. And ironically it had been a job he didn't even want; until she was part of it.

He was used to being the guy that nobody wanted to see. As a business consultant he was generally there to help a place run more efficiently, which often meant changes that weren't popular on the ground. Being unpopular came with the territory, but Matthew was always open with everyone about what he was doing and how it would affect them. It was a style that had earned him a solid reputation for being a straight shooter; someone who could streamline businesses whilst ensuring the people on the front line were at the very least, accepting of change, if not always happy about it.

From time to time over the course of his career he'd come across the type of slash and burn CEO's who simply wanted an outsider to blame for driving their businesses to the wall. After ten years in the field he had become adept at side-stepping any such projects. This was different.

Despite the fact that Gerry had professed a great affection for the resort and its place in his father's heart, Matthew wasn't convinced. Suspecting there was a lot more to this project than a creative accountant and some potentially undervalued leases, his professional antennae had told him to steer clear. But that was all immaterial once he realised that Jem had a business in Pine Tree. If Matthew didn't take the role, there would be no chance of protecting her from whatever was coming down the line. At least this way, there was a possibility he could influence things.

Jem's attitude at the meeting had stung though, he wouldn't deny it. Travelling back to London after the meeting three weeks ago he'd decided she was right, he should steer clear of Pine Tree. Of *her*. Pissed off and angry he wondered just who the hell she thought she was giving *him* a hard time. Especially when she'd been the one to leave London twelve years ago without even so much as a goodbye? Just when he'd finally thought they were on the same page… Only to arrive home to a letter saying she was running off to the coast with Bear.

That letter had torn him apart. But, exhausted from years of wanting someone who'd never been his in the first place, he'd reluctantly accepted what he'd known all along; Jem would never get over Nick. He had to respect her wishes and let her go. And just maybe, without her constant presence in his life, there was a chance he could move on. The moving on part had not been as hard as he'd imagined – he'd made good decisions, made a good life for himself – even if his heart had never quite managed to catch up.

What it all came down to, was one moment. That first day – when she had lain injured on the stone steps and Nick had introduced them. Matthew, on the phone, could only look over and smile. And she had smiled back. That warm wide smile; grey eyes shining out from a mass of dark curls. Something had happened. Something that, try as he might, he would never be able to put into words. Something physical – visceral even – that had flipped everything on its head. She'd felt it too. It was impossible that she hadn't. But whatever it was that had passed between them, it was lost in all that came after. Nick swept Jem off her feet and Matthew had had to watch from the sidelines – wondering why it should be this way with the one person he couldn't have.

Here in her cafe, with the aroma of coffee beans and the rustling of pages, he reminded himself that he *had* stayed true to the promise he'd made when she left London. He had let her go. He had let her get on with life and he had *never* gone looking for her - no matter how desperately he had wanted to. And whilst some strange twist of fate had brought them together, he was only here to head off whatever might come down the line from Gerry Monroe. Nothing more.

He had his own new chapter to write and this job was also part of enabling that. Jem's reaction when he'd first turned up in Pine Tree had confirmed one thing; whatever it was he had once imagined was between them, he'd been wrong.

Jem

After her run, Jem showered in the garden apartment. When there were no guests she often used it to get ready if she was going out somewhere nice after work. That would have to change if Matthew was renting it. She reminded herself that that was never going to happen; she had yet to think up a plausible reason why.

Once she'd towelled off, Jem quickly pulled on the fresh clothes that she'd brought with her that morning – jeans and a cashmere sweater – the cashmere just the right shade of heather to highlight the grey-blue tones of her eyes. She pulled her unruly curls from their pony tail and gave them a shake. The effect was a bit wild looking but it would have to do. After a coat of mascara and a slick of lip-gloss she practised her smile in the mirror. Yes that would do nicely – she was all set for the charm offensive.

Striding into the café, she felt confident and there was a slight buzz humming though her veins. Not about the prospect of seeing Matthew obviously, it was purely down to the post run endorphins. But she would not be frosty with him this time, she needed to get him onside. And she supposed she was genuinely interested in what had happened to him in the intervening years. But she mustn't forget that she was here to find out about Gerry's plans. Perhaps she should get Matthew into a more relaxed frame of mind, yes she should suggest they have dinner…

Jem stopped in her tracks. *What the…?*

Matthew was sitting with Kate – the woman from Coastguard's. Their heads were angled closely and they were both laughing uncontrollably at something on his laptop. Jem tried not to feel irked as the thought of how good they looked together crossed her mind.

In the weeks since the town meeting, Kate and Jem had exchanged pleasantries – Kate was a regular in the cafe – but Jem had studiously avoided striking up a friendship with the newcomer. She was very aware of having *overshared* with Kate; the woman had caught her at an unguarded moment and Jem now felt, somehow, at a disadvantage.

Kate's beatnik style irritated Jem too. The girl always managed to look so urbanely cool. Today she was wearing a leather biker jacket with three quarter sleeves over a long sleeved Breton t shirt and skinny jeans. An oversized scarf and beret lay on the seat between them and Matthew was crying with laughter at whatever was playing on the laptop. Jem supposed it was only inevitable that the two city types would be natural friends for each other. Neither of them had wasted any time though, she thought to herself huffily.

'Well this certainly looks like *fun*.' Jem immediately regretted the bitchy tone that sprang from her mouth as she neared their table.

'Jem!' Kate looked up from the laptop, still laughing. If she had caught Jem's tone she certainly didn't let on. 'I was just showing Matthew here the Halloween video that Rab has posted on YouTube. Did you see it? He and all the staff at The Smugglers have done a cover of 'The Monster Mash' for the festival? He's taken the production to serious heights. It's like a Heart music video from the 1980s!'

Matthew turned to Kate wiping away tears of laughter. 'That's the best laugh I've had in ages,' he chuckled. 'This guy has a serious talent, I can't wait to meet him.' Finally he looked up at Jem, his eyes still crinkled with laughter. 'Jem, perhaps you could take me down to The Smugglers this evening and introduce me to the legendary Rab?'

She would do no such thing. Who did he think he was rocking up and expecting her to drop everything and take him out on his first evening in town. Ok so she had actually been considering asking him to join her for a quick bite this evening but *he* didn't know that.

'Matthew,' she said, somewhat sniffily, 'Isla told me you were here and I thought it might be a good time to go over what you're proposing to do here over the next few months. I'm just breaking for lunch – care to join me?' She raised her eyebrows and pointed her thumb in the direction of her study. Christ, even to her own ears she sounded like a headmistress who's just caught two school kids bunking off.

'Sounds great.' Matthew looked around him at the many customers in the place. 'But I'm loathe to give up this very comfy little nook and leave myself with nowhere to work for the rest of the afternoon, so perhaps you could join me instead?'

Jem wanted to point out that, as it was her café, wherever they sat *he* was technically joining *her* but she let it slide and gave a tight smile in agreement.

Kate who had been watching the interchange between them with an intrigued smile on her face, hopped out of the booth. She wound the oversized Alpaca scarf around her neck and secured the black beret over her long blonde hair saying, 'Right, that's my cue to skedaddle.'

'Really?' asked Matthew. 'You're welcome to join us you know?'

Jem echoed the sentiment with as much enthusiasm as she could muster but Kate waved the notion away. 'No, no that's fine, thanks, I have a Pilates class at The Barnacle Spa in half an hour so I need to head off. Catch you both later. Enjoy!'

Feeling that she had somehow landed on the back foot, Jem slid into the seat opposite Matthew. He closed his laptop, leaned his head back against his seat and held her gaze a fraction too long before saying, 'So….'

She returned his gaze levelly, and refused to acknowledge that the air was suddenly being sucked out of her lungs. 'So…?' she countered breezily, keeping the intonation light.

Jem was not going to allow herself to be reeled in this time. *Move forwards not backwards* she reminded herself. But it was difficult. He looked good. Too good. *Dangerously* good. A light tan and a honed physique, probably from a summer spent indulging his passion for kiteboarding. Fit, healthy, his dark blonde hair still thick and slightly dishevelled, despite the fact that he must have turned forty in the past year. He had shrugged out of a thin woollen zip-up and the t-shirt he was wearing underneath left nobody in any doubt that he kept himself in shape. All this and a successful career in management consultancy, Matthew was clearly a man at the peak of his powers. It was a derailing thought. *Focus on the town. Focus. On. The. Town.*

She shifted in her seat. 'So then,' she twiddled her earring hoping it made her look casual and chilled. 'What's your plan for looking at each of the businesses?'

But Matthew was having none of it. 'We'll get to all that in time, let's just….' He ran his hands through his hair, seemingly searching for the right words. 'Can we just catch up for a bit first?'

'Ok.' She reminded herself that she was on a charm offensive. 'But first let's order some of Jamie's delicious food, I've just got back from a run and I'm starving.'

By the time Jem and Matthew had polished off two huge slabs of pumpkin and beetroot quiche with a green salad, they had moved into much easier territory and despite herself, Jem had lowered her guard sufficiently to start enjoying Matthew's company. He gave her the highlights of the last ten or so years; how he'd stayed in London, left banking to build up a freelance career in management consultancy, still indulged his passion for kiteboarding. He brought her up to speed on some of the people they had both known and then he finally told her about his divorce.

It was clearly painful for him as he briefly described the way things ended, 'We had a good relationship, we were the best of friends but in the end it just wasn't enough.'

He looks like a man who thinks he's failed, Jem thought to herself but she said nothing.

'For a long time I kidded myself that ours was as good as any other marriage, I guess compared to our friends it probably was. But Lissa, she needed – no that's not fair – she *deserved* better. I was working away all the time and she was in London with her own social circle and well, you know how it is.'

Jem didn't. She'd managed to avoid all that. Instead she asked, 'How did you meet in the first place?'

'Lissa was a member of the legal team in a large tourism company that I was working with. Unfortunately, she was made redundant as part of a revised structure they wanted to implement. We'd become friendly over the course of my work there so the day they told her she was being let go, I offered a shoulder to cry on and it just took off from there.'

Typical Matthew, thought Jem resisting the urge to roll her eyes, never knowingly leaving a damsel in distress; it was probably his Instagram bio.

He fiddled with a sachet of sugar that sat in a jar between them. Jem made a mental note to bin it later. 'Lissa said she'd always felt there was something, some sort of an *issue* that got in the way....' He paused, as if he wanted to say more but then he shook it off and changed tack. 'Anyway,' Matthew straightened up, bringing his mind back to the present, 'enough of my miserable story, what about you? Isla mentioned something about... is it Finn? The outdoor pursuits guy? I met him briefly at the town meeting.'

Jem made a further mental note to throttle Isla when she next got hold of her. 'We... er... see each other from time to time, yes. It's not a relationship as such.'

Something flickered across Matthew's face and then was gone. He looked around the shop in admiration. 'You know, I can't believe we've sat here for over an hour and I haven't told you how amazing this place is. I'm blown away. You've built something really special.' Then looking back at her, 'You should be really proud of yourself.'

'I guess I am,' she said self-consciously. 'If that doesn't sound too big headed. But I think that's also why I'm a bit over protective about the place, about the whole town really...' She was heading back to the sticky issue of business again and, for now at least, decided to tail off.

'So how on earth did you end up living here?' Matthew asked. 'Last I heard you were in Appledore.'

So he *had* known where she was. Jem was more certain than ever that she'd done the right thing in leaving London. God the relief he must have felt.

'This is where my grandmother grew up.'

'Marcia was from Pine Tree?'

Yes, well, the *original* Pine Tree. When she was here back in the fifties, it would have been just the pub, the harbour and a handful of shops and warehouses. When she died she left me her house. It's a mile or so along the bay with all the other old cottages and villas. It was rented to a lady by the name of Mrs MacBride. She'd been in the old house for years and Marcia left explicit instructions that she wasn't to be turfed out.' Jem smiled remembering Marcia's veracity on this subject. 'But then Mrs MacBride needed to downsize, so I decided to sell it. Once I got here I just fell in love with the place on sight. It must be in the genes.'

'I didn't realise there was such a personal connection. But yes, now you say it, it makes a few things clearer.' Matthew's eyes twinkled mischievously.

'What's that supposed to mean?'

'Look,' Matthew set his cup down and grinned to take the sting out of his next comment, 'don't go all prickly on me again, I'm just saying, it explains why you feel so protective about the town and the people who live here. Which you clearly do.' He stared at her frankly. 'And for which you have my great admiration by the way.'

She was only slightly mollified. 'Well it's not like London. People really care about their neighbours around here.'

'That's hardly fair,' he said raising an indignant eyebrow.

She laughed. 'Don't tell me you're still running the Sunday lunch club for the Camden pensioners?'

'Well, to be completely honest I was always away so one of my neighbours ended up running it, *but* I do still give lifts when I'm there.'

'Ooooh, Saint Matthew.' Jem leaned across the table and started to chuckle. 'Do you remember that old lady who peed in the back of Nick's Volkswagen?'

They both collapsed into giggles at the memory of Nick, hopping mad that an old lady with a bladder problem had defiled his new car. As their laughter subsided, Jem fiddled with her coffee cup gathering herself to ask the next question but Matthew spoke first.

'You're still wondering if I know where he is aren't you?'

'To be completely honest Matthew, seeing you again, it's kind of hard not to.'

'Did you ever receive a letter I sent to your London flat after you left?'

She reddened slightly. To admit she had received his letter was also to admit that she had never responded. 'Yes it found me on a redirect, in Appledore,' she said quietly.

'Well then, you know everything I know. His parents contacted me a few weeks after you left to confirm that Nick had called. All Nick would say was that he was out of the country and wasn't coming back. They said he refused to tell them where he was. Of course they may have known and decided not to tell me, but his mum grilled me so hard about whether I could think of anywhere he may have taken off to, I think they were telling the truth. She asked me to let you know. I told her I'd write to your old address – figuring you'd be back there at some point – and that's what I did.'

They were both silent for a moment and then Matthew spoke again, more brusquely this time. 'I'm sure Nick had his reasons for what he did but quite frankly, I stopped caring where he might be a long time ago.'

The way he held her gaze, as if challenging her to agree, had Jem scrabbling around for something to break the tension. She landed on the first thing that came to mind. 'So, Isla said you're interested in renting the garden flat?'

'That's right.' Matthew handled the change of direction smoothly. 'She said you have nobody booked in for the next few months. Would I be able to see it?'

Silently berating her jumbled brain for settling on the first thing that came into it, and being unable to think up a convincing excuse as to why it wasn't available, Jem found herself offering to show it to him.

'I can't right now.' Matthew looked genuinely sorry. 'I really need to get some files over to Gerry before the end of the day.' He laughed apologetically. 'Working in your café is proving way too sociable for getting any actual work done.'

She laughed. 'I know what you mean, which is why my study is out of the way of everyone who comes in here.'

'What about tonight for the flat?' he asked.

She shook her head. 'It's going to be full on with the whole Halloween extravaganza at The Smugglers so come round tomorrow evening instead?'

'Oh I've, er, just promised Kate I'll have dinner at hers tomorrow night.'

Despite the irrational thud that landed in the pit of her stomach, Jem didn't miss a beat. Of course he had a date with the most attractive girl in town. It was classic Matthew. Remembering the ease with which he had slipped in and out of relationships in his twenties, it made sense that he would return to that now his marriage was over. Sliding out of her seat Jem's voice became businesslike. 'Well look, don't worry we'll catch up at some point when you're free over the next few days. It could do with a duster before it's ready for inspection anyway.'

'Well, you don't need to bother on-'

'I'll let you get on now Matthew,' she said briskly. 'I'm stacked in the office anyway.'

'I might see you at The Smugglers tonight then?' He sounded hopeful but she was already walking away.

'Probably,' she tossed over her shoulder, not offering to accompany him as he'd initially asked her to. She marched off in the direction of her study feeling irrationally miffed and only slightly appeased by the exasperated sigh she heard him aim at her departing figure.

Matthew

Matthew hit send on the email he'd been crafting for the past half-hour.

He knew he wasn't telling Gerry what he wanted to hear. This whole assignment baffled him. Even a cursory glance at the financial reports confirmed the resort was holding its own – just from the existing lease charges. But, even if those charges were increased, the resort was never going to throw off the level of turnover that would warrant such close involvement from someone at Gerry's level.

The acting head of a multi national conglomerate the size of Monroe Holdings had any number of executives they could turn this small scale stuff over to. Matthew could see the man had no great affection for the place so what was the deal? To add to that, Gerry was clearly steering Matthew in the direction of an exit proposal; he wanted to sell the resort off. All the more reason for the acting CEO to distance himself, not be so personally involved with the locals. None of it was adding up. Yet.

Matthew stretched his arms above his head. His muscles felt tight. He'd been working in the café all day and needed to close his laptop, gather his papers and get out of there. Isla had explained it didn't usually stay open past seven but they wanted to provide refreshments for the trick or treaters who'd finished making their way along the bay. It was a good decision by the looks of things – the café was still heaving. Mind you, the festivities of the day, not to mention the sugar intake, seemed to have taken its toll on some of the children; the shrieks of laughter were slowly descending into tantrums and wails. It was definitely time to make tracks.

He would go off in search of Jem's office and see if she was still around. Despite promising himself that he wasn't here to pursue Jem, he was pretty sure that the mention of his dinner with Kate had pissed her off. He was indulging himself with the notion that she might be jealous and couldn't help smiling at the thought.

Threading his way through the rows of bookcases Matthew came to a door marked *Private*. Through the glazed half he could see a desk with a laptop and an empty chair. It was clearly Jem's office but she wasn't there. He was about to retreat in search of her when something caught his eye. Going into the room he took the postcard from her desk and moved toward the lamp that sat behind Jem's desk for closer inspection. A wet nose nuzzled his hand and he looked down to see that a hopeful Bear was checking his pockets, bending slightly to scratch the dog ears he continued to look at the postcard intently.

'You see it too?' Jem's voice came from the doorway.

'Is it from him?' he asked not looking up from the card.

'I have no idea where it came from Matthew. It was hand delivered about three weeks ago in an envelope with my name scrawled on the front. There was nothing else, no note and obviously no post mark to go by.'

'It certainly looks like…I don't know…it's these colours, the brush strokes. I lived in student houses littered with paintings that looked an awful lot like this for almost three years. I think I'd know his work anywhere. And the subject matter?' He turned to face her. 'It just seems like too much of a coincidence.'

Jem let out a large sigh, 'I'm so glad it's not just me. I thought I was going a bit crazy. I don't know, possibly seeing things that weren't there? Out of hope or something?'

Hope. Matthew felt crushed by the word but when he spoke his voice was even. 'Have you done any investigations into who it might be by?'

'I wouldn't really know where to start.'

'How about searching online for impressionistic paintings of St. Paul's and seeing what comes back?'

'Well it would be a starting point I guess.'

Matthew returned the postcard to the table. 'I just came to see if you wanted to walk down to The Smugglers together, but I can see you're busy so I'll-' he made for the door.

*

Jem didn't want Matthew to leave. She reminded herself that she was supposed to be on a charm offensive. What was it to her if Matthew was planning to shack up with Kate whilst he was here? Jem wanted *information* from her old friend, nothing more. 'No, you're right… It's a good idea. I can introduce you to some of the locals,' she said reaching for her coat.

Matthew

Stepping out of the cafe, the sweet aroma of toffee apples and burning lanterns combined to permeate the damp night air. Jem laughed as Matthew wrinkled his nose.

The town seemed to be overrun with trick or treaters. Children clamoured at the beach side cabins unable to decide between the variety of sickly sweet goodies on display and hundreds of candlelit pumpkins flickered from every shop front that lined the shore. Matthew could only hope that the nearest fire-brigade was on standby.

Everyone seemed to be either shrieking or wailing as they raced on by. Witches and goblins collided with phantoms and ghouls and Matthew expertly side stepped a group of Harry Potter characters careering past him with wands aloft shouting, *'Expecto Patronum!'*

Jem called out cheerily to a corpse bride and groom that she recognised as they glided by silently without cracking a smile. Matthew was impressed by the the town's commitment to the occasion.

'Well one thing's for certain, Pine Tree Bay knows how to do Halloween,' he said, taking it all in. 'It's a real achievement – getting everyone so firmly behind it.'

Jem grinned. 'They wouldn't dare do anything else. Madeleine Beaver's orders! The town is pretty special that way though. It's one of the reasons I moved here in the first place. As soon as I arrived and people found out that I was Marcia's granddaughter they treated me like family. I'd never had that before. Growing up I always wished I could belong to one of those large extended families where there are lots of get togethers with cousins, aunts and uncles – you know, that sense that there are more people to go round than you could ever need – this felt pretty close to that almost as soon as I got here.'

Matthew thought about his own upbringing with his Irish parents, which had been pretty much what Jem had just described, and suddenly realised how lonely she must have been as a child. 'I can understand that,' he said. 'But it's a rare thing for a town to have this kind of community spirit these days.'

'It comes from being part of something that's busy and thriving. So many coastal towns struggle, trying to run businesses from dilapidated buildings that need more investment than the owners can support. Cuts in the grants available and a reduction in lottery funding. Not to mention the hoops you have to jump through to get credit from the banks these days. It's just become that much more difficult to start up any kind of business. And if people do manage it, the work is so seasonal. Some people really struggle to make it through the winter. Frank's investment here is what gives Pine Tree Bay a better chance than most. Well, look who I'm talking to… you've must have seen the figures.'

'I have,' said Matthew, narrowly avoiding an ill placed pumpkin. He felt conflicted. He hadn't meant to stray into this territory so soon and he didn't want to discuss the business economics of the town with Jem – not because of any particular loyalty to Gerry – but because he hadn't worked out what the man was up to just yet.

'And?' she was calling him out for being cagey.

'And, from what I've seen, it all looks very sustainable as you say.'

She went to say something then clearly decided not to push it, much to Matthew's relief.

'Ok, I'll let you off for now, Mr non-committal,' she said teasingly.

Look who's talking, he couldn't stop the thought.

As they neared the pub, Jem asked Matthew to hold on for a second. She dodged across the road to a motorhome which was parked up along the sea front with a long queue of customers waiting outside. A woman, whom Matthew took to be a fortune teller of some sort was standing at the door. She was dressed in long purple robes, sporting the worst excuse for a wig he'd ever seen. Just as she was crooking her finger theatrically, to beckon the next customer, Jem interrupted and pulled her aside for a brief word. The older woman nodded and then resumed her duties and Jem ran back across the road.

'That's Beryl, aka Madam Zelda, she might join us later if she gets chance.' Jem smiled up at him slightly out of breath. 'But she predicts that she will.'

'Oooh clearly she's very good then! Mind you judging by the roaring trade she's drummed up…' he nodded towards the queue.

'Yeah,' Jem sniffed evasively, 'apparently she's quite good.'

They finally reached The Smugglers which, having been dressed as Captain Jack Sparrow's *local* for the last month, was now Halloween on steroids. They opened the door, ears ringing from the familiar 'Mwah-Ha-Ha-Ha!' which rang out, and were both temporarily blinded by a cloud of atmospheric green fog which billowed out onto the street. Unable to see a thing, Matthew and Jem made their way tentatively into the candle-lit pub.

As soon as they came through the door, there was a chorus of, 'Watch out for-!'

Too late. Matthew was suddenly sprawled across the entrance having tripped over a hotch-potch of plastic gravestones positioned just inside the door.

'Rab, ye need to move these bloody gravestones!' a disembodied voice from deep inside the pub shouted. 'Ye're an ambulance chasers dream so ye are!'

A barely recognisable Rab, complete with dreadlocks, a bandana and an eye patch came bustling through the fog to help Matthew to his feet.

'For God's sake! You need to look where you're going man!'

'I'd take your friend's advice if I were you,' said Matthew, wiping the dirt off his knees. 'Either that or notch down the dry-ice a bit.'

'Aye, well, come inside and you can have the first drink on the house,' grumbled Rab, snatching up the plastic gravestones on his way back towards the bar.

'I can't seem to walk into this pub without causing a scene,' Matthew muttered. Jem, looked as if she was trying very hard not to laugh.

Bear led the way to the bar – there was no fog thick enough to come between dog and gravy bone – and as he and Jem drew nearer, Matthew recognised Isla and Finn enjoying a glass of some sort of Halloween Punch which Rab was clearly peddling to anyone and everyone he could offload it to. Jem introduced a tall attractive, willowy lady as her great friend Helena. The punch must have been a potent brew as, to Matthew's practised eye, they all looked half cut.

'Cheers!' shouted Helena, holding up her glass as they were introduced, she gave him the once over and wore what Matthew could only describe as a lascivious smile. Coupled with her glassy eyes it was quite unnerving.

Matthew held up an imaginary glass. 'Cheers,' he said, joining her in the toast. Helena didn't seem to notice his hand was empty.

'Rab promised us it was a treat!' She indicated the red coloured drink in her hand which, Matthew was alarmed to note, was currently fizzing and giving off a bright pink vapour. 'But we're all beginning to suspect it's a bleedin' trick!' She let out a raucous laugh at her own bad joke.

'She's in full Barbara Windsor mode tonight.' Finn muttered close to Jem's ear. He followed the comment with a surreptitious kiss on her neck which, in the low light, Matthew suspected he alone had witnessed. He couldn't help wishing he hadn't.

Then Jem was leaning towards him to ask if he wanted a drink. Matthew's instinct was to insist on getting the round in but this was Jem's local and so he simply nodded and asked for a bottle of Becks. As he spoke, he looked around and his attention was momentarily diverted toward Helena. She was pointing exaggeratedly in his direction whilst giving Isla a thumbs up, mouthing, 'I see what you mean.'

Jem ordered the drinks accompanied by Bear who happily chomped away on his gravy bone, wagging his tail and generally enjoying the high spirits of all the humans around him.

As the evening wore on, Matthew found himself enjoying the easy banter of Jem's friends catching up on the news of the town. He didn't mind that he was unable, for the most part, to join in. It gave him chance to observe and suss things out.

About half way through the night, Rab commanded everyone's

attention and announced a brief hiatus in service whilst he and his team carried out a 'costume change'. The broadcast was met with a collective groan.

'What's going on?' asked Matthew, sensing that something was clearly afoot.

Jem leaned in toward him and raised her voice above the music, 'Well, you know that video you were so taken with earlier?' Matthew nodded. 'You're just about to catch the live show.'

Ten minutes later amidst cries of, 'About bloody time!' from customers holding empty glasses, Rab reappeared. More moaning followed however, as the music that had been blaring out of the speakers suddenly stopped and the floor was cleared so that Rab and his mortified bar staff could perform their Halloween extravaganza.

If Matthew had found the video amusing, it had nothing on the live re-run. By the time the performance was finished, everyone in the pub was crying with laughter because an over exuberant Rab had split his trousers whilst climbing out of a coffin at the beginning of 'The Monster Mash' and unwittingly mooned everyone throughout the entire song.

'Rab, ye might want tae think twice about going commando next time!' someone shouted as the music came to an end.

'Now get some bloody trolleys on and get us all a drink!' shouted another.

Towards the end of the evening, when their stomachs ached from laughter and the alcohol had well and truly taken hold, a small elderly looking lady, made her way through the crowd to join Jem and her friends. Matthew, though slightly merry by this time, recognised the clairvoyant from earlier. Thankfully she'd ditched the unfortunate hair piece.

'Matthew!' Jem touched him on the arm and shouted over the music to get his attention. 'This is Beryl, the lady I was telling you about earlier. The lady who reads Tarot cards.' Jem tactfully steered away from using the term *fortune teller*.

Matthew stretched out his hands to shake Beryl's in greeting and as he did so, he felt a small crack of electricity pass between them.

'Well I'll be buggered!' the old woman shouted over the loud music, 'If it isn't the The Knight of Pentacles!'

CHAPTER SEVEN
1st November

Matthew

'Have you even looked at the cost initiatives I suggested?' Matthew could hear the irritation in his own voice but he wasn't about to roll over for Gerry at this early stage. The man was refusing to see sense. Matthew was not feeling as patient as usual – having spent the entire day nursing a hangover – they certainly knew how to party in this town.

'Just a quick heads up Matt.' Gerry's tone suggested he resented sparing five minutes for the tedium of Pine Tree Bay. 'The last thing we want is for you to waste time investigating avenues I'm never gonna walk down. I've looked over the note you sent yesterday – you're in danger of steering wildly off brief.'

Well that might be true – thought Matthew – if Gerry had ever given him a brief. 'Gerry, with your leverage, greater economies of scale could be exploited. You're paying far too much for-'

'I should have thought it would be clear by now – I'm not interested in implementing new initiatives,' Gerry snapped. 'Look, you seem to be a little slow in catching on so let me spell it out, I'm looking to sell off the resort. What I need you to do now is confirm that those property leases are undervalued. Most of the agreements for the commercial premises are due for renewal in April and if they're undervalued, I can drive up the price of the resort.'

Matthew felt frustrated. 'But any increase will be notional,' he argued. 'You'd need a couple of years trading figures to be able to raise the price of the overall businesses. Any company in a position to buy the resort will drive a hard bargain precisely *because* the new lease terms are unproven. It loads too much risk into the deal. Any commercial lawyer worth his salt will spot that and the buyer will use it to drive you back down on price. You'd be much better holding off on a sale for another couple of years at the very least.' *And with any luck your father will have recovered and this whole idea will be toast.* Matthew thought to himself.

'Leave the negotiation strategy to me Matthew. I've actually done this before believe it or not. Are we done here?'

'And is your father on board with this?' Matthew hadn't wanted to play that card just yet but sound, commercial logic clearly wasn't cutting it.

He detected a slight pause but Gerry ploughed on regardless. 'My father is a businessman, he knows when it's time to cash in and he knows that time is now.'

'I'm hearing from the people here that the town means much more to your father than just a financial vehicle.'

'I'm paying you to make objective business recommendations. I hope you're not developing personal connections which might cloud your judgement. Because if that's the case I'm more than happy to look else-'

'That won't be necessary.'

'That's great to hear Matthew. Now if you can start to assess the properties individually from Monday, I'd like some initial views by the end of next week.'

As Matthew ended the call he shook his head in disbelief. None of this made any business sense. He asked himself for the hundredth time what the guy was up to.

He checked his watch and cursed. He'd been due at Kate's cottage a quarter of an hour ago.

Kate

Thank goodness Matthew was running late, thought Kate, as she hastily dried her hair and applied a coat of mascara.

It had to be said, Pine Tree Bay agreed with her. A month of daily walks together with Pilates and swimming at the Barnacle Spa were resulting in a much longer, leaner version of herself than she'd seen in the mirror for years. The fresh air seemed to be buffing her cheeks into a healthy glow and her complexion was definitely clearer. A month of early nights had cleared the persistent dark circles from under her eyes. There were certainly some benefits to being exiled to the coast.

Though she would never admit it to any of her London friends, Kate had been increasingly surprised to find that she wasn't missing the city anything like as much as she'd expected. The troubles that she'd arrived with were all still there of course, but just as she'd originally hoped, the distance from her home and her work had begun to shift her perspective on life to a certain degree. Now that an established routine had emerged – dedicated mostly to mind and body – what she'd been doing for the last ten years did not look quite so attractive. It didn't look healthy either.

But it paid the bills. And more than that – she had to admit – it gave her the sense of being part of something. Something quite big and important. In London, she had only to say what she did for a living to prove her relevance in the world. Head of Corporate for Allocott Finance. Six words amounting to the professional equivalent of 'I'm the dog's bollocks' or some more ladylike accolade.

This honest appraisal of her own ego hadn't left her feeling, exactly, proud. But she couldn't deny that the status her role brought was an attractive part of the package. The only problem was that this neat label – this efficient encapsulation of her place in the world – took every hour of every day. And quite a few from the night too. So she'd been asking herself, was it worth it? Working her arse off for the buzz of knowing she had some relevance, some importance in this world? Did she really love what she did? Enough to dedicate every waking hour to it? She hadn't quite worked out the answer yet.

Here in Pine Tree Bay, people glazed over when she explained what she did in London. It was genuinely the first place she'd spent any length of time where it was patently obvious that no-one cared a jot for what you had or how successful you were. Here you were judged on your worth to the community and little else.

She'd mentioned as much to her sister on the phone last week when Suse had dryly observed, 'Careful Kate, people will accuse you of growing.'

Now, opening her wardrobe, she took a few moments to consider the appropriate outfit for a relaxed dinner with a new friend. She picked out a pair of dark indigo skinny jeans and a black silk Hugo Boss shirt which were casual enough for an evening in, but still looked like she'd made the effort. She wasn't exactly sure where the evening was headed but if her suspicions were right, she wouldn't be needing to wriggle out of anything in a hurry.

More's the pity, she thought to herself, but you couldn't win them all. She teamed the outfit with a tortoise shell belt and nude flats and – pleased with the effect – started to straighten up her bedroom, leaving the book she was currently reading on her bedside table. Sadly it was likely to be her only bedtime companion that evening.

And that was another thing; she'd actually read a number of novels in the time she'd been here. Usually her reading was limited to company reports or a flick through the financial press. Since arriving in Pine Tree Bay she'd swapped *The Financial Times* and *The Economist* for the contents of Penny's bookcase. She'd just finished *Wuthering Heights* and *Rachel's Holiday,* each one an equal classic of its time in her opinion.

As a child, Kate had been an avid reader of fiction. In truth, she'd been an avid fan of lots of things and the last few weeks had caused her to question where that enthusiasm for life *outside* the office had disappeared to? From this distance she could see that the demands of her job had been gradually increasing over time, until there was no room left for anything other than work.

Even the man she'd been seeing was unavailable. Had that been a conscious choice on her part to ensure she wasn't expected to be around more than an evening here and there?

Not that she would be confiding his existence to anyone here – she doubted that the locals in Pine Tree would approve of a woman who dated married men. And the thought of Tom coming to stay was, quite frankly, laughable. With nowhere to pick up his daily wheatgrass shot and insufficient bandwidth for his Peloton, he'd be on the first train back to London in no time. Anyway it was all moot because, barring the first day or two when he'd tried, repeatedly, to contact her, all his attempts to get in touch had ceased.

And there was the other unpleasant thought that had been running around her head for weeks now. With the exception of her assistant, no one at the office had tried to contact her since the day she was suspended. What shocked her most was that she fully understood why.

During the course of her career Kate had seen people give their life to a company, only to walk into the office one day and find their face didn't fit with the latest senior star. There was nothing more pitiable than the forced jollity of a departing colleague spouting demob happy clichés whilst barely concealing their bewilderment that the firm had decided it could get by without them. Kate had been an onlooker to this type of descent down the greasy pole on more than a few occasions. And yes, she'd felt sorry for these people, but she'd never imagined she would become *one of them*.

Those dispensable colleagues had somehow brought it on themselves hadn't they? They'd taken their eye off the ball, become too complacent, failed to stay ahead of the fluctuating politics of the senior team. Kate was too smart to make any of those mistakes. What's more, she could recognise that same quality in others. She had always been drawn to driven, focused, unequivocal types. People who fitted her definition of perfection. Matthew Albright seemed to fit the bill on that score, but there was one major fly in the ointment; he was quite clearly in love with someone else.

Kate did a quick time check as she spritzed some scent on her wrists, happy to be diverted from thoughts of her mind lingered on Matthew. The way he talked about Jem Small indicated a lot more than just friendship in their past. And of course the chemistry between them was unmistakable; they were so awkward with each other it spoke volumes.

It was just as well that Kate had clocked this early on, as with his looks and physique, together with his background in business, she would have been tempted to make a serious play for him. It could have been embarrassing. As it was they seemed to have struck up an easy friendship – probably due to the fact that they were both city escapees navigating the politics of a small town.

Kate was glad to have someone to hang out with. Yes it would have been fun to have a bit of a fling whilst she was here but in reality, what she was missing most was the company of someone who understood the corporate world that she was usually such a part of.

She headed into the kitchen to pour herself a glass of Chablis and instructed the smart speaker to play some chilled Henry Green. She then put a match to the wood burner and set the oven to preheat, ready for the pan roast panzanella topped with butter baked cod loin that she would be serving up later. It was her fail-safe supper dish that didn't involve any more preparation that the chopping of a few ingredients which were then shoved into the oven. Casual, rustic and packed with flavour, it never failed to impress.

After lighting a few candles and plumping the cushions there was nothing else to do so she picked up her phone to check her incoming messages. There was just the one. From a number not stored in her contacts list.

Kate this is Paula.
Can't write too much here but we need to speak!

Call me on this number!!

Why was her assistant texting her on a Friday evening... from someone else's mobile? Then the doorbell rang and Kate cursed the timing. Intriguing as the message was, Paula would have to wait until later.

Matthew

'Well, that's the last of the Chablis.' Matthew turned the bottle upside down in the wine cooler.

'Hey Albright, you're not in a restaurant. Put the empties in the recycling whilst I grab another bottle from Penny's state-of-the art chiller.'

'It certainly has all the bells and whistles this place doesn't it?' Matthew called over his shoulder as he rooted around the utility room in search of the recycling bin.

'Yup.' Kate got up slightly unsteadily from the table. 'It's Penny's haven for stressed out executives who have little time and lots of cash, so it needs to be top spec I guess. She's letting me have it at a discount but I could still be in the Maldives for a couple of weeks with what I'm paying each month.'

'So why aren't you?'

'Let's just say, whilst I haven't actually been asked not to leave the country, it wouldn't look good if I did.' Kate took her head out of the chiller cabinet to find Matthew looking at her in mock horror.

'You're not in one of those witness protection programmes are you? Because I think the idea is to keep it to yourself.'

She laughed, bringing the wine to the table. 'No it's a bit simpler than that. For some reason, that has yet to be fully explained to me, I've been given a forced leave of absence from my job.'

'I thought you were on sabbatical?'

'Yes, and that's what I'm telling everyone here, so if you can keep all this to yourself I'd be grateful.'

'Of course, that goes without saying, but what happened?'

Kate uncorked the bottle and over their next glass of wine filled Matthew in on what had happened to date.

'But, legally, aren't they compelled to give you some sort of explanation?' he asked, after she'd given him all the details.

'Apparently, if the company can solidly justify that telling me why would pose a risk to their investigation, then they don't have to.'

'So have you any thoughts on what it might be related to?'

'If you're asking me if I think I've done anything wrong then the answer's no. But the way they've gone about things and the length of the suspension suggests they suspect some misconduct that reaches outside the organisation.'

'And you've no idea what that is?'

'None whatsoever. I deal with external contacts every day. I don't do the actual deals at my level, but I'm involved in an oversight capacity. It could be any one of them.' She shook her head. 'And, as I don't have my laptop or business phone to check back, it's a waste of time trying to think about who it could involve.' She took a deep breath. 'I've decided to surrender to it and enjoy the break. I'll drive myself crazy if I think about it non-stop. I know in here,' Kate tapped her chest, 'that I haven't done anything wrong and in time, they'll know that too and this will be over. So I might as well try to enjoy the break.'

'Will you go back once they clear everything up?'

'Probably.'

'Really?' Matthew was surprised. 'You don't feel like the working relationship's soured?'

'It's just business. I'm more worried about my professional reputation. The best way I can prove I did nothing wrong is to carry on working with the company once things are cleared up. If I leave there'll be a smell about it that I'll never be able to shake off.'

Matthew sensing she was ready to change the subject decided to run his own concerns by her. 'Talking about bad smells, I spoke to Gerry Monroe this evening, that's why I was running slightly late.'

Kate laughed at his segue. 'Do I detect some friction between you and Mr Monroe?'

'Well, as of this evening, yes. Am I right in thinking I can speak to you in confidence?

'Of course, I've shared *my* secret so I'm more than happy to keep yours.'

'You *are* the one person I can off-load to I guess. You're not personally invested in the town to the extent that anyone else is.'

'You don't need to worry. I'm well practised at being discreet where business is concerned. So what's the deal with Gerry?'

Matthew exhaled slowly. 'Ah now that's the question… What *is* the deal with Gerry?'

'I don't trust the man.' Kate shook her head slowly.

Matthew sat back in his chair suddenly realising how welcome another professional opinion would be. 'Go on.'

'Ok, so why don't I trust him?' She contemplated this for a second or two, working through her own logic. 'Well, I have to admit, it's mainly gut feel. The only time I've seen him in action was at the town meeting – where I thought he was generally patronising.'

Matthew was about to agree but Kate her held her hand up to signal that she hadn't finished her point. He closed his mouth and suppressed a smile.

'But if I were to talk specifics, these are the things I noticed. First off, he makes too many references to being "on the level". In my experience, someone who does that is seriously trying to pull the wool over your eyes. He's also rattled by challenge.' Kate looked at Matthew squarely. 'And he's *really* rattled when that challenge comes from your friend Jem Small.'

Matthew raised his eyebrows. 'You think?'

Kate nodded, taking another sip of wine. 'Before you came into the meeting that first day, Jem was challenging Gerry on his accusations about under-reported profits, and she was doing a good job. He looked very uncomfortable. When you walked in it saved him from having to squirm any further.'

Matthew looked at the ceiling as if something had just dawned on him. 'Ah… so that's what he was up to.'

Kate smiled. 'He gave you the wrong start time for the meeting didn't he?'

'How did you know?'

'You looked slightly thrown when you came though the door. The thing is Matthew, when you walked in, it really threw Jem too. I think Gerry was satisfied with that reaction.'

'You think he orchestrated it?'

'Perhaps. But then how could he know that you and Jem had history? I guess it's more likely that telling you to turn up late was probably a bit of insurance in case people turned nasty at hearing his announcement. It would provide a distraction.'

Matthew spoke more hesitantly, 'So… you know Jem and I go way back then?' He wondered how she could have found out.

'She told me that you were best man at the wedding where her fiancé didn't show up.'

'Is that all she said?'

'She said you helped get her through the difficult time afterwards.'

Matthew nodded but didn't speak for a moment.

Kate, seemed to read his mind. 'Anyone who sees the two of you together can tell it's more than that Matthew, but that's all she was prepared to tell me, a stranger.' She waved her hand in an impatient gesture. 'Anyway we're getting off track here. You asked for my impressions of Gerry Monroe, how do they fit with yours?'

'Well, for starters, I share your concerns about whether he can be trusted. When I took the assignment he told me he wanted an assessment of the resort from a commercial perspective. I started, as I normally do, by looking at the previous years' accounts and even without the increased marketing spend of the last two years, it's a great business. It doesn't cost Monroe holdings anything, pays for itself, but that's not where the resort's real worth lays.

He leaned in to emphasise his point. 'From a reputational standpoint it's *gold*. It's the Monroe's 'get out of jail free' card whenever the media throws accusations of corporate insensitivity at them. In the scheme of their global business, it's financially insignificant but that just makes Monroe Holdings look all the better for supporting a small community like Pine Tree.'

'So it's valuable in the wider sense, surely Gerry is interested in that?' asked Kate, sipping her wine.

'It's strange. In some ways, given his position in the company, he's *too* interested. He shouldn't be personally involved at his level. In terms of where this ranks in the overall scheme of things, it's such a low priority. And yet he wants to work one on one with a business consultant, you've got to admit that's unusual.'

'Agreed. But if he's interested, that's good, so where's the problem?'

Matthew hesitated. 'I'm breaching all sorts of protocols here as it is…. Oh what the hell, I'm going to take the risk that I can trust you. I've been given a pretty heavy steer that I just need to assess the financials in preparation for an exit.'

'So he's selling the resort off?'

'Pretty much, yeah.'

'Is that even your speciality?'

Matthew raised his eyebrows at Kate's rather dismissive tone. Did she think he was some kind of amateur?

'Sorry.' She closed her eyes apologetically and put her fingers to her lips. 'That came out all wrong. You'll have to forgive me – I'm like a dog with a bone when I'm discussing a professional conundrum! I just mean, in his position, I would have headhunted someone who specialises in that field.'

Matthew took a moment to think about this then smiled. 'You make a good point. In answer to your first question, I've dealt with this scenario before but I prefer to work with clients who are looking to turn their business around. Sometimes it just turns out this way, but I don't normally sign up for a project where a sell off is the only option on the table. And Gerry – despite what he's saying to the community – is not looking for any other solutions.'

'If he just wants to sell the resort, maybe that's why he's so personally involved. Men like him *love* the deal making side of the operation.'

'Possibly.' Matthew wasn't convinced.

'Would there be financial penalties if you terminated the assignment?'

'You think I should get out?'

'I'm just wondering what your options are,' she said evenly.

'He as good as threatened me with the sack if I don't get on board fast, in which case he would have to pay me out for the full contract term.'

'So why not just leave then?'

Matthew rubbed his hand across his jaw. 'It's not as simple as that.'

'Ah,' Kate understood. 'Jem?'

Matthew nodded.

'You want to try again there?' Kate raised her eyebrows. 'Assuming you've tried before…'

'I'm not sure that's ever likely to happen.' He shook his head. 'But if I stay I might be able to influence the way all this unfolds. If I just accept the money and go, Gerry will find someone else to prepare the commercials ready for a sell off to the highest bidder. He's sticking to his story on the undervalued leases and he wants my work to back that up so he can drive up the price of the resort.'

'If the leases do increase do you think the town can survive?'

'You know it yourself Kate – in all good businesses there's got to be something in it for everyone. If those leases are increased, Pine Tree Bay will become just another town that's breaking its back for a profit and people will stop renting the premises. Over time the resort will likely turn into a collection of run down outlets that attracts few visitors.'

Kate with her business hat on, assumed the habitual role of devil's advocate. 'These premises though, they're coming up what thirty years old? And the ones that were renovated are much older, so there's about to be some increased costs for the resort owner in maintaining the buildings as they start to age. Isn't it just what would happen in any business situation as dilapidations increase?'

'In a resort situation like this, where there's only one land-owner, you'd normally see a maintenance charge alongside the lease. The people leasing the premises pay in every year and when something needs fixing, it comes from that pot. From what I can see, Frank never structured things that way. For him, Pine Tree Bay is his own back garden, he's happy to maintain it.' Matthew shook his head slowly. 'Gerry's changing the goal posts.'

'So, instead of hiking up the lease costs, you think Gerry should introduce a maintenance charge?'

'That would be much better for the business owners because there would be a guaranteed fund for repairs. But, for Gerry, increasing the lease charges looks the better option because it makes the resort look more profitable and therefore, more attractive to a potential buyer.'

Kate nodded. 'I can see why you're suspicious of Gerry's motives. Surely Frank can't be on board with all this?'

'I can't believe he would be, but I've no way of getting to him directly. If he's a sick as he's reported to be and Gerry takes the reins, that might be irrelevant anyway.'

Kate reflected for a moment. 'I know I've only been here for a month, but this place has really gotten under my skin. It's one of those communities that you always wished you belonged to but suspected didn't really exist anymore.' Kate laughed self consciously. 'I've even daydreamed about moving here one day, which, if you knew me, you'd realise is quite something!'

'It certainly *has* something, this place' Matthew agreed.

'And for you, is that Jem?' Kate questioned gently. 'Because you seem to be going way out on a limb here for a town you've spent about three days in in total.'

'Oh I don't know.' Matthew looked sheepish. 'I've always been a bit of a sucker where Jem's concerned. She clearly loves it here. It's where her grandmother grew up. She told me it felt like coming home when she first arrived and yes I do care about her, about making sure she's ok. But genuinely, I hate to see a good business that works for everyone get screwed up, and that's what's going to happen here.'

'Will you tell Jem all of this?'

'No, I don't want to worry her. I'd rather work out a way to change Gerry's mind.'

'Ok,' Kate nodded. 'I get it. But for what it's worth I think she's tough enough to handle a bit of worry. She can handle Gerry Monroe and that takes courage. Don't treat her like she's fragile because from what I've seen she isn't. And she might not thank you for it.'

'Noted. But will you keep all this to yourself for now.'

Kate nodded. 'So, as I know the rest I might as well ask, what happened with this Nick guy that Jem was going to marry? She told me that she never saw him after the day he stood her up at the church?'

'Nobody has.'

'Was it treated as a missing persons report?'

'Not officially – though in the confusion some of Jem's contacts in the London press got the wrong end of the stick and wrote it up that way. They gave it this whole "Runaway Groom" angle – but it was all rubbish. Nick did get word to his parents to let them know he wasn't coming on the day. He got cold feet and it was as simple as that.' Matthew was lost in his thoughts for a moment. 'You know, he was my best friend for *ten years*. Still today, I can't believe he just disappeared like that.'

'What do you think happened to him?'

'I have no idea. He told his parents that he left the country.'

'Do you think there was anyone else involved?'

'I think there may have been.' Matthew shifted uncomfortably. 'But I've never shared that with Jem.'

'You know Matthew, it seems that you're telling me an awful lot of things that you should be telling Jem.'

Matthew shrugged. 'I know. I've always just… wanted to protect her.'

Kate drained her glass and set it back down on the table. 'Maybe that's where you're going wrong.'

CHAPTER EIGHT
2nd November

Jem

'She's not coming back you know Jem.' Jamie was furiously whisking eggs and spilling half of them down his apron.

'Jamie, I hate to sound unsympathetic but will you go easy with those eggs! There isn't going to be enough left in the bowl to fill a quiche case if you carry on at this rate.' Saturday morning in the cafe was always manic and Jem was losing patience with her head chef. They'd been going over the same ground for weeks now. 'If you want any chance of getting Lorna back you have to be patient,' she said more gently, rinsing out pots and stacking them in the drainer. 'You have to prove to her that you're not going to immediately rebound to the first girl who gives you the eye! And once she sees that, she'll maybe start to trust you again. She's giving you the rope, all you have to do is *not* hang yourself.'

'Aye I know that, but it's taking so long. I-'

'Jamie, it's been a month.'

'Nearly five weeks now.'

'Give her time. Anyway, I'm sorry to sound harsh but the choice isn't yours anymore. Your only choice is whether you move on or wait. And you can't do both! If you choose to wait you need to be single whilst you go about it. You know what the bush telegraph is like around here. She might be miles away at her mum's but I'll bet she still hears if you even so much as sneeze.'

'Well I hope she knows how hard I'm trying. I've not so much as talked to a lassie since she left.'

Though this wasn't exactly true, Jem had to admit that Jamie *was* trying. Especially given the number of attractive women who'd shown more than a passing interest in him during the festival. However, she chose to say nothing as she finished the last of the pots and dried her hands. 'Right I'm off to show Matthew the garden flat.'

'Speaking of second chances,' Jamie muttered under his breath.

'Pardon me?' Jem, already on her way out, turned sharply.

'Nothing boss.' Jamie poured out the egg mixture he'd beaten half to death.

She was heading into her office to collect the keys to the garden flat when her mobile buzzed. It was Jeanie – the daughter of Mrs MacBride who used to rent Withershins – so Jem answered the call with a smile. 'Jeanie! How are you? Are you in the area?'

'No but I'm planning to be over in a week or so. I just wanted to ask you a favour.'

'Of course, what can I do for you?'

'It's my Gordon. He's doing some family history research and he wants all my dad's old army papers. I think mum must have left them in the attic at Withershins because I haven't been able to find them anywhere. I know it's a long time ago but do you think they could still be there?'

'It's worth a look I suppose. There are boxes in the attic I've never looked through but I thought they were all belonging to Marcia. I've been meaning to do a clear out up there myself to be honest but it's so busy here in the café, I never seem to get around to it.'

'No problem, just when you've got a spare minute hen.'

'I'll give you a call once I've had a good look around up there and let you know if I find anything.' She ended the call and made her way out to the cafe garden.

The apartment was nestled behind the herb patch and sheltered by a tall hedge. With shuttered floor to ceiling windows opening out onto a side lawn, it was more of a studio than an actual apartment; one large open space with birch wood flooring and a vaulted ceiling – built and decorated to a beach house design.

The large open space of the studio room now housed a king size bed and a French style cream armoire. There was a kitchenette and a separate shower room off to the side. It didn't have a sea view, but neither was it possible to see the café from any of the windows, and this lent an air of seclusion that guests loved to retreat to after a day spent in the hustle and bustle of Pine Tree Bay. Despite the cool November morning, Jem left the patio doors ajar. Someone along the back lane was burning leaves and the sweet aroma floated in on the breeze as the jagged caw of a rook pierced the dank morning air.

Jem laid the fresh coffee, croissants and fruit she had brought on the counter with the idea that she and Matthew could breakfast whilst discussing the terms of the let. She still wasn't exactly sure how long he was going to be in town for and she was confused to find herself hoping it would be more than a couple of weeks. Only two days beforehand she'd been so annoyed to find him back in her life. Determined to deal with him only in so much as would be useful to the preservation of her community. What was happening to her steely resolve?

Thursday night was to blame; Matthew, fitting in to her group of friends as if he'd known them forever, winning everyone over with his easy charm. And Jem didn't want to dwell on the number of women she'd noticed casting an appreciative eye over him. Even Helena and Isla hadn't been immune. Then there was Beryl with her Knight of Pentacles rubbish. Mind you she wasn't wrong. Solid reliable type? Tick. The one you can count on? Tick. Trouble was, Jem had been so busy remembering *that* version of Matthew, she'd forgotten what great fun he was too.

And something else strange had happened. When the old Matthew had surfaced on Thursday night – the Matthew who'd been her best friend for so many years – she'd remembered what great fun *she* could be too. It had been exhilarating to let her hair down, dance a little, laugh a lot. She busied herself laying out the croissants, spooning coffee into the cafetiere.

The unavoidable truth was, Thursday night had done more than just break the ice between Jem and Matthew. It had *woken her up*. To the fact that she was thirty-nine not seventy nine. In fact, there were probably lots of seventy nine year olds out there who were living it up far more regularly than she currently was. Whilst it was probably for the best that her days of dancing on tables were behind her, she used to know how to have a good time.

Once again, Madam Zelda's words came back to her. What was it she'd said? That everything was about to change. Was she about to change? Did she *want* to change? Three days ago the answer would have been an emphatic *no* but–

'This looks nice.'

Jem had been so deep in thought that she hadn't heard Matthew coming into the studio until he was right behind her saying, 'And the breakfast looks good too.' She jumped and he put his hand on her shoulder, laughing. 'Sorry, did I startle you?'

She shook her head and grinned. 'No I…yes I…was just miles away.'

His eyes went to the breakfast she'd laid out on the counter. 'Fresh coffee, croissants *and* strawberries? Is this one of those estate agents tricks where you fill the place with nice smells so that I don't notice the leaky roof?'

'Now why would I need to use tricks when I can rely on my own natural charm?'

'Yeah, probably a good job you brought the food.' He teased, then dodged a playful punch that she sent his way.

She stood back and took in his dishevelled state. *And how annoyingly great it looks on him*, she thought to herself. 'Have you just come from the gym or something?'

He had the decency to look bashful. 'I came straight from having a run. Don't be annoyed but the only non-negotiable for me on a place is the shower, so I know it's really cheeky but I thought I'd bring my stuff and shower here to 'try before I buy'. You don't mind do you?' He gave her his most disarming smile.

'You're right. It *is* really cheeky!' she said with mock outrage. 'Ok fine but you should know that if you don't like the shower and you turn this place down, I'm going to make you clean that bathroom from top to bottom in preparation for the next guest.'

'Deal.' He grabbed his bag and headed into the shower room.

Jem poured them both a coffee and when Matthew emerged a few minutes later in a t-shirt and jeans, rubbing his hair vigorously with a towel, she had a job to drag her eyes back to the counter.

'Did the shower pass muster then?' she asked, diligently focusing on the strawberries she was hulling.

'With bells on! Nearly threw me to the other side of the room, which is just what I'm looking for.'

'Oh really?' She widened her eyes, unable to resist. Good God now she was flirting. *Stop flirting with him!* They burst out laughing at the same time then Jem said, 'Well, what you do on a weekend is your own affair Mr Albright.'

'Actually,' he said, coming over to the counter and placing his hands either side of her. 'I was rather hoping that next weekend it might be yours too.'

Jem swallowed. 'You did?' Her voice sounded weird. Why had it dropped a couple of octaves? And now she was suddenly short of breath.

Matthew moved in, a teasing look on his face, and she tilted her head to look up at him. Oh God. She hadn't been able to think of anything else but kissing him since he'd come out of the shower. What should she do? Should she give in to it? What on earth did he use that made him smell so good?

'You're playing it safe. I can tell. I think that it's high time someone helped you out of your comfort zone.'

'You do? And who might that be?' she asked in a husky sounding voice that she had definitely never heard herself use before.

Matthew pretended to looked around him. 'Well I'm the only one here so…' he grinned.

'So what's your plan?' She parted her lips. She hoped they looked inviting. To hell with it. She was going to do this.

'Kiteboarding!'

'Eh?' Jem blinked rapidly. 'Oh… kiteboarding?' Had she heard him right?

'Yeah it'll be just like the old days,' Matthew said excitedly. 'A drive out to the coast on Saturday morning, me and you, riding the waves.' He stepped back from the counter and bounced on his feet. 'What do you reckon? You up for it?'

It would seem I am. Jem hastily buried the thought.

As they sipped their coffee and nibbled on the croissants, Matthew outlined his plans for the following weekend.

'So you're seriously asking *me* to come kiteboarding?' Jem asked doubtfully.

'Why not? You've done it before.'

'A *lo-o-ong* time ago.'

'It's like riding a bike, you'll be back into it in no time. Apparently the conditions a little further up the coast here are really good for beginners. It'll be the ideal place for you to get back into it.'

'I'm not sure.' She scanned her mental list of excuses. 'Oh no, I won't be able to – can't leave Bear for the whole day.'

'Who's talking about leaving Bear? He's invited too. In fact,' Matthew pretended to look awkward, 'truth is I only asked *you* because I want to spend the whole day with *him*.'

Jem laughed.

'Seriously, he'll love a whole day out at the beach and we can take it in turns to surf whilst the other looks after him.'

'Matthew it's November, it'll be freezing.' She swallowed the last of her croissant.

'Since when have you been bothered about cold water? You used to make us all swim in the Serpentine in January. You've still got a wetsuit right?'

He was right, she *did* used to drag them all out to swim in the colder months, she had forgotten that. But she'd been a lot younger and a lot fitter then. She had to admit though, there was something slightly intoxicating about looking at herself through Matthew's eyes. He still thought of her as the girl who was adventurous and fearless. Jem didn't even know if that girl was still in there… But suddenly, she wanted to find out. She drained her coffee cup and placed it firmly on the counter. 'Right, you're on. Bear and I are in!'

'Really? He looked genuinely thrilled which made her stomach do some kind of funny flip flop thing. 'Great, I'll sort all the equipment for us.'

'How was your dinner last night?' She didn't really want to know but, needing to derail her increasingly steamy thoughts, this was the next best thing to chucking a bucket of cold water over herself.

'Oh it was great! We definitely drank a few too many glasses of wine though,' Matthew groaned. 'What with the night out at The Smugglers and the late night at Kate's, I really needed to clear my head with that run this morning.'

It was a late night with Kate then was it? 'How nice.' Jem dusted the crumbs from her lap and jumped down off the high stool she'd been perched on.

Matthew looked at her carefully, a faint smile tugging at the corners of his lips. 'Are you upset that I had dinner with Kate?'

'Of course not!' She started briskly gathering plates and coffee cups and taking them to the sink. 'Why would I be upset about that?'

'I don't know, but you're doing that thing where you go all business-like and efficient,' he said in an amused tone.

'And so I should as we came here to discuss a business transaction,' she smiled primly. Wiping her hands on the tea-towel, she rested against the work top then folded her arms. 'Now, are you going to be renting my flat or not?'

'Oh I see, you've buttered me up with breakfast and now it's time for the hardball negotiations. Ok, here we go. Right, first things first, what's the rate?'

'That depends. How long are you staying?'

'Until Christmas. Maybe longer...'

Her heart sank remembering that Kate was staying until the spring, was this why he was changing his plans? But she refused to get side tracked. She tilted her head to one side and narrowed her eyes. 'Who's paying? You or Gerry Monroe?'

'I'm part expensed.'

'Well in that case...' She quoted an inflated figure which he agreed on without hesitation and she held out her hand to seal the bargain.

'I think I'm going to be very happy here.' Matthew murmured holding on to her hand a moment too long before casting his eyes around the apartment and coming back to rest on hers.

Jem suddenly needed some air. Handing him the keys she smiled cheerily and said, with forced brevity, 'Lovely! Nice doing business with you Mr Albright.' She threw the tea-towel at him. 'Dishes are in the sink!'

Heading back up the garden path to the safety of the cafe, she let out the breath she hadn't even realised she'd been holding. What had she been thinking back there? For God's sake... If Matthew was going to be staying just moments away from her business, she needed to get a grip of herself. Fast.

Matthew

Matthew watched Jem weave her way through the herb garden and back through the gap in the hedge. She'd agreed to come out for the day – that suggested something didn't it? And was it his imagination or was she jealous whenever he mentioned spending time with Kate? Perhaps he could take that as another encouraging sign.

He mooched around the studio apartment opening drawers and cupboards, checking out the wardrobes.

Though he tried hard not to let them, the memories filtered through. Their breakfast today had reminded him of another morning almost twelve years ago now. A much fresher, sunnier day, when Matthew had run down to the street to pick up coffee and pastries still hot from the oven, with a lightness of step that hadn't been there before.

They'd polished off breakfast in bed. And when they'd eventually decided to get up, hours later, they'd enjoyed showering the crumbs from every inch of each other. It had felt like the perfect morning after the perfect night before. And he knew in his heart that Jem had felt the same way too. You couldn't fake that.

For the rest of the day he'd wandered around on cloud nine, couldn't get the smile off his face. After so many years of reconciling himself to the fact that it would never happen, suddenly and wonderfully, it had. And Jem had been the one to instigate it.

Then he'd arrived home to the letter. It was a complete blindside. He'd read it in a daze. They'd spent four months in each other's company every day and – he wasn't imaging it – they'd been building to something. They *had* built to something. Because whatever else the previous night had been, it had not been casual, not for either of them. But even so, she had left him.

He eventually found out through some mutual contacts that she was in Devon but by then he'd made the decision not to follow her. The madness had to stop. Jem knew where he was if she changed her mind. It had simply been time to get on with his life and stop chasing a figment of his imagination, something that was never his in the first place and never likely to be for that matter.

But for some reason, when it seemed impossible to get things to work with anyone else, he wondered. Was it down to *that* morning? Is that where it had been hatched? This secret conviction that one day, given the right conditions, it could work between them? Last night, over dinner with Kate, Matthew had silently asked himself why he couldn't just give it up – this ridiculous obsession. Because whichever way you looked at it that's what it was. Wasn't the definition of madness to keep doing the same thing, expecting to get different results?

Look at Kate for instance – she was great company, she was stunning – and they got on like the proverbial blazing house. She was single. And they had the same background in business. They even lived in the same *city* for God's sake. Any sane person would be telling themselves to at least consider asking her out. Why wasn't he doing that? What was wrong with him? What was wrong with Kate?

It always came back to the same thing; she wasn't Jem.

CHAPTER NINE
4th November

London *Kate*

Ten in the morning, the following Monday and the British Library was already heaving with the usual apposite blend of remote workers and tourists – plus the odd researcher thrown into the mix. Kate moved through the throng and scanned the tables in the cafe.

Idella Achike had arrived early, bagging them both a table next to the mountainous wall of ancient books that towered above the low-lit refectory. *Look at her*, thought Kate, spotting Idella at the table; *head buried in phone, completely oblivious to the number of heads she's turning.* Kate hurried over to greet her old friend.

'I took a punt,' said Idella, indicating the pot of steaming peppermint tea which sat on the opposite side of the table.

'And you were right.' Kate smiled, taking off her coat and sitting down. 'As always.'

'I've been wondering when you'd get round to giving me a call.' Idella, never one to waste time on pleasantries, came straight to the point.

'Like I said on the phone, I didn't want to involve you right off. I thought this was all going to blow over fairly quickly.' Kate chewed on her lip and looked at her friend. 'Now I'm just not so sure.'

'You should have come to me straight away. This is the time when you call in favours.' Idella's shrewd eyes narrowed. 'You know that as well as anyone.'

'I didn't want to take advantage, you're always so busy and honestly, I honestly thought it would take Allocott a matter of weeks to realise they've made a mistake.'

'Ok ok.' Idella shook her head, already bored with the preliminaries. 'Now bring me up to speed and don't leave anything out.'

Kate relayed all the details surrounding her suspension and her friend listened with forensic attention. There was no need to take copious notes; Idella had a remarkable memory.

Kate had known the strikingly attractive woman sitting across from her for ten years now. Their paths had first crossed when Idella headed up an IT security audit for the company that Kate worked for at the time. As their careers had progressed they'd become friends – borne out of a mutual respect for the operating style of the other. Idella was now a freelance corporate investigator, charging mega bucks to companies, mainly law firms, who needed her technical expertise to look into the activities of the organisations they were building a case against.

Idella had a quiet reputation for being able uncover information quickly, always ensuring she left no trail that would put her, or the people who hired her, on the wrong side of the law. And whilst the information that she uncovered wasn't always admissible, she could at least advise her clients where to focus their research, which was ninety percent of any legal battle anyway.

Kate knew Idella had to use somewhat subversive methods to get the results she did and this was the reason she hadn't turned to her immediately. Every time Idella carried out an investigation she took a personal risk. Kate didn't want her friend out on a limb for something that was likely to turn out to be nothing more than a misunderstanding. But after speaking to Paula on Friday night, it was clear that she needed help.

After saying goodnight to Matthew, she had called the number in Paula's text. Her assistant had picked up almost immediately.

'Paula I'm so sorry to call this late. I saw your message just before my dinner guest arrived and he's only just left.'

'Oh really?' Paula's croaky London accent brought an unexpected lump to Kate's throat. She had obviously been asleep but she rallied quickly at the sound of Kate's voice. 'Blimey, you haven't been letting the grass grow have you?'

'Ha Ha. Very funny.' Kate chuckled. 'It's platonic.' *More's the pity*, she thought to herself. She'd enjoyed Matthew's company tonight.

'Sorry for all the cloak and dagger stuff with the burner phone,' Paula said yawning. 'I'm still not sure where all this is leading and if Allocott requisition *my* phone records I could get in trouble just for contacting you.'

Kate's heart sank. She'd been hoping all evening that Paula was going to tell her they'd found out the suspension was a huge mistake. Followed by a call first thing on Monday to offer a full apology. Clearly *that* wasn't about to happen.

'Of course,' was all Kate said, then, 'So you still don't know what's led to the suspension?'

'Not a clue,' Paula sighed, 'but Emma cocked up today-'

'Emma Perkins, from Human Resources?'

'Yeah, that's what I wanted to tell you. I had to use the executive copy room and she was already in there when I arrived. We got chatting and I thought she looked a bit jumpy. Anyway, after she left I noticed that the copier had jammed. It must have happened on the last couple of pages of her document, so I located the jammed copies and that's when it all made sense.'

'What?'

'She was copying something about you – that's why she was jumpy. I only had the last two pages to go on, but it looked like they were employment termination papers. Your name was on the header.'

'Fuck.' Kate felt a hammer blow to her chest.

'I know! I honestly can't believe it Kate.'

'Was there anything within those pages that gave any clue as to what they are sacking me *for*?' asked Kate urgently.

'No, it was all generic stuff about intellectual property and equipment. I'm so sorry Kate.' Paula sounded upset. 'I can't get any information from anyone on what this is about and believe me I've tried.'

'You can't afford to lose your own position over this Paula. Just keep your head down. At least if they're drawing up papers this thing is coming to a head and they'll have to start talking to me soon. Maybe I'm just going to have to let this play out and see what they think I've done.'

'Kate, there's just one thing. I could be making a massive leap here but…'

'What is it?'

'Well, I went into to Tom's office on Wednesday.'

Paula had been re-assigned to work directly for Kate's boss whilst the suspension was ongoing. Thankfully her assistant had never found out that Kate had been sleeping with Tom or she might well be uncomfortable confiding things about him. 'He had his back to me so he didn't realise I was there.'

'Ok…' said Kate, wondering where this was going.

'He was on his mobile. And he was getting pretty antsy with the person on the other end of the line. He was talking about the CMA.'

'The Conduct and Markets Authority?'

'Yes. Then he said something about how he wasn't about to lose his job over something *'she's done'*. I think he was talking about you.'

Kate immediately knew it had to be more than just a coincidence. If the CMA were involved it was serious. But why would Tom think that he could lose his job?

'Paula, listen, whatever you do, don't tell anyone else what you've just told me. It looks like this is all going to come to a head one way or the other. Just let me handle it from here on in ok?'

'Ok Kate. I just want you to know I'm on your side.'

'I know. And thanks… You know, you're the only person who's even bothered to get in contact.'

'You know what folk are like Kate. Scared they won't know what to say.'

More likely scared of being tainted by association thought Kate privately. The two women chatted a little longer about things other than work before Kate brought the conversation to a close.

Even though it was late when she put the phone down, several things had crystallised in her mind.

Firstly, Allocott must be in possession of some physical evidence of misconduct on her part – most likely something that was traceable digitally – otherwise they would have needed to question her first before drawing up termination papers.

Secondly, if the CMA were involved, it was probably because the alleged misdemeanour was connected to some kind of prohibited business practise, most likely a breach of anti-competition regulations.

And whilst she couldn't be sure of anything at this point, there was one thing that *was* for certain; she couldn't possibly defend herself whilst stumbling around in the dark the way she had been up to now. Her reputation in the city was going to be ruined if she didn't do something, fast. It was time to fight back.

First thing on Saturday, she had called the only person she could think of who might be able to help her do that. Now, sitting in the British Library cafe, she was relaying the stark facts to her.

Idella's first question was predictable. 'Who in the office has access to either your computer or user log-in details?'

'No-one. I'm meticulous about not sharing my password. Paula has access to my email, yes, but in that case the digital footprint shows that *she* has operated the mail account on my behalf. If they're looking to sack me on the back of some technical evidence, it's because that was done when *I* operated my account.'

'Could you have left your machine unlocked when you were away from your desk? Could someone have used your PC when it was left unattended?'

'Again no, it's Pavlovian these days – I automatically hit control-alt-delete and lock the screen whenever I get up from my desk. Too many horror stories about all-staff emails offering to buy everyone a drink! I'm paranoid about it.'

Idella was nodding. 'It's the right way to be. And I know you well enough not to doubt you on it. What about when you've been working from home?'

'Well, you know I live alone, there's no-one who-' Kate stopped suddenly, remembering something from a few months previous.

Idella gave her a moment, watched the cogs turning in her friend's head, then said, 'Spill.'

'Well, it was back in August… I've been seeing someone from work. It hasn't been common knowledge because he's married. He's my boss. Such a cliché.' Kate felt embarrassed.

'Is this the real reason you didn't involve me from the get-go?'

'No, I-'

'Kate,' Idella cut in, leaning across the table, 'I'm not here to judge your personal life. Just tell me what happened.'

'We were working on a proposal together, Tom, that's my boss was presenting and I was helping him with the underlying information, but we were drafting it on my laptop. He got up to pour us both a drink so I went out to use the bathroom. I locked my screen because it was such a force of habit. Or at least, I thought I did. It sticks in my mind because, as I made my way to the bathroom, I remember thinking that Tom would think I was paranoid to lock my screen when there were only the two of us in the flat.

'So you definitely locked it? There's no chance he used it whilst you were in the bathroom then?'

'Yes, but that's just it. When I came back my email account was open. The screen was unlocked.'

'Is there any way this Tom could have somehow known your password?'

'He could have watched me type it in earlier I guess.'

'Well that's as good a place to start as any.' Idella pushed a notepad over the table. 'I need his full name, mobile numbers and email addresses – business and personal – the date and rough time that this happened.'

'Idella, it's Tom. We… we were close.' Kate knew she was sounding naive. 'I just can't believe he would-'

'And that's exactly why he's the first place I need to look.'

Kate chewed on her lip as she wrote the information down.

'Now, this Paula girl, your assistant, can we trust her?'

'Yes absolutely. But I don't want to get her involved. She supports her husband… he's… it's a long story but she can't afford to lose her job.'

'We won't ask her to do anything that's going to get her into trouble. But we might need someone on the inside. You can't tell her I'm involved though.'

'Of course not.'

'If I dig up any information you can use, I can't afford any of it to be traceable back to me for obvious reasons.'

'No, of course not. Idella, I do realise you're going out on a limb for me here.' Kate wondered if her disclosure about Tom had caused her friend to doubt her good sense.

Idella sighed. 'Sorry, I know I don't have to say any of that to you, it's just force of habit. Don't get all offended on me ok?'

'Ok.' Kate smiled, used to Idella's forthright approach.

'So,' Idella put the pad and pen to one side. 'Let's forget all this for a minute. Tell me how you're coping with the self-imposed exile?'

Kate laughed – it was the description she had used for her retreat to Pine Tree Bay too. 'I'm actually really enjoying it – believe it or not. There's more going on in a small town than you might think. Even you might be intrigued at some of the stuff I've been privy to!'

'I'm listening.' Idella leaned in.

Kate gave her a brief overview on the meeting with Gerry Monroe and Idella looked suitably impressed. She made her friend laugh with her caricature of the awful Madeline Beaver and then she mentioned the dinner with Matthew.

'Oh yeah?' Idella leaned across the table. 'Hot?'

'Very.' Kate fanned herself theatrically. 'Sadly he's a one woman man... and the woman isn't me. He's got it bad for someone in the town that he goes way back with. She's nice but she's carrying some pretty heavy baggage.' Kate filled Idella in on the runaway groom story and Matthew's role in it all.

'Certainly sounds like he's got it bad... It's funny you should mention that name though. *Nick Townsend*. I remember him coming up in one of my investigations when I was auditing.'

'You're joking?' Kate was astonished. 'It must be a different guy. Apparently, the one I'm talking about left the country.'

'Nope,' Idella shook her head. 'It's the same guy. Always stuck in my mind because it was a really strange scenario.'

'How so?'

'It's years ago now... must be what? Twelve years or so... back when I was still doing the digital auditing. A royalties firm hired me to look into the systems activity of an employee who'd done a bunk. Some woman who had worked for them for about two years then one day just didn't turn up for work. They couldn't trace her and the woman's family said they couldn't confirm her whereabouts. Anyway, because she had worked in the accounts department, the firm hired me to make sure she hadn't run off with any of their cash. They were all over the place to be honest. You wouldn't have had to be Einstein to fleece them and get away with it.'

Kate was all ears, but she still didn't understand how this could be related to Nick Townsend.

'I ran a full check over her systems activity,' Idella continued, 'but she was totally clean. Interestingly though, I turned up a few external emails to a Nick Townsend at one of the major banks. It rang alarm bells because I'd been reading about the disappearance of a man with the same name in *The Metro* a few weeks prior. I checked it out and it was the same guy.'

'Yes Matthew said there'd been something written up in the London press – someone reported this Nick's disappearance as a missing person story by mistake.'

Idella nodded. 'Anyway, this woman at the royalties firm had opened an account at the bank where this Townsend guy worked, so at first I thought I'd hit the jackpot; that she'd been using the relationship as a way of transferring cash out of the company. But there was absolutely zero evidence of anything dodgy. Nothing had been stolen. And that was all this royalties company were interested in, so I filed my report and that was the end of it.'

'Incredible!' Kate was flabbergasted. 'Do you remember her name?'

'Yes it was Zara Harper.'

'God you've got an amazing memory.'

Idella grimaced. 'You always remember the one that got away.'

'So you think she *was* guilty?'

'Of defrauding the royalties company? No. But when two people who are connected like that just happen to disappear around the same time? Well there's almost certainly a story behind *that*.'

'But you didn't investigate further?'

'Anything unrelated to the royalties company was out of scope. And you know me... If I can't bill for it...'

Kate laughed at her friend's mercenary approach, but she couldn't help being intrigued. 'What did the emails say?'

'Well, that was the odd thing, apart from the documentation to open the bank account, which all turned out to be legit, the rest were what you'd call... pedestrian. Just emails about meeting up after work and such.'

Kate then asked cautiously, 'Would you mind if I mentioned her name to Matthew, just to see if it rings any bells?'

'Sure, enough time has passed now, but be discreet.'

'Thanks Idella, and please don't worry, you're a ghost in all this I won't mention your name. I'd just be interested to see what Matthew knows about this Zara woman.'

Kate poured the last of her peppermint tea from the pot with a heavy sigh of relief. 'I can't tell you what a weight it is off my mind knowing I've got you in my corner with the suspension. I really feel as if someone's trying to fit me up.'

'Only one way to find out,' Idella said, draining her coffee. Getting to her feet she asked, 'You got time for another?'

Kate looked up at her friend gloomily. 'All the time in the world.'

CHAPTER TEN
6th November

Scotland   *Matthew*

'How old did you say this step ladder was?'

The following Wednesday, at Jem's house, Matthew had arrived to help out with the search for the old MacBride army papers. He was delighted she'd asked for his help – at least up until the point when she'd shown him the dodgy ladder that was supposed to get them both up to the attic.

Propped in a manner which could only be described as 'suicidal', with the top resting against the loft hatch and the bottom wedged against the bannister, it reminded Matthew of an episode of *999 What's Your Emergency*. He pictured himself weeks from now talking to a camera in a full body cast.

'It's solid enough,' insisted Jem. 'Stop being such a wuss.'

'Says the woman who's frightened of going into her own attic,' Matthew muttered, testing his foot gingerly against the first rung.

'What can I say? It creeps me out!' She watched him climb the ladder. 'I saw a film once where a woman went up into her loft and someone broke into the house then locked her up there and, well, you can imagine the rest. I wouldn't be able to focus on looking for Jeanie's documents if I were listening out for some mad axe murderer.'

'I can see what you mean,' said Matthew, now at the top of the ladder and making his way into the attic. 'I mean it's not as if there's a window you could climb out of or shout for help or anything is there?'

Jem reached the top of the ladder where she was met by an amused looking Matthew opening the attic window and letting some much needed fresh air into the loft space.

'I said it creeps me out, I didn't say it was a logical,' she mumbled shirtily.

'So what are we looking for again?' Matthew surveyed the room. It was actually very spacious and high enough that a person could stand up without having to duck. Someone had clearly once used the room as a study or perhaps a library; one gable end had floor to ceiling shelves which were now stuffed with old books, ornaments and boxes labelled up as Christmas decorations and other such paraphernalia.

At the other gable end, there was an aged desk above which hung an old map of the world tacked to some very faded willow leaf wallpaper. Matthew wondered who had sat there dreaming of far off places.

Along one of the eaves there was an ancient art deco style sofa in a mustard velvet with brown piping – probably the height of fashion in its day. It was draped with a silk shawl. The effect was rather more *Rising Damp* than The Ritz but, Matthew thought to himself as he looked around, Virginia Woolfe would have looked at home writing her novels here.

All this sat now amidst cardboard boxes of papers and various other forgotten things which must have once amounted to someone's life. There were a few lamps dotted around the room and Jem moved about, dodging boxes and switching each one on, grumbling that none of her predecessors had bothered to install an overhead light. The day outside had turned dreich and dark which would only make their task even harder in this dimly lit room.

'I think the idea was to be cosy,' said Matthew. 'Someone once created a little haven away from the world up here.'

'It was my great grandmother, Marcia's mum, she was a writer. She's the one who changed the name of the house to Withershins. Marcia hated the name. She said it was unlucky.'

'Yes, it's a strange word. I presumed it was an old family name or something.'

'No but I wish it was because that would be so much easier to explain,' Jem groaned. It's an old word meaning time running backwards or counter clockwise. My great grandmother took it from a Yeats poem because she hosted a literary group up here but Marcia said it was really because she was stuck in the past. Marcia thought the whole thing was morbid to be honest.'

'Well I hope her literary group had a head for heights.' Matthew grinned referring to the only route up there. 'Sounds like an interesting woman though, maybe that's where you get the writing gene from?'

Jem groaned. 'See what's happened? The spell is already cast. This is what attics do to you; they pull you back in time. We've only been here two minutes and we're already back a hundred years. She rolled up her sleeves and started hefting boxes. 'Right, you start with this one.' Jem plonked a large box down in from of him. 'We're looking for anything related to the MacBride family. Jeanie is looking for old army papers belonging to her father but anything we find of theirs needs returning so let's just keep it all to one side.'

'All right, I think I can do that boss,' Matthew chuckled.

'First job for me is to go down and make us both a cup of tea.'

'Then what? You're going to climb back up with two mugs in your hands?' Matthew looked doubtful.

'Nope, I have a cunning plan.' Jem disappeared down the ladder.

Matthew started to sift through the paperwork from the box she had deposited at his feet. The first thing he came across were some letters addressed to Marcia and so, realising it was clearly not a MacBride box, he put it to one side and started on the next one.

Jem appeared ten minutes later, with a rucksack full of flasks, plastic sandwich boxes and a blanket. 'Right the deal is, we do an hour of sifting then we get to have the attic picnic.'

'You clearly read far too many Enid Blyton books as a child.'

They'd been working away companionably for around forty minutes, Matthew pausing to ask Jem for clarification on whether something might belong to Mrs MacBride every now and then, at which point Jem reached for the box that Matthew had first started with.

'It's ok I've checked that one; it's a Marcia box, there's some letters in it addressed to her.'

'Letters?' Jem frowned and opened the cardboard flap. 'I never saw any letters when I was up here before.' She delved in and started to retrieve them whilst Matthew pulled another box from the pile.

Opening it up, he quickly realised it was full of Jem's old writing notebooks and he couldn't resist picking one up and flipping through it. As he did so a piece of paper slipped to the floor, he picked it up, slowly, a small current of shock running through him as he realised what it was.

'Matthew come look at this!' Jem said urgently from the other side of the room. Hastily pocketing the small piece of paper he hurried over.

Clutching several pages of the letters that Matthew had originally found, Jem was almost shaking. 'These letters to Marcia, they're dated back to 1955. Marcia must have been what, nineteen years old? They're from someone she had a holiday romance with here in Pine Tree.'

'She always was a good looking woman – I bet she was a stunner at nineteen. I should think there was more than one holiday romance for Marcia.'

'Matthew, they're from *Frank Monroe!*'

'*What?*'

Jem showed him the front of the envelope, 'Canadian postmark.' She flipped over the handwritten letter and pointed to the sign off. 'See here... "Yours always, Frank" followed by what has to be said are, a large number of kisses.'

'But that doesn't prove it *is*-'

'I know what you're going to say but there's this.' She pointed at a paragraph and read aloud, "We Monroes have always been a stubborn bunch..."

Matthew sat back on his heels and let out a low whistle. 'Well I'll be damned. They *are* from Frank Monroe.'

'He can't have been much older than Marcia at the time.'

Matthew scanned the letter. 'He was pretty keen on her if this is anything to go by.'

'Yeah, look here, he's asking her to go to Canada. I think things must have been quite serious between them.' Jem was still trying to take in the revelation.

'Did she ever mention any of this to you?' asked Matthew.

'No never. But then, I mean, I'd never heard of Frank back when she was alive so it would never have come up.' Jem stared at the letter in her hand. 'I guess this was just a teenage romance that she had all but forgotten.'

'Yes but that doesn't make sense. Frank created the resort back in 1993, and even then he was a pretty big fish, I would have thought it was the type of thing Marcia would have dined out on. "The billionaire I could have bagged" – it's the type of wheeze Marcia would have loved.'

Jem considered this. 'You know, you're right… I'm going to give these a proper read tonight see if I can get any clues as to what went on.'

'Well, I don't know about you but all this searching has given me an appetite.' Matthew said, looking longingly at the rucksack. The light drizzle outside was working its way up to a deluge and he crossed to shut the window before spreading the picnic blanket out onto the floor.

As Jem unscrewed the flasks and Matthew opened the Tupperware boxes, he asked carefully. 'Have you had any more postcards?'

'No,' she said quietly, handing him a flask. 'It's strange though how we both had the same reaction don't you think?'

Matthew nodded, selecting a cheese and pickle from the plastic box. 'What I think is even stranger, is that barely a week after you received that postcard, I turned up on the scene.'

'You think the two are connected?' Jem looked surprised.

'I have no idea how they could be, but it seems a bit of a coincidence.'

Jem swallowed a mouthful of sandwich, trying not to think about Beryl's reading. 'And now here's another mystery with this whole Frank and Marcia business.'

They sat in silence for a while, munching on their sandwiches and listening to the rain hammer on the roof when, changing the subject Jem said, 'I heard that Kate's gone back to London?'

'Yeah, just for a couple of days.'

'Oh.' Jem's voice sounded flat.

Matthew, caught the tone, it was the third time that she had sounded prickly about his friendship with Kate. He could let her wonder about it, in the hope that a little jealousy might jolt her into finally lowering her guard around him, but it wasn't his style. When he spoke his voice was even.

'Kate and I are just friends, you know that don't you?'

Jem shook her head and laughed 'Matthew, you forget we spent five years hanging around the beaches of Devon together. She is absolutely your type. Blonde, attractive, easy to talk to. Of course you're more than friends. You don't need to hide it from me.'

He experienced a momentary flicker of irritation that she was writing him off as some player, based on the way he had handled relationships in his twenties. There was a reason he had only ever indulged in casual flings back then.

His voice took on a quiet tone that commanded her attention. 'Kate and I are friends and only friends. It's important to me that you understand that.'

Jem nodded, unwilling or unable to say more, but he decided to take it as a sign that she believed him.

'Anyway,' Matthew said trying to lighten the tone, 'would you just look at us, eating an attic picnic with mysteries to solve all around us; all we need is a collie and a few mates and we really could be in the *Famous Five*.'

'It would have to be *Five Go Boozing* if we're recruiting any of my lot,' Jem murmured then reached for a piece of flapjack. 'You know, just to add even further to the mystery, I *could* tell you that I was warned about everything that's unfolding here by a fortune teller.'

'No way!' Matthew roared with laughter. '*You* went to see Beryl? Sorry I mean,' he waved his hand in a mystical flourish, 'Madam Zelda?'

'Yes,' Jem laughed. '*I* went to see Madame Zelda.'

'Well all I can say is, having met the lady in question, I already believe everything she told you.' Matthew nodded sagely. 'Is she Romany?'

'I think she's more Bradford-y,' Jem deadpanned. 'But whatever she is, she certainly saw you coming.' She reached for the last piece of flapjack but Matthew beat her to it.

'Oh yeah?' His eyes were full of merriment.

As Jem started to tell Matthew about Beryl's reading he struggled desperately to keep his face straight.

'Right that's it!' Jem shouted as she brought the story to a premature close. She grabbed a cushion from the sofa and gave him a swipe. 'I know it all sounds far fetched but everything she has predicted has come true in one way or another. *And*,' Jem went on, wide-eyed, 'she told me to be on my guard for forces working against me.'

'*Forces working against you?*' Matthew's efforts to keep his composure finally collapsed and he dissolved into laughter.

Jem pummelled him repeatedly with the cushion. He fell over in submission then reached up to grab her forearm in defence at which point she lost her balance and collapsed on top of him.

The kiss that followed was so unexpected that Matthew had to stop himself from catching his breath. Jem had instigated it but there was certainly no hesitation on his side. When they finally drew apart he gave her a slightly amused look and murmured, 'Well, that's one way of shutting me up.'

'I wouldn't be too flattered,' Jem replied dryly, 'I was just trying to retrieve that last piece of flapjack.'

*

Later, after Mrs MacBride's boxes had all been located and Matthew had made plans to collect Jem for their trip up the coast on Saturday, he made his way along the shore road. All he could think about was the kiss. Was she finally ready to lower her guard around him? Had she really thought he was just a player first time around? Those comments about Kate suggested as much. He'd been so wrapped up in how it was from his side of the fence, he'd never considered how his behaviour might look from her perspective.

Perhaps that was it; he needed to show her that where relationships were concerned he was prepared to be all in, prove that he could be trusted.

Unfortunately, stuffing someone's private papers into your pocket was not the way to go about it. Pulling out the document that had been burning a hole in his jeans all afternoon, he halted under a streetlight to give it a closer look. His first impression had been right; it *was* a sonogram. A sonogram with Jem's name at the top left hand corner, dated twelve years ago; just a few weeks after she'd left London – and Matthew – for good. Jem had been *pregnant*.

Matthew was so wrapped up in his thoughts, he didn't see Kate until she was right beside him. He stuffed the piece of paper back in his pocket and they greeted each other warmly.

'You're back?' He was surprised that Kate hadn't taken the opportunity to catch up with friends in London for a few days.

'Yeah, I missed this place funnily enough. It must have grown on me more than I realised,' she grinned. 'I'm glad I ran into you though as I need to have a word. I found out something when I was in London that I think you'll be interested in?'

Matthew peered at her looking slightly puzzled. 'Sounds very intriguing... Look I'm just on my way back to the flat, do you want to join me and perhaps I can repay you for your hospitality the other night? Though I warn you, it's a toss up between omelette or beans on toast.'

Kate fell into step beside him. 'Two of my favourites.'

Jem

Jem danced around the kitchen. She felt as fizzy as a glass of champagne.

Had she actually planned on kissing Matthew? She probably had; she just hadn't shared that fact with the sensible head girl who ran the decision making side of her brain. Mind you the head girl *had* earned a day off – she'd been running the show for the last twelve years.

The radio was blaring out a feel-good anthem and Jem sashayed around the table a second time. Bear sauntered in and immediately picking up on the good vibes, started to wag his tail. She bent down to give his ears a good scratch and he closed his eyes in ecstasy, treating her to his big panting smile.

'Don't worry,' she said in the gentle voice that was only reserved for Bear. 'You're still my number one boy'. He continued to wag his tail lazily, loving all the adoration.

She was looking forward to one of her favourite rituals that evening; a long soak in the tub, with a gorgeous smelling Lush bath-bomb. And yes, she was going to treat herself to a glass of something sparkling too, to echo her mood. She would light some candles and sink down into the warm water whilst catching up with the latest episode of Radio Four's *A Good Read*. The perfect night in. Though this afternoon might well signal there were other perfect ways to spend an evening...

Jem was more than aware that her calm, orderly approach to life could seem a bit boring to others but by and large she'd been happy in her contented bubble. The way she was reacting to Matthew's reappearance in her life, however, felt like something beyond her control. She felt looser, she was letting her guard down. For once, the cautionary voice in her head was not the loudest, increasingly drowned out by the over excited one that was telling her to *go for it*.

She'd overheard the low murmurs of approval from a few of the local single women when Matthew came in to the cafe. Though she would never admit it, they had brought out a slightly possessive streak in her. Even when she'd been with Nick, she was the only female constant in Matthew's life, and rather unreasonably, she'd always felt he was, somehow, *hers*.

Jem finished pouring herself a glass of Prosecco before going to answer a knock that came from the back door. Looking through the glass she could see Finn. The excitement flooding her body was immediately swamped by guilt. The result was a slightly jittery cocktail.

'Celebrating something?' He smiled indicating the glass as she let him in.

Jem had the ridiculous feeling of being caught out and laughed self-consciously. 'I was just about to take it upstairs to drink in the bath.'

'Oh really?' Finn raised his eyebrows in a playful gesture that suggested he might join her. It wouldn't have been the first time.

She pretended she hadn't picked up on his intonation.

'Yeah, I'm really grubby. I've been in the attic all day digging through boxes for some of Mrs MacBride's old documents. Jeanie's husband is doing some kind of family history project.'

'You should have said, I would have come round to help. I know how you hate going up there on your own,' he chuckled.

'Oh it's ok, Matthew gave me a hand.' At the sound of Matthew's name, the frequency in the room changed and Jem scrambled to fill the sudden chasm that seemed to open up between them. 'Yeah, he wanted to see Bear again, so I thought, whilst he was here, you know…' Why was she gabbling? She reminded herself that if she wanted to have Matthew in her house that was *her* business and she didn't have to make excuses for it.

Finn's whole posture had tightened but he didn't speak. He'd stood in her kitchen a hundred times before but this familiar scene suddenly felt uncomfortable.

'Cup of tea?' she offered in a desperate attempt to breeze through the awkwardness. He nodded and she busied herself filling the kettle and placing it on the Aga, arranging mugs; anything to keep her hands busy and her eyes averted from his.

Finn, so confident and capable with his tall strong legs and broad shoulders not to mention his ability to turn his hand to anything, had been her only date for the last two years but she had always been clear with him; theirs was a strictly casual arrangement. Had she been kidding herself? If she was honest she'd suspected for a while that his feelings for her were deepening.

It wasn't that she didn't think the world of him, she did, but try as she might she had never quite managed to fall in love with him. Before Matthew had reappeared on the scene, she took that to be just the way she was nowadays – it was all just down to having grown up. A fact of life. She wasn't in her twenties anymore and so all the excitement of love's young dream was over. This was just what happened when you approached forty. For *that* person, *that* version of Jem, Finn had been enough.

But Matthew had her stomach doing somersaults like a teenager. She was frightened of the feeling but at least she *was* feeling. It was a wake up call. She had no clue how this attraction for Matthew was going to play out but she was slowly realising something; whatever happened she *was* capable of being truly excited about someone again. Surely that was preferable to bending a friendship into something it wasn't?

'Jem,' Finn began in his warm Scottish brogue.

Please don't ask where we are headed, prayed Jem silently as she retrieved the whistling kettle and poured water into the mugs.

But Finn took the conversation in another direction. 'What do you really know of this Matthew? I mean, yes you knew him years ago and all that, but what do you know of him *now*?'

'Well, to be honest, from what I've seen he doesn't seem to have changed all that much over the years.' Jem tried to sound casual as she returned the kettle to the stove.

'Do you think he's on the level?' Finn asked.

Jem turned around now to face him; she was simultaneously relieved that the conversation wasn't about the two of them, yet perturbed to find herself discussing Matthew with Finn, especially after what had happened this afternoon. She shrugged, 'Well, like anyone, he has his moments... but when it comes down to what really matters, I would say he *is* on the level, yeah. He's always been one of the most straight up people I've known. Why do you ask?'

'It's just that,' Finn sighed, clearly hesitant to broach the subject. 'He's been visiting the business owners in the town this week, part of his review for Gerry. I'm getting feedback that he's asking some very leading questions.'

'In what way?' Jem frowned.

'He's been going over his profitability forecasts for each business with the owners to get their agreement, and some people are saying that his projections are, let's just say, on the *optimistic* side.'

'But he's probably factoring in the increased marketing spend that Frank introduced for the whole resort,' said Jem quickly. 'That investment is only just starting to kick in. You know as well as I do that the overseas visitor numbers have been up four fold for October and it looks set to continue that way across the winter events that we've got planned. Bookings are well up on last year...'

She knew she was talking too quickly. Defending Matthew more vigorously than someone who, only weeks ago, had been just as suspicious of his motives as everybody else. 'Anyway,' she went to pour milk into the tea, 'if people have concerns they should just let him know directly what they think and see how he reacts. He doesn't bite you know.'

Finn was looking at her with an unreadable expression, his chin slightly raised. 'Well, I'm sure people *will* raise their concerns but I just thought I'd sound you out. At the outset you seemed as keen as everyone else to make sure Gerry Monroe wasn't about to use Matthew to pull a fast one on us.'

'And I still am!' Jem felt her cheeks redden. 'Just because Matthew and I are friends it doesn't mean my loyalty to this town is any less. Hell, three weeks ago everyone was looking at me like *I* was the frosty fish because I wasn't welcoming an old friend with open arms. People should make their mind up about what they want from me.'

'And I suppose by *people* you mean *me*?'

'Well you were one of several who questioned why I wasn't more gracious with Matthew at the beginning.'

'That wasn't because I was worried about *his* feelings.' Finn said quietly.

Shit! She'd blundered into the very conversation she'd been trying to avoid. She turned to attend to the cups so he wouldn't read what was written all over her face.

'The things is Jem, I *do* know what I want from you,' Finn said, laying his hands gently on her shoulders. 'But the more important question is, do you know what you want from me?'

Jem stiffened. Her mouth suddenly felt dry. She wasn't ready to do this. She wanted more time to plan something eloquent and considered. She *could* tell Finn she wanted for things to stay the same between them, wanted what they already had, but after today, she didn't know if that would be true. With her back still to him, she placed the spoon on the counter and took a deep breath. 'I want your friendship Finn.'

'And what if I said I wanted more?' His voice sounded strained behind her.

Jem turned around slowly to look up at his face. 'And what if you didn't say that?'

He closed his eyes for a moment then looked toward the ceiling. 'Message received loud and clear.' He turned swiftly and made for the door.

'Finn, please.' Jem shot forward and placed a hand on his arm. 'Above everything we're *friends*. We have *always* been friends.'

'Well as a *friend*, I'll ask you this, whilst you're here defending Matthew Albright in one breath and finishing things with me in the next, do you know where *he* is?'

Jem looked incredulous, 'It's got nothing to do with me where-'

'He's in *your* apartment with Kate Parker. I saw them not half an hour ago. By all accounts he was with her on Saturday and they're together again, two minutes after she's back up from London! I hope you're not falling for him Jem because he's going to make a bloody fool out of you… and quite possibly all of us!' He shrugged her hand from his arm and stormed out into the night.

Jem closed the door after him with a shiver that was not entirely caused by the cold night air. She'd never seen Finn so angry. He was one of her best friends and she didn't want to lose that. But he was also a proud man, and she couldn't bear to think how much she was hurting him right now.

That wasn't the only reason for feeling like the rug had been pulled out from under her though. Finn's words had landed like a blow. What was Matthew playing at? After *that* kiss he had waltzed off to meet *Kate*? The whole afternoon they'd been together and he'd never mentioned that he had plans with her this evening.

She looked at the three untouched drinks on the counter top and reached for the glass of Prosecco. Taking a huge gulp she grimaced as the liquid went down; all its earlier fizz replaced by something tepid and flat.

Matthew

Much later that evening, Matthew stood at the open patio doors of the garden studio.

Kate had headed off an hour earlier – in need of an early night after her long trip north – and now he was taking a moment, looking out on to the garden, listening to the rain as it poured through the trees and bounced off the deck. Matthew let the soothing, rhythmic beat wash over him and tried to organise his thoughts. This had certainly been a day of revelations. Over a quick bite to eat, Kate had downloaded what she'd found out from one of her friends in London.

So Nick had been in contact with Zara Harper in the weeks leading up to his disappearance?

It was a name Matthew hadn't heard since his uni days. Zara had been the 'it girl' during their time at LSE. The one everyone in their year *and* those above and below, would have given their student loan to go out with. Matthew had fancied her along with everyone else at first, but once he got to know her a little better, the attraction waned. Not Nick though. He developed the worst type of crush. He saw other girls yes, but the way he followed Zara around like a sick puppy meant those relationships soon fell by the wayside once the girl in question got wind of where his real affections lay.

Nick wasn't completely to blame; on and off Zara had reciprocated his feelings and they had long periods where they were, to all intents and purposes, a couple. Until, just like that, Zara would cool off. Matthew later found out the reason for the sudden deep freeze; Zara had her sights set on someone else. A very wealthy, well connected guy who was a friend of her – similarly well connected but much less well-off – family. The times when Zara and Nick were apart she was spending with the rich kid; she was ambitious and he was her first choice, it was as simple as that.

Matthew told his best friend what he knew and Nick confronted Zara. She had admitted there was someone else and, what's more, she said she'd managed to bag him. Nick was history. That was the day that Nick put Zara behind him once and for all – at least that's what Matthew had always believed. Now he thought back to the very last day that he'd seen Nick before his disappearance.

Arriving at the tailors in Saville Row to collect their wedding suits, a few nights before the ceremony, Nick hadn't looked like a man who was happy to be getting married in three days time. In fact, Nick had been so preoccupied, he hadn't even noticed that Matthew was being slightly cold toward him. The tailor regarded them quizzically; two men who looked to be planning a funeral rather than a wedding.

'Pint?' Matthew had asked, as they headed up Piccadilly. He had needed to get something off his chest and the street wasn't the place for it.

'I need to get up to Highbury. I'm picking up a puppy for Jem.' Nick's face had brightened for the first time that evening.

'A quick one won't hurt, come on.' Matthew remembered steering his friend into the Wolseley. And once they were seated with drinks, his friend had tried to muster up the persona of an excited groom; rubbing his hands together and saying jovially, 'So, *best man* are you all ready for Saturday-'

Matthew had to cut him off sharply. 'Look Nick, I'm just going to come straight out with it. We've been friends for over ten years and I've always considered you as one of the good guys...' He had looked down at his pint then back at his friend. 'So I can't understand why, only three days away from getting married you're screwing around with someone else. What the *fuck* are you thinking?'

Nick went pale and his eyes started to widen but Matthew shook his head in a warning gesture. 'Don't even bother trying to deny it. Tony Partridge saw you coming out of the Four Seasons with a red haired woman this afternoon. At the same time you told *me* you were meeting Jem. You're lying to me, to Jem.... Plus you've been looking as shifty as hell ever since we arrived at the tailors.'

Nick paused as if considering how much to tell. 'Matt, it's not how it looks,' he said finally.

'Well how is it then?' Matthew inhaled sharply. 'Because from this side of the table it looks like shit.'

'I was there to... *end* something.'

'So there was something to be ended then?' Matthew didn't bother to hide how sickened he was by Nick's admission. 'No, don't even bother answering that one.' He held his hand up. 'I don't want to know all the sordid details. And just so you know, Jem called looking for you, whilst you were off "ending" things.'

Nick who had been staring guiltily into his pint looked up sharply. 'You didn't...?'

'Don't worry, I covered for you. I suddenly remembered that you were sorting a surprise for her but Jesus Nick-'

'Well that's perfect actually, you know for the surprise, the puppy-'

'This is so *fucked up*! I'm not going to sit here and pretend this is all business as usual. That we're two mates getting excited about what's planned for the big day. Can't you see how unbelievably pissed off I am with you for this? I feel as if I don't even know you.'

'If you let me explain. It hasn't been going on for long... I-'

Matthew quickly drained his pint then slammed his glass down on the table. Standing abruptly, he reached for his coat staring furiously at Nick.

'Do you know what I can't believe? I can't believe you're doing this to her. *It's Jem for Christ's sake.* After everything she's been through these last few months?' He raked his hand through his hair. 'And worst of all, I can't believe that knowing all that, I have to stand up in three days time and tell everyone what a fantastic bloke you are. Tell Jem what a stand up guy she's marrying, just because-'

'Just because I got there first Matt?' Nick's voice had been full of menace as he lifted his head from his pint. 'Isn't that what this is really about? Taking the moral high ground when what you'd really like to take, what you've *always* wanted to take, is something else all together?'

Matthew had looked at his friend with something approaching pity. 'If that's all I was interested in Nick, wouldn't I have just told her the truth when she called this afternoon?'

Nick's pale complexion had turned even paler and whatever fight had been in him, left as quickly as it had come. Matthew pulled up the collar of his woollen overcoat ready to brace the winter chill. 'I'll see you at the hotel on Saturday morning as planned,' he said, 'but after that, I'm done.'

But Nick had not been at the hotel. Nor the church. And the rest was history.

And Matthew wondered now…. *A redhead. Had that been Zara?* She was the only woman he could imagine Nick ruining things with Jem for. But it seemed so unlikely. Yes, she'd had an unhealthy hold on Nick at university, but at the time of the wedding they wouldn't have seen each other for years?

If Zara *had* turned up on the scene, and from what Kate said it looked like she *had*, well, for the first time in twelve years, Nick's disappearance was making some sense. But until Matthew could find out more it was probably best he didn't mention anything to Jem. For one thing he didn't have all the facts and, slightly selfishly, he didn't want any further reminders of Nick hanging between them – the postcard was doing a good enough job of that already.

He padded back to the fridge and took out another bottle of Becks. If he *were* to act on this knowledge, it would be to close things off once and for all. Today Jem had instigated that kiss. If she wanted to pick up where they had left off in London he would be ecstatic, but this time he had to be sure that the shadow of Nick wasn't hanging over them.

And then there was this other thing; Matthew took the sonogram from his pocket. He shouldn't have taken it. It was an instinctive reaction because he somehow thought the baby might have been *his*. It was clear from the dates though that this was Nick's child.

What had happened? He hated to think about Jem going through the loss of a baby alone. But how could he broach the subject with her now? He smoothed out the paper and placed it carefully inside a file within his satchel. He would pick a good moment to raise it with her, carefully, and hope she could forgive him for taking it in the way he had.

He picked up his smart phone and set it on the dock to play his music library at random. The raw edginess of Nickelback's 'How You Remind Me' floated out past him into the night air. He stood with one arm raised against the open door jamb and listened to the lyrics as the rain hammered onto the deck. Twelve years on and he was still playing the same song.

As the words washed over him, he thought back to this afternoon; Jem and the kiss. Were they having fun? He hoped to God it was more than that.

Otherwise he was just torturing himself all over again.

Nick

Spain

Nick turned the light out in the en-suite and padded through to their generously sized bedroom. Zara, in bed reading a novel, reclined against plumped white pillows, with her tumble of red curls looking even more striking against the crisp, white cotton, allowed her eyelids to droop. As soon as the lamp was out, she would be wide-awake. Zara's insomnia wasn't the only third party in their bed.

Closing the book she'd been pretending to read, she placed it on the bedside table along with her reading glasses. 'Any news from Perry whilst I was away?' she asked through a stifled yawn.

'He's been on at me to accept that commission again.'

'That's good,' she said absently. Nick knew she was only half listening.

'I'm not accepting it.'

'No?'

'Remember, they wanted me to deliver it personally?'

'What?'

Oh yes that *would* get her attention. Even though he hadn't mentioned that part before, she so rarely listened to what he said, he could get away with insisting he'd told her pretty much anything.

'Surely they realise you work anonymously?' she scoffed.

'I think they were after some kind of publicity coup.'

She relaxed, took a tube of cream from her nightstand and began rubbing it into her arms. 'Still...' she looked doubtful. 'Who was it, one of the London galleries?'

'No it was... oh just some business tycoon.'

'How much were the offering to pay?'

'A hundred and fifty.'

'*Thousand?*'

'What else?'

Zara stopped massaging her hands for a moment and stared at him. 'You never mentioned that before. Jesus, how badly did this guy want to meet you?'

Nick laughed. 'It's crazy isn't it? You know, I got such a kick out of being offered that sum but....' He walked over to the window and looked down at the distant lights that dotted the coastline. 'Isn't it ironic the way things have turned out?' He searched for the right words. *Tread carefully.* 'Coming here in the way we did because we saw a chance to escape. And now, that decision has led to more of everything than we could ever need.' He paused. 'I don't know, I sometimes wonder if we would have got here anyway, without–'

Behind him he heard her usual exasperated sigh. Why did she always always became defensive when he tried to explore these feelings; he was an artist, and art had to ask questions of life, surely she realised that.

Zara spoke slowly, with the tone of an impatient mother. 'Nick, you're a great artist. That's why you decided to take the risk and come here with me – so that you could stop being a boring finance man in a grey suit and realise your artistic potential.' She took a deep breath. 'But the truth is, there are a million great artists out there. Perry has created a *brand* for you, a lucrative *anonymous* brand, and when he coupled that with the type of work you produce, he struck gold. We *all* struck gold. You know how the art world works – it's the combination of the concept and the work that commands the price. When are you going to grow up and accept your part in it?'

'*My* part in it?' he hissed. His eyes flashed dangerously but he didn't dare go any further, not with Sophia only metres away.

'Oh for Christ's sake not *this* again.' Zara rolled her eyes. 'Face it Nick. I offered you the chance of a great life, doing exactly what you most loved doing. And, after wrestling with your conscience for all of about thirty seconds, you snapped my bloody hand off! But now you're making legitimate money you can't stop bleating on about how it was all *my* idea. Change the record will you. It's fucking boring!' She turned on to her side and slammed her head into the pillow.

God she was a bitch. He stalked into his dressing room and pulled on a tracksuit. 'I'm going to the den.'

'Well don't wake me when you come up,' she grumbled to his retreating back.

They both knew she would be lying there awake regardless.

Zara

Zara had stopped sleeping because of the affair. It had been going on for around eighteen months and to begin with was just another fun diversion from the endlessly boring days of her life in Andalucia. Back then she was still sleeping through the night.

It wasn't her first affair. Jeremy was just the next in a long line of clandestine liaisons that added a bit of spice to her life. You could pick them up everywhere out here, Zara's type: young men with good breeding who looked after themselves. She approached affairs in the same way she would buy a horse; teeth, tone and temperament were all important. The last thing she needed was a nag who might try to entangle her in something heavy; she had Sophia to think about.

But then, ironically, it was Sophia who had led her to Jeremy. Zara's daughter, a keen rider with her own pony at livery, had badgered her mother for Polo lessons. Zara had taken her to the local club just to shut her up but when she met Sophia's instructor, she'd been more than happy to sign her daughter up for any number of lessons.

Lean and strong and a good eight years younger than Zara, Jeremy was everything that Nick wasn't; athletic, healthy and well connected with a blissful absence of any brooding Byronic tendencies. He was everything that Zara looked for in her young companions. She fully expected it to burn out as quickly as it started – the way of all the others – but, to her complete surprise, their mutual infatuation had matured into something deeper, and now she lay awake most nights contemplating her next move.

Returning today from two incredible nights in his company – under the guise of a trip to check out a horse for Sophia – she had much to keep her awake. 'I've been offered a job in Gloucester.' Jeremy had come straight to the point over dinner last night, 'I want you to leave Nick and come with me. With Sophia of course.'

She'd been about to tell him it was impossible but instead found herself wondering if that were strictly true. So now there was a choice to be made.

Telling Nick about the affair wasn't the problem – their relationship was long dead. She could probably even bear to uproot her daughter, though that would be harder. The real cause of her anguish was the fact that a move back to England would force her to come clean about everything. She would have to tell Nick that the last twelve years of his life had been one big *lie*.

Her little outburst just now was part of a well worn routine; a reminder for Nick that he was part of their little scheme to flee to Spain too, but there lay the problem; in truth, he wasn't. And, when it came down to it, neither was she.

Twelve years earlier, when Zara had learned that Nick was about to be married to Jem, she'd gone through what she now thought of as some kind of *temporary insanity*. At the time, her first marriage to a well connected family friend – which she had clung on to with all the tenacity of a tick – had finally come to end. To add insult to injury, that end had been bitter, and his wealthy family had instructed their lawyers to 'do whatever it took to get shot of her'.

Zara had emerged bruised and rejected; not to mention an ugly sense of having been "scraped off". But, thanks to a talented divorce lawyer, she also emerged *wealthy*.

Zara wasn't one to wallow; she immediately cast her eye around for people and things that would plug the hole of her broken marriage and act as a salve for her injured self-esteem. Her thoughts had quickly returned to old flame Nick Townsend; the back-up plan. The best looking guy at university who she'd fancied the arse off but had ultimately passed over as a bad bet financially. In her wounded state, she was suddenly convinced that Nick was the one she should have chosen all along.

She tracked him down through mutual friends and was surprised to find him even more attractive than she remembered. He also worked for a major bank. Tick. Tick. But though he seemed genuinely pleased she'd made contact and agreed to meet her for a drink, he made it clear from the outset that he was soon to be married and was only available as a friend.

It was a gauntlet.

In the following weeks, Zara became quietly obsessed with hooking her old flame and slowly, over a period of months she was thrilled when her efforts began to pay off. Fortunately for Zara, Nick's intended was spending all her time with some conveniently sick grandmother. Leaving Nick with lots of free evenings to fill. Add that to the fact that he still looked as if he wanted to eat her every time they met and bingo! It was only a matter of time before he capitulated. Back at her flat one night Zara finally got him into bed. She felt triumphant but, from the moment it was over, Nick had been full of remorse.

Zara wasn't worried, the initial breach had been accomplished and the hard work was over; it was only a matter of time before he was hers. But, infuriatingly, Nick had started to prove her wrong.

The more he pulled away, the deeper Zara's fixation rooted. Nick had grown in confidence since his days at university and she was highly attracted to this new wolfish, cocky version of the younger man it had been so easy to cast aside. As the chance of securing his affections started to look increasingly remote, she convinced herself that she couldn't live without him.

When she looked back on it, twelve years on, the mania that had possessed her was ludicrous. Now of course, with enough experience to recognise and temper that compulsion toward unavailable men, she could see her obsession for what it was. But the twenty-nine year old Zara was convinced that Nick was the only man she would ever want.

She tried every trick that had ever worked on a man to convince Nick of the same, but though she could get him into bed she couldn't *keep* him there. The dawning realisation that she was hoping for on his part – that she was 'the one' – would just not materialise. Devastatingly, after the fourth time they had sex, a guilt ridden Nick had ended things once and for all and stormed out of her apartment.

At work the next day her insides had churned. Why was she so singularly obsessed with a man who would cheat on the woman he was just about to marry?

But the answer to that question lay at the heart of the whole intoxicating mess: here was a man who wanted her at the cost of all reason. She saw the physical power she held over Nick; the way he wrestled endlessly with his conscience when he was in her company; the way he had to stop himself from touching her, from leaning in to kiss her. And she craved that power to the point of addiction.

But wasn't this obvious struggle on his part also proof that he was on the wrong track? That he was going to end up married to Miss Goody Two Shoes out of a sense of loyalty, or duty, when what he needed was someone who lit a fire in him the way *she* did.

He just needed an added incentive, that was all. Something that meant he had no choice but to back out. It could be her gift to him…

A plan began to form in Zara's mind, prompted in part by her workplace; the royalties office where day after day she processed cheques that had been returned, uncashed, in the mail. It was just a temp job whilst the settlement for her divorce came through and she couldn't wait to get out, but what then? What would she do with herself all day?

The returned royalty cheques, her divorce, Nick. It was then that the idea came to her; the answer to the conundrum she'd been wrestling with all day

All Nick needed was an incentive, a way out.

Twelve years ago, Zara had seen to it that he had one.

Nick

Nick's den was every man's dream; a total lad-pad, complete with light grey walls, dark cedar floors and matching shutters. Along the back wall a huge, worn, leather sofa took up most of the room. It was the soft buttery type of hide that you sank into, not the cheap plastic looking crap that your arse slid off. Of course, there were all the obligatory boys toys too: games consoles, VR headset, a state of the art sound system and a widescreen TV for his growing Netflix addiction.

It was midnight and, despite the underfloor heating, the room was chilly so he lit a fire and searched for some music to suit his mood. Settling for the mournful solace of Beck's *Sea Change* before opening up his MacBook and navigating to a private browsing window, he searched for Pine Tree Bay Resort, then clicked on Jem's blog.

Surprisingly, in the current image obsessed world, there weren't that many pictures of her, but she was all there in the words. Her warm, witty and, at times, irreverent writing style made for amusing articles about local life, coupled with a collection of more nostalgic pieces that she'd obviously worked on with visitors who were tracing their family history. He could see why someone would want to visit Pine Tree Bay after following the blog; probably feeling they knew half the town before they even arrived.

His eye was drawn to an article where Jem was pictured facilitating a workshop with local writers. In full flow, addressing the group, she stood before them gesturing with pen in hand. It was the Jem he remembered; capturing the passion she had for whatever she did in life.

Throwing back the duvet he padded over to the small drinks cabinet he'd installed in the corner of the den and poured himself a measure of his favourite eighteen year old Glenfiddich. Taking a long sip he contemplated the flames that were casting shadows around the darkened room.

Jem had realised her dream, just as he had realised his. She had a bookshop and a café overlooking the sea and she was running writers' workshops. It was the picture of the future that she'd described to him many times but *she* hadn't screwed anyone over to get it.

Zara's words floated back to him like an icy draft. *Accept your part in it!* He *had* accepted his part. He had learned to live with it… hadn't he? Or what else was he doing stuck out here day after day?

His part was far from blameless but in the end it came down to one thing; he'd swapped the best girl he would ever know for financial freedom and a seedy obsession – one that had burned itself out within less than a year. And now all he had was the question; had it been worth it?

He went back to the laptop and navigated to the comments section at the bottom of the blog post. He had made his choice. He had let Jem go in favour of another life. She was living her dream without him and that was all he had ever wanted to know wasn't it? That he hadn't ruined her future. Now, knowing that, he could rest easy, close the laptop and draw a line under that niggling doubt once and for all.

But he couldn't stop himself... He felt ridiculously charged as he typed a simple line of text into the comments box and pressed enter. And then he realised something – typing those few words was about the most thrilling thing he'd done in years.

He needed to get a life. Because this one sure as hell wasn't what he'd had in mind.

CHAPTER ELEVEN
9th November

Jem

With freedom, books, flowers, and the moon, who could not be happy?

Jem stared at the anonymous blog comment. Two things were immediately strange. Firstly, the article she had written was quite old and the comment was new. Most comments were generated around the time of the blog posting or a few weeks after. Of course it wasn't unheard of for a new reader to stumble across an article and add a note, but that was usually the case on evergreen topics such as climate change or local history. Events at the bookshop rarely generated comments much after they had occurred.

The second, and more important thing was the very personal choice of message. The comment was an Oscar Wilde quotation and yes, of course, everyone used his epigrams for speeches and philosophical sound bites, but this particular quote was one that was very close to Jem's heart. These were the words that Marcia had written in Jem's graduation card and Jem had quoted them often over the years.

The fact that the comment had been added to the article about the writers group that she facilitated seemed deliberate and calculated but…

'Ugghh…' she let out a groan and closed her laptop harder than she should, before climbing out of bed. She was not going to think about this now. She didn't have time for one thing. Today she was meeting Matthew and despite the fact that she still wasn't clear on what was between him and the annoyingly gorgeous Kate Parker, she was nonetheless determined that she and Bear were going to enjoy a day off, away from Pine Tree Bay and all the tensions that were running through the resort just now.

Bear, who had very naughtily, crept up on to the bed in the night, stretched out on his side with an ecstatic sigh that flapped his roomy jowls like pants on a washing line.

'Sorry pal but there's no lie-in for either of us today,' she said giving his neck a scratch. He proceeded to lie there like a dead weight, luxuriating in the softness of the feather duvet. She showered, dressed and packed her wetsuit, made enough sandwiches to feed an army and heated up soup for a flask. On the spur of the moment she grabbed a bottle of red from her wine rack – she would give it to Matthew as a thank you for the day out. And who knows? Maybe they would drink it when they got back?

Then she remembered that he had got drunk on wine last Saturday with Kate Parker and almost took it out again. Exasperated at the extent to which this thing between Matthew and Kate seemed to be occupying her thoughts, she went round the house and drew the blinds. It was starting to get light outside which meant she was going to be late.

Running out into the dark November morning, a cool wind whipped her hair about her face and a blizzard of autumn leaves flurried from the trees and crunched under her feet. She hoped that the weather forecast was right. Were they really thinking of kiteboarding this late in the season? At least they would have the water to themselves she supposed.

Jem, hurried now and after hastily shoving the food, towels, wetsuit, spare clothes and blankets she had gathered into the car along with a huge bag of dog treats, she and Bear took off at speed for the short drive to the cafe.

Parking up she decided to pop in and check that Isla and Jamie had everything they needed for a day without her. Coming through the door she was surprised to find Matthew already at the counter. She detected immediately he was excited, fired up, at the prospect of their day out. The upbeat jokes with Isla and Jamie, the over animated way he was regaling them both with a story. It all gave him away.

She was surprised at just how good that made her feel and the way he casually placed his arm around her shoulder, kissed her on the cheek when she reached the counter, it all felt so… natural. She must remember her resolve; be cautious.

As they drew apart, Jem, feeling slightly hot and bothered made a deliberate effort to avoid catching her head waitress's eye. Isla's knowing expression would just make her flustered and she was determined to be cool. But it was Jamie who spoke first. Grinning from ear to ear he said to Jem, 'Boss you've been holding out on us! Matthew's just been letting on what an expert kiteboarder you are.'

Jem laughed and rolled her eyes. 'Yeah, I'm almost pro.' She turned back to Matthew and patted him on the chest. 'Don't worry, once I've out-surfed you I'll get you home in one piece.'

'You think she's joking!' Matthew raised his eyebrows.

'Have you checked the wind conditions up there?' Jem asked.

'I checked first thing. It's looking like a cross on-shore so the conditions will perfect.'

'Now you're just showing off with all the fancy jargon,' jeered Jamie. 'Away with the two of you, we're bored already.'

'Ok we're going, we're going,' said Jem. 'I have my phone so just call if there's any emergency.'

'There'll be no emergency,' said Jamie. 'Just get on and enjoy yourselves!'

Jem, Matthew and Bear headed for the door.

'And don't bother rushing her home before midnight Matthew,' Isla shouted. 'She won't turn into a pumpkin!'

'If I never see a pumpkin again it'll be way too soon,' Jamie muttered as they went out the back.

'Wow, I can't believe she's still on the road,' Jem ran a hand along the blue and cream paintwork of Matthew's camper van. 'You've done an amazing job with the finish, she was mainly rust the last time I saw her.'

'I know, cost me a fortune. I could have traded her in and bought something brand new for what I've spent on getting her to this condition.'

'Why didn't you?' she asked, hefting her gear in the back then getting in the passenger side.

Matthew slammed the rear doors and made his way round to the drivers seat. Fastening his seat belt he said gently. 'I guess once I find what I'm looking for, I have a hard time letting it go.'

The morning was perfect.

Seventy miles of coast and country which was way more fun than Jem expected; a mini road trip. Drinking coffee, munching through pastries and chatting amicably, she was reminded of the blisteringly sunny weekends when their little trio would leave London and head for Devon – high on the prospect of a couple of days with the surf crowd.

Today, arriving at the beach that Matthew had chosen, they found it deserted. For once the weather forecast had delivered on its promise and the sun was the only thing to be seen in the sky. The wind conditions were ideal too; gentle white caps cresting a pale green surf that was every boarder's dream.

'We don't want to get too cold setting up,' Matthew opened up the back of the camper.

'I haven't forgotten everything about boarding you know,' Jem grinned, climbing in past him.

'Sorry forgot I'm dealing with and old pro for a minute.' Matthew looked suitably chastised.

They giggled, stumbling around in the back of the camper, trying not to stand on a disgruntled Bear, whilst climbing into their wetsuits then pulled on neoprene hoods, boots and gloves to ensure their extremities were protected.

Jem, no longer owning a board or kite, listened as Matthew talked her through the kit he had brought for her. Jem didn't ask how he just happened to have a board and kite suitable for her weight and size but she knew he had brought them with him on the drive from London. She guessed they might have originally belonged to Lissa. Perhaps Matthew's ex hadn't taken to the sport. She didn't ask; didn't want to cast shade onto their perfect morning.

After carrying their kit down to the beach, they agreed to take it in turns to help each other launch then agreed that each one would ride whilst the other sat with Bear. Jem's four millimetre neoprene wet suit kept the worst of the cold at bay and, when it was her turn, after a few reacquainting false starts, she was amazed to find herself flying across the waves in the shining sun, skilfully manoeuvring her kite to catch a smooth, even ride.

Gaining in confidence with each turn, Jem started to perform a few basic hand drags and tricks. Landing effortlessly without losing her balance, a bubble of euphoria formed somewhere in the pit of her stomach. It swelled within her, rising and rising until suddenly she let out the the most joyous scream that was immediately whipped from her mouth and out into the ocean. Her body remembered how to do this! But she remembered it too – this feeling, this *freedom* – the exhilaration of the ride. Adrenalin coursed through her veins and for a few blissful minutes, her kite, her board and her seemingly weightless body flying across the waves, were all there was.

Finally, and reluctantly, she rode in toward the beach to give Matthew his turn. She was grinning from ear to ear feeling lighter and freer than she had in years, as if something had been shed out upon the water. Matthew leapt up to help her land the kite and Bear ran along side, playing in the shallows, picking up on Jem's infectious good mood.

'Look at you doing the tricks!' Matthew shouted to her across the beach as they manoeuvred the kite into the correct position and brought it to rest safely on the sand.

'I was surprised how easy it all came back,' she shouted back, the high of the ride still coursing through her. 'I was definitely surprised that I can manage it without taking too many dives!'

'It was never in doubt! And at this time of year it's definitely a plus.' Matthew laughed.

'Jees, I can feel it in my upper body and core now though,' she said as Matthew caught up to her. 'Come on I'll help *you* launch now, I can tell you're desperate to get back out there.'

Watching Matthew ride was a master class. As he manoeuvred expertly through the water, the result of many years practise and a few summers teaching in the Dominican Republic, it came back to her. The memory of how she'd always liked to watch him ride when they first met. The tricks and turns he could perform were always smooth and graceful. He made it look effortless. The same way he made everything look effortless. It was an annoying quality but it also made her feel somehow... she searched for the right word... *Safe?*

As she watched him out on the water she thought back to that night... the night before he had suddenly reappeared in her life. When she had found the photograph just before Beryl knocked at the door.

Out of nowhere, Beryl's voice was in her head. A forgotten question floating in on the ocean breeze. *Why do you think Marcia was so insistent on this Matthew…?*

Suddenly Jem was shivering and she snuggled closer into Bear. Her eyes followed Matthew, as he rode back and forth along the water, her racing mind mirroring his speed across the waves.

Was this what Marcia had been signalling all along? Marcia, who had always known Jem better than she knew herself? That night, when Jem had asked her to be honest about Nick? How like her not to come straight out with it; to plant a seed that wouldn't take root until the ground had shifted into perfect alignment for it to grow.

Jem's eyes continued to travel left and right across the horizon, mesmerised by Matthew's swiftness, his power, his speed and she knew, suddenly, what Marcia had been trying to say. But before she had time to consider it any further, Matthew was heading back toward her. She sprang to her feet to help him land his kite.

'Think we better call it a day at that,' he shouted. 'The wind seems to be moving slightly offshore.'

She gave him a thumbs up to signal agreement. A cold day like this one was definitely not the time to risk getting dragged out to sea.

After ensuring their kites were resting in the correct position for the changing wind conditions, Matthew bounded over to join Jem and Bear on the picnic rug. Shoulders touching they sat clutching enamel mugs of hot soup, staring out at the waves and reliving the ride. Bear nestled under their knees in his fleece lined doggie jacket, happy to help warm his companions.

After a long pause in the conversation Matthew turned to check she was alright. 'You ok? You've gone very quiet.'

Jem deflected with a smile. 'Sorry. I forgot how much I enjoyed this part,' she murmured, sipping from her mug. 'I'm just relishing the warm afterglow of the post surf high.'

'You looked to be having a lot of fun out there.'

'I forgot how much I enjoyed that too,' she said wistfully. 'I've forgotten a lot of things as it turns out.'

She turned to look at Matthew, and found he was already searching her face for clues as to what was behind her confession. The mixture of hope and concern in his eyes took her breath away. Perhaps it was a good time to put her cards on the table.

'Matthew-'

'Hi there!' A voice from behind them interrupted her speech. 'And I thought *I* was the only round here mad enough to brave a November ride! Gorgeous day like this can't go to waste though right?'

They turned to see a young lad of around seventeen or eighteen approaching. He raised his hand in greeting,

Matthew got to his feet, brushing the sand off the back of his wetsuit. 'It *was* a gorgeous day for it,' he said. 'But the wind switched to an offshore about half an hour back and it's pretty strong so we decided to call it a day. Shame though, you missed a good morning.' Jem detected that Matthew was holding back on directly advising the boy not to ride, suspecting it would likely to be treated as a challenge, but the boy carried on anyway.

'Ah no bother. I ride here all the time in all conditions,' he said confidently. 'I'll just need a hand launching if you wouldn't mind.'

Matthew looked uncomfortable. When he was teaching he would never have launched anyone in these conditions unless they had a rescue boat tailing them, and not knowing the lad's capabilities it was clear he was very hesitant to be the one to help him into the water. In the end he levelled with the boy and told him as much and waited for the onslaught.

But the young man simply nodded good-naturedly. 'No worries. I'll self launch off the post up the beach there. I do it all the time. Just take me a bit longer that's all. See you.' And then he set off back up the beach where several wooden bollards marked the entrance to the dunes.

Matthew turned to Jem. 'I'm not happy about this.' He looked around the beach, there wasn't another soul in sight and certainly no other kiteboarders. 'If he gets into trouble there's nobody here to even call the coastguard.'

Jem agreed. 'Look, let's hang around a bit,' she said despite the fact she was starting to freeze. She could see Matthew felt anxious about leaving. 'He looks like he knows what he's doing but we'll leave our gear out just in case.'

'Thanks,' said Matthew. But noticing the strength of the wind increasing he shook his head. 'Look at the size of his kite, it's way too big for these conditions. I hope to God he knows what he's doing.'

They carried on as before, chatting and sipping hot soup to keep themselves warm but all with one eye on the boy who had now managed to self-launch the kite without a hitch, hopped on his board in the shallows and ridden off fairly expertly. Matthew's shoulders relaxed. The young man could ride but this *was* a moderately high wind and Jem could tell he was uneasy.

After a few minutes of watching the boarder move both downwind and upwind, Matthew commented to Jem that they may have been worrying over nothing when a large wave jerked the boy awkwardly and sent his control bar spinning. The kite suddenly went out of control.

Matthew jumped to his feet – it was what all kiteboarders dread – a repeating death loop, which if the boy didn't act quickly, would drag him further and further out to sea.

Almost immediately however the young rider pulled hard on the furthest steering line and the kite instantly dropped out of the sky. Jem and Matthew simultaneously exhaled, the boy had reacted correctly and quickly. He now needed to untangle his lines and re-launch, but in this temperature and with a cross off-shore wind which could drag him out to sea within minutes, a rescue was his best option.

Matthew and Jem both saw the potential for danger at the same time.

Without speaking they ran to Matthew's equipment and after completing their safety checks as quickly as they could, Matthew's kite was airborne and he was on his way to where the boy was still in the water and clearly unable to re-launch his kite. Jem retrieved her phone ready to call the coastguard at Matthew's signal.

Matthew was there within seconds and circled around the boy, keeping his own kite at a safe distance to remain upright. From her position on the beach Jem could see that the boy was arguing with Matthew who she guessed was telling him to cut the lines to his kite so that Matthew could drag him safely back into shore.

With each passing moment, the boy was being pushed further and further out to sea and the swim distance was looking increasingly dangerous. Jem was starting to feel frantic. The first rule of kiteboarding was that you never went out further than you could safely swim back to shore. In offshore winds where the waves were driving back off the beach that was likely to be half the distance you could normally swim – at best.

He must know that this is serious! Why isn't he cutting the lines?

She wasn't prepared to wait any longer. She dialled the coastguard.

'The boy has been in the water for around ten minutes trying to relaunch the kite,' she shouted above the noise of the crashing waves. 'My partner is trying to rescue him but the boy is refusing to leave his equipment and there's an offshore wind. I'm worried. They're both moving further and further out to sea.' The coastguard calmly took the relevant details and assured her a lifeboat would be launched immediately from nearby.

Bear, picking up on Jem's nerves, started to whine and, still clutching the phone in one hand, she bent to give him a fuss with the other. When she straightened up, she was able to breathe a sigh of relief. Finally! The boy seemed to have at last seen sense. He was free of his equipment and was now clinging to the handle at the back of Matthew's harness. Jem's heart was in her mouth as Matthew, navigating the tricky conditions with a deadweight pulling him backwards, tried to tack them both safely back to shore. It was a risky procedure that should only ever be performed by a super experienced kiteboarder and it wasn't something Jem would ever have attempted herself – especially in these conditions which no sane rider would ever have gone out in in the first place!

She sent up a silent prayer of thanks as the lifeboat came speeding into view. Matthew, clearly exhausted and at the limit of his strength, immediately powered down his kite and sank into the sea. He and the boy clung to his board then finally and mercifully the two fatigued riders were hauled to safety aboard the RIB.

Burying her head in Bear's fur she suddenly gasped as her boy started to lick the salty tears – tears she hadn't even known she'd been crying – from her wet cheeks.

Jem

Later that afternoon after Matthew had been checked over by a medic, warmed up and taken back to his camper, he chastised himself for even attempting the rescue; berating himself for not calling the coastguard straight away.

'Ah don't be so hard on yourself, everybody loves a hero,' Jem tried to lighten the mood. 'Bask in the glory for a few hours!' But it wasn't going to work; Matthew clearly needed to process the ordeal. 'Look,' she said more gently, 'you knew you could get to him faster than the lifeboat. It was the right call.'

'Well thank God you had more sense than I did and phoned it in. I was really struggling.' Matthew's teeth chattered as he spoke. 'Bloody stupid kid could have drowned both of us.'

They were now sitting in the camper van, and, having changed into dry clothes, Jem had brewed up a scalding cup of Bovril from an old jar she'd found at he back of the van's tiny store cupboard.

'This will help replenish your energy,' she said as she handed him the cup. 'Think I remember reading once that it's good for lost electrolytes or something.' She took a sip. 'Tastes a bit funky mind.'

Matthew, lost in thought, didn't answer.

'Did he apologise at least?' Jem grabbed a teaspoon and stirred her Bovril which seemed to be congealing at the bottom of the cup.

'The rescue team gave him a pretty severe bollocking, he's a regular here apparently – one of the rescue crew knew his family.' Matthew shook his head again. 'He at least had the decency to look ashamed. I don't think he'll be kiteboarding on his own again any time soon.'

They had all seen in the past how quickly situations could turn. Matthew's anger at the boy was understandable – for ignoring his advice in the first place and not reacting quickly enough in the second.

'You know there was a moment when I was shouting at him to cut his lines when he actually started shouting back about how expensive his kite was?' Matthew looked at her in disbelief. She could see the frustration in his eyes. She let him talk. 'When he finally got his hook-knife out of his harness it took him an age to cut himself free. Clearly some bloody rusty old thing that he hadn't checked in months.' He took a deep breath, sipped on his Bovril, obviously making a determined effort to stop ranting and calm himself down. 'I suppose everyone got out alive that's the main thing.'

Bear, ever the emotional barometer for any situation suddenly stood up and rested a woeful head on Matthew's knee, earning himself a scratch behind the ears in the process. Jem saw the tension start to ease from Matthew's jaw. Realising for the first time what Marcia – with her uncanny ability to see right into the hearts of people – had so shrewdly observed. A man who was strong in every sense of the word. Of body, of heart, of principle yet also – she now saw – with a rarely glimpsed vulnerability.

Jem came to a decision. 'Come on, drink up,' she said, holding her hand out for his cup. 'Let's get ourselves out of here. I know a nice spot a little further up the coast where we can catch the sunset.'

Matthew

Jem took the wheel and drove further up the coast to a deserted stretch of beach that was peppered with sand dunes. Having first stopped off to stock up on more hot drinks and provisions, she and Matthew now sat in the belly of an egg shaped dune, tired but grateful to be in one piece after the day's dramatic events.

Watching the sun as it slipped slowly toward the darkening ocean, they sat on a picnic blanket –both swaddled in jumpers, woolly hats and gloves – with their fleece-lined Dryrobes draped around them for extra warmth. The sun had mercifully shone all day and the earlier wind had blown itself out. Sheltered by the dunes they were snug, comfortable and the campfire they had built was beginning to warm their bones.

The post mortem of the day's events had continued on the journey up the coast and Matthew's mood was now much more relaxed, having had the chance for a good rant to clear the anger out of his system. With faces glowing golden pink in the setting sun, they sat in silence for a while, just enjoying the sound of the waves and the whispering grass – as well as the odd snuffle from Bear who was snuggling contentedly in his doggy fleece beneath a blanket.

Taking a deep, jagged breath, Matthew finally broke the silence. 'I'm sorry,' he said. 'You were on such a high earlier. This is not at all how I wanted this day to pan out.'

'How *did* you want it to pan out?'

'I wanted you to…forget…' Matthew tailed off, grappled for the right words, started again. 'You know what today is of course?'

Jem nodded. Though she had hoped that neither of them would choose to openly acknowledge it – today was the same Saturday that she was supposed to get married to Nick twelve years ago.

'I don't know Jem, I see you after all this time… and I think you're still, you know, *carrying* at lot… inside I mean.' She didn't look at him. She was staring into the distance, twiddling the butterfly on the back of her earring. 'I think you do a good job of keeping life at arms length.' *Careful* he told himself as she frowned slightly. 'But today I wanted you to be distracted. Not to have to remember what happened. I just wanted you to ride a wave and ride it really well, and think of absolutely nothing else. The pure joy on your face when you came back in.' He watched her closely as he spoke. 'That's what today was supposed to be about.'

She turned slowly to face him. 'You've always had that gift of really seeing people Matthew, even when we think we're hiding things really well. It's like that kid today. You knew from the word go he was going to act from a position of ego even though he was all humble and competent sounding. How do you do it? How do you *always* see it?'

He was surprised at the question. 'It's not... I don't do anything special. I suppose I just want to help.'

Jem took a deep breath. 'But you know, not everyone needs or wants to feel like they're being looked after all of the time.'

Now it was his turn to frown. He shook his head a fraction about to question what she meant, but Jem carried on quickly; 'Sorry, that came out wrong. What I'm trying to say is that sometimes it comes across as if you're acting out of responsibility. Everything is not always *your* responsibility.'

'But the boy was... Look I know it was foolish but I couldn't just-'

'I'm not talking about the boy!' She cut across him and the note of exasperation in her voice brought him up short. He turned to face her but she wouldn't meet his eye.

Staring out at the vast beach before them she said, 'Do you know why I left London twelve years ago?'

'It was a difficult time. You were still hurt from being-' he didn't want to use the word *jilted*. 'From what happened with Nick and the wedding. You were right. I needed to back off. Give you space to come to terms with things-'

'Matthew, I left London because I couldn't stand the thought of you stepping in to do the right thing,' she interrupted him. 'You were trying to clean up Nick's mess. You always did. You were looking after me, making up for him...'

Matthew was silent. Maybe it was better to let her think that.

Jem continued quieter now. 'And I couldn't let you do that when...'

She was going to tell him she had been pregnant. 'I know,' he hung his head sheepishly. Now was the time to tell her about the sonogram, 'I know that you were-'

'I left whilst I still *could* Matthew,' Jem's sudden confession crowded his out. 'Before I fell for you so hard that I let you to step in and take over where Nick left off.'

He wasn't sure he'd heard her correctly. 'What-'

She held her hand up to counter any interruption. 'No Matthew. Just let me get this out, before I have chance to decide I can't.' She took a deep breath. 'When I left London, I was falling for you. And that wasn't fair to you. Because I know you would have stood in for Nick. Gone along with the relationship just to ease my grief, even when that wasn't what you'd ever signed up for.' She had tears in her eyes.

'But-' Matthew jumped to his feet, running his hands through his hair. He turned his back so she wouldn't see the pain on his face. All this time he had thought that she left because she was still in love with Nick. The idea that they could have been together was almost unbearable. 'Why didn't you just say something?' He asked, barely concealing his frustration. 'At the time?'

'Have you not been listening at all?' she asked heatedly.

'Yes!' He realised he sounded angry but he couldn't help himself. 'But I still don't get why didn't you just *talk to me* – back then.'

'Because of what I just said! I didn't need someone stepping in to look after me on Nick's behalf. You're a good man Matthew. And I know that however much you might have wanted to carry on with your bachelor lifestyle, you would have sacrificed that to get me through that first year. I couldn't stand knowing how sorry you felt for me. Trying to make up for the way Nick had let me down. I couldn't take *that* from someone I'd…' Jem faltered for a moment, losing her nerve momentarily before continuing, 'After you and I slept together…after I realised what it could be like, I had to get away. It would have been so easy to just give in to it all. Let you do the right thing. But it would never have been enough for me. Not in the long run. It was better to be on my own. On my own there was no risk. No…' she cast around for the right words. 'No waiting for it to happen all over again.' She brushed away an angry tear.

Matthew couldn't believe what he was hearing. *All this time…*

'But you couldn't have got it more wrong!' He urged himself to calm down. Crouching before her he gently took her face between his hands. She tried to turn away, embarrassed by her tears, but he held her fast. 'Look at me.' He said it quietly, urgently.

She did as he asked.

'Jem, that day at the church, I wasn't doing anything out of a sense of *honour*. I was devastated for you yes, you were my best friend but–' he faltered. 'Look, all the time we spent together afterwards – I loved every minute of it – not because I was *helping* you but because I was *in love with* you.'

The look of surprise that crossed her face was quickly replaced by doubt. 'But… then, why did you never follow me to Devon?'

'I thought you went there because you were still in love with Nick.'

'I went because-'

He put a finger to her lips. 'It doesn't matter why you left.' Matthew didn't want this moment, fragile as it was, to be put under any more strain. Everything was suddenly coming right. He couldn't risk losing this chance amidst the hurt of what must have happened afterwards. There was time for that later.

He moved his finger to her chin and tilted it up towards him. 'Look, let's stop talking about the past. All that really matters is where we go from here. Just tell me one thing. Do you want to give it a proper try? This? Us?' He searched her face, willing her to say what he had wanted to hear since the day he first set eyes on her.

'I do,' she whispered.

'Then let's start with this.' He brought his lips to hers. Her arms wound around his neck, pulling him in close but, as she drew him toward her, Matthew lost his balance falling sideways, out of her embrace and onto the sand.

'Well this *is* a promising start!' Jem shrieked and they both started to laugh; maybe it was something to do with the years of pent up tension that caused them both to crack-up uncontrollably.

When the laughter subsided and they had each caught their breath, Matthew went to sit along side her, moving his body in close. It was dark now but he could make out her features in the glow of the fire. A breeze stirred the grass that bordered the sand dunes and ruffled the curls that tumbled from her beanie. Her eyes sparkled as she stared deep into the fire. He could see her mind whirring in time with his own – there was a lot to consider in the new light of what they'd just confessed to each other.

He took her hand, reached over to kiss her cheek, her neck. 'It's *always* been you,' he whispered close to her ear.

She turned to seek out his lips. And this time it was no laughing matter.

CHAPTER TWELVE
21st November

Kate

'Finn, hi!' Kate waved as Finn came striding towards her down the high street.

'So you found our local metropolis then?' he smiled.

'I certainly have,' said Kate returning his grin. She had decided to take a trip out to the county's bustling market town that grey Thursday morning because the moody weather had brought on a bout of cabin fever. 'Although I'm loving Pine Tree Bay, it's nice to get in the car and break out once in a while. Don't tell Jem but I called into the charity shop and couldn't resist picking up this lot for a quid a piece!' Kate held up her shopping basket which was bursting with second hand books. 'Having read nothing but crusty financial reports for the last ten years, I'm rediscovering a passion for thrillers.'

Finn's face clouded over at the mention of Jem's name and Kate suspected she knew why. After a trip up the coast a few weeks back, Matthew and Jem had both been walking around Pine Tree Bay like a couple of love-struck teenagers. She was pleased for her new friend Matthew, who had clearly been in love with Jem for years, but at the same time it had to be hard on Finn.

From what she had seen of Finn so far, he seemed like a nice enough guy. He clearly cared about the people of the town and he seemed genuine, not to mention she thought to herself now she was looking at him properly, easy on the eye. Jem might have had a harder time letting him go than Kate had imagined… but then, the unfinished business between Jem and Matthew had been clear for everyone to see from the start.

She took pity on the man before her. 'Anyway, I was just about to head into The Lighthouse for a coffee do you fancy one?'

Finn looked a bit taken aback; Kate was forgetting that she wasn't in London where women routinely asked men for coffee all the time. 'It's no problem if you're busy,' she said, giving him a way out.

'No, no I'm not. I was just on my way to the bank but a coffee sounds good.'

They found a table quickly and both asked for a latte when the waitress came to take their order.

'Share some cake with me so I don't completely stuff my face?' she asked him pleadingly.

He laughed. 'Of course, choose anything without nuts.'

She ordered a Victoria sponge and turned to Finn as the waitress left them. 'You're allergic?'

'Highly.' Finn took an epipen from his pocket. 'Unfortunately, I can't go anywhere without this.' He smiled ruefully. 'It doesn't exactly chime with the image I'm trying to project for the backwoods experience, but I've taken the view that visitors will overlook that in favour of me staying alive long enough to guide them back to civilisation.'

'I couldn't agree more,' Kate said, pulling out an asthma inhaler from her bag to show solidarity. 'Imagine having to chug on this whilst you're convincing the head of a global conglomerate to invest his surplus millions with your company.'

'You didn't!'

'I did!' She laughed. 'I wanted the deal and it was unlikely to come off if I collapsed in the middle of my pitch.'

Finn's eyes creased at the corners as he pictured he scene. 'Well, I second that.'

Their coffee and cake arrived with two forks and Finn politely allowed Kate to tuck in first.

'Speaking of millionaire investors,' Kate said, hastily swallowing a forkful of Victoria sponge, 'what's the latest on Frank Monroe? Is he recovering from his illness?'

Finn looked wary but he answered straightforwardly nonetheless. 'It's difficult to say. It's never happened before, but all direct channels of communication with Frank seem to be closed. Obviously he's not the kind of bloke who just hands his personal number out to all and sundry...'

'I can imagine.' Kate nodded sympathetically.

'...But we've always been able to chat to him when we wanted to in the past. We just call or email his assistant and he generally gets straight back. Last week I tried again but I just got a response from Marcus saying that he's on the mend and for the time being everything will continue to go through Gerry.' Finn leaned back in his chair. 'To be honest, it seems a bit odd. Frank loves Pine Tree Bay like it's his home town. If he was well enough to talk he would speak to us. To my mind he's either *not* well enough or....' He stopped.

'Or what?' Kate paused, a forkful of cake midway to her mouth.

Finn bit down on his lip and stared at Kate for a long moment. She recognised the look; he was assessing whether he could trust her.

'Honestly? Given your relationship with Matthew Albright, I'm reluctant to divulge,' he said evenly.

For Kate, there was a lot to digest in this one sentence. '*My* relationship with Matthew?'

'You've been seen spending a lot of time together.' Finn spoke in a slightly lofty manner.

Kate felt suddenly incensed and cautioned herself to hang on to her – rarely lost – temper. She lowered her fork to the plate and regarded him cooly. 'I hadn't realised we were under surveillance.'

'I seem to have touched a nerve. I'm sorry.' Finn held his hands up in surrender. 'It's really none of my business.'

He doesn't look sorry at all, thought Kate, *he looks smug.*

Fixing him with a glacial stare Kate resorted to a well worn tactic, 'That's correct Finn, it is none of your business. What *is* your business is to be some kind of leadership figure to the community of Pine Tree Bay. That's going to prove difficult if you spend all your free time sniffing around the rumour mill for small-town tittle tattle. And here's me thinking you were a sensible man above such nonsense.'

Finn flushed with embarrassment. As Kate had intended, the blow had landed slap bang in the middle of his machismo.

'Well what's Matthew playing at?' he snapped. 'First he sets his sights firmly on you, then he goes after Jem, and I won't even go into some of the coercive tricks he's been trying with the business owners.'

Kate was exasperated. 'I think you need to decide what your beef is Finn. Is it Matthew or I or neither of us that you can trust? Are you worried about the business owners or is this all just some petty jealousy over Jem? Because right now you're sounding very muddled and, I might add, just a touch paranoid.'

'And what if I am paranoid?' Finn leaned across the table. 'A lot of people I care about stand to get hurt if Matthew Albright turns out to be Gerry Monroe's axe man. You're just here for an extended vacation Kate. It doesn't matter to you if the business leases get hiked up and the town is leached of its livelihood. You'll be back in London at your next job and Pine Tree Bay will just be a holiday resort in your rear view mirror.'

Kate prickled at the picture he was painting but she had to admit that there was some truth to his perspective.

Finn carried on. 'And let me ask you this – if anything happens to this town and Matthew Albright has a hand in it, do you think Jem will ever forgive him? She stands to get hurt all over again and, after what her fiancé did, I don't think she'll bounce back from another betrayal. So forgive me if I'm a little paranoid here but there's a lot at stake here for *all* my friends.'

Kate's anger dissolved as quickly as it had arisen. Whilst he may be going about it slightly cockeyed, Finn's concern for his friends was admirable; plus from what Matthew had said it looked as if his fears about Gerry Monroe were spot on; he just didn't know that Matthew was trying to work from the inside, to *help* the town rather than destroy it. But she couldn't share any of this without betraying Matthew's confidence and she wasn't about to do that.

'Look,' Kate said in a placatory tone. 'I get it. You're worried. But all I can say is this – in my opinion Matthew is one of the good guys. I haven't known him long but he's someone you can reply on to do the right thing; someone I would class as *a friend.*'

Finn remained silent, brooding.

'And that's *all* we are,' Kate blurted, then frowned; *where had that come from?*

'Well I'm glad to hear it!' Finn shot back looking equally puzzled.

As they simultaneously reached for their coffees, each privately wondered at the need there had been to clear that up.

Helena

'Finn's trying to hide it, but he's got himself into a bit of a state.' Rab was offloading his worries to Helena as they jostled the Christmas tree into position overlooking the garden at The White Pebble Gallery. Helena was planning to sit it in the window as always and by nightfall there would be hundreds of twinkling fairy lights garlanded around its boughs.

'This is going to be a funny old Christmas.' Helena straightened up, slightly out of puff from her exertions. 'There seems to be so much change in the air. But then, I guess there was always going to be uncertainty once Frank took a back seat. The reason we've had it better than most is all down to his backing if we're honest.'

Rab stepped back to take a look at the tree from a few feet away. 'I sometimes wonder if hiring a fortune teller for the festival brought bad luck to the town.'

'Beryl? Bad luck?' She placed her hands on her hips. 'Rab Carmichael, I have never heard such rubbish in all my life. What next? Smudge cleansing rituals down at the harbour? The only bad luck around here is Gerry Monroe. He's never been interested in this place and with Frank out of the way he's seen his chance to milk us. He's a greedy bastard and if he can make a case to jack up the leases he will.'

Rab was quiet for a moment, seemingly lost in thought.

'Come on, out with it!' Helena demanded, sensing a gentle prompt was not going be enough to encourage Rab to offload whatever burden he was carrying.

'I don't know…' He continued to sound troubled. 'Finn shared a lot of things over a pint last night and it's got me thinking.'

'Thought I could hear the sound of machinery turning.'

'Did Jem ever tell you that Gerry Monroe propositioned her?'

'Good God no?' Helena was suddenly serious. 'I got the impression he was sniffing around at one point earlier in the year but when I mentioned it to her she said she'd given him the cold shoulder. I just assumed he'd eventually taken the hint and backed off.'

'He backed off all right. Straight onto Jem's kitchen floor…. When Finn landed one on him.'

'What?' Helena was incredulous. 'Finn *punched* Gerry? Jem never mentioned a thing.'

'Well, there's a reason for that.'

'What do you mean?'

'People round here would just love to know that Finn had given Gerry Monroe a good hiding. Especially when they found out it was because he got a bit over friendly with Jem. And can you imagine how vindictive Gerry would be if he thought the whole town was laughing at him?'

'"Over friendly"? I don't like the sound of that. What exactly happened?'

'It was early on this year. Finn turned up at Jem's and found Gerry in the kitchen. Gerry wasn't taking no for an answer… All Finn would say is that he had his hands on her-'

'Gerry attacked Jem?!' Helena practically shouted.

'Shushshsh,' said Rab nervously.

'Why are you shushing me?' Helena looked around, bewildered. 'The shop's closed God's sake!'

'You've got one of those posh voices that travels.' Rab grumbled.

'Well it'll be travelling all the way down to Jem's cafe and asking her what all this is about if you don't get on with the story.'

'Don't you dare!' Rab countered. 'Look, Finn said the way Gerry pursued Jem had her completely freaked out. She tried to handle it quietly by herself but he wouldn't take no for an answer. Finn went round one night and found him in her kitchen. Gerry had a tight hold of her by the arm and she couldn't shake him off. Finn just saw red, punched him and threatened him with the police.'

Helena looked dumfounded. 'I just can't believe it. I mean I knew Gerry was a snake and it's been clear for a while now that he's taken a sudden disliking to Jem but I just thought that was because she challenges him about his ideas for the resort-'

'The word Finn used was *predatory*.'

'That's a strong word.'

'Aye, but you know Finn as well as I do. He doesn't do drama. If he says Gerry is or *was* obsessed with Jem – and he seems to know all the ins and outs of it, most of which I'm sure he didn't tell me – then I'm inclined to believe him.'

'Well, you're right on that score at least,' agreed Helena.

'The thing is, Finn is suspicious about Matthew too. Thinks Gerry has put him up to something.'

It was no surprise to Helena that Finn didn't like Matthew – given that the man had waltzed in and swiped his girlfriend from right under his nose – but she resisted saying as much to Rab. Instead she asked, 'Like what?'

'Fabricating figures to make the resort look like a good prospect for a sell off, as well as doing a number on the person who's likely to be the most powerful opponent of such a move – Jem.'

'Oh Rab that's ridiculous,' said Helena. 'And you should know better than to indulge in such gossip. Jem would be furious. You've seen how she's been since Matthew arrived. I have never seen her as relaxed and happy as she is right now, please don't spoil this for her.'

'I'm just looking out for her that's all. We don't know this Matthew from Adam.'

'But *she* does, she's known him half her life Rab and she's a grown woman capable of making her own decisions, just wish her well and let her enjoy this!'

Rab went silent and Helena wondered if she'd been a little too harsh. 'And look on the bright side.' She came towards him and held out her arms. 'Whilst the town is preoccupied with all these shenanigans nobody but nobody is going to even think to look in our direction.'

'Every cloud I suppose,' his face finally softened, drawing her close. 'You have to admit though,' Rab continued, 'this situation with Gerry – whatever he's up to – puts all our livelihoods in jeopardy.'

'Well I can't argue with that,' Helena sighed. Considering all that was good about their community, Helena saw the threat for what it was but she had a deeper worry. If Jem *had* turned Gerry Monroe down in the way that Rab had described, that wouldn't be the end of it. Helena was certain. That man had a darkly vindictive streak running through him – a deep, malign crevice that he would mine thoroughly in a bid to get even with Jem and Finn. She hoped that Jem was on her guard and, as she thought this, a shiver ran through her.

'Come on, you've got goosebumps,' Rab said, guiding her into the room at the back of the gallery where a fire blazed in the hearth. She allowed herself to be led, thinking out loud, 'Frank would never allow this happen. If only we could get hold of Frank.'

CHAPTER THIRTEEN
25th November

Matthew

Spying Jem stacking a pile of books at the back of the store, Matthew crept up silently then placed his hands around her waist, leaning in to nuzzle the nape of her neck. Jem shrieked delightedly and Matthew felt the thrill of being able to act on impulse around her. She swivelled to face him and, after checking that there were no customers in sight, instigated a long, delicious kiss.

Alluding to the section of the store they were standing in Matthew gave a low chuckle as they broke apart, 'Mmm, I've always wanted to make out in "Health, Mind and Body" he murmured.

'Is that right sir?' Jem played along, allowing her eyes to flick briefly downward before saying, 'Are you sure I can't direct you to "Personal Growth"?'

Matthew roared with laughter and reached for her again but she placed her hands on his chest. 'Matthew Albright! I have work to do. You'll have everyone branding me as the town floozy if you carry on like this!'

'Nah… Jamie's already claimed *that* title!'

'I heard that!' Jamie's voice came from somewhere behind Matthew.

'I think you were meant to,' Jem laughed, as Matthew turned around to feign innocence.

'And here's me coming back here, out of the goodness of my heart to see if my hard working boss and her man are in need of a brew.'

Matthew grinned. He could certainly get used to being called Jem's 'man'.

'Jamie, you're a lifesaver. I'm so thirsty after unpacking all these dusty boxes. Peppermint for me please.'

'Builders for me,' said Matthew.

'Thanks to God you're a man who likes a good strong brew. I could'nae entrust the boss here to a fellah that drinks that herbal shite.' Jamie stalked back off towards the kitchen.

'I can't work out whether he's worried that I won't be able to defend you or defend myself *against* you,' Matthew said, watching Jamie retreat.

Jem smiled sweetly. 'The latter. I'm a real ball-breaker.'

'I can believe it.'

'So, where were we?'

'I believe I was ruining your reputation.' He pulled her toward him and they carried on from where they'd left off. With some effort, they finally drew apart and Matthew cleared his throat. 'Christ, I don't know about *your* reputation but we're going to have to stop this or I'll be in danger of being arrested.'

'You know,' she said in a sly voice, resting her hands on his chest, 'I was just thinking today that your apartment might be overdue for a landlord's inspection?'

'Oh you *were*, were you?'

'Mm-hmm. I was thinking lunchtime today?' she nodded, treating him to a deliberately flirty look from beneath her lashes.

'Well, obviously I will need to be there,' he said earnestly. 'Can't have you rifling my things whilst I'm out.'

'So you'd prefer I rifled your things whilst you're in?'

'Stop!' A low rumble of laughter vibrated through his chest. 'Now, there's only so much sexual harassment a tenant can take, so let me tell you what I really came to see you about-'

'Spoilsport.'

'I finally read the letters we found in the attic - the ones from Frank to Marcia.'

'You did? That's great! What did you think?'

'Well, I agree with you. I think it's pretty clear that there was something between them.'

Jem nodded. 'I know right? I got the sense that if he hadn't been so busy with the family business, he would have been back here like a shot.'

'It's such a shame we can't see Marcia's side of the conversation. What do you think she was saying to him in *her* letters?'

'I'm guessing she told him that she was planning to leave Pine Tree.'

He nodded. 'I tend to agree. He says more than once that if she is planning to leave, she might as well come to him in Canada. It was definitely a serious offer for her to move over there.'

Jem shook her head in puzzlement. 'I wonder why she didn't go? Though, it's possible she may have asked him to come *here* instead you know.'

'You think?'

'Yeah.' Jem nodded, thinking aloud whilst reaching for more books to stack. 'Although he doesn't directly refer to it, it's something in the way he keeps re-iterating his need to be in Canada. She may have asked him to come back here but knowing Marcia, she wouldn't ask twice. When I think about it in that light, his repetition looks a bit like guilt to me.'

'Ah well, on that point, did you get the sense there was some other possibility too?'

Jem's head snapped up from the pile of books.

Matthew smiled and raised his eyebrows. 'Ahh, so you *did* notice.'

'You first.' Jem rolled her lips together as if to stop herself from saying more.

'Ok.' He pulled a letter out of his back pocket and flicked through the pages. 'It's here… where he says; "*I'm sure you'd tell me if I have created any responsibilities that I'm not there to see through, but I'll spell it out clearly nevertheless – you can count on me to do the right thing."* I think it's pretty clear from this that they must have slept together.'

'Who slept together?' Jamie had sidled up behind them without either of them noticing and, at the prospect of some town gossip, was now all ears. Jem looked at Matthew sharply – with a widening of her eyelids and the slightest shake of her head she signalled that he was not to divulge the name of the person they were really talking about.

Matthew stuffed the letter back into his pocket and said the first name that came to his mind. 'Oh…er Gerry Monroe.' *Gerry? Where had that come from?*

'Gerry Monroe? This *is* good gossip, who did he sleep with?' Jamie was now all ears.

'Er…' *What was he supposed to say?* 'Er… his assistant.' Matthew nodded authoritatively, 'Yup, Gerry has been sleeping with his assistant.'

'Gerry's gay?' asked Jamie.

Shit! Thats right Gerry's assistant was Marcus…

Jem looked on in bewildered amusement as Matthew floundered. He bowed his head and rubbed the back of his neck to avoid Jem's gaze.

Without waiting for Matthew to answer, Jamie rested the tray of mugs on a nearby table. 'Well, not that it matters either way o'course. But to think, I always suspected he fancied my Lorna?' He made his way back to the kitchen, shaking his head.

'Great work genius!' Jem slapped Matthew on the back. You've just outed your boss, who for the record, is not gay or, to the best of my knowledge, bi-sexual.'

'Oh God. I just said the first name that came into my head. And I forgot that his assistant is Marcus.'

'I just hope, for your sake, that Jamie keeps that little nugget to himself.' Her voice was bubbling with amusement.

'Well *you* got us into this mess. Why couldn't we just tell him about Frank's letters?

'Because,' Jem lowered her voice, 'if our suspicions are right, Frank Monroe just might be my grandfather. And if that *is* true, I would rather that Frank finds out before the whole of Pine Tree Bay.'

'Ah, good point.' Matthew tilted his head considering this. 'Didn't Marcia always say she only met your grandfather *after* she arrived in London.'

'Yes that's what she always told me. But when I rang Jeanie MacBride to tell her we'd found her family documents, I managed to get her talking. She as good as admitted that her mother told her there was a local rumour that my grandmother had been sent to a relative in London because she was expecting. It was the 1950s Matthew, it would have been a real scandal at the time if Marcia had been pregnant with no husband in sight.'

'So what did Marcia actually tell you about your grandfather?'

'That he died in an accident at work when my dad was three years old.'

'Did she show you any pictures or anything?'

'I remember a few grainy black and white ones years ago, at the London flat, but I haven't seen those for years.'

'What about your father's birth certificate?'

'I can't recall ever seeing it, but I could order a new one from the national records office.'

'Good idea,' he nodded.

But Jem didn't answer. She was still thinking things over.

'What?' he asked picking up his mug. 'Is there something else?'

She chewed on her thumbnail. 'Come into my office and I'll show you.'

Once in her office Matthew hovered behind Jem as she fired up the laptop. Navigating to the Pine Tree Bay Blog she said, 'I've had a few strange comments added to my blog-posts in recent weeks, I just want to get your take on them.'

Matthew was puzzled yet intrigued. He wasn't sure how he would be able to help but he hoped she wasn't being targeted by some creep who was messing with her over the ether. Reading the comments in question however, he immediately saw what was on her mind.

'You think these are from Nick?'

'Interesting that his is the first name to come to your mind too.'

'Well, the Oscar Wilde quote seems a bit of a coincidence.' He drew his thumb back and forth along his his jaw. 'I would say, at the very least, they're from someone who knew all three of us back in the day, judging by the comments on the kiteboarding article.'

Jem had written a blog piece about their day out at the beach and added the shots they'd taken of each other out on the water. There were also snaps of Bear and a couple showing Matthew's vintage camper van. Matthew's name had not been specifically stated in the article but a comment had been added at the bottom of the post. '*The Three Must Kite-eers... almost.*'

'I suppose it could be someone from the old crowd that we surfed with in Devon.' Matthew tried to sound convincing.

'But why the cloak and dagger approach if that's the case? I also did some more digging on the postcard too.' Jem tapped the keyboard as if about to show him something else.

Matthew tried to look interested but inside of him something was dying. After everything they had shared together in the last few weeks she was still looking for Nick? Surely it didn't matter now? Why should either of them care *where* that jerk was?

For the first time since they had both opened up to each other at the beach, Matthew was niggled by a sense of insecurity. Had he got this totally and utterly wrong? After everything she'd said, was he still just the consolation prize?

Even to his own ears, his voice sounded hollow when he said, 'So, what else did you find?'

'Not a thing.' She closed the screen and spun in her chair to face him. 'And anyway. I think it's high time for that landlord's inspection don't you?' she asked, grinning up at him wickedly. It didn't take much effort for Matthew to push his worries to one side.

But later that night, as Jem lay sleeping in his arms, the niggling fears were back. Their earlier conversation played on a loop in Matthew's head.

Why was it that *he* could move on from his marriage – which ended only a matter of months ago – but Jem couldn't seem to let go of Nick after *twelve years*?

Despite appearances, it hadn't been an easy few months. The breakup with Lissa had ripped him apart and like any wound it would leave its scar. But he had no doubt it was over. Final. And as such the best way to deal with it was to look ahead. But Jem was still looking over her shoulder. Why was that? Why did she even care about messages that may or may not be from Nick?

Today Matthew had come to realise something which surprised him. He needed to know if, given the chance, Jem would choose Nick over him. Matthew had spent half of his life wanting her, but in truth he didn't think he could give it his best shot until he knew with some finality, that he wasn't competing with a ghost. But how to achieve that? When nobody knew where Nick was?

Being careful not to wake her, he gently disentangled himself and climbed out of bed. Retrieving his hastily discarded pile of clothes, he dressed quickly and after whispering to a hopeful Bear that he should stay and look after Jem, he pulled on his insulated jacket and stepped out into the blisteringly cold night air.

A million stars twinkled in a cloudless sky as he made his way down to the sea, his feet echoing along the pavement. The town was silent, save for the distant tide, the sound of his own footsteps and the warning hoot of an owl.

Suddenly, through the silence, he heard the low distant hum of music. At first he couldn't work out where it was coming from but as he neared Beryl's motor home he realised that she must still be awake – and listening to The Stones by the sounds of things.

Matthew increased his pace and almost by their own volition, his feet took him straight to her door. After a brief knock it opened almost immediately and, expecting to see Beryl, he was startled to be greeted by a man of a similar age to the fortune teller, wearing a smart shirt and tie.

As soon as the man saw Matthew he shouted over his shoulder, 'Eh-up Beryl! I told you last time, absolutely no more threesomes!' Then, seeing the look of horror on Matthew's face, he collapsed into wheezing, phlegm filled laughter which turned, somewhat alarmingly, into a bone rattling cough.

'I am so sorry-' Matthew flushed with embarrassment at having disturbed what was clearly a romantic evening but Beryl bustled the man out of the way and ushered Matthew inside.

'Oh don't mind him love, he thinks he's on Live at the Apollo! Come in, come in. This is Billy – one of my oldest friends. Popped in on his way north.'

'Pleased to meet you son.' Billy held out his hand and Matthew, thinking of all the germs this debonair looking man must have coughed into it just a moment ago, didn't remove his gloves before shaking hands.

'I won't keep you Beryl,' Matthew said quickly now. 'I was just out for a stroll and heard your music playing so I thought I'd just knock and say hi.' It sounded lame but it was better than the truth. *I'm out walking at midnight because I'm totally muddled and confused and – even though I don't believe in all this fortune telling stuff – right now I'm prepared to give anything a try.*

Beryl handed him a glass of whiskey but it was Billy who spoke. 'Don't you worry son, she's been expecting you for the last hour.'

Matthew looked quizzically at Beryl and she waved her hand dismissively in Billy's direction, 'Ah, take no notice, I just had an inkling that's all.'

But Billy was having none of it. 'It's as true as I'm standing here lad. Earlier on she says to me, she says, "Billy, don't you be polishin' off all that whiskey, we're gunna have a visitor at midnight." So I says, "What visitor? It's dead round here. Who's gonna be knocking on at midnight round these parts?" And she says – all mysterious like – "Just you wait on," and then you turned up almost as the clock struck twelve. I tell you lad, as long as I've known her, I'll never get used to it! She's got proper gift she 'as.'

Billy then turned and raised his whiskey glass in a salute to Beryl.

Matthew picked up on an almost imperceptible exchange between the couple, suggesting there was more to this brief tribute than met the eye. 'Stop now, you're embarrassing me!' Beryl chided and then to Matthew, 'Anyway it's good to see you and share a nightcap with you lovey.'

'Well thanks,' said Matthew, raising his glass to them both and taking a warming sip. It was welcome after the bracing walk. After a long pause – Billy's initial outburst over, he now seemed to be struck dumb and both he and Beryl were looking at Matthew expectantly – he cleared his throat, thinking desperately of something to say. 'So… well… it must be nice for you to catch up. How do you two know one another in the first place then?'

'Oh it's a lo-o-ong story.' Billy closed his eyes as he drew out the word and then opened his mouth ready to launch into the tale.

'Oh Billy, the lad's just being polite, don't start bletherin' on.' Beryl cut him off.

'No, I'd really love to know.' Matthew cupped his whiskey glass and settled himself onto one of the bench seats.

'Well, it was the middle of winter fifty years ago-' Billy started.

'Billy, it was the height of summer and it was *forty-nine* years ago!' Beryl cut in again.

'Well go on – *you* tell it then!' Billy grumbled and folded his arms.

'Ok I'll tell it.' Beryl glanced sideways at Billy, she seemed to be deciding how much to reveal, but eventually she leaned in and started the story.

'It was the summer of 1970, boiling hot it was, I remember cause I spent most of it in a halter neck top, denim shorts and wedges! Not at my job mind – I was working as an ambulance driver in Bradford. Billy was working as a roadie for a band that was playing at St. George's Hall.' She nodded her head, lost in the past.

'It was one of these prog rock bands. All the way from California they were. Anyway, the lead singer took a few too many of the old *smarties* – if you catch my drift – and collapsed on stage. So we got called out and Billy was the only one out of the lot of 'em that we could get any sense out of-'

'I had to give him kiss o' life!' Billy cut in 'The lead singer! Right up there on stage with the crowd cheering me on-'

'Anyway to cut a long story short,' Beryl reclaimed the floor rolling her eyes, 'Billy asked me out and I agreed to meet him at the end of my shift. So, that's how we met – whilst the hospital were pumping out the lead singer's stomach, we headed off to a club.'

'No way.' Matthew grinned picturing the two pensioners back in their twenties dressed like a couple of new age hippies and dancing to "The Age of Aquarius" at Bradford's premiere nightspot.

'The thing was,' Beryl said looking sheepish, 'neither of us told the other we were engaged to be married. Billy was only in town for one night as he was touring as a roadie all the time. And so I thought well, why mention it? I just slipped my engagement ring on to my other hand. And after that, whenever Billy came back to Bradford we'd meet up. He never mentioned that he had a girl in Sheffield and I never mentioned that I had a fiancé. But even though we never said anything to each other, we both knew. It was just a bit of fun though – that what's we thought of it as. So, best to say nothing and then there'd be no harm done.'

'Famous last words.' Billy said ominously.

'What happened?' Matthew asked looking from one to the other.

'Well, we carried on like that for five years, you know meeting up like that, not often – just every six months or so. We were both married by then and we knew it was wrong but we just liked each other's company. And we really did think we were doing no-one any harm…'

Beryl smoothed her dress before continuing. 'But, well, after five years my marriage wasn't a happy one and my husband wasn't stupid, he could tell my heart wasn't in it anymore. I think he sensed I was looking for a way out and one night, when I was going to meet Billy, I must have let it show that I was excited about where I was going…' Beryl tailed off and looked at Billy with a sorrowful expression. 'Anyway, as we found out later, my husband followed me. The thing is, I used to get a funny feeling about things. I didn't know how to work with the gift then, but I could always sense when something bad was coming, but this… there were *some* signs but I didn't recognise them.' She shook her head looking anxiously at Billy.

Billy reached over and put a hand on Beryl's shoulder as her voice wavered. 'Come on love. Don't upset yourself it's all water under the bridge now eh?'

'Beryl, I'm so sorry.' Matthew reached forward and squeezed Beryl's soft, lined hand. 'I would never have asked you how you met if I thought it would cause upset.'

'Oh, don't be daft love.' Beryl reached for a tissue to dry her eyes. 'It's just such a long time since I've talked about it, that's all.'

'What she's trying to tell you, is-'

'No Billy, let me finish.' Beryl halted her companion with a gentle hand on his arm. 'So, the final time we met up, my husband followed us.'

Matthew was silent. Beryl was now scrunching the tissue she was holding. 'And when he saw us together, he went absolutely berserk. He started knocking me about. I didn't know what had hit me at first – there seemed to be twenty fists coming at me from all angles. I thought there would be nothing left of my face when it was over. Billy was at the bar – it was like my husband had waited until he thought I was on my own to lay into me – but a woman started screaming and Billy turned round and saw what was happening. He flew over to drag my husband off of me.'

Matthew, taking in Billy's broad shoulders and big hands had no doubt he would be able to.

'He threw him backwards and my husband went through a glass

door.' Beryl's voice broke again and she couldn't go on.

Billy went to put his arm around Beryl's shoulders. 'I killed him,' he said in a low strong voice. 'I didn't mean to, but I did. And I paid for it with five years in prison for manslaughter. As God's my witness, I never meant to kill that man, but I don't know that I'd do anything different if I saw it happen again today.'

'But surely it was a case of you defending Beryl,' said Matthew. 'It sounds like her husband is likely to have killed *her* if you hadn't been there!'

'The law didn't see it that way lad. I could still be there now if it wasn't for the witnesses in the pub that night – all of whom stood up for me. I already had a couple of convictions from one or two previous rumbles see – just the usual cut and thrust of life as a roadie back then – but the police had me pegged as a violent criminal.'

'I was depressed for a long time afterwards.' Beryl was fighting the tears again now. 'There I was walking free and Billy had gone to prison for defending me. And then Billy's wife wouldn't let him see his son.' She looked at him through watery eyes. 'It still cuts me up that you lost your family because of me.'

'I took the decision to keep meeting up with you all those years. That's on me not you.' Billy made it clear he could take responsibility for his own actions.

The air in the motorhome had become heavy and Matthew attempted to lighten the mood. 'Have you ever wished you hadn't asked a question?' he said looking from one to the other with a rueful smile.

Billy let out a shaky chortle. 'Well lad, to tell the truth, we haven't actually talked about this since we met up again a few weeks ago. I have to admit it's been the elephant in the room. And, as you can imagine,' Billy made a show of looking around the small confined space, 'there's not much room for one in 'ere!' They all laughed and the tension eased. 'No Matthew,' Billy continued, 'you've done us a favour in letting us talk about it tonight.'

Beryl nodded in agreement. She looked at Matthew. 'Jem told me you have a way of working out what people need. Tonight I see what she means. Mind you, I've often said that there's always a bit of the gift in them that are blessed with a truly good soul.'

'I honestly can't take any credit,' said Matthew. 'I just asked what you'd ask any couple you saw together for the first time.'

'Hear that Beryl! He's calling us a couple,' Billy said with a huge grin.

'You're on the couch. End of!' Beryl pointed to the pull out bed and winked at Matthew who checked his watch and said he really should get going.

Billy stood up. 'I'll walk a little way with you while Beryl gets kettle on,' he said cheekily. 'I could do with a breath of fresh air.'

Matthew kissed Beryl on the cheek and hugged her warmly before ambling up along the shore with Billy.

'That's some story,' Matthew said after they had walked a short way.

'It's not something I spend a lot of time thinking about these days, but it taught me to keep my nose clean.'

'What do you do now?'

'I travel around doing casual work – it's not easy once you've got a criminal record like mine so I just pick up bits and bobs where I can. Getting a bit long in the tooth for it now mind.'

'Sounds exciting, living the carefree bachelor life on the road, "wherever I lay my hat" and all that?'

Billy stuffed his hands in his pockets as they walked. 'Aye maybe – for some. But that's not what it's been about for me.'

'No?'

'It was to start with. Or at least that's what I thought. No ties. Nobody to let down when you can't catch a break. Then one day someone mentioned a fortune teller who toured around the country in a motorhome. After a bit of detective work, I had a pretty good idea they were talking about Beryl. And after that, the travelling wasn't really about the work. I was mainly moving around to look for her. I've been looking for her ever since.'

Matthew stopped in his tracks. 'You're kidding? How long ago was this?'

'About twenty years.'

'*Twenty years?* You've been looking for Beryl for twenty years?'

'Probably longer. You try tracking someone down when you're both off grid. It's not easy I can tell you. I kept turning up places and finding out she'd been there the previous year or a few months prior. But I could never seem to land in the same place that she was at the same time. About a month back I decided to throw in the towel.' He shook his head thinking back to it. 'Then a young girl in the pub I was working in convinced me to put myself on a dating website.' Billy chucked. 'I didn't even realise they did 'em for blokes my age! She showed me how to use the computer and helped me get one of those smart phones and what not. Who do you think the first person to contact me for a date was?'

Matthew laughed. 'Beryl!'

'I couldn't believe it – as soon as I stopped looking, there she was!' He shook his head in disbelief and the two men walked a few steps in silence before Billy said quietly, 'But even though I told myself I'd stopped looking for her. I knew I hadn't really. You *can't* stop looking. Not when it's like how I feel about Beryl. I'm not being overly soppy or anything, that's not my style lad.' Billy gave a jocular snort. 'It's just...

Well it's like I don't have a choice in it. Simple as that.'

Matthew, knew only too well. But he said nothing and the two men walked on in companionable silence for a while.

'So what will you do now?' Matthew asked when they reached the end of the road. The two men had come to a halt, each preparing to head off in separate directions to their seemingly parallel lives.

'I have to be careful with Beryl.' Billy put his hands in his pockets and jangled some loose change. 'She values her independence above everything. But I like to think she'll want to have me around. I'd love to see what it could have been like if we'd been brave enough to say "bugger it" and make a go of things forty nine years ago. But that's up to her really.'

'Well I hope to see you around Billy.' Matthew held out his hand to shake the big man's bear paw. 'And I won't mention anything of what you've told me tonight. You know what these small towns can be like.'

'Appreciate it son.' Billy shook his hand then headed back off in the direction he had come.

Matthew crossed the road toward Small House Book & Brew and made his way around to the back gate. He hesitated before letting himself into the garden studio. Billy's words were bouncing around his brain like an echo. Was he going to wake up one day in his seventies to realise he'd spent his whole life chasing a pipe dream? Matthew was glad that Billy and Beryl had found each other again but whichever way you looked at it, theirs was the kind of love that had had them both wandering around in limbo for the majority of their lives.

Yes, he and Jem seemed to have found happiness in the here and now but he had to be honest with himself; until he was sure that it was really him she wanted to be with, he would never be on solid ground. And he was surprised where that thought led him. Surprised to find that he did not want to suffer the torment of that.

Matthew reached into his inside pocket for his phone and typed a message to Kate, asking whether they could meet the following day. This time, for once, he would let his head lead the way.

CHAPTER FOURTEEN
26th November

Jem

The following morning Jem awoke to the sound of rainfall hammering on the roof of the garden flat. She snuggled down into the duvet, in no rush to leave the warm comfort of Matthew's bed. Turning onto her side she reached out for a cuddle but instead was greeted by the big furry face of Bear.

Matthew was already out of bed and at the breakfast counter. 'Ready for a cuppa?' he asked, throwing teabags into mugs. Jem was about to ask him how long he'd been up but his phone started buzzing on the nightstand. She felt irrationally irked when she read the display – Kate was calling rather early.

'Chuck it over will you?' Matthew asked from across the room.

Jem got out of bed, retrieved the phone and handed it to him across the worktop. 'Here. Far safer.' She placed it in his hand like a disapproving headmistress.

Matthew answered the call and Jem headed into the bathroom with feigned disinterest. Once inside she lingered near the door unable to resist listening in to the conversation. Matthew was arranging to meet Kate and seemingly – from his side of the conversation at any rate – had texted her the previous night.

Jem picked up her toothbrush. She couldn't really put her finger on why Kate Parker felt like a fly in the ointment. It was unsurprising that she and Matthew should have become friends – as outsiders to Pine Tree Bay they had bonded over the fact they were both Londoners with a background in business. But Jem sensed that Matthew saw Kate as a sensible sounding board, a woman with a smart head on her shoulders; the thought that he might prefer to discuss his professional concerns with *her*, well – she scrubbed her gums a little too vigorously – what could she say? It rankled!

Matthew ended the call in good spirits just as Jem emerged from the bathroom. 'Guess what? Kate's roped me into a body pump class at the Barnacle this evening, should be fun.'

'It's a good class,' Jem nodded taking a mouthful of the tea that Matthew had made whilst chatting to Kate. It tasted bitter after the toothpaste. 'I try to do it regularly myself.'

'Great then come with us!' Matthew grinned and raised his eyebrows suggestively. 'Then maybe afterwards we can compare muscles?'

'No can do I'm afraid Arnie,' Jem said dryly. 'I'm meeting Helena for dinner at The Bistro.'

'Call in here afterwards?' he sounded hopeful but Jem shook her head. For some inexplicable reason she was desperate to take the air out of his balloon.

'Bear needs his own bed for the night and I could do with a good sleep too.'

'Ok I get the hint,' said Matthew good-naturedly.

It wouldn't do him any harm to miss her for an evening or two – Jem thought as she popped some bread into the toaster – and it wouldn't do *her* any harm to have a breather either.

Matthew

'So how did you find that?' Kate asked later, as she and Matthew were making their way out of The Barnacle gym and on to a side street.

'I suspect I might have some difficulty walking tomorrow.' Matthew winced as he slung his gym bag over his shoulder. 'I put far too many kilos on my bar.'

'Typical male approach to body pump!'

'Don't worry, I'll pay for my hubris in the morning,' he said ruefully.

When they reached the bottom of the road, a decision was required – their respective houses lay in different directions. Matthew had an idea. 'How about we get some tapas at The Wine Bar? That way neither of us will have any washing up to do.'

'Sounds like a good idea, I haven't been there yet. Thought I might look a bit sad going in on my own.'

'I'll warn you though, we might look a bit out of place in our gym gear,' Matthew cautioned.

'Would you prefer to go to The Smugglers instead?' Kate asked.

If he were honest, Matthew was avoiding the pub. It was starting to feel a little uncomfortable venturing into the haunts of the locals just lately. It was clear that there was some mistrust brewing, and he could understand why. He was trying to remain upbeat and brush it off but knowing you were the subject of a lot of the town's ill feeling was exhausting. He could do with an evening away from all that; The Wine Bar was mainly a tourist hang out. This was all something he could discuss with Kate later but for now he said, 'Nah, let's do The Wine Bar.'

The Wine Bar was housed in one of the town's few original buildings. When Frank Monroe had first bought up the properties and the land in Pine Tree, the town had consisted of just one street which led from the road skirting the Pine Forest at the top of the town, all the way down to the sea. At that time the street had just a handful of rustic looking eighteenth century properties and the new resort had been built up around these. But the old warehouses and barns which had stood for centuries had been fully restored as part of the resort development. The building which Matthew and Kate now found themselves in was one such property: an old trading post warehouse that had been used for goods storage for the harbour.

The exposed brickwork and wooden floors were a nod to what the building had once been but the ceilings had been lowered to provide a much more intimate setting that was perfect for the wine bar vibe. Low level jazz music, industrial lighting and the buzz of customer chatter, gave it a relaxed feel which, Matthew observed, wouldn't be out of place in Smithfield Market.

Kate approved. 'This *is* nice,' she said looking around her and reaching for a menu. 'And you were right, it's totally relaxed enough to pop in on your own. I could see this becoming my regular. Although,' she leaned forward, clutching the menu to her chest, 'I would miss Rab's penchant for fancy dress. I hear he's got something very special lined up for St. Andrew's day on Saturday night.'

'Well, that's one of the things I wanted to talk to you about actually… I've found myself avoiding The Smugglers in the last few weeks. I get the sense I'm not entirely welcome there.' Matthew detected that Kate was considering how best to respond, which indicated she too sensed the locals' reservations about him. 'It's not that I blame anyone for feeling they need to be on their guard,' he added quickly. 'It's what I've come to expect. It's just becoming a difficult tightrope to walk.'

The waitress appeared and took their orders, leaving a carafe of water with fresh lemon. Kate poured them both a glass. 'Have you had any luck in changing Gerry's mind? Does he still mean to sell off the resort?'

Matthew was thankful that Kate was keeping her voice low to avoid being overheard. 'I haven't been able to get hold of him *at all* these last few weeks. He seems to be completely stonewalling me at the moment.' Matthew rested his elbow on the table and circled his temple with this thumb. 'I'm not sure I'm ever going to convince him that selling is not his best option. I've prepared two scenarios; selling and retaining. The second option makes more financial *and* reputational sense but you know, I'm beginning to wonder if he's even interested in the commercial arguments.'

'What do you mean?'

'Nothing I say makes any difference to the way he looks at this. It's as if there's something personal driving his actions… some kind of obsession.'

Kate took a long drink of water, thirsty after the workout. 'So why hire you in the first place if he's not interested in receiving any real recommendations?'

'I've asked myself the same question and I can only assume he wanted to distance himself from the decision, or at least suggest there's some rigour behind it. It lends a more professional veneer.'

Kate and Matthew paused their conversation as the waitress appeared with their drinks. Once she had retreated Kate leant across the table and said in a low voice, 'But why does Gerry need that? He runs the company after all. Who's benefit is it for?'

'His father? The people in the community? His investors? If he was seen to make arbitrary decisions without the proper due diligence it would make his investors nervous. He has to make his business dealings look like thoroughly analysed decisions across his entire empire. His reputation is at stake too here.'

Kate nodded allowing Matthew to continue.

'That's why I thought I'd be able to convince him to hold on to this place. Like I said before, the fact that Frank supports a whole community and the hundreds of people who come to work here each day is a really valuable asset. The fact that it's a community that his ancestors came from – it's a living breathing symbol to his investors that he has heart, that he hasn't forgotten his roots and that family comes first.'

'As a business woman even I would say that's a card worth having in your deck when people are assessing your company's values. Or at least the *appearance* of them,' Kate added cynically.

'Precisely.' Matthew reached for his beer and took a large chug, drawing his thumb across his lip. 'For Frank it's more than that, he really does seem to care about this place, but for Gerry...' Matthew shook his head feeling something close to despair. 'He's just not prepared to listen'.

Kate eyed him over the rim of her wineglass. 'This place has really gotten under your skin hasn't it?'

'I'm sort of hoping it might become home.' He was almost too scared to admit it.

'Me too.' She said it quietly.

It was Matthew's turn to look surprised. 'What? You're thinking of moving here too?'

'Yes, or perhaps my second home. I haven't quite figured it out yet.' Kate looked slightly bashful. 'And, to that end, I wanted to ask you for a favour.'

'Of course.'

'I'm going to look at a house tomorrow and I was going to ask you if you would come and look at it with me, give me a second opinion... and to stop me getting carried away.'

'I can't imagine you, of all people, having anything but a level head when it comes to a financial transaction of that scale,' Matthew laughed.

'Property is my weak spot.' Kate smiled wryly. 'I can force myself to be objective in almost any situation but when I fall for a house, I fall hook, line and sinker.'

'Would you ever think of moving here full time?'

Kate cast her eye around the room, clearly she was still thinking this over. 'I'm not sure to be honest. I don't know if I'm ready to leave London behind completely. But one thing this break has taught me is how easy it is to get back and forth from here to London. And I certainly couldn't afford a property like the one I'm about to look at tomorrow anywhere in the South.'

'Is it here? In Pine Tree Bay?'

'Have you seen the villa at the top of the cliff, overlooking the town?'

Matthew knew the house that Kate was describing; a generously proportioned shingled property that was perched at the very top of the town looking proudly out to sea. 'Who could help but notice it? It's one of the most beautiful properties around here,' Matthew said before adding, 'You know who owns it don't you?'

'No.' Kate leaned forward eager to hear more. 'But clearly you do.'

'It's Gerry's house. He built it when the resort was first developed. From what I can work out, he doesn't spend any time there so it should be like new,' Matthew added drily.

'Ah, that makes sense; I wondered why it wasn't advertised anywhere. I only got a viewing because I called all the agents in the area directly asking what was for sale. I was basically told that the house is for sale at the right price but it's not currently on the open market.'

'He probably doesn't want to advertise the fact that he's off loading his assets just yet,' Matthew said bitterly. It didn't bode well for his chances of changing Gerry's mind about a sell off. Not wanting to labour the point with Kate however he steered the subject back to her. 'So what *are* your plans – if you were to buy?'

'Well I haven't seen any particulars or anything yet but…' she paused. 'Can I tell you this in the strictest of confidence?'

'Of course.'

'I was thinking about possibly running a bed and breakfast.'

'That house would make a fantastic place for guests,' Matthew agreed. 'All those windows looking out to sea. And the wrap around verandah…'

'This doesn't bode well for tomorrow, you're supposed to be talking me out of it!' Kate laughed.

'Plus the views from up there are amazing – you'll be able to see all the way over to the Lake District.'

'You *can*! I took a walk up there yesterday. It is *the* most stunning aspect. And because it's set so high above the town it feels more remote and away from everything but with an easy walk down to all the shops. I think it's got real business potential.'

'What about your job? London? Your life there?'

Kate considered the question. 'All my life I've known from a really early age that I wanted to move to London and be part of the big corporate machine. And, you know, London totally lived up to the hype. It was all I thought it would be and more and for my twenties and most of my thirties it's been right for me. But I wonder now if, for the last few years anyway, I've just been putting one foot in front of the other without thinking about where I'm going?'

'And being here has given you chance to step off the treadmill and wonder if that's still what you want?'

Kate nodded. 'I don't know that I want to cut all ties with London but I *do* know I want to make a change.'

'Well,' said Matthew, 'I'm definitely intrigued to see what the house looks like inside.'

'Ok, well that's a date then. The viewing is at nine thirty tomorrow morning. Walk along to mine and we'll drive up from there?'

'I'll be there,' Matthew said. Their tapas arrived and Matthew idly moved his gambas around the plate. 'There's something else I wanted to talk to you about.'

'Oh?' Kate looked up from the heap of Padrón peppers she was all set to devour.

'I wanted to ask you to go over again exactly what your contact in London told you about Zara Harper.'

'Why?'

'Someone has started to leave mysterious comments on Jem's blog. I think it could be Nick.'

'Really?' Kate sounded intrigued. 'What makes you think they're from him?'

'They're comments that only someone who knew us both from the old days would make.'

'Why do you think he would come out of the woodwork after all this time?'

'I have absolutely no idea. Maybe he's been following Jem for a long time. Maybe me being on the scene has prompted him to step out of the shadows? It could be any number of reasons.'

Kate chewed slowly on her food, mulling things over. 'Matthew, if you don't mind me asking, hasn't it occurred to you that all this is a little coincidental? You and Jem haven't seen each other for twelve years and you suddenly find yourself in the same town. Now the mysterious Nick seems to be communicating through the ether?'

The very same question had been running through Matthew's head all day. First Jem received the postcard, a few days later Matthew had arrived at Pine Tree, then within weeks the comments started appearing. Three people who had disappeared completely from each other's lives were suddenly being drawn back together.

'Well, that's kind of why I need to ask you about Zara...'

Zara

Spain

'I've made my decision, I'm telling him tomorrow.' Zara draped the white cotton sheet around her breasts as she watched Jeremy walk toward the shower room.

It stopped him in his tracks, as she had known it would, and he turned to face her. 'Honestly?' His face lit up with delight and he sprinted back toward the bed and launched his naked body on top of hers.

'Yes!' She couldn't help but laugh at his ebullient reaction. He was like a boy sometimes but, thankfully, not where it counted. 'Now go jump in the shower and we can talk about this over a drink.'

'Sod the shower!' He leapt off of the bed and opened up the mini bar then pulled out a bottle of champagne.

'You know the hotel are going to fleece you for that.'

He laughed. 'Who cares? We're going to live together! In England! This is fucking huge and we are celebrating.' He popped the cork and poured the over priced fizz into the little glass tumblers that the Granada Palacio provided in all their rooms. Zara would have preferred to drink from a flute but she consoled herself with the knowledge that the Palacio always stocked a very decent vintage.

Handing her a glass and coming to lie on the bed, Jeremy touched his tumbler to hers. 'To us.'

'To us,' she echoed.

'And Sophia,' he added and she loved him for it.

She would have dearly loved a cigarette but there was no question of that in front of Jeremy. The man's physique was the living, breathing embodiment of a thousand *Men's Health* articles. Even the champagne was something of a concession – a departure from his strict, professional fitness regime. She would buy a pack of Marlboroughs on the way home all the same, because one thing was for sure, she needed one before she spoke to Nick tomorrow.

She couldn't leave it a day longer. She had to get away. And she was taking Sophia with her to live with Jeremy in the handsome Cotswold stone house that he had shown her on the internet the night before.

Gloucestershire. She was thrilled at the idea. It was a million miles from this dusty, arid, desolate, arse-end of the world and she couldn't wait to get there. Just thinking of the proper traditional Christmas that she and Jeremy were planning for Sophia, not to mention all the glittering events that his new polo club were laying on, galvanised her wavering nerve and shored up her resolve.

There was no way around it; she was going to have to confess *everything*. It would be horrible, but it was worth it to be with Jeremy and oh, the luxury of being within a train ride of London, not to mention the beautiful villages of the Cotswolds with their small, trendy boutiques and wine bars. It was going to be heaven. She so longed to be back in the rolling countryside of her beloved Britain. How could she have ever imagined *this* would be enough?

There was just the thorny issue of bringing Nick up to speed first. Obviously he was going to go ballistic. Anyone would. Not only was she about to tell him she was taking his daughter away, she would have to confess that she had conned him into coming to Spain in the first place.

She was about to tell him that the 'fraudulent activity' which had forced them to disappear was all an invention on her part. That the money that brought them here was a marriage settlement not a stolen royalty cheque. And though she was adept at playing him by now, this one was going to require a bit of thought if she was going to emerge with the upper hand where Sophia was concerned. He would fight that one tooth and nail but, then again, maybe she could work that to her advantage.

She had always got her way where Nick was concerned and she had no doubt she would manage it again - despite the certain shock of what she was about to reveal. When she thought back to it now, she really must have been quite unhinged to go to such lengths; thank goodness those reckless days were well behind her.

It all began that morning – after Nick tried to end things once and for all. Bereft at his rejection, she'd been simultaneously heartbroken *and* dying of boredom; working at the royalties company she was simply treading water until her divorce money came through. As she processed the latest pile of returned cheques sent up from the mail room, she refused to accept that Nick really was going to choose Jem over her. There must be some way to make him see sense.

And then she'd had a brainwave.

Just three weeks earlier, Nick had completed all the paperwork and fast-tracked the opening of an offshore account for Zara at the bank where he worked. She hadn't told him at the time but the account was for the payment of her divorce settlement – which was to be considerable following the sale of her ex's Chelsea mews house.

Her lawyer had managed to secure the full proceeds of the property by having Zara agree to relinquish all claim to any of her ex's future income. It had been a good deal for Zara (and an even better deal for her ex) and the two million pound settlement that was due had gone some way to restoring her faith in the institution of marriage; if only for what one could get out of it once it was over.

Of course she could just tell Nick about the settlement and ask him to come away with her on the proceeds…. The trouble was she was pretty sure the answer would be a resounding no. He was still hell bent on throwing his life away on the safe option. But Zara was about to make him see the light.

After a few nail biting weeks, the divorce settlement finally hit the offshore account just four days before Nick was due to be married. And Zara had breathed a huge sigh of relief that everything had completed in time; it was the cue for her plan to be set in motion.

On the Wednesday before his wedding, Zara called Nick and told him to meet her at the Four Seasons Hotel near Aldgate. Anticipating that he would refuse, she told him that she had some important news; rightly guessing that he would fear she was pregnant. Nick took the bait and agreed to meet her that afternoon.

Zara dressed in a low cut silk shirt tucked into a tight mini; then hid it all beneath an expensive cashmere overcoat. It was November after all.

When Nick arrived at the hotel and was unable to find her in the bar, he called her mobile. She gave him the number of the hotel room she'd booked. Predictably he refused to come up but when she said coolly, 'Trust me Nick, you don't want to do this in public,' he relinquished. Within minutes he was at the door of the room.

As planned she ushered him inside and waited until he was perched on the edge of the bed before slowly shrugging out of her overcoat. Her outfit had the desired effect and despite his obvious anger at being summoned like a schoolboy, his eyes roved her body and his pupils dilated. He licked his lips nervously and once more she felt the intoxicating rush of the sexual power she held over him.

He tried to avoid eye contact but when he spoke his voice was raw, 'So? Why all the cloak and dagger shit? What do want to tell me?'

Zara stayed silent for a moment, bit her bottom lip. This would work best if she seemed unable to get the words out.

Nick raked his hands through his hair. 'Oh God is this…? Is this all to get me to change my mind? It's over Zara, I've told you. Whatever madness this has been on my part, I'm done with it. I'm marrying Jem in *three days time*. I'm not going to change my mind on that.'

'No. It's not that. It's…' She pretended to search for the right words and start again. 'Look, I think it's only fair I give you the heads up on… I've done something,' she blurted out at last, trying to look worried and contrite. 'I didn't intend to mix you up in it but something went wrong at the last minute and I think I might have implicated you into a situation I never meant to.'

'What?' Nick's eyes widened in horror. *He's worried I'm going to tell him that Jem has found out about us*, thought Zara, *but in about five minutes he'll think that would have been preferable.*

She spoke slowly. 'Do you remember me telling you about the returned royalty cheques at my office?'

Nick looked at her as if she were speaking a foreign language. He frowned and shook his head in puzzlement. 'What the fuck are you going on about Zara?'

Zara took a deep breath. 'Do you remember me saying that these huge cheques the company was sending out just kept being sent back to the office, and nobody was bothering to check out a forwarding address for them?'

'Possibly...' Nick was losing patience. 'But what the hell has that got to do with us?'

'Well, I... I've been so desperate lately. The divorce, that shitty flat I'm living in. Not to mention that boring job... I couldn't take it anymore Nick. It's all such a come down. Compared to what I thought my life was going to be like.' She acted the part of a desperate divorcee fallen on hard times and just crazy enough with despair to do something unthinkable. 'I... I changed the payee for one of the returned cheques, on the system at work. The money is now sitting in my account.' She bowed her head.

Nick blinked at her in astonishment. 'Wha...?' The disbelief was written large across his face. 'Well, good luck *in prison* Zara, but I have zero interest in sharing your illegal secrets. Why are you even telling me this? I'm getting out of here.' He made for the door.

'Nick wait!' she shouted after him. 'I paid the money into the account that you opened for me. At your bank.'

He paused, his hand on the door handle, and turned slowly to face her, his voice was low. 'I'll deny any involvement Zara. And what's more they'll believe me because it's the truth. I'm leaving this hotel and going straight back to my office and tell them – and the police – that you're a fucking thief and that has *nothing* to do with me.'

'Nick, calm down. Just think about this for a minute.' She assumed a breathless tone. 'If you do that then yes, I'll most certainly be arrested *but* if I am, there'll be a huge investigation. They'll look at all the e-mails and text messages that have passed between us. Didn't you tell me that you bent the rules a little? Used an old authority you still held to fast track the opening of that account for me and avoid some of the paperwork? What's that going to look like to your employer?'

Nick swallowed as he thought about this and Zara saw him processing what she had said. He collapsed on the bed and put his head in hands, running them back and forth across his face, realising what this might mean for his job, his whole career...

Zara sensing her advantage, pressed her point home mercilessly. 'If you go to them and tell them what I've done, it will all come out Nick. You'll lose your job. You'll lose Jem.' She walked over to him and placed a hand on his shoulder. 'I'm so sorry, I didn't mean for the money to go to that account. It was a mistake.'

Nick sprang up and grabbed her by the shoulders, throwing her against the wall. 'You bitch! You lying bitch! You've done this on purpose because I ended things between us. You're fucking crazy and you're going to ruin both our lives!' His face was contorted in anger and for a moment Zara wondered if she'd misjudged things horribly and he was going to hit her.

She decided to change tack. Suddenly breaking down she started to sob hysterically. 'Do you think I wanted to have to admit this to anyone?' Zara hissed through her tears. 'I should be long gone by now. I'm just giving you a heads up to save your skin you selfish prick. I should have just fucking hung you out to dry.' She struggled to get out of his grip, and frightened as she was by his anger, the tears were flowing easily.

He relinquished her shoulders and she collapsed onto the bed, great heaving sobs racked her body and, as she knew he would, he came to her. He took a deep breath and, unbelievably, her outburst seemed to have worked – Nick held her whilst her sobs subsided.

Eventually she spoke, 'Nick, that royalties company are all over the place. The only way they'll even bother to look into this is if the artist who was supposed to receive that cheque comes looking for it. I'm not stupid, I checked it all out carefully. The guy it was meant for is some obscure song writer who's been dead for over fifty years. No-one is looking for his money. Once I cashed the cheque, I amended the system back again, to keep doing what it always did. Chances are it'll never come to light and if it does, I'll be long gone and you can just deny everything.'

Nick looked like a deflated balloon and when he spoke his voice was full of despair and frustration. 'But Zara there's a financial trail,' he explained weakly. 'You don't just get away with fraud. Not these days. Not without being a lot cleverer than you've been. You've made no attempt to hide this. You've paid it into an account in your own name for Christ's sake, an account I opened for you! Shit…' He stood up and started to pace the room. 'Don't you see that once all this comes to light, even if they believe I had no part in the theft, I broke the rules when I opened that account for you. Link that to a fraud and,' he shook his head despairingly, 'whether I had any hand in it or not, my days at that bank are over. And nowhere else will take me after being sacked for financial misconduct. I can kiss goodbye to any hope of a career in business – any hope I had of making any real money.' Massaging his temples Nick continued to pace the floor as he tried to think his way out of the nightmare situation.

Zara could practically hear the cogs whirring in his brain. Now was the time to strike. 'Come with me,' she whispered, as if the thought had only just sprung to mind, her voice still hoarse with tears. 'I have somewhere we can go. In Spain. I know people there, the right kind of people to help us become invisible.'

He shook his head.

'Just think about it,' she urged. And then, as if this was all just a spur of the moment idea, she continued, 'You could... you could paint!' She grasped his arm as if warming to the theme. 'All day, every day. We'd be free. No commute. No shitty air-conditioned offices, chained to a desk for fifty hours a week. Isn't that what you said you wanted? Well what if you didn't have to wait? What if you could have all that now?'

Nick groaned, sat back down on the bed and pinched the bridge of his nose. Zara stood before him, took his chin between her perfectly manicured fingers and tilted it upwards. 'I'm so sorry,' she whispered. 'I'm so so sorry.' And then she brought her lips to his. He didn't resist. She still remembered it vividly to this day – the sex that had followed had been like nothing before or since, as if he couldn't decide whether to screw her or slap her. But afterwards, as she watched him laying there breathless and wrecked, she knew she had him.

And when she thought back to it now, she realised, that this was the moment the excitement had started to wane – it had been a lot like breaking a horse. That incendiary passion which had fired between them that day at the hotel had quickly faded. As the force of Nick's initial rage gave way to a resigned self loathing, he began to repulse her; his wolfish confidence usurped by a brooding introspection that would, quite frankly, bore anyone to tears.

Nick wasn't the great love of her life after all. He was a temporary obsession. Like the many who came after, and, as with those affairs, she quickly lost interest. But this time *was* different. Jeremy was different. He was younger. She had to work harder and that was never going to change. Just the thought of his youthful muscular body beneath her fingers caused the blood to rush to her head – and other places. Zara found the challenge of maintaining the younger man's interest endlessly exciting. She took a deep breath; only one more day to hold on. She was telling Nick everything tomorrow.

Jeremy's voice broke into her thoughts. 'When we get to Gloucester, I'm going to bring you champagne for breakfast every morning,' he said, nuzzling her neck. Zara felt a minor flash of irritation then quickly smothered it.

Jeremy *was* the one. He was. She wouldn't risk Sophia's happiness for anything less.

CHAPTER FIFTEEN
27th November

Jem

Scotland

The next morning, Jem was late leaving Withershins. Again. It was the third time this week that she would miss her early start. All the late nights she'd been spending with Matthew had finally caught up with her and she hadn't even opened her eyes until gone eight a.m.. What was happening to her beautifully ordered schedule? Mind you, this was perhaps was less of an issue at the moment; early mornings were for writing and she was in no rush to add any further comment fodder to her blog right now.

Despite the fact that it was now well past nine, Jem didn't rush to the cafe. Instead she took the steps down onto the beach and walked slowly, enjoying some much needed one on one time with Bear. He was in his element; snuffling around the bladderwrack and filching out dead crabs, delighting in the occasional ball of decaying whelk husks. In Bear's book, it was a case of the smellier the better.

Jem bent her head and tucked the curtain of curls that fell forward back behind her ears, searching for any nice pieces of sea-glass that might catch her eye… She was currently on the hunt for deep blue chunks to add to the jars of white and aqua pieces which she used as shelf decorations in the café.

Whilst she tried to get her eye in for these smooth sea jewels, her mind wandered back to the conversation with Helena over dinner the previous evening. As was often the case, Helena's sharp insight had homed in on all the issues that were weighing heavily on Jem's mind and although she knew it hadn't been Helena's intention to unsettle her, she had come away from her friend feeling more uncertain than she had for some time.

It had all come to a head when Jem confided in Helena about the website of artist's work she had found; the style of painting very similar to that on the anonymous postcard. As they sat in The Bistro together, Jem had brought up the website images on her smart-phone and held them up for Helena to see.

'Look here. This guy paints under an anonymous pseudonym – they call him 'The Ghost.' She swiped through the images on the website. 'And see here, this series of paintings? They're called *Surf Girl.*'

Helena peered at the images and studied them carefully, 'You think these might be of you?' she asked.

Jem responded hesitantly, 'I don't know…I guess…it's possible. What do you think?' She had expected her friend to be intrigued but, instead, Helena had sounded annoyed.

'Jem, why are you persisting with this wild goose chase? Everyone can see how happy you are with Matthew. What does it matter now where Nick is?'

Jem put her phone face down on the table and frowned. 'I suppose the two are not mutually exclusive in my mind. I mean, I can be happy with Matthew *and* still want to know what happened to Nick can't I?'

'Yes but it seems to me like this is more than a passing interest in someone you used to know.'

Jem became defensive. 'I'm intrigued that's all.'

'And Matthew understands all this does he? This need to keep searching?'

'To be honest when I showed him the blog comments – the ones I thought *could* be from Nick – he just sounded a bit bored, so I didn't show him the website.'

'You think he was "bored"?' Helena asked shaking her head.

'What are you trying to say? That I've read him wrong?'

'I would put my gallery on it!' Helena laughed tucking into the large bowl of spaghetti that had been placed in front of her.

'So, what? You think he's annoyed with me?'

'I think if I was head over heels with a guy and he started showing me messages and pondering the possible whereabouts of his ex, I might be ever so slightly er, I don't know? *Pissed off?*'

'But it's not like that with us of course.' Jem had gestured emphatically with her fork. Surely Helena could see how this scenario was different. 'Nick was Matthew's best friend so he's equally invested in his whereabouts.'

'And yet he sounded *bored* when you mentioned all this to him?'

Jem sat back in her chair and thought for a moment. 'So you think Matthew is under the impression I'm still hung up on Nick?'

Helena stared at her friend for a long moment. 'Are you really this dim?'

'What?'

'Can you honestly tell me, hand on heart, that some small part of you isn't hoping that Nick Townsend comes riding in to Pine Tree Bay one day to tell you that running out on you was the biggest mistake of his life?'

Despite the emphatic 'No' she had given to Helena last night in the Bistro, Jem had to acknowledge privately, here, alone on the beach, that she'd been so wrapped up playing Miss Marple, she hadn't even considered this question.

If she were to be completely honest, she did think about Nick Townsend. Though she would never have admitted it to anyone, he had, over the years, occupied her thoughts far more than he had any right to.

Where he was; why he had not shown up for the wedding; what their life would have been like if they'd got married. These were all things she pondered but surely that didn't mean she was researching the strange events that had happened because she still *wanted* him? Because she didn't. Did she?

And on top of all this, there was the additional news that had landed in her inbox this morning. Frank Monroe was *not* her grandfather. The copy of her father's birth certificate had been emailed through to her and she was shocked at how disappointed she felt at the realisation. She supposed she had looked back over her relationship with Frank, brief and distant though it had been, and seen something that wasn't there – she'd imagined a sort of paternal concern for her wellbeing. Jem had left a message for Matthew with the news but she was yet to get a response.

Because Frank was ill, she'd been feeling some small sense of urgency about things – fancying she would need to get the news to him before it was too late. Now she felt silly to have thought they could have been related in the first place.

The man whose name *was* on her father's birth certificate was Job Kintyre. It wasn't a name she was familiar with and she didn't know if she even had the heart to go looking for a man who was, in all likelihood, long gone. If he was in the area then he would know her, and who her grandmother had been, everyone knew everyone around here. It wasn't as if he'd been in any rush to seek her out, whoever he was.

Suddenly voices from above the beach broke into her thoughts. She looked up and was shocked to see Kate and Matthew emerging from Kate's house. Her heart hit her belly like a stone. Was that why he had not taken her call this morning? Finn's words were suddenly in her head *'He's going to make a fool out of you…'*

Jem pushed down the spike of jealousy that reared its ugly head but the arm that Matthew casually placed around Kate's shoulder, giving her a little shake, caused it to resurface. Before she could spy on them any further however, Bear started barking in joy, having seen another dog coming towards them on the beach. It was Jeanie MacBride's lurcher, Sorrel. Bear and Sorrel went racing off together towards the waves and Jeanie made her way over to where Jem stood. It was impossible for Jem to continue watching Matthew and Kate without drawing Jeanie's attention but she was vaguely aware that they had jumped into Kate's car together and were speeding off, up out of town.

Jeannie and Jem chatted amicably for a few minutes before Jem plucked up the courage to ask the older woman if she had heard of a man called Job Kintyre.

'*Job?*' Jeannie frowned, considering the name for a moment. 'There's a *Joe* Kintyre who lives out on the old military road but he'd be well in his eighties now. Why do you ask?'

'Oh it was just a name I came across when I was going through my grandmother's things in the attic,' Jem lied.

'Hmmm, I guess they would have probably known each other, being around the same age and living round here before it was as busy as it is now.'

'It would be nice to look out one of Marcia's old friends. He's still alive you say?'

'I believe so,' said Jeannie. 'He wasn't one for mixing much mind. Always kept to himself after his wife died. I'm not sure he keeps too well to be honest but I certainly haven't heard anything to suggest he's passed on – and most news filters through to me.'

I bet it does, thought Jem cynically, the way the jungle drums work around here. She took details of the house that Job lived in from Jeannie then the two women said their goodbyes. If this man kept to himself as Jeannie suggested, it would certainly explain why she hadn't heard of him before now.

Instead of heading to the café as originally intended, Jem retraced her steps back to Withershins and loaded Bear into the back of her car. There was no time to worry now about what Matthew was up to – she could deal with that later if she needed to – but if she wanted to meet her grandfather it sounded like she needed to get a move on.

Madeleine

That same morning, over at Magnolia Mansions, Madeleine Beaver's husband was ignoring her. Worst of all, she realised, he didn't even *know* he was ignoring her.

There was a time when, at the sound of her voice, he would have put down the newspaper, pulled his reading glasses to the end of his nose and asked, 'What's that you say darling…?' Even though he had no real interest in a word that came out of her mouth. But over the last few years he had ceased to bother even with this pretence. Now her voice seemed to have merged with all the other background noises in life to the point where it was no longer capable of completing the journey to his ears; her words floating in the air like planes in a holding pattern looking for somewhere to land.

She eyed the top of his balding head resentfully. She could reel off a blow by blow account of having been ravaged by six lusty fishermen around the back of the community centre and he wouldn't raise and eyebrow.

Closing her laptop she stood and smoothed the creases from her Ann Taylor skirt then walked from the orangery – where she'd been enjoying her morning espresso in the warm November sunshine – all the way to her study located at the back of their large manor house. This room was dark and dingy at this time of year, and possibly (she wrinkled her nose) slightly damp. It was nowhere near as pleasant as the sunny room she had just exited but, if she was going to be ignored, she would be ignored on her own terms thank you very much!

It really was very tiresome to have no-one to talk through the concerns of the Pine Tree Bay Community Council with. How was she supposed to resolve this current dilemma without so much as a sounding board? The council members had made it abundantly clear what they thought of her objections to that fortune teller over staying her welcome. They had only just stopped short of calling her a snob.

She, Madeleine Beaver – who since arriving in Pine Tree Bay had devoted herself to the well being of this community – branded as an elitist! They hadn't actually said as much but she knew that's what they were all thinking. Well now they would have to eat their words.

Hadn't she been the one to point out that if they allowed Beryl to stay in Pine Tree Bay it would only be a matter of weeks before more of these unsavoury 'off-grid' types turned up? And hadn't she, this very morning learned that this prediction had indeed come to pass? Beryl Clutterbuck wasn't the only woman around here who was able to see into the future! According to Madeleine's ultra reliable informant – Sherry Crombie, waitress and beauty therapist at The Barnacle Spa – Beryl had been *entertaining a gentleman* in her motorhome for the last few days and the talk throughout the town was that he would be staying with her 'indefinitely'.

This was all very disheartening in itself but worse had been to come: when Madeleine had contacted one of her husband's Westminster colleagues to discreetly check out the name that Sherry had so helpfully supplied, the situation had shocked her to the core. Beryl Clutterbuck, whom everyone had been so quick to defend; whom everyone had practically sung the virtues of had brought a convicted murderer into their midst!

And there was no doubt her Westminster contact had unearthed the correct man because Beryl's name had been mentioned in the court case. Oh yes, that lopsided excuse for a wig and the humble vernacular may have everyone else hoodwinked around here, but Madeleine Beaver was nobody's fool. And once they all found out that *Madam Zelda* was one half of a criminal duo, the people of the town would be forced to admit that Madeleine had been right all along.

But how to go about things without looking like it was all a case of sour grapes? This was the question she had been trying to raise with Bernard. After a lifetime in politics he had developed the oily sheen of a crow – everything simply slid off him – but he had absolutely no interest in assisting his wife in what he called 'the tedious business of the community council'.

She looked around her office, ignoring the mounting pile of paperwork that demanded her attention, and tried to come up with a solution. Her eyes fell on a newspaper cutting the she had proudly clipped from the Galloway Gazette a month or so earlier. The grainy, black and white photograph of the handsome business tycoon exiting a helicopter after landing at one of the local country estates. It gave her a sudden flash of inspiration.

She sipped her coffee and felt a small frisson of excitement. This was just the opportunity she had been looking for – an excuse to liaise confidentially with the man himself. And once he realised that Jemima Small was a staunch advocate of Beryl's, she was sure to get his backing to boot the old bird out – taking that murderous boyfriend with her!

With a glint in her eye that had not been there when she entered her study, she thumbed her ancient rolodex for the number of Gerry Monroe's personal assistant.

Matthew

Matthew looked out over the vista that lay before him. 'Kate this place is amazing, if you don't buy it, I just might.'

'It would make a fantastic bed and breakfast wouldn't it?' Kate sighed dreamily. 'Imagine the guests eating an informal breakfast back there in the kitchen-diner, with a fresh sea breeze blowing in through the French windows. Then they could stroll out here with their coffee to sit on the verandah and take in the view.'

'To hell with the guests, I'm coming here for *my* breakfast to do that,' he laughed.

But Kate, lost in the land of her imagination, wasn't listening to a word he said. 'Tea roses and hydrangeas in pinks and creams would look lovely against this paintwork and I could get a couple of rockers and a porch swing... Oh Matthew it would be so fabulous.' She just stopped short of clapping her hands together and tried to keep her voice low so the estate agent wouldn't realise how much she wanted the place, but her excitement was bordering on uncontrollable.

'You weren't exaggerating when you said your business brain goes out the window where property is concerned were you?' Matthew laughed.

Kate tried to look indifferent and said more loudly, 'Yes it's ok I suppose, but there would be several changes that I'd need to make. I'd need to think about whether it's quite what I'm looking for.'

Matthew said softly, 'Some things are just meant to be... I can see how animated you are about this, which suggests to me that this might be one of those times when you should follow your heart rather than your head. Subject to all the necessary surveys and legal searches of course,' he added quickly.

Kate laughed at the caveat. 'What a lovely blend of providence and prudence! Do all your aspirational speeches come with a disclaimer?'

'Sorry,' he made a rueful face. 'Force of habit. Speaking of which however.' Matthew turned around to check they were out of earshot of the estate agent then drew Kate over to the railing that ran the length of the verandah. 'I filed my final recommendations with Gerry this morning.'

'And?'

'Well, like I said last night, the management summary I've put together basically outlines the two approaches open to him – retain or exit. The option to retain the resort is my recommended course of action.'

'Do you think he'll take it?'

'I honestly don't know.' Matthew shook his head slowly, 'But I found out late last night that there are several long-term business deals currently on the table for Monroe Holdings. If he dumps Pine Tree Bay resort now, he risks portraying himself as a man who favours quick profit over long term partnership and that could potentially jeopardise these more lucrative deals that are in the pipeline.'

'So you're basically telling him that a decision to sell the resort when it's about to start needing more investment looks like a shitty move on his part.'

'Yeah, basically.' He grinned. 'But in slightly more professional terms.'

Kate looked doubtful. 'There are those who might think his own track record speaks for itself. The man's a billionaire after all.'

'No Kate – he's the *son* of a billionaire.'

Kate smiled, the penny had finally dropped. 'Ah, so what you're *actually* suggesting is that dumping Pine Tree could spook potential business partners into thinking Gerry's *not* the honourable man in business that his father is.'

'I haven't come out with it in so many words but I've made a strong case that the timing is off just now.' Matthew looked out over the town nestled at the bottom of the hill below them. 'I know I'm never going to change his mind but if I can at least buy the community some time, Frank might rally from this illness and put a stop to Gerry's plans.'

'One thing's for sure - Gerry won't want to come off worse when it comes to comparisons with his father. You've probably found the one visible chink in his armour.' Kate's voice was full of admiration.

'I hope so. I've also tried to *tactfully* point out that investors won't be happy if he risks the share price of Monroe Holdings over some insignificant part of his global empire. Not right now; let's face it – his father's state of health will be making investors jittery enough – start disposing of assets and it's going to set alarm bells ringing.'

'God he's going to love you.' Kate sounded amused. 'He's brought you in to look at what he probably thinks is some two-bit part of his multi-billion dollar operation – and here you are suggesting he could bring the whole empire to its knees.'

Matthew chuckled. 'He's going to hate it. But it's my honest opinion that this *is* his best option. I mean, in his shoes, wouldn't you just leave well alone? Selling off assets makes no sense right now. Not when you consider what's at stake for him? There's no profit in a sale, relatively speaking, but the risk to the rest of his business would be reckless. Whatever's motivating him, it's not common sense.'

'Maybe it's a simple fact of him having a warm lead? Another big fish who's looking to expand their holiday resort portfolio? If he has someone on the hook, he'll want to capitalise on the timing. These things often happen that way.'

'Possibly…' Matthew wasn't so sure. 'Anyway,' he shook his head, 'my report is confidential so, he could just ignore my recommendations and nobody will be any the wiser. I'm just hoping the fact that he hired me in the first place means he really *is* interested in a professional opinion.' Matthew ran a hand through his hair. 'Well, I submitted the report this morning, I've done all I can now. The rest is up to him.'

'So what next for you? Things are going so well with Jem, I'm guessing you're sticking around for while?'

'I'm heading back to London today.'

'What?' Kate sounded shocked.

Matthew leaned on the rail and looked out to sea. 'I just don't think Jem and I can move forward until we've put this whole Nick business to bed. Or at least *I* can't. Those comments on the blog weren't the only suggestion that Nick's been trying to get in touch. Just a day or two before I arrived here, Jem received an anonymous postcard. The print on the front had all the hallmarks of a painting by Nick. Ever since then she's been trying to trace the painting and who it's by. She's clearly still looking for him.' Matthew's mouth twisted bitterly.

'That doesn't necessarily mean she's still hung up on him.'

Matthew hoped that was true but... 'You never met him Kate. He wasn't the kind of man that women get over easily.'

Kate touched his arm and he turned to face her as she said, 'Well, all I can say is, you must have been quite the duo when you hung around together.'

Despite the gravity of the situation Matthew laughed. 'Thanks, my ego needed that!'

'You really think that, after all this time, she's still in love with him?'

Matthew shook his head. 'I honestly don't know. But if *I'm* enough, would she still be looking for...whatever it is she's looking for?'

Kate tilted her head to one side. 'Shouldn't you be asking Jem that?'

'I've thought about asking her. Trouble is, I know that whatever she tells me, Nick's always going to be the ghost hovering between us. I *am* trying to see it from Jem's point of view – anyone in her shoes would want to know what happened.' He took a long ragged breath. 'That's why I'm going to London today. After you told me about the Zara Harper emails I started to do a bit of digging. I've managed to track down Zara's sister to an address in Barnsbury. I'm going to go round there tomorrow – see if I can find an address for Zara. There's no trace of her anywhere – none of our friends from university has seen her in years and she's not on any social media, well not with her maiden name anyway. It must be more than just a co-incidence that she and Nick disappeared at the same time.'

'Well not everyone wants to live their life on social media I guess.'

'Believe me, if you'd known her.... She'd be on every platform going.

She always knew how sensational she was and boy did she enjoy the adulation.'

'Have you told Jem?'

'Not yet, I'm going to text her from the train and say it's a last minute thing. I just don't want to tell her until I have something concrete.'

'I'm not sure it's wise to keep all this from her.' Kate cautioned.

'Tell me about it. But what's the sense in setting hares running until I know something for certain? The real reason for Nick's disappearance? Gerry's potential sell off of the town? I can't tell her anything concrete about either of those things yet.

'She's not a child Matthew. She's a full grown, capable woman who might well be able to help you with all this if you would just let her.'

'I'm just worried she'll get scared again… back off like she did last time.'

'Matthew if you *don't* share this with her she's more likely to feel patronised when you actually do let her know what you've been beavering away on.'

Matthew leaned forward on the handrail and looked out to sea, 'Yes, but by then I'll have all the answers.'

Kate grasped his arm and shook it gently, 'No, by then *you'll* have sorted things *alone*… with no input from Jem. Good relationships are about being one half of a team; stop shielding her from bad news like she's a child or I'm telling you now, it's going to seriously backfire.'

Matthew paused for a moment, thinking about Kate's words. 'I know you're right, I'm just seriously worried about risking the fragile ground we've gained over the last few weeks…' He tailed off then held up a hand in surrender. 'But you make a very persuasive argument. I'll tell her everything once I get back tomorrow.'

'Thank you.' Kate, clearly relieved, looked around her. 'Ok now we've got that sorted, where's that hideous estate agent gone?'

Finn

Finn pressed the accelerator on his Mitsubishi L200 and felt a sense of satisfaction as it climbed easily up Pine Cliff Road – taking him out of the town and toward the sprawling pine forest that reigned majestically above the bay. He was desperate to lose himself in its wilderness, blowing away the cobwebs and clearing his head.

It was always a good time of year - with all the bracken and foliage died back – to check out new camping hideouts for his backwoods tours. He generally scouted out his wilderness camps – and the hidden tracks that lead the way to them – in late autumn. Then he continued to walk those same tracks throughout the winter months, making sure they were obvious and easy to find once the dense woodland carpet started to grow back in Spring; getting lost in the forest was bad for business when you were the tour guide.

Getting lost on those tracks didn't sound so bad right now - he could do with some head space. Everything seemed to be changing and Finn was not a man who liked change. Who honestly did? He couldn't help feeling that his business was under some kind of threat, but it wasn't just that, look at the way things had come to an abrupt end with Jem too.

Six weeks ago he'd been enjoying his life and looking forward to taking the next step with the woman he had thought of as his girlfriend… now all that prospective happiness seemed to have dissolved in a cloud of autumn mist.

There was no getting away from it; the way Jem ended things had stung. Ok so she'd always *said* that she didn't want anything serious but her actions had suggested something different. They'd grown close over the two years they'd been spending time together; Finn was the one she relied on for help, the one she shared her secrets with – look at the whole Gerry Monroe incident. They were the only two people who knew that Gerry had been practically stalking her. Up until a few weeks ago, he'd sensed that she was on the brink of opening up to the prospect of a relationship but now… it had all come to nothing. After two years didn't he deserve a little more than a conversation in her kitchen about wanting to be friends?

Feeling frustrated he geared the truck down forcefully and it crested the rise smoothly, levelling out just at the point where Gerry Monroe's villa looked out to sea. The steep incline had slowed the car and Finn's eye was drawn to a couple looking out over the rail of Gerry's veranda. The unmistakeable figures of Kate Parker and Matthew Albright stood deep in conversation. Kate had a steadying hand on Matthew's arm and their heads were close together. A third figure in a business suit, who Finn couldn't quite make out, lurked inside.

Suddenly Finn's mind was whirring. Was it more than a coincidence that Kate and Matthew had become such good friends in such a short space of time? Secret meetings at Gerry's house with another businessman? Could it be possible that they were *both* on Gerry's payroll?

Look at how Kate had 'accidentally' bumped into Finn over in town and invited him for coffee. Gerry knew fine well that his strongest opponents to any change within the resort would be Jem and Finn, together they had always been the galvanising force behind any community action within the town… Was this all an attempt to divide and conquer? Kate and Matthew always seemed to have their heads together and Kate's rather convenient sabbatical had just happened to dovetail with Gerry's hiring of Matthew for an 'economic review' of the resort?

Finn was starting to see things with a clarity that had hitherto evaded him. The trouble was, if he tried to share this with Jem she would, in all likelihood, side with Matthew. No, more evidence was needed before going to her with his theory.

He resumed his journey into the woods; he could immerse himself in nature whilst he chewed this new insight over in his mind. He needed time to think. How best to gather the facts he needed? The answers weren't about to simply fall into his lap now were they?

Gerry

London

Gerry was on his way to the video conferencing suite when the call he had been waiting for came through.

'Mr Monroe.' Marcus's voice came down the line. 'As requested, I'm just letting you know that Mr Albright's final report has arrived in your inbox.'

'Thank you Marcus.' Gerry acknowledged the confirmation. He checked his watch. 'Now, please tell the chair of my next appointment to postpone for twenty minutes whilst I attend to some urgent business.'

'Would you like me to forward the document on to your father sir?'

'My father is still not to be disturbed under any circumstances, is that *clear*?'

'Yes Mr Monroe.' Gerry heard his assistant hesitate. 'I, er... All communications to your father are still being redirected to your email account do you want the diverts to remain in place?'

'Of course!' Gerry shook his head at the stupidity of his assistant. 'I'll let you know once the old man is well enough to return to business.' He was becoming agitated at the protracted call.

'Certainly, I'll make sure the tech guys know to extend that. And how is your father sir?'

'He's returning to health, but as his doctor's have stated, he's still *not* to be disturbed by *any* business affairs. You make sure and deliver on that Marcus or I'll know who to hold responsible.'

'And will your father's assistant be returning once he's fully recovered?'

Gerry inhaled sharply, what had gotten into Marcus today? 'Miss Hoskins has demonstrated all too clearly that she doesn't have my father's best interests at heart and she will not be re-joining the company. Please continue to deflect all attempts to contact my father and let me know of any persistent offenders who you think I need to deal with personally. Understood?'

'Understood Mr Monroe.'

'Thank you Marcus. I know I can rely on you to help with Frank's recovery.'

Gerry ended the call without bothering to listen to Marcus's reply.

'Recovery'. There's a word he'd hoped he wouldn't be using to describe Frank any time soon. But the old man had surprised them all by rallying from this latest health scare. Now Frank was getting stronger and more belligerent by the day.

Currently, the doctors were playing into Gerry's hands by insisting his father continue to have complete rest from the business and, so far, Frank had been happy to comply. But now the cantankerous bastard was itching to get back up to speed with all current projects and Gerry was having trouble keeping him from sticking his nose where it wasn't wanted.

Last week, Frank's assistant, Barbara Hoskins had almost put a spanner in the works: sending emails out to Gerry's team requesting information on the key projects currently underway. After a difficult phone call in which she argued that Frank had a right to be given the information he had requested, Gerry had had to insist she took a forced leave of absence until the doctors confirmed that Frank was well enough to conduct business again.

That would have to do until he could fabricate some evidence to support a misconduct claim and get shot of her for good. For now, Marcus had been assigned her workload, which was limited to blocking all access to Frank and diverting any documentation that came through for him, over to Gerry's personal email account. It was the only way that Gerry could ensure he had complete and unobstructed control of all areas of the business.

When it came to his little side project – Pine Tree Bay – Gerry just needed a few more weeks. For several months now he'd been courting a venture capitalist who was looking to acquire holiday resort villages with growth potential. The man in question had a reputation for maximising profits through increased property leases and stripping of costs. The latter they managed by setting up minimum wage maintenance teams to manage repairs, negotiating bulk deals on low cost materials.

Once the model was at peak profitability they sold the resorts on… and made a killing into the bargain. Historically, many of the resorts ultimately went into decline – low quality offerings that failed to attract holiday makers. By the time that happened to Pine Tree Bay, both Monroe Holdings and the venture capitalist in question would be long gone, each having wrung all the juice out of the business and onto their balance sheets. Gerry loved making money almost as much as he loved getting even. And with this deal he was managing to achieve both.

Retracing his steps back to the corner suite of Monroe's London offices he looked out over one of the richest patches of real estate on the planet. He considered the billions of dollars that were travelling through the ether all around him at this very moment; all you had to do was reach out and take it. But when you had everything you needed and more, when you could afford anything you wanted, the zeros really did become meaningless; they existed just to prove how clever you were, how much bigger your dick was compared to all the other players. Ludicrous as it was, you could stick any number of zeros on to the end of a deal and it wouldn't give Gerry half the satisfaction that he was going to get from getting even with a couple of small town hicks who thought they could humiliate him.

He opened up his laptop and scanned the recommendations provided by Matthew Albright. When he came to the end he grinned, satisfied that it wasn't going to prove too difficult to rip the information he needed into a new document under Matthew's name.

All the pieces were aligning perfectly for what Gerry had planned and he was amused at how smoothly it had all played out. His cell buzzed in his jacket pocket and he took it out to check the display. The name 'Tasha' flashed up on the screen. He answered immediately, 'Tasha. I need someone for tonight.' There was no need for pleasantries.

'Gerry…' The hesitation in the woman's voice irritated him, he hoped the woman wasn't going to be difficult. 'Gerry, we need to talk first. It's Celine. She's in a bad way. She's talking about going to the police. I've been with her all morning. I've only just managed to convince her not to report it.'

'I thought I made it clear. With the amount I'm paying you I don't expect complications. I thought you said the girl was aware of my preferences.'

'You asked for some light role-play Gerry. The girl looks like she's been hit by a bus.'

'That's a wild exaggeration and you know it.'

'Not that far off.' He heard her mutter down the line.

'I expect better from you Tasha,' he said with just the right amount of menace. 'So tonight then. Ten p.m. at my apartment.' It wasn't a question.

'Gerry,' he was glad to hear her voice take on a more conciliatory tone. 'Look, I'm telling you this for your own good. You've been… sailing a bit close to the wind just lately and well you must have seen the media around this type of stuff right now. If Celine were to go to the press…'

For a moment he let the silence speak for itself. 'That sounds an awful lot like a threat to me Tasha. Even *you're* not stupid enough for that.'

She didn't respond to the insult. 'It was nothing of the sort Gerry. No-one is immune is all I'm saying. I'm giving you good advice here.'

'Don't fuck with me Tasha. I can make life very difficult for you if that's the way you decide to play it.'

'Ok ok,' she sighed, capitulating.

'Ten sharp. And Tasha? Make sure she's fully prepared.'

The woman took a deep breath. 'I'll see what I can do.'

'Ok. *Madam.*'

* * *

*

At the other end of the line Tasha Carmine ended the call in no doubt that Gerry had used the slur to put her in her place. She knew what she was, and if she'd been sensitive enough to take offence when people called her on it, she would have been out of this game a long time ago. No, of far greater concern was the escalating zeal with which that man was pursuing his own, very particular, predilections.

Gerry Monroe, who, up until a few months ago she would have listed firmly under the category of 'vanilla', had started to insist on a very strict set of criteria. He wanted a definite look – dark curly hair, grey eyes – slim. Most worrying of all was his requirement for the girls she sent him to act out a fantasy where they resisted his advances. He had started asking for different girls, sometimes on consecutive nights, whereas previously he would 'date' the same girl for a couple of months. It was as if he was suddenly chasing a high that couldn't be satisfied. The situation gave Tasha a bad feeling in the pit of her stomach.

Gerry Monroe may be her wealthiest client but she'd been in this business long enough to spot crazy when she saw it. She thought back to the dark, angry bruise on Celine's cheek this morning, the girl who suddenly wanted off her books after three years as an escort and just one night with Gerry Monroe. Tasha Carmine made a decision. None of her girls would be travelling to that man's apartment tonight, or the night after. She located his contact details on her phone, took a deep breath and selected to *Block Contact*.

Jem

Scotland

Jem was in danger of breaking the speed limit and applied the brakes slightly. These country roads drew you in with their wide-open vistas and before you knew it you had rounded a corner to find yourself rear-ending a tractor. She'd waited thirty-nine years to meet her grandfather, an extra ten minutes wasn't going to make any difference. If this guy even was her grandfather; which was highly unlikely.

In this frame of mind she pulled off the military road and into the driveway of the squat Galloway cottage that Jeanie had described to her. The recently whitewashed cottage sat back from the road and was fronted by a pretty, well kept garden. There was evidence of raised beds and fruit nets, now empty as they headed into in the depths of winter, but clearly this patch of green was Joe Kintyre's passion in the warmer months. The iron gate clanged shut behind her, announcing her arrival and she made her way down the garden path and knocked lightly on the pale blue wooden door. Almost before she had finished knocking, the door swung open and a tall, rangy man with a thick shock of white hair stood in the doorway looking at her inquisitively.

'Hello there,' Jem said in her friendliest voice. 'My name's Jemima Small I'm looking for Job Kintyre.'

There was the slightest raising of the eyebrows and then the man exhaled resignedly. 'Well looks like you've found him,' he said before starting to make his way back down the hallway at a surprisingly pacey shuffle. Jem felt slightly nonplussed. She hovered on the doorstep for a moment until the man stopped and turned around.

'Are you coming in or not?'

'Yes, yes.' She followed him down the hallway to a small kitchen. 'I'm sorry Mr Kintyre, it's just that, well, I'm a bit er... don't you want to know who I am and why I'm here?'

His response was to limp about the cramped kitchen – which was neat and orderly and smelled pleasantly of pine fresh cleaning spray – filling an electric kettle and pressing the switch with trembling hands he took down some old tan and brown mugs from a dresser and filled them with teabags. Lifting milk from the fridge and pouring it into a jug, he said, 'Please call me Joe, everyone else does. And, I know why you're here.' Returning the carton to the fridge before straightening up with a heavy sigh he finally turned to face a dumbstruck Jem. 'I've been expecting you for the last ten years or so if I'm honest. I was getting to the age where I thought *I* might have to be the one to come to *you*. I wouldn't have liked to leave this world without knowing you had the truth.'

Jem said nothing but watched the old man squeeze the teabags with a silver teaspoon and lay them carefully in a glass bowl that was sitting beside the kettle. *Yes,* she thought to herself, *I can well imagine that this meticulous man would not be comfortable leaving any loose ends.*

He placed the two mugs on the small scrubbed kitchen table and motioned for her to take a seat.

'So-o-o,' Jem started tentatively, 'I'm right in thinking you *are* my grandfather then.'

Joe Kintyre blew on his tea then shook his head slowly. 'Sadly no lassie, I'm not.'

Jem was confused. 'It's not your name on my father's birth certificate then?'

'It *is* my name on the birth certificate.' He took a long sip of his tea and shook his head slowly. 'But if you've come here looking for your grandfather, well, I'm sorry to tell you that's not me.'

Jem frowned. Was he telling the truth? Did he think she was going to want something from him if he admitted to being her grandfather?

'But you knew my grandmother, Marcia?'

'I did. In fact I don't mind admitting to you that many years ago I *loved* your grandmother. Now that's surprised you hasn't it?' He said, when her eyes widened slightly at his confession. He cast his gaze out over the garden, and she could see his mind travelling somewhere far away from this tidy little kitchen. 'Aye, I loved Marcia. I even offered to marry her. It would never have mattered to me that the baby wasn't mine, I would have raised him as my son in a heartbeat. I just wanted Marcia to stay in Pine Tree. I would have done *anything* to get her to stay.' Jem looked into his aged, watery eyes and knew he was telling the truth.

'So my grandmother *was* pregnant when she left Pine Tree Bay back in the fifties?'

'Aye lass, she was.'

'And you know who the father of her baby was?'

'I do.'

Jem, impatient as she was to hear the answer, saw the old man's eyes grow wistful. She sat back in her chair, letting go of her frustration and allowing Joe to wander back through time and tell the story at his own pace. 'Your grandmother and me, we knew each other all our lives. She was always so feisty – if anyone tried to bully someone, maybe a young lass who was a bit soft say, she was straight in there – taking them to task.' He laughed at the memory, then returning to the present momentarily, he raised his mug in Jem's direction. 'I've seen you in action at the Pine Tree Bay meetings with Gerry Monroe, you're a lot like her.'

Jem reddened slightly. 'Well I try to live up to her example.' She smiled warmly at the older man. 'This is the first time I've heard about her as a young girl though, I'm fascinated.' She leaned forward, resting her chin on her hand, eager to hear more.

'Well, your grandmother and me, we were pretty much inseparable from the age of about thirteen years old. We were best friends, nothing more mind. Everything was done proper in those days and the whole town had their eye on us young ones. It was a much smaller place then and everyone looked out for the kids of everyone else.

'Anyway, when we turned fourteen, we both got weekend jobs up at Dalrigg Farm. I helped out in the dairy and she looked after the horses. Every lunchtime, we'd have our sandwiches together in the hayloft and talk about all the plans we had for the future.' Joe, spoke more hesitantly for a moment. 'I'm not sure that your grandmother's home life was the easiest…she was very taken with the idea of getting away. She talked about that a lot; had big plans to go to university and be a lawyer. Said she liked a good argument and she might as well get paid for it.'

They both laughed. 'Sounds about right.' Jem agreed. Given that Marcia had ultimately spent most of her career supporting women who were fighting domestic violence cases through the courts, none of this came as a great surprise but it certainly made some things a lot clearer.

'But her dad didn't approve of her going off to get an academic education.' Joe shook his head bitterly. 'The most he would agree to was a commercial college in Edinburgh so, whilst we ate our sandwiches in that hayloft, Marcia would tell me all the things she was going to do once she got there.

'I remember her eyes lighting up when she described it all to me. A flat share in Haymarket, a different film every night at the New Vic picture house and dancing every weekend at the Palais.' He smiled to himself at the memory.

'She had it all planned out your grandmother.' Joe removed his spectacles and took a neatly folded cloth from his pocket to rub the lenses clean. 'She painted such a great picture of it all that I had it in mind that *I* would go too. So I left school as soon as I was able – later that year – and started saving up. When the time came I fancied I was going to tag along with her. It all came to naught mind.' He shook his head sadly. 'Marcia's dad, your great grandfather, changed his mind. She wasn't allowed to go to college on account of your great grandmother's declining health. By then Marcia didn't want to leave her mum anyway. I often wonder if that man drove his wife to depression just to spite Marcia – and what he called her "grand ideas".'

'Are you saying my great grandmother suffered some kind of mental breakdown?'

Joe popped his clean specs back onto his nose. 'These days they would probably call it nervous exhaustion. I hate to be the one to tell you this but your great grandfather was a rotten man. He took a bright, talented, vibrant woman for his wife and sucked all the life out of her until there was nothing left but a hollowed out shell. Everyone said it was the injuries he brought home from the war that changed him, but I was too young to know him before that and he just seemed to have cruel bones to me.'

Jem thought about the attic room that had once been her great grandmother's sanctuary, possibly the only part of Withershins that her injured husband couldn't reach.

'I wonder that Marcia never told me all this.' Jem shook her head.

'Well, she wasn't much one for looking back was she?'

'No that's true,' mused Jem. 'So, if Marcia stayed here to support her mum through mental illness rather than go to do a secretarial course, did she work at all?'

'Yes, she continued to work at the stables until she was nineteen, taking holidaymakers out horse-riding and what not. It worked out well because it was a couple of hours here and there and she could look after her mum in between times. But that's also how she came to meet Frank Monroe.' Joe Kintyre's jaw tightened slightly. 'I knew from the first moment I saw them together that I'd been kidding myself all along. I'd never seen her glow like she did in his company. And who could blame her? Here he was, this young cowboy, straight off a ranch in Canada looking and talking like one of the film stars we spent our Saturday night's watching at the Electric Theatre in Dumfries. I woke up from that dream there and then.'

Joe Kintyre rubbed his left wrist with his right hand; perhaps a touch of arthritis Jem wondered. 'Anyway, everyone realised Frank and Marcia had gotten close. He was here for the summer to "check out his roots" as he called it, and Marcia took him everywhere, the two of them on horseback. Thankfully no one mentioned it to your great grandfather or there would have been hell to pay.

'But at the end of the summer, Frank went back to Canada and Marcia, well she just went back to being Marcia. Then one evening, at the farm, she came to me and told me she was pregnant. That's when I offered to marry her. I said we'd go to the registry office the very next day. But she wouldn't hear of it. I'd just started courting my Betty see, and Marcia told me if I broke that lovely girl's heart she would throttle me.' He laughed at the memory. 'She knew what was right for me better than I did. But I would have married her in a heartbeat to stop her from leaving.'

Jem reached over and briefly put her hand over the old man's. He reddened slightly but continued his story. 'She was planning to run away to London, but she was worried that if Frank's family found out that the baby was his, with all their money and wealth and she a single mother, they might be able to come and take the infant away from her. All she had come to ask from me was that, when the baby came, she could put *my* name on the birth certificate. She said it was the one thing I could do for her. So, of course, I agreed immediately.'

'So Frank *is* my grandfather then?' Jem thought back to the letters – she and Matthew had been right.

Joe nodded. 'Yes, he is.'

'But I have old letters from him written to Marcia. He asked her to come to Canada. You said she glowed when she was with him. Why didn't she just go?'

'And turn up pregnant? Giving him no choice but to marry her? Stuck on a ranch with his disapproving family, miles from anywhere in a foreign country? You knew Marcia. Even at that young age she had far too much pride for that. No matter how much she loved him – and I know she really did love him – Marcia refused to turn into her mother; trapped in a marriage gone cold. No, she was determined to live life on her own terms. So I gave her the money that I'd been saving and that was enough to get her started in London. She was some woman your grandmother.'

Jem marvelled at Marcia's courage. 'And Frank never came looking for her in all that time?' she asked.

'Ah, well… That's the one thing I don't reflect too well on if I'm being honest,' said Joe shaking his head. 'Frank wrote to me the year after Marcia left. He had lost all trace of her. He'd continued to write to her at Withershins but the letters began to be returned to him unopened. I thought he was just looking to line up another summer fling for himself so I told him she was married and living in London, with her new husband… and that took care of that.'

Jem thought about this for a moment. 'You know, I genuinely think, from the letters I've seen that he really wanted to be with her.'

'Eventually I came to realise that lassie – especially as Frank told me as much himself… thirty years ago when he eventually came back here.'

'What? 'Jem sat up straighter in her chair, 'You mean he told you he'd been in love with her?'

'What do you think Pine Tree Bay Resort *is* Jem? I suppose if Frank Monroe were a poet he would have written a sonnet for Marcia, but he's a property developer. The resort was his gift to her.'

'But he built it in the nineties… when my grandmother was still alive…?'

'*And*, when he found out about the baby, your father… and you.' Joe's eyes glistened.

Jem didn't know what to say.

'I wrote to him and told him everything after my wife died.' Joe explained. 'Betty made me promise before she passed away, said I'd carried it around for so many years it had begun to throb like a splinter. She was a wise lass my Betty.' He became misty eyed at the memory of his long dead wife and, after all these revelations, Jem was in danger of joining him.

'So, after you wrote to Frank, he came here?' Jem asked.

'Yes, in the letter I told him everything. That Marcia had had his son. That she hadn't gone off and got married. I felt so ashamed when he arrived here and told me how much he had thought about her over the years.'

'I wonder why he never contacted Marcia in London?'

'Well, I suppose neither of us knows that he didn't.'

Jem hadn't considered this. 'There's just so much to take in,' she said shaking her head. 'If Frank *knows* that I'm his granddaughter then why has he never said anything?'

'Maybe that was how Marcia wanted it.' Joe drained his cup and got up to rinse it out at the sink then laid it face down on the drainer before turning to look at her. 'But he's looking out for you. In the best way he knows how.'

That night, Jem tossed and turned in her bed; every time she closed her eyes Joe Kintyre's words repeated in her head over and over again. On top of that she felt as if she were coming down with something. Her throat was scratchy and sore and she ached all over.

She threw back the duvet and padded down to the kitchen where Bear snored next to the Aga. He opened one eye and beat his heavy tail twice in appreciation of her company, before allowing the land of nod to reclaim him. Jem bent to scratch his ears, feeling slightly envious of her boy's ability to sleep anytime, anywhere.

Rummaging around in one of her kitchen cupboards she rooted out a packet of Lemsip that on inspection was well past its sell by date; a testament to how rarely was she ill. She mixed up the hot drink regardless and then wrapped herself in a blanket, taking her steaming mug over to one of the sofa's in the conservatory, she snuggled down in the dark to look out over the moonlit bay.

She considered the events of the past twenty-four hours. There was a lot to process. Frank Monroe was her grandfather. And, from what Joe Kintyre had said, was pleased to be so. Not only that, but Joe had said that building the resort had been Frank's tribute to Marcia. To Jem, this was what made the current state of affairs in Pine Tree Bay so confusing.

If what Joe had said was true, and she could see no reason to doubt him, then surely Frank would never allow Gerry to do anything to harm the future of the resort. Seen in this light, the review that Gerry had Matthew conducting became totally redundant, wholly inconsistent with Frank's vision.

Gerry surely didn't know that she was Frank's granddaughter either. The man was capable of a lot of things but he would never have pursued her had he known she was, in effect, his *niece*. Aside from the 'ick' factor, imagine the danger to his reputation if that one ever got out.

It seemed very likely that whatever he was up to, Gerry was acting independently of his father, and whilst this might be comforting on one level, it did not bode well for the businesses of Pine Tree. It signalled that the town was, somehow, no longer under the shelter of Frank's protection.

Jem had to find a way to contact Frank directly; she would go and see Finn tomorrow. Hopefully they could put their differences over Matthew aside to work out a way to get an audience with Frank. Knowing what she did now, she felt sure Frank would want to speak to her if he were well enough.

Had Frank longed for Marcia all these years? And how much easier might it have been for her grandmother if she had just told him about the baby?

Even though Jem fully understood why Marcia had resisted the temptation to jump from one bad family situation to another, she was in awe of her grandmother's mettle. Few young girls would have had the courage to strike out on their own when the chance of wealthy life with a handsome Canadian rancher was the alternative. But, for all that she had kept the romantic attachments in her life at arms length, Marcia had been a very happy, fulfilled woman.

Which led Jem to consider the other bombshell of the day; Matthew's text telling her he was going to be in London for a few days, a last minute urgent appointment. No phone call. No response to Jem's earlier voice message. A text. And coming as it did, on the back of what she had seen that morning, Jem had to concede that her faith in Matthew Albright was wavering.

Ok, so there were probably many valid reasons why Matthew should spend the evening with Kate and then be leaving her house early the next morning – but why was the only reason that sprang to mind the very worst one? Why was she suddenly remembering Matthew's laddish days down on the beaches of the Devon coast?

Jem banged her cup down on the coffee table with a frustrated sigh. Why could she not seem to escape this incessant back and forth where Matthew was concerned? Hadn't the last few weeks been wonderful –

precisely because they'd both finally broken free of all that?

She needed to make her bloody mind up. Which one was he? The ultra-reliable, too honourable friend or the ladies-man? And why was it that neither one could measure up? Both being equally handy as an excuse to push him away.

Last night she had defended Matthew to Rab and Finn, not to mention the others in The Smugglers who seemed hell bent on running him down. She had cast them all as blinkered sheep, following the rest of the small town flock, hungry for some conspiracy or drama to liven things up.

Yet here she was, in the dead of night, with her own doubts rushing to the surface – wondering if they didn't all have a point.

CHAPTER SIXTEEN
28th November

London *Matthew*

Matthew stood outside the lavish London townhouse and checked the scrap of paper he was holding. This was definitely the right address. He resisted the urge to whistle as he took in the grandeur of the building; clearly Zara's sister had married well. With its tall shuttered windows and Juliet balconies, not to mention the potted bay trees standing sentry on the scrubbed stone steps, every detail of the house had been staged within an inch of its life – right down to the generously stuffed Christmas wreath which currently adorned the glossy front door.

All the way from the tube station, Matthew had been rehearsing exactly how he would introduce himself, so it was a shock when Rebecca Harper opened the door, recognised him immediately and ushered him into the house. He followed her down a long hallway to her kitchen at the back of the house, confused by her warm, chattery welcome. Had he got this completely wrong or did she seem to be expecting him?

At university Rebecca had tagged along to a number of parties with Matthew when Zara and Nick had been together, but he hadn't expected her to remember him so readily. She certainly assumed a greater familiarity than their previous fleeting encounters would suggest. Even so, he didn't jump straight in; politeness dictated that he should start by asking her how she was and what she'd been up to since university. So, whilst she busied herself rustling up coffees on her state of the art Gaggia, she filled him in on life events since they had last seen each other.

He was impressed to hear that after a brief fling with advertising she had set up her own fair-trade children's clothing company, which Matthew – recognising the brand – knew to be *hugely* successful. Matthew felt momentarily ashamed for jumping to the conclusion that the beautiful house must be all down to a wealthy husband; Rebecca was clearly, in every sense, a self made woman.

Matthew was just wondering how to turn the conversation to the subject of Zara when Rebecca took that burden from him; placing two mugs down in front of them both she hopped up on the stool at the opposite side of the island and said, 'So I take it you're here about Zara and Nick?'

Thankfully, Matthew had a mouthful of coffee and before he could reply and Rebecca started to answer her own question. 'Honestly Matthew what a complete and utter mess. I thought *I* was the only one that knew about them, but, well you and Nick were always so close, I always did suspect he'd confided in you too. Anyone in their situation would go mad without someone to offload to. Zara always had me, but I used to worry for Nick I really did. Anyway,' Rebecca blew on her latte, 'I guess it doesn't matter who knows now does it?'

Realising he was on the brink of discovering something momentous, Matthew forced his features not to betray his surprise. He shook his head gloomily, detecting that this was the appropriate response. Buying some time, he took another long sip of his coffee which gave him an excuse not to answer. If he just kept quiet he might actually find out what was going on here.

'If you've come to give Zara a piece of your mind, I'm sorry to disappoint but she's gone straight to Gloucester. With Jeremy and Sophia of course. They left from Malaga last night.' She tilted her head to the side and rubbed her forehead with her index finger. 'I don't blame you if you want to have a go at me. God knows I've had a go at myself enough times. I honestly did wrestle with the prospect of telling Nick the truth you know. But then Sophia came along and well, he and Zara seemed happy at that point and I always think it's better for a child to have both parents around don't you?'

Matthew nodded, praying that would be enough to get her to continue. So Zara and Nick *had* run away together. To Spain? And now they had a daughter? Had Nick got Zara pregnant was that it? What did Rebecca mean about not 'telling Nick the truth'?

'Then of course it all happened for Nick with the success of his work,' Rebecca continued. 'And he seemed genuinely happy. What did it matter if it was all built on a lie? He wanted the financial freedom to paint and he'd got what he wanted hadn't he? I mean… that's all he ever went on about wasn't it?' She looked at Matthew for confirmation.

This was, at last, something he could comment on with absolute certainty. 'Certainly was. If he wasn't kiteboarding he was painting.'

'Exactly!' Rebecca looked relieved to have Matthew's agreement. 'So what Zara did, it… well it gave him what he always wanted didn't it? He got to spend his days painting. And then his work started changing hands for tens of thousands of euros. So the end justified the means wouldn't you agree?' She looked at Matthew expectantly again.

'You've clearly spent a lot of time thinking about this,' he said diplomatically.

Rebecca groaned. 'You honestly don't know the half of it. I did nothing *but* think about it some days – because I couldn't *tell* anyone – not even our parents. My father always suspected that Zara had mental health problems. I swear he would have tried to have her sectioned if he'd known about this. I'm just glad Mum and Dad both passed away non the wiser.'

Matthew chanced a question, 'And Nick? Have you spoken to him?'

Rebecca frowned. 'Haven't you?'

He recovered quickly. 'Yeah but it was so garbled I couldn't-'

'Hardly surprising under the circumstances is it?' She took a sip of coffee and looked despairingly out over the back garden.

'I guess not...' Matthew was hesitant. 'But now I can't get hold of him and, we haven't kept in touch all that much recently so I'm a bit out of the loop. Hence coming here.'

'It's the thought of losing Sophia isn't it? You know how much he loves his little girl. He'll be desperate. No wonder he wasn't making sense. What did he say exactly?'

'I couldn't make head nor tail of it.' Matthew massaged the back of his neck and looked at the floor unable to meet Rebecca's eyes with such a barefaced lie. He hoped the gesture would be passed off as worry about his friend.

'So you don't know then?'

'I don't know anything other than what we've discussed today.' It was, at least, the truth.

Rebecca leaned in towards him. 'So you don't know then? About the fraud? The reason they left the country in the first place? It was all made up. Zara invented it. That's what I meant when I said this entire thing was based on a lie. There *never was* any fraud. The two million they ran away with came from Zara's divorce settlement, not the royalties company. That's what Zara has had to come clean about now she wants to come back to England with Jeremy. She made it all up because she simply couldn't stand the fact that Nick was so firmly set on marrying that other girl.'

'Jem.'

'Yes that's it, Jem.' Rebecca leaned in closer. 'Zara said that when she finally came clean – when she confessed everything to Nick last night – he went berserk. He just started screaming Jem's name at her. Anyway it's not surprising that you can't get hold of him if he's on a flight to Scotland.'

Matthew's heart missed a beat. 'Scotland?'

'Yes, apparently that's where this Jem woman lives now. Nick's on his way to tell her what really happened.'

Jem

Scotland

Jem strode out along the shore road and up the steep incline of the Pine Tree Bay High Street. She was experiencing a renewed burst of energy after clearing her mind of its clutter in the early hours of the morning. She greeted friends and neighbours, slightly out of puff, as she climbed the hill towards Finn's outdoor equipment shop.

The shop also doubled as Finn's office and Jem knew that at this time of year she was sure to find him sitting at the counter, mapping out routes or working on his latest marketing strategy to drum up business for next year's excursions.

She still felt a little sad at the loss of their old routine – they had been in the habit of breakfasting together once a week. Every Thursday morning Jem would drop in to Finn's shop with coffee and croissants, and they would go over whatever community business they needed to plan for the week ahead. On weeks where the schedule was empty they would just chew the fat with town gossip, usually having a good giggle at whatever ancient festival Rab was trying to resurrect as an excuse to get into fancy dress!

She missed the ease and camaraderie of those days and she hoped that soon they could get back to that easy friendship they had always enjoyed. Maybe today was the day to give it a try.

The shop wasn't open so Jem – hands laden with a conciliatory breakfast – knocked as best she could to get Finn's attention. As Finn looked up from the counter, she could see, even from this distance, that he was ashen faced. At first she worried that his expression was a deliberate attempt to carry on his coolness towards her, but it was clear, as he ushered her through the door, that his worry was down to whatever he'd been reading on his computer moments before she'd turned up.

'What on earth has happened?' she asked. 'You look terrible.'

And then she realised that Finn was not upset – he was *angry*. 'I told you what he was up to Jem. I take no pleasure in being right but if you had just listened to me!'

Jem had never seen Finn in such an agitated state. He was usually so laid back. So calm. So... unflappable. 'Finn, what's happened? You're speaking in riddles.'

'Thanks to your bloody boyfriend–' Finn began but Jem cut him off. She raised a warning hand. 'Finn, I did not come here for a fight. I came because–'

'Read this!' He swivelled his laptop around so she could read the screen.

Jem didn't want to get dragged into Finn's paranoia about Matthew and she scanned the screen briefly. 'What exactly am I supposed be looking at?'

'Read the title of the document Jem.'

She leaned closer so that she could see the font and slowly read the words aloud, 'Recommendation for the... Sale of Pine Tree Bay Resort?' She turned to face Finn, incredulous. 'Where did you get this from?'

'I was blind copied into an email sent out from Gerry this morning; it had *this* report attached. His covering note makes it clear he's addressing the board of directors for Monroe Holdings so I think we can assume I've been copied in error.' He sighed. 'I suppose you've seen who the author of the report is?'

'Matthew obviously! Look, I'm not naïve enough to think he wouldn't have had to float a sell off as part of a suite of options for the resort but... Have you read the whole thing? Are there other options?'

'Yes, I've read the whole thing and no, there aren't any other options. Face it Jem, your boyfriend has fucked this town over.' Finn so rarely swore that Jem was doubly shocked.

'I just refuse to believe it Finn. I know Matthew and he is not underhand in this way. Look, you... you said it yourself, Gerry's had it in for us since February. He was never going to take it lying down was he? Me rejecting his advances. You having to forcibly remove him from my house. What did you say at the time? "We'll pay for that one way or another." Gerry's behind this not Matthew.'

'Wake up woman! Look whose name is on the report. It may be Gerry firing at us but Matthew has handed him all the ammunition.'

She blew the air out of her cheeks and shook her head. 'Just tell me what it says.'

'Read it for yourself.' He angled the laptop towards her.

Jem settled down at the laptop and read through the document, fully expecting to finish it and berate Finn for over-reacting. But after she'd finished she put her head in her hands. How could Matthew betray them all in this way, treating them all as commodities to be bought and sold, without so much as a heads up.

Before she could find the words to express her upset, Finn said 'I wouldn't be surprised to find that Kate Parker is in on this too.'

'What?' Jem raised her head to look at him, wondering if she should have asked that question, if she could handle another blow.

'I saw them both, yesterday morning, along with another suit. They were gathered on the verandah at Gerry's villa.'

So that's where Kate and Matthew had been going when she had seen them together yesterday morning? Is that why they'd looked so chummy? No, she simply would not believe it. Knowing Matthew for as long as she had, it just wasn't his style to be so underhand.

But then immediately after that meeting, Matthew had shot off to London with only so much as a brief text. Was he avoiding speaking to Jem because he was ashamed of what he'd done?

Jem needed to think but Finn was in her ear. 'They've taken us all for bloody idiots. I'm going to go down there and give him a piece of my mind!'

'He's in London. Went yesterday – probably just after you saw him with Kate in fact,' Jem said quietly.

'How convenient for him.' Finn said bitterly, but his shoulders visibly relaxed at this piece of information and Jem could see he was trying his best to calm down. 'Did you come in here looking for my help with something?'

Jem instincts told her this was the time to confide everything in Finn so that they could try to contact Frank together but there was a growing niggle at the back of her mind that made her pause.

Frank must surely know what was going on in Pine Tree – yet he was doing nothing to prevent it. Either that, or his condition was so serious he couldn't be disturbed. Neither circumstance encouraged her to contact him if she were honest. And then there was the worst scenario of all. What if he was well enough. What if she did manage to contact Frank and he did nothing? It would feel like another rejection. And right now, she wasn't sure she could handle one.

She just needed to sit with this a while, until she could think it all through. Before she did that however, she needed to find out what Matthew was playing at. She forced herself back to the present and to Finn's question, which still hung in the air. 'I just came to try and bury the hatchet,' she said weakly.

'If I can lay my hands on a hatchet, I'll be burying it all right,' said Finn disappearing into the back of the shop. 'I'll be burying it right up Matthew Albright's...' Jem didn't catch the rest.

Jem left the shop and headed straight back to the café but she entered via the back entrance and went directly to her study. Reaching into her office drawer she unlocked a small metal box and quickly retrieved the spare key to the garden flat.

Yes, she acknowledged to herself, she was about to cross a line. To go through Matthew's things whilst he was away *was* a massive invasion of privacy but to hell with it. She'd had enough of questions and uncertainties to last her a lifetime.

Making her way up the path she let herself in to the garden flat, taking a moment just to look around at Matthew's things, at the way he had left it. The bed was made, a breakfast dish, plate and mug sat on the drainer, there were some jogging pants and a t-shirt laying on the edge of the bed, but generally there was nothing remarkable. She made her way into the bathroom and all Matthew's toiletries were still stacked tidily at the side of the sink. The smell of his aftershave lingered in the air and she suddenly felt a pang of involuntary longing for him. She pushed the feeling aside. She was here to establish facts. It certainly didn't look as if he had left in the sort of hurry that his text had suggested.

As Jem retraced her steps, something caught her eye; Matthew's old, battered satchel was hanging on the coat rack directly behind the front door entrance. She almost jumped, wondering if Matthew might have returned to Pine Tree Bay without telling her. But, she checked again, his coat and overnight bag were definitely gone. No, Matthew must have left *without* the satchel. This was odd in itself as he took it everywhere with him for business. Did this mean the reason that Matthew had travelled to London wasn't work related as he had suggested?

If she was going to find anything, it would be in that satchel. She crossed the room, took it from the door and laid it on the bed. Unfastening the leather straps from the worn brass buckles, she felt suddenly overcome with a wave of shame that stopped her in her tracks.

Who *was* this person? The girlfriend rummaging illicitly through her partner's things – looking for scraps of evidence that proved or denied her suspicions but in all likelihood would just spawn more doubt and distrust? Wasn't this what all her years of strictly managing her romantic attachments had been about, avoiding this type of pitiable scenario? She didn't need to look through the contents of this bag; she needed to take a long hard look at *herself*. Because this person sitting on the bed, reduced to snooping for answers was not consistent with any version of herself that she recognised.

Suddenly, Jem couldn't wait to be out of the flat. She jumped up and hurried to the door then flung the strap of the satchel back over the coat hook with a force that, together with the weight of the documents inside, caused the twenty-year-old leather to finally give up the ghost. The shoulder strap snapped and the contents spilled out and scattered all over the floor.

Jem moaned in horror, she had forgotten to do up the buckles! Dropping to the floor she rushed to repack the contents of the bag. Feeling increasingly grubby and underhand she just wanted to stuff everything back in and get out of the flat as quickly as possible, but she needed to rearrange the documents in some semblance of the order they had originally been in – if she could work out what that was! Thankfully it was possible in most cases to tell which manila folder each document had slipped out of.

As she reached for the final flimsy folder, the single document it held, slipped from the cover and floated to the floor. She knelt to retrieve it, but the blurry photocopy of a foetus image with her own name at the top, brought her up sharp. She covered her mouth with her hand and stared at the sonogram. She had not held this piece of paper for many, many years but she hadn't needed to. Each blurry line was etched indelibly on her memory.

The blood now rushed inside Jem's ears. She had no idea what this, the only picture she would ever have of her lost child, was doing here, in Matthew's satchel. Had Matthew stolen it? What the hell was he playing at? The anger that rose up within her was overwhelming. How could he take this precious image and wedge it unceremoniously between spreadsheets and financial reports like some old expenses receipt?

Jem brushed a tear from her cheek. Thinking back over the last few months and the ease with which she had allowed him back into her carefully organised life, she felt so gullible. With a sudden clarity she saw that she'd allowed herself to fall for the *memory* of Matthew. What did she really know of the man in the here and now? That he stole documents from her, that he spent evenings (and mornings it would seem) confiding in another woman, that he was in the employ of a seedy businessman who stalked her and threatened her livelihood. Because she'd been wedded to the image of him as the one person who got her through the most difficult time in her life she'd let her guard down too easily; Finn and the others in the pub had warned her to be careful but she hadn't wanted to listen.

In alarming detail Beryl's tarot reading flashed before her eyes. The Ten of Swords – the man lying down with all the knives in his back. What was it Beryl had said? *Someone who's working against you.*

Finally, Jem gave in to the tears and let them flow unchecked as she knelt on the floor, bent double over the picture that had slipped from Matthew's satchel. And, as she clutched the blurry black and white image, she wondered for the millionth time if the baby would have changed everything; if the baby would have been somebody to love, wholly and unreservedly. She couldn't stand it. The constant loss of the people she let in. She gave in to the tears. Wave after wave of them as she keened and wailed noisily, bent double on the floor.

Jem wasn't really sure how long she stayed like this but at length, the noisy sobs turned to snivels and sniffs, until finally, all cried out, she exhaled a noisy blast of air then forced herself to rise up off of her knees and onto her feet.

Enough. She brushed the last tears from her cheeks and opened the wardrobe doors. One by one she took each item of clothing from its hanger, folded it carefully and placed it in Matthew's suitcase.

Nick
Malaga, Spain

The airport was heaving. Christmas music was playing and all the outlets were trying to outdo each other with the most extravagant decorations. Flashing fairy lights and foil stars were blinding him at every turn and the screams of over excited children, fired up with the festive overload around them, had his already frayed nerves in tatters.

Unable to get a flight from Grenada this late in the year he'd made the two and a half hour trip to Malaga airport in something of a daze. He was having trouble processing the conflicting melting pot of emotions that had been surging through his body since Zara had confessed everything to him the night before.

In true Zara style, she hadn't been in the least bit contrite. She'd just come out with it, in the kitchen, as he was fixing himself a drink. Over the years Nick had come to realise that Zara had, what some people might describe as, a fragile relationship with reality. She created drama around herself whenever the opportunity arose, like a character from one of the Spanish soap operas that she insisted she only watched to improve her language skills.

The trouble was, he'd been so infatuated with her in the early years, he'd been all too ready to overlook the warning signs. As their relationship progressed, he'd learned to weather the tempest of her volatile moods, admittedly by staying out of her way as much as possible, but he had never expected the level of insanity she'd laid out before him last night.

The volatility that had become so tiresome over the years had finally peaked. The reckless wild streak all too evident as she told him she was leaving – with all the care of someone announcing a trip to the supermarket.

He already knew about Jeremy of course; the latest in a long line of playboys who'd been servicing her. Though Nick had assumed the polo instructor was just another in her stable of conquests - another diversion until she got bored. And there had been some strange reassurance in that; due to their unique situation she would never be able to make any of these affairs permanent and take Sophia away from him. But in that, like so many other things, he had been wrong.

Nick had not been able to process what she was telling him at first. 'Oh, you're moving back to the UK with lover boy are you?' He knitted his brows in mock concern, 'Have you forgotten about the small matter of er... I don't know... you being *a criminal* perhaps?'

Unbelievably she had started to laugh. Then, just as he was

beginning to think she really was unhinged, she blurted it out.

It had all been a game.

She had swept her hand around the kitchen in a grand gesture, indicating the house and all its fancy contents, and explained how twelve years ago when they had left the UK, it was *not* on the proceeds of some long dead song writer's talents, but *her divorce settlement*. There never had been any fraud in the first place.

The ground had shifted beneath him. It was such a physical sensation he'd had to put a steadying hand on the worktop. And all the while Zara had been sitting there, sipping a glass of champagne, not her first of the day judging by the way she was swaying around. But it was more than that – she was overflowing with excitement, charged with that wound up manic energy she always gave off when she was creating drama.

Whilst Nick responded in stunned silence she continued to taunt him. How Nick should be flattered that she had gone to such lengths to secure him; about the way her actions had freed him from the corporate prison he would have been locked into for the last twelve years.

When Nick finally did find his voice, he said very quietly, 'You seem to think this is some kind of celebration.'

She waved the champagne glass around. 'Oh, come *on* Nick. We've been miserable for years and you know it. I've just signed the release on your prison sentence. You should be happy. And besides,' she wagged a drunken finger at him 'you've emerged from this a much richer man than you came into it. You're a celebrity in the art world. In fact if anyone's had the rough end of the deal it's me. Stuck here in the back of beyond for all these years!'

This was no performance. She actually *believed* what she was saying. He could see it in her eyes. As his anger swelled like a tumour, threatening to consume him, she carried on. 'It's time for *me* to have what *I* want now.' She flapped her hand dismissively. 'You can run off and find that little writer girl you were so fond of.'

She was on the floor before he even realised he had lashed out. 'Jem! Her name is Jem!' he'd screamed, towering over Zara as she lay on the floor. And he would have said a lot more, if Sophia hadn't run in and thrown herself down onto the hard porcelain tiles to shield her mother against him.

'Daddy, daddy please, no! Please don't hit mummy!' She screamed as tears poured down her face.

Nick caught the triumphant glint in Zara's eyes. His heart blown to smithereens by the fear he saw in his daughter's eyes. He left the kitchen and went to throw up in the downstairs bathroom.

And that had been the worst of it. Not Zara and whatever nasty insanity propelled her to do the crazy things she did; not the twelve years he'd lost, hiding in Spain, cutting himself off from his friends, his family, everyone and becoming a ghost. No, the worst of it was the knowledge that his daughter, the pure, true and absolute love of his life, now saw him as *a monster*.

He would never be able to undo what he had done. She would never be able to 'unsee' what she had just witnessed. It was there, permanently bookmarked in the story of her childhood, forever. *My father hit my mother.* And Nick knew well, from listening to the childhood accounts of friends who had been through it, that this one memory would endure; would crowd out all the others and forever define for Sophia who her father really was, deep down. It didn't matter that men who beat women were the lowest of the low in Nick's view, he was now one of them.

Nick wasn't about to paint himself as the victim. He'd played his part in it all right enough. If he hadn't cheated on Jem, Zara would never have been able to deceive him in the way she had; and if he hadn't found the lure of what she offered – on all counts – irresistible, he would not be in this mess and that was all there was to it. But to lose Sophia…

His daughter had gone with Zara last night and now Jeremy would get to be the hero, for a while at any rate; rescuing them both from the abusive husband. Nick had played right into Zara's hands – he had to hand it to her – she always managed to get things her way.

Nick wasn't about to simply roll over and let Zara take his daughter from him but, for Sophia's sake he would let things take their course just now. Before she left he had let Sophia know that he would be coming to see her in Gloucester just as soon as she was settled. He felt tears pricking the back of his eyes as he remembered the look of distrust plain on her face. He needed to think about something else, quickly.

A thankful distraction came in the form of a call coming into his mobile. Perry's name flashed up on the screen. Nick had an hour to kill before he needed to board – might as well get this over with now. He selected the button to answer the call and Perry's American accent hurtled down the line. 'What the hell Nick? I just got your message. You're heading to Edinburgh? What's going on?'

Nick took a deep breath and explained to Perry the events of the past twenty four hours.

'Jesus,' Perry gasped when Nick finally came to the end. 'Sure sounds like Zara did a number on you. But why in God's name are you on your way to Scotland?'

'I need to see someone. Someone I hurt a long time ago. I always promised myself that the first chance I got to apologise I would – but I was never able to in the past. Now I can.'

'Is this the girl you ran out on?' Perry ventured.

Nick was silent. He had never told Perry about Jem.

'Zara told me about it,' Perry explained. 'She said it had made the news at the time due to some dumb missing persons story. I looked it up.'

'Yes that's the one.'

'*Surf Girl?*'

'How did you guess?'

'Because it's the best of your work. It's all there on the canvas.'

'When did you speak to Zara about this?' Nick felt immediately suspicious.

'I haven't spoken to her in weeks Nick. She told me this a while back.'

'And you never said anything? What else did she tell you?' Nick didn't think he could stand finding out that Perry had been in on the deceit too.'

'That's *all* she told me.' Perry sounded insistent. 'But she asked me not to mention it. This whole ruse of hers though, well, it makes sense to me now. I always thought you must be on the run from something. No other way to explain the paranoia, the need to remain anonymous.'

'Well that part worked out pretty well for both of us.'

Something in Nick's voice must have alarmed Perry. 'You're not thinking of doing anything stupid now like telling this Jem who you are in the art world?'

'Perry I have to. Look, I'm not expecting her to welcome me with open arms but I don't intend to go to her and apologise for all this deceit under the shadow of another lie.'

Nick heard Perry take a sharp breath. 'Now look Nick. I know this is a watershed moment for you and all, but I urge you not to throw the baby out with the bath water here. Once you tell one person, especially someone who very likely holds a sizeable grudge against you, then there's a good chance that this great thing we got going is gonna blow up in our faces.'

'I'm just not bothered about that anymore Perry. That's out the window for me now… The Ghost angle – it was only ever there for one reason. That reason's gone. I just want to start again with a clean sheet.'

On the other end of the line Perry sighed, but he didn't argue further.

'I expected you'd take a little more convincing than this,' Nick ventured.

'Well, I've known you for twelve years Nick. And once your mind is made up I know *I* ain't gonna be the one to change it,' Perry said resignedly.

'Thank you.' Nick was grateful not to have to fight this one out with his agent.

'So, where exactly are you travelling to in order to make this big apology anyways?'

'Well, it was you who tipped me off to Jem's whereabouts to be honest.'

'Really?'

'Do you remember the Frank Monroe commission? Pine Tree Bay in South West Scotland?'

'How could I forget?'

'Well that's where Jem is. I looked up the resort after your call and it just so happens that Jem runs a book shop there.'

He sensed Perry hesitate on the other end of the line. 'And you think this is a coincidence?'

'Whatever it is – that's where I'm headed.'

'Well I guess… small world and all that. Now, you don't happen to have a piece of art work in your suitcase that we can charge them for do you?' Perry asked wryly.

'With everything that's been going on Perry, that might have just slipped my mind.' Nick managed to laugh.

'Do you think this Jem woman is gonna be pleased to see you?'

'I doubt it.' Nick's throat tightened. 'But at least I can apologise and we can both get some closure on what happened.'

The two men said their goodbyes and Nick ended the call. Typical Perry – always thinking of the bottom line.

*

Over in Atlanta, Perry Charles hung up the phone slowly and stared at the blurred photo of Nick on his computer screen – the Nick that he'd first met twelve years back – the young, nervous man who had introduced himself as Carl. The photo shone out, in a bluey white glow from his computer screen, accompanied by an archive newspaper article. The mystery of the runaway groom who had disappeared through a pair of closing tube train doors, never to be seen again.

Perry clenched his right fist and swore – kicking the waste paper basket that sat beneath his desk and scattering the contents all over his office floor. It was over. Just as the really big money was about to start rolling in, Nick was turning the off the damn faucet. *Shit!* He banged his fist on the desk. Perry had honestly begun to believe that his investment had paid off.

He'd gotten off his ass and scouted for talent. Paying expensive airfares all over the world when he could ill afford to. Then he'd found the golden ticket; someone with real talent who couldn't afford to play the temperamental artist. Someone who had no choice but to get on board with Perry's plans. All Perry had had to do was create the buzz and wait for the the money to roll in.

He sat and considered what he was about to do. Nick was a fool. This woman from his past was living in the same town where he'd been asked to *personally* deliver a commissioned work, and he was treating it as a coincidence? There was something strange afoot. Perry had no idea what that was – but he sure as hell knew a PR opportunity when he saw one.

Flicking through the contacts on his phone he found the person he was looking for. Arts correspondent for several of the UK broadsheets, Peter Shackleton. Stories sold art. A mystery story sold it even better. There was still something to be made from this situation and Perry needed to get on that – fast.

He brought to mind a homecoming exhibition, visualising the show in his mind's eye: *'Resurrection'* or some such title that allowed him to wring the last few drops from the whole *Ghost* concept he'd come up with in the first place. But to really make money, Perry knew that he first needed to create some buzz, some kind of sensational reveal.

Peter Shackleton answered on the first ring. 'You ready to give me a name Perry?'

'I can give you more than a name. How fast can you get to South West Scotland?'

Matthew

Somewhere between London and Lockerbie

Matthew politely refused the offer of coffee from the First Class train steward with an equanimity he didn't feel. He went back to staring at his screen. He couldn't believe what he was reading. His report, the one he had submitted to Gerry yesterday morning, had been butchered into a one man treatise on a Pine Tree Bay sell off – with Matthew's name against the title.

His mind – a tangled mess of injustice woven with frustration – had not stopped racing since he'd closed the door of Rebecca's Barnsbury terrace and hailed a cab to race him down to Euston Station. The revelations of the morning, together with the report he was staring at now, increased the anxiety that had begun to gnaw away at his solar plexus.

He'd toyed with the idea of flying but Euston had been only minutes away and he knew, having checked the journey times previously, a flight wouldn't have been any quicker. Now, however, due to overhead power line issues caused by a raging storm further north, the train was crawling along a branch line at an agonisingly slow pace. A pulse in Matthew's jaw twitched as he tried to keep his mounting frustration at bay.

Where was Jem? She wasn't answering his calls. It was possible she was busy in the cafe he supposed – but he needed to warn her about Nick's imminent arrival. He didn't want her to feel ambushed by the enormity of what was about to be thrust upon her but it wasn't the type of news you could just casually drop onto a voicemail.

Rebecca had said that Nick was flying from Malaga. Matthew had checked the flight times and by his calculation, even if Nick took the earliest flight, he couldn't get to Pine Tree Bay before late afternoon. Matthew had banked on being back by four but now, with the rail issues, that was looking optimistic.

Matthew wasn't worried that Jem was about to fall back into Nick's apologetic arms any time soon, she had far too much self respect for that – especially if Nick came clean with her about where he'd been for the last twelve years. But why was she ignoring his messages? He'd asked her to call him. She wasn't responding. Despite how urgent he'd told her it was.

He mulled it over in his head, drumming his fingers on the table until the passenger opposite gave him a look that said '*Really?*' at which point he picked up his phone to call the only person in Pine Tree he thought might feel disposed to help him.

Making his way out into the corridor so as not to be overheard in the relative quiet of the first class carriage, he realised he was going to have to share the truth with Kate. She answered almost immediately, and she was practically speechless once Matthew had filled her in on everything he'd found out from Rebecca.

After a pause she found her voice. 'Well, God knows what this Nick must be thinking. I mean his wife sounds like a first class bitch and let's be honest, not just a little bit crazy, but I don't think turning up here is going to improve things for him.'

'There's an added complication too. Rebecca told me that Nick is apparently something of a big deal in the art world. I've never heard anything about him but within certain circles his work is, according to Rebecca, highly sought after. She said he's been producing artwork under some sort of pseudonym – *The Ghost?*'

'You mean that anonymous European painter?' asked Kate.

'You've heard of him?' Matthew sounded surprised.

'One of our clients at Allocott was a collector of his work. What has Jem said about it all?'

'That's the problem. I can't get hold of her. I've left numerous voicemails and texts but she hasn't got back to me. You haven't heard that she's unwell or anything have you?'

'No, in fact I saw her going in to Finn's shop just this morning.'

'Would you do me a favour and pop into the café, see if you can get her to call me. I don't understand why I can't get hold of her.'

Kate paused and Matthew sensed the hesitation. 'Kate, are you still there?'

'Yes, I'm here. I was just thinking… I heard something in The Barnacle today that *might* explain why Jem is avoiding your calls.'

'What?' Matthew felt alarmed.

'It's just a theory but… There's a rumour floating around the village that Finn was accidentally copied in on an email with your final report attached. It hasn't gone down well with the locals.'

Matthew's heart plummeted. 'It's not my report Kate. Gerry's butchered it and distributed it to the board under my name. He's made it look like I'm recommending that Monroe Holdings sells off the resort with no other considerations.'

Matthew moved to the side to let another passenger go by and tried to balance as the train rounded a corner at high speed. At least the driver was picking up the pace again. 'Look, I just need to speak to Jem personally and explain all this. It'll be fine once I can speak to her directly, she knows what Gerry's capable of. Would you just go down there, to the café, and ask her to call me?'

'Sure, I'll head over there straight away.'

Matthew ended the call and as the ground lurched and tilted beneath his feet, he couldn't decide whether it was the motion of the train or the knowledge that Jem must think he had betrayed her that was making him feel nauseous.

Scotland *Jem*

Fortunately – or unfortunately as she would later come to look at it – a very busy afternoon was in progress at the café. Jem was in need of distraction after the morning's upheaval. She had returned from Matthew's flat mentally and emotionally exhausted and the simple and industrious task of serving up coffees, cakes and the odd panini was exactly what she needed to take her mind off things.

Even if she was unable to shift the feeling that a stone had lodged itself firmly in place of her heart, taking positive action had always brought her a sense of fortitude; having packed up Matthew's things and made the decision to eject him from both her flat and her life she was currently experiencing a small measure of relief. This feeling was just an interval – she understood that – later the sense of loss would take over and the hurt would have to be endured. But for now she could distract herself with action.

Ever since Matthew had come back into her life she seemed to have known little peace. With this temporary madness behind her, she could switch into operational mode and turn her attention back to more important things – such as her business. She had been a little lax in that department lately but in the capable hands of Jamie and Isla the cafe had not suffered however, it had to be said that lazy mornings and long lunches had led to the shelving of some of Jem's responsibilities – and now it was time to get on with things. Not least garnering some kind of opposition to Gerry's plans to offload the resort.

A customer signalled for Jem's attention. 'Excuse me but do you think I might get the scone I ordered before I've completely finished this coffee here?' the man grumbled.

'I'm so sorry that must have somehow been overlooked. I'll sort that for you right away.' Jem conjured her most contrite smile. 'I'll get you a fresh coffee on the house at the same time.'

Jamie heckled as she made her way into the kitchen. 'Here she is! Hey boss, Isla and I were just saying we haven't seen Matthew around here for the last few days. Where's he been gallivanting off to then?'

Ignoring the question Jem said, 'Isla, I forgot the scone for table five. Can you get me one with all the trimmings whilst I do a fresh americano? I can just see the review on Trip Advisor – *Sieve-Headed Owner Forgot Scone!*'

'Sure,' said Isla flashing Jamie a warning look that told him not to push it any further. Jem was well aware of what had passed between them

— honestly, they were about as subtle as a kick in the crotch. She knew it was just a taste of what was to come; nothing escaped the notice of the hawk-eyed locals of Pine Tree Bay.

'There must have been a rare bird sighting up along the cliffs or something.' Isla changed the subject. She raised her voice over the sound of the Magi-mix that Jamie was currently feeding with vegetables.

'Why do you say that?' Jamie shouted back then turned off the motor.

'All those fellas out there with cameras.'

Jamie looked at Isla as if she had finally lost it. 'Are you bevied? This is a tourist town - people are always in here with cameras.'

'Yes, I know stupid!' Isla momentarily broke off her task to flick a tea-towel at his thigh. 'But you can always tell the twitchers from the usual tourists because they sit waiting with those fancy cameras, the ones with the long lenses.'

'Aye, all right Miss Marple.' Jamie rolled his eyes.

'Where are we on that scone?' Jem asked wiping her hands and picking up a tray with the coffee. She wasn't in the mood for the usual banter this afternoon.

'Here you go Jem.' Isla put the scone along with small pots of jam and cream on the tray and Jem swept out of the kitchen and into the café. Having delivered the order, Jem set about clearing the tables that had been vacated whilst she was in the kitchen. Her arms were laden with a tray of empty cups, plates and dishes as Kate came through the door and made a beeline for her.

Oh God not you. This was the last thing she needed. She'd hoped for a little more time to regain her composure before she had to face either Kate or Matthew – and also to think of something suitably cutting to dispense when that time came. Before she could escape Kate rushed over. 'Jem, Matthew's been trying to get hold of you, he asked me to come and check you were ok.'

'Did he?' Jem looked evenly at Kate, 'Well I'm just fine, thank you.' She managed a curt smile and hoped that would be enough to signal that the conversation should end there.

She tried to move forward, toward the kitchen, but Kate blocked her path. 'Look, I can see you're run off your feet...' Kate held up her splayed her hand in a gesture that said she just needed a second then smiled understandingly, '...I'm sure you haven't had time to even listen to Matthew's messages. But it's really really urgent that you call him.'

With her blonde, highlighted, hair that swung in its ponytail and her wide generous mouth full of straight white teeth, Kate looked like someone from a toothpaste commercial; fresh, attractive and brimming with health. Jem was shocked at how strong the desire was, to wipe that cheery smile right off her face. How dare she walk in here and tell Jem what to do, after the way she and Matthew had gone behind everyone's back? Treating Kate to her iciest stare and her steeliest voice, Jem said, 'What? So he can feed me even more lies to disperse around the town? I don't think so.'

Kate took a deep breath. 'Oka-a-ay,' she said hesitantly. 'I can see that you're upset about something and I don't want to get in the middle of things- '

'Don't you?' Jem raised an eyebrow so sharply it was in danger of catapulting off her face.

Kate, clearly taken aback, frowned. With some steel of her own she said, 'And what exactly is *that* supposed to mean?'

The atmosphere in the café was suddenly charged as customers stopped their chatter to tune into the conversation between the two women. Jem's extremely strained length of rope finally snapped. 'Oh come off it Kate! You were seen yesterday morning! First at your house, then during a business meeting at Gerry Monroe's villa. The *jig*, as they say, is up! So you can stop this whole 'friendly gal on holiday' act you've got going, because everyone knows that you and Matthew have only ever been here to put Gerry Monroe's plans into action.'

Isla, who had just emerged from the kitchen, stood stock still with a tray full of crumpets and eyes like saucers.

Kate pulled herself up to her full height. 'I don't know who's been filling your head with these ridiculous notions but I can assure you – what you're describing is absolute fantasy.'

'So, let's be clear,' Jem said, raising her chin. 'You *didn't* leave your house with Matthew early yesterday morning and go for a business meeting at Gerry's villa?'

Kate looked uncomfortable, 'I'm not saying that-'

'So you did leave together?'

'Yes but-'

'And you went straight to Gerry's villa for a meeting?'

'Yes.'

'And Matthew stayed the night at yours.' Jem thought she might as well confirm her suspicions whilst she was on a roll.

'No! Jem-' Kate's eyes widened.

Kate

Kate didn't get the chance to protest her innocence however, because the next moment – just as she heard the café door creak on its hinges – Jem's eyes fell on whoever had just walked through the door. Kate watched as the woman's jaw fell open and all the blood drain from her face.

With shaking hands, Jem slowly placed the tray of cups and plates on to the table, never once taking her eyes from the door. At the same time, Kate noticed out of the corner of her eye, the two men sitting at the tables to her right had raised their cameras and trained them on the doorway.

As if this were all happening in slow motion, Kate turned to see a tall, strikingly handsome man with longish, dark wavy hair that was threaded with a few grey strands at the temples. He wore a calf length, grey woollen overcoat that looked about two sizes too big for him, but in a good way, Kate decided. With his dark brown eyes and his gaunt expression, the man had an unmistakably, brooding appearance. *My God,* thought Kate, *Heathcliff has just walked into Small House Book and Brew.*

The man towered for a moment in the entrance, his eyes focused on Jem as if she was the only person in the room and then he walked slowly towards her. 'Jem,' his voice cracked as he said her name. But Jem simply held her hand up as if cautioning him not to come any further. She looked, thought Kate, like a woman defeated.

The man stopped in his tracks and Jem, still with her hands raised in warning, shook her head slowly, her voice was thick with emotion and when she finally got the words out, they were low and strained, 'No Nick.' She shook her head emphatically. 'No no no, not today. I can't....' She hung her head and her voice broke. 'I can't do this today. I *won't* do this today.' She whispered before making her way into the back of the shop.

As soon as Jem started to speak, the men with the cameras had sprung into action, seemingly intent on capturing every moment that passed between the couple. Kate guessed what had happened – someone must have leaked to the press that Nick Townsend, *The Ghost,* would be turning up at Small House today. It was the type of story the public would devour – the famous artist relinquishes anonymity for the love of his life. That's how it would be written up throughout the arts' media this evening, with all the inconvenient parts of the story blithely cast aside. Oh God, Matthew was going to be devastated thought Kate.

Nick, made to go after Jem but Kate blocked his path saying firmly, 'You heard what she said.' Taking in Nick's distraught expression, she said more softly. 'I think she probably needs some time to process this, don't you?'

Nick turned to Kate as if noticing her for the first time. 'I *have* to see her. I have something important to say and I've waited a long time to say it.' He started again in the direction that Jem had gone but Kate pressed her hand into his chest.

'You might have something you're ready to say, but Jem's not ready to hear it. I think you'd be better waiting until she is.' Kate then lowered her tone even further. 'Now,' she said, looking around hastily, 'there seem to be a couple of people in here who are keen to take snaps of you and I'm sure they would love nothing better than some ghastly scene to splash all over the media. Can I suggest you leave without fuss and come back when things have calmed down a bit.'

'Impressive,' mumbled Jamie, who, alerted by Isla had rushed out from the kitchen, clearly with a view to protecting Jem. Seeing Kate had it all in hand, he addressed Nick in the friendly yet no nonsense tone he usually reserved for the drunks he helped Rab to clear out of The Smugglers, 'Come on pal. You don't want to get on the wrong side of this one.' He inclined his head toward Kate. 'You'd best be on your way aye?'

Nick's shoulders slumped and he turned toward the door then back to face Kate. 'Can you just tell her I'm here to apologise that's all… I'm just here to say sorry… and to explain.'

Kate looked into his haunted face; it was no co-incidence that someone had come up with the moniker of *The Ghost* for this man. 'These guys here are Jem's team,' she said, inclining her head toward Isla and Jamie. 'They'll make sure she gets the message after you leave.' After their earlier exchange Kate doubted very much that Jem would want to receive any such message directly from her.

Nick, looking just as defeated as Jem, finally left the cafe. It was no surprise to Kate or anyone else when the two men with the cameras followed him. The café resumed a slightly heightened buzz and Kate followed Jamie and Isla back behind the counter.

Isla let out a low whistle. 'So that's the one and only Nick Townsend? He's got a nerve walking in here like that after what he did.'

Kate didn't want to waste time with a post match analysis. Neither did she want to put herself in a situation where she had to divulge the information that Matthew had told her about Nick's whereabouts for the last twelve years.

'Do either of you have media alerts set up for this place?' Kate asked.

Jamie looked nonplussed by the question but Isla confirmed she had an overarching alert set up for any news about Pine Tree Bay. 'I take it you're referring to those photographers?' she added.

'I am,' said Kate and both she and Isla filled Jamie in on how the men had sprung into action when Nick walked into the restaurant. 'It looked like some kind of tip off to me,' Kate surmised.

'Why would photographers be interested in Jem's ex?' Jamie asked looking perplexed.

'Beats me,' Kate lied. 'But can I suggest we all keep an eye out for anything that pops up on-line for the rest of the day. Isla can you keep me in the loop if those reporters come back?'

'I can,' said Isla, then pursed her lips as if she were considering her next words very carefully. Finally she said, 'I have to say this though, I'm not sure whether your interest in the reporters stems from a concern for Jem or from worry about what any adverse publicity will do to Gerry's plans for a sell off.'

Kate sighed, 'I can't even begin to tell you how wrong everyone is about this.'

'But you admitted that you and Matthew were at a business meeting at Gerry's house yesterday? If you're not both working for Gerry then what other explanation can there be?'

Kate looked uncomfortable. She wasn't ready to share the fact that she was thinking of buying Gerry's villa with anyone. Firstly because she didn't want to tip people off to the fact that it was for sale, but secondly, she had yet to fully understand how her own situation with Allocott was about to play out… Until she knew more she wasn't going to make any concrete decisions or tell anyone in Pine Tree Bay what she was contemplating. Besides, if this afternoon had taught her anything it was to think very hard about the wisdom of moving to a community that could clearly turn against you at the drop of a hat!

When Kate didn't speak, Isla shook her head, 'Well I guess that's our answer.'

Kate felt exasperated. 'Look, I asked about the reporters because Matthew is a friend and, despite what everyone around here thinks, he'll be worried sick about Jem when he hears about what happened just now. He's currently on a train heading north. I don't want him to find out about all this on some media feed. As for the other thing, well you can jump to whatever conclusions you like, all I can say is that I'm not working with Gerry, or Matthew for that matter, and whether you decide to believe me or not is up to you.' With that she picked up her gym bag and walked out of the café, thinking that the first thing she needed to do was to contact Matthew and bring him up to speed with the afternoon's events.

She pulled the phone from her bag; she could speak to Matthew whilst she completed the mile walk back along the shoreline to her cottage. As she did so her eye was drawn to the bus shelter on the opposite side of the road. Inside, Nick Townsend sat huddled into his coat, his eyes trained on the café, seemingly oblivious to the fact that snow was starting to fall softly and heavily all around them.

Kate decided to walk on, she needed to get home before this weather turned into a blizzard. She had done all she could to keep the man away for the time being. It was up to Isla and Jamie to shield Jem now.

It wasn't as if anyone around here seemed grateful for her help anyway.

Matthew

Scotland

Matthew hated to think how many speed violations he might have clocked up on the drive back from the railway station if it weren't for the fact that his old VW camper van refused to go anywhere near the national speed limit. The windscreen wipers worked away valiantly in the drifting snow and Matthew desperately hoped it wouldn't settle on the tarmac as he rounded the tight corners of the windy roads that spiralled their way down to Pine Tree Bay.

Ever since Kate's call his insides had been churning with the knowledge that Jem, and half the town, now believed that he'd been working against them. Gerry's butchered version of his report had somehow been circulated around the town.

And to top it all Nick was there. In Pine Tree. It set Matthew's teeth on edge. Did the guy really think he could just turn up out of the blue, say sorry and think that would make up for the last twelve years? If he even bothered to apologise that was. Knowing Nick he would have some creative way to side step the more grubby issues of his disappearance. Matthew had wanted closure where Nick was concerned; to understand which one of them Jem would pick given the choice. But that had been so much more palatable when Jem *wasn't* labouring under the misapprehension that Matthew was trying to sabotage her community.

Even now, after all the things Rebecca had told him, Matthew wasn't sure he would come off best in that contest. Somehow, Nick had managed to turn up just as the whole town had decided that Matthew was an underhand bastard. Why didn't that surprise him given the way it had always gone between the two of them? One thing was for certain, he would make damn sure Jem got the full story. The thought made him press even harder on the accelerator.

The camper van did its best and fifteen minutes later Matthew finally pulled up in his usual parking spot at the back of the café.

What the…?

He was shocked to see his suitcase and all his gear leaning against the front door of the apartment underneath an inch of snow. Brushing it away he lugged the suitcase, together with his wetsuit and the surfing equipment that had been unceremoniously dumped beside it, into the van and made his way into the back of the café. The twin emotions of incredulity and anger were starting to rise within him. Was Jem actually throwing him out of the flat? Based purely on a rumour that was circulating the town? Or was that just convenient grounds now that Nick had crawled out of the woodwork? Well, whether she liked it or not she was going to have to listen to what he had to say.

He entered the café via the garden entrance. She wasn't hard to find, he could hear raised voices coming from her office. He inched down the corridor and saw the two of them, Nick and Jem facing off against each other. For a brief moment Matthew stood outside the door watching, listening to the exchange. It felt surreal; like travelling back in time to before, when Jem had been Nick's girlfriend and there was nothing he could or *would* have ever tried to do about it. It wasn't his style, to lurk around eavesdropping, but he needed a moment, just to see for himself what the interplay was between them.

Nick had always been a tall, good looking bastard and time only seemed to have enhanced that, Matthew observed. He had developed a kind of weathered, haunted look, finally accomplishing that tormented artist appearance he'd always tried so hard to cultivate when they were younger. For most men, the years of living under the threat of exposure and possible imprisonment would have worn away their sanity to such an extent it would have affected their looks. Whatever it had done to Nick, it suited him.

Jem was standing with her back to Matthew but he could tell from the set of her shoulders and the violent shake of her head that she was listening to Nick with a sense of anger and defiance.

'Just give me a chance to explain properly.' Nick was saying - it didn't sound as if he'd been there long.

'What do you think you could possibly come up with that would excuse what you did?' Jem folded her arms and titled her head to one side. '*I'm sorry but the dog ate my vows?*'

'Jem, please-'

'You left me at the church Nick! Left me to face everyone on my own. You ruined my life. I loved you and I trusted you and you just ran out on me without a backward glance.'

'If you only knew how wrong you are Jem. There's not a day-'

'Don't tell me there's not a day you haven't thought about me for the past twelve years because I think if that were true, you might have at least managed to pick up the phone, don't you?' Jem said bitterly. 'Was I that insignificant to you? How long did you wrestle with your conscience before deciding not to go through with it? Because I need to know Nick, what was so important that you could just throw me away like that?

Matthew suddenly decided he wanted to be in the room to hear Nick's answer.

'Oh great,' said Jem as he walked in. She turned her back on them both and went to stare out of the window.

Nick and Matthew looked each other in the eye for the first time in twelve years. Matthew saw a mixture of shock and irritation on Nick's face. He clearly wanted this private moment with Jem and it was a real pain in the arse Matthew turning up and ruining his prepared speech. *Likewise*. Matthew set his jaw.

Nick recovered quickly however. 'It's been a long time mate.' He managed a weak smile then held out his hand awkwardly. If there had been any lingering doubt in Matthew's mind that Nick had been the one to add the anonymous comments to Jem's blog posts, it vanished. Nick's face showed no surprise that his old friend was in town too.

Matthew didn't take the proffered hand and after an awkward moment, Nick let it drop to his side. He made it clear, however, that he wasn't going to give any ground, 'I need a private moment with Jem if you don't mind.'

'I do mind,' said Matthew, noticing Nick's eyes widen fractionally. 'Jem and I are together now. If you've got something to say to her then you can say it in front of me. If Jem wants to see you in private then, by all means, but until she says otherwise, I stay.' Feeling emboldened by the fact that Jem hadn't contradicted him, he followed this up with, 'I think you owe both of us an explanation don't you?'

Nick's eyes darkened. 'Oh come off it Matt,' he said wearily. 'Don't give me all this sanctimonious crap. The best thing that ever happened to *you* was me not turning up at the church that day and you know it. You couldn't wait to step into my shoes. You thought you were hiding it so well but it was so fucking obvious to everyone that you had a thing for Jem. I bet you couldn't wait to go running to her with the news I'd been seen with another woman.'

At these last words Jem swung round and fixed Matthew with a vicious glare. 'You *knew* Nick had been seeing someone else before the wedding and you've never thought to tell me? Not through all those months we spent together afterwards when I was tearing myself apart, wondering what had gone wrong? Not now during these weeks we've spent together?'

Matthew felt a frustrated outrage at the way things were suddenly backing up on *him*. He held his hands up in defence, 'Don't anyone think of turning me into the bad guy here!' Flashing a look of irritation at Nick, he took control of his temper and said to Jem more evenly, 'Yes, a few days before the wedding someone at work told me that Nick had been seen with another woman. I never told you because I never had any idea who it was. I didn't even know for sure that this woman was the reason Nick had called off the wedding. And I thought the only thing to be gained from telling you was more heartache. It wasn't going to provide any answers for you Jem, it was just another question that would drive you crazy because you would never be able to know for sure.' He crossed the room, placed a hand on her shoulder. 'After Nick didn't show up, seeing how devastated you were, I made the call not to tell you at the time and then… well there didn't seem any point in dragging the whole thing up again later on.'

Jem shrugged out of his touch. 'You know what I realised whilst you were away these past few days Matthew?' She looked at him scathingly, 'I have absolutely no idea who you are.'

Matthew stepped back as if he'd been stung. The sheer unjustness of the way this was turning out was beyond belief. Suddenly he'd had enough. When he finally found his voice it was low and even, 'Well, you know what? Right now, that feeling is pretty mutual.' He saw that his words had hit their mark and he couldn't stop himself from letting everything rip. 'You say we're a couple Jem, yet at the first sign of trouble what do you do? You believe what everyone else has to say about me and give me no right to reply. You're running around town listening to rumours and gossip and when I try to give you my side of the story you won't even pick up the phone.'

Matthew gripped the back of a chair, trying to steady his anger before he continued, 'Since coming here, I've done nothing but try to help this town. I've worked my backside off to stop Gerry from selling off this resort. Is that because I love this community? No, but because *you* do! I spent yesterday in London because there was someone there who could tell me what had happened to Nick. Did I give a shit where he was? No! But it would have meant closure for *you*! A clear way forward for *us*!

'All I ever wanted to do was to be with you Jem. All those girls I went out with, when you and Nick were together, do you know what that was? A distraction; a way to stop myself going insane watching Nick have the life that I wanted – with *you*! And just the vague, slim hope that someone might show up who took that feeling away. You know, someone who would match up.' Matthew ran a hand through his hair, let his arm fall to his thigh and slowed his breathing. Finally he said, 'But you know what? That stops here, right now. I'm through trying to be with you.'

He didn't wait to see her response. Instead, he walked toward the door before stopping half way, 'And as for him?' Matthew looked at Nick then back toward Jem. 'Well he's got one hell of a story but I'll tell you this before I leave – there are no circumstances in the world that could have forced me to treat you the way that he did.'

'Oh no?' Jem finally found her voice, but it sounded uncertain. 'Then what do you call Kate Parker?'

Matthew looked incredulous, ready to defend himself, then, thinking better of it, he shook his head, 'You know what? Think what you like. That's what you always do anyway.'

Jem seemed intent on keeping Matthew in the room, 'So, what should I think about finding this in your things?' She pulled the sonogram from her desk and thrust it in front of him, with fierce triumph.

Matthew looked at her with hollow eyes, all the fight having left him. 'You should think that the man who loved you thought you might once have been carrying his child.' He looked from Jem to Nick and shook his head again. 'You chose badly once. You're free to do it again. You're both clearly incapable of real love and you might just deserve each other.' He closed the door gently on his way out.

*

Jem thought she would much rather he had slammed it.

The finality of Matthew's icy words hung in the room. She wanted to run after him, to tell him he was wrong, she *was* capable of love. But all the things she'd learned about him that day kept her rooted to the spot. Instead she turned to face the man who stood before her. This tall, dark haunted version of the fiancé that she'd last seen stepping onto a train twelve years ago. This older, more mature man, even more devastating than his younger self.

The corners of his mouth curved almost imperceptibly and a warm glint flickered briefly in his dark eyes. It was like watching a fleeting echo of the old Nick dance across his features – that devilish quality she had always found so irresistible.

A single thought began to float above the jumbled sea of all the others, demanding to be heard. Nick was back. Nick was *here*. He was back – and he wanted her. She felt the potency of it.

The fact was, Helena had been right; Jem *had* fantasised about this very scene. This moment of reckoning when the tables would be turned and Nick's future would lay in her hands. But even though she'd played it out in her head a hundred times or more, she realised now she'd never nailed her part. Nick was here, he was apologising, he was begging her forgiveness. What should she do? Just like in the fantasy, the only thing she was sure of was her anger.

Jem looked at Nick coldly. 'I think you should follow your old friend's lead don't you?' she said, opening the door.

But Nick wasn't going anywhere.

Matthew

An hour later Matthew was clutching one end of a string of fairy lights whilst Kate Parker held the other. Pacing back and forth as Kate tried to arrange the bulbs into an even garland around the Christmas tree, he knew he was not helping her quest for symmetry. She threw her hands up in surrender and told him she was going to pour them both a very large glass of mulled wine. The lights could wait.

Matthew hadn't been able to stop ranting since arriving at Kate's. He realised it wasn't much fun for her, but he was so full of pent up indignation, he badly needed to let rip with the only person in the village left to offer him a sympathetic ear. Now, the energy was gradually draining out of him, like a clockwork toy on its final revolution – one glass of mulled wine and he would more than likely collapse. He accepted the offer regardless.

Just as Kate headed into the kitchen, his phone vibrated and he was irritated to see Gerry's name flash up on the screen. He knew that he should wait until he felt calmer before he spoke to the man but to hell with what he should and shouldn't do. He answered curtly, 'Gerry.'

Gerry's oily voice sounded jovial for a change. 'Well, hello there Matt, I'm just calling to thank you for your final report. It was just what I was looking for, very *thorough*.' He lingered on the word, pronouncing it 'thurrow' which incensed Matthew even further. 'Thank you for a solid piece of analysis,' he finished.

'You're right Gerry. It was a solid piece of analysis. It's a shame you only published a fabricated version of it.'

'Well that an interesting take Matthew.'

'It's the only take there is Gerry. The email you sent out today, completely ignores my final recommendations. Selling off the resort is one of a whole suite of options. And as, you well know, it's not the path I recommend. It might look good on this year's balance sheet, but it doesn't make long term financial sense for Monroe Holdings.' Matthew played his final ace, 'Not to mention what it could mean for *your own* credibility in future corporate negotiations.'

Gerry's hoarse laughter came down the line. 'Well, you've got balls I'll give you that much. But I think you're forgetting a few things. Like who you're dealing with for starters. I operate on a global business stage Matt – and nothing – certainly not *this* little sideshow of a deal is gonna change that. The second thing that seems to have slipped your mind is that I'm the owner of the resort and I can do what the hell I like.'

Matthew wanted to call Gerry an imperious prick, instead he said,

'Except you're not are you? The person who owns the resort? You father is. What does Frank have to say about all this I wonder?'

Gerry sighed audibly and Matthew knew the tactic was designed to convey the gargantuan gap between the two of them. 'Not that it's really any of your business Matt, but I have my father's full authority to act as I see fit across all operations. I hardly need point out to you that this type of low level deal is not something that someone in my position would usually involve themselves in. I have taken a personal interest in this project simply because the town is so close to my father's heart and he wants to ensure our exit is handled sensitively-'

'Good God,' Matthew interjected scathingly, all pretence at civility abandoned. 'I've heard some bullshit in my time but this is beyond belief. Now, I don't care what crap you want to peddle to the people you're looking to sell this place to, but I do object to you butchering *my* work to make it look like *I* was the one to recommend the sell off. I thought I was here to produce a work of fact not some fiction you've cooked up to suit your own questionable decisions.'

'These are some very wild accusations Matt.' Gerry sounded amused. 'I wonder that you've been in business so long. You're exhibiting all the naivety of a college graduate. Although, perhaps I shouldn't be surprised at that, given the way you dress.'

Matthew knew better than to rise to such a low blow but the response was out before he could check it. 'If the way I present myself is such a problem for you Gerry, I'm surprised you hired me in the first place.'

'Well,' Gerry's tone suggested that Matthew had played right into his hands, 'I'll leave you with that little conundrum shall I?' There was a long pause before the line went dead.

Kate who had been hovering outside the room whilst Matthew took the call, now came in to find him staring curiously at his phone.

'I take it Gerry doesn't have any intention of letting everyone know what you really recommended.' Kate filled a punch glass with mulled wine and handed it to him.

'No,' Matthew said hesitantly, still thinking about Gerry's words. 'But it's not that.' He frowned. 'Gerry said something about leaving me to work out why he hired me in the first place.'

Kate took a sip of the mulled wine, grimacing slightly at the concoction. 'Well you've said before that it was a bit of a coincidence-' Kate stopped mid sentence as if something had just occurred to her. She narrowed her eyes.

'What?' asked Matthew.

'I didn't put it together at the time, but today I overheard one of the girls from The Barnacle talking about something…'

Matthew, who couldn't think where this was going, raised his eyebrows questioningly.

Kate continued, 'It might be nothing.' She shook her head. 'There's a girl called Sherry – real piece of work – she didn't realise I was in the waiting room and I heard her confiding in one of the other girls. She was boasting that Gerry had taken to calling her. He was particularly keen to know about the movements of one particular woman in the town. I didn't hear who she was talking about and I dismissed her as a bit of a show off at the time, but… could it have been Jem do you think?'

'What else did she say?'

'I only heard snippets, but the gist was that Gerry had approached this woman once too often earlier on this year and the boyfriend had had to step in.' Kate's hand went to her mouth. 'Oh God I remember now – she referred to the boyfriend as 'Bear Grylls'. I bet she was talking about Finn.'

Matthew's jaw started to pulse. He put his glass down on the kitchen island and started pacing again, suddenly he got it. 'Christ,' he said, shaking his head and feeling incredibly stupid. 'No wonder he called me naïve. It all makes sense! Gerry's motivation for this is not *business*. It's personal. I *knew* it wasn't natural for someone at his level to be so personally involved. This is a vendetta against Jem and Finn.' Matthew started to piece things together. 'Jem said he was a 'creep' but she never went into detail. He must have come on to her and Finn must have warned him off… bruised his ego. A bit of background research on Jem would have thrown up her past and, of course, hiring *me* was the perfect way to get to *both* of them. That bastard set me up…. I have to do something…I have to tell Jem.'

Kate put a steadying hand on Matthew's arm but he continued to pace, to think…

'Matthew, …Matthew, stop!' Kate had to shout to get his attention. 'You're reaching. You don't know for definite that any of this is true.'

'But it all makes sense, don't you agree?'

'I do, but..' she squeezed his arm, 'let's just take it down a notch. Think it through. Don't you think you've suffered enough for one day?' she asked gently. Suddenly Matthew saw himself from Kate's perspective and he let his hand drop to the counter in a gesture of defeat.

Kate sighed. 'Look, I'm not saying that you should do nothing but you just don't have to do anything right now that's all. It's been a *massive* day for you, on both the personal and professional front. You need some rest, some food… a shower…' A smile played around her lips. 'Because to be honest you do stink a bit.'

Out of nowhere Matthew laughed and she was so relieved to see his blue eyes crinkle and his mouth widen into a smile. He put his head in his hands and leant back against the worktop. 'Arghhh…. I'm so sorry Kate.' It was a cross between a laugh and a wail. 'I've turned up at your door, ranting like a raving lunatic. I haven't once bothered to ask about your situation with work or your plans for the villa, I've just offloaded all my drama without considering all the shit you're dealing with too.'

'Well there's time for all my drama don't you worry.' She rubbed his shoulder in solidarity. '*Plus* I do have some ideas on where we might go from here. But first, you have to jump in the shower and freshen up whilst I rustle us up some pasta and,' she waggled the glass of mulled wine and grimaced, 'swap this shit for a proper drink.'

Matthew laughed, looking into the punch glass. 'Yeah, it's bloody vile, what's it made from?'

'Gerry Monroe's scruples?'

'Ahh so that's where they went…' Matthew threw it down the sink before grabbing one of the suitcases he had brought in earlier and heading off in the direction of the shower.

Jem

Bear was chasing rabbits in his sleep. His paws twitched and he made tiny yelping noises as if he were dreaming of his younger years, bounding through the forest, his nose mere inches away from a white bobbly tail. It was a sight that always made Jem smile, but tonight even this couldn't raise her spirits.

Earlier she had returned home, completely shattered, and slowly walked through the house completing her usual routine. Turning lamps on, lighting the wood burner in the lounge, feeding Bear. Pouring herself a large glass of Merlot, she had eventually plonked herself down at the kitchen table, turned on a Radio Four programme and immediately tuned out of whatever the presenter was saying.

Bear, living up to his Labrador credentials, had finished his bowl of food in around thirty seconds flat but instead of going to lie down on his bed as normal he first came and rested his chin on Jem's lap and wagged his tail slowly whilst looking up at her adoringly in an effort to bring his human some cheer.

'You know me better than anyone don't you?' She scratched him just below the ear and in raptures, he closed his eyes and titled his head, pressing it into her hand until, satisfied that she must be feeling better, he wandered over to the Aga where he could collapse and snooze off his tea. And now Jem was watching him chase rabbits in his dream whilst asking herself, *What the hell happened today?*

Over the years she had played out the scene of Nick's return so many times in her head. He would appear at her door, looking terrible, regretful, citing some kind of panic induced moment of madness that had caused him to run. And in some ways that's exactly what had happened. But in all her wildest dreams she could never have conjured the story he told her today.

When he'd first walked into the café she'd been overwhelmed by the visceral reactions he still had the power to set racing within her. For a long time he'd been just a figure of her imagination, a character in the melodrama of her twenties; someone she had loved absolutely, but had come to despise. She hadn't expected to feel the tug of attraction, the flicker of something she thought his callous actions had long since extinguished. Not that she'd revealed any such feelings to him; but they were there all the same.

She'd forgotten things about him. The qualities she was always unable to resist. His voice for starters; those beautiful, well-bred tones that were irrevocably bound to the first memory she had of him, when she was regaining consciousness on the day they first met. His voice had been the force that brought her round after the fall and she'd never had been able to resist it after that; that was how he'd been able to persuade her to do almost anything, always getting his own way.

Six years of loving him, trusting him, thinking he was the one – the man in her corner. It had all come rushing back. What it felt like *to believe in him*. And some mad, destructive part of her wanted to believe in him again. Even as her head told her otherwise, her heart whispered *what if…?* And although she had acted as she should and sent him away with a very large flea in his ear, she wanted to slap the part of herself that was awakened by him, no matter how small and well hidden it was.

But all of that had nothing on the one image from today that would haunt her for the rest of her life; Matthew's face as he'd walked out of her office. The hurt in his eyes, the disbelief, the injustice – it had all been there. Had she got this very badly wrong where Matthew was concerned?

A knock at the back door interrupted her thoughts and she switched off the radio then hurried to open it.

'Oh. Helena, it's you.'

'Yes it is.' Helena, bustled past her clutching two bottles of wine and a bulging shopping basket. 'But that note in your voice suggests you were rather hoping it was someone else.'

'Definitely not! I've never been so relieved to see anyone in my whole life.' She greeted her friend with the tightest hug. 'But part of me wondered if it might be Matthew.' Jem bit down hard on her lip. 'It's over. And I'm glad of it, I am. But it ended in the most horrible way.' Helena gave Jem another large hug and the younger woman's lip wobbled. 'Don't be nice to me or I'll cry,' she whispered, dissolving into tears.

Once she was over the worst of the sobbing, Helena guided Jem to the table and poured them both a large glass of red. She laid out the olives, bread and hummus she had brought, saying in a motherly fashion, 'I'm guessing you've had nothing to eat. Get some of this down you and if you're still hungry at the end of it, I'll whip us both up an omelette.'

'Did you bring chocolate?' Jem asked through hiccupy tears.

Helena pulled out a box of Fortnum & Mason's pink champagne truffles. 'I brought in the big guns.'

Jem managed a watery smile. 'I love you'.

'You're just trying to get into my truffles. Savoury first. Sweet later.'

'Spoilsport.'

'Now come on, get yourself a hunk of that bread – I bet you've had nothing to eat all day – and start talking. I want to know everything. The Pine Tree Bay bush telegraph has gone bonkers – not to mention the social media pages – but I want to hear it all from the horse's mouth.'

Jem filled Helena in on the whirlwind events of the day – from Finn's revelations about the report that morning, through to finding the sonogram, followed by Nick's sudden appearance in the middle of her argument with Kate – and of course the appearance of the photographers. As she relayed the details of her row with Matthew, a fresh bout of tears threatened but she managed to keep it together and give Helena a rundown of Nick's final, lengthy confession about what had happened twelve years ago.

Helena gave a low whistle and reached for the box of truffles. 'Blimey! I take it all back. Darling, have as many as you like.'

'Thank you.' Jem ignoring the box of truffles, reached out to squeeze her friend's hand. 'Thanks for coming round and just making everything a bit more bearable.'

Helena squeezed back. 'We've been through some stuff together Jem.' Her eye went to the sonogram that Jem had pulled from her pocket when relaying the day's events. She took a large sip of wine and swallowed it quickly. 'And whilst there's clearly a lot to unpack in all this, in reality, it's just more 'stuff' and you'll come out the other side. You always do.' Helena paused. 'At least you have the answers now, to all the questions about Nick that have nagged away at you for the last twelve years.'

Jem pushed an olive around her plate. 'But I felt somehow, I don't know, *drawn to* him Helena.'

'Who? Nick?'

'Yeah, I felt an old stirring of attraction.'

'Honey, I saw the pictures on-line. You'd have to be dead not to. I'm only half joking when I say that I'm not the least bit surprised that this Zara woman went to the lengths she did to nail him. I can't believe you never told me how devastatingly handsome he was.' Helena fanned herself comically.

Jem laughed despite herself then with a puzzled expression. 'He was always handsome but…he seems to have become more so with age.' She shook her head as if trying to clear it of cobwebs, 'I'm annoyed at myself for thinking that way. After everything he's done to me, how can I be attracted to him? What does that say about me?'

'Oh Jem, it says he's an attractive man and you have a pulse – not to mention history – that's all. This attraction. Is it strong enough that you want to act on it?'

'I couldn't, not after everything that happened.' Jem sounded certain but a shadow of doubt crossed her face.

'Look, don't beat yourself up about it. Trust yourself. You'll make the right choices.'

'But that's just it.' Jem wailed in frustration. 'I can't trust myself Helena. I keep making the *wrong* choices.' She threw a screwed up napkin onto the table and dusted her hands off. 'I should have just stayed with Finn, it was so much easier.'

'But you said yourself you could never fall in love with Finn.'

'That's what made it easier.'

'Jem, you know as well as I do that nothing worth having is easy.'

'That's what Marcia used to say! And that's exactly the kind of thinking that has got me into this mess.' Jem took a large gulp of wine and reached for a cheese stuffed pepper.

Helena, guessing what was really behind Jem's outburst, waited a moment then said quietly, 'You know, for what it's worth, I don't subscribe to this version of Matthew that's being bandied about the town.'

The lump was rising in Jem's throat again and she swallowed hard. 'I wish I could say the same. But I've seen everything with my own eyes. The report on Finn's computer, the sonogram that he took from *my* things, he even admitted himself that he knew that Nick was seeing someone days before the wedding. Why did he never tell me about that? Why did he leave me wondering? I might have been able to handle things better if I could have put Nick's disappearance down to another woman. All these years I've wondered if it was a breakdown of some sort. If I had known there was someone else it might have given me some kind of closure.'

Helena nodded, 'Fair point. I can see that. But if I'm being honest, you're not always the easiest person to talk to Jem. Matthew may have felt he needed to tread carefully with you. You're very easily spooked you know.'

'What's that supposed to mean?' Jem asked crabbily.

'It means that as soon as discussions stray into uncomfortable territory, you have a habit of closing down.'

Jem was quiet for a moment as she processed this. She decided to confess something to Helena. 'On the beach, when we went kiteboarding that day, Matthew told me he'd been in love with me since the first day we met.'

'Well there you go then,' said Helena as if this settled everything.

Jem's bottom lip wobbled again. 'I believed him. But now I'm not so sure. It could all have been a line. To get my trust. To distract me from what he was really here to do.'

'You don't really believe that.' Helena sounded incredulous.

'I don't know what to believe...' Jem hiccuped and her eyes swam with tears. 'You should have seen him today Helena. I've never seen him so angry.'

'Jem, if you loved someone, I mean completely, *all in,* loved the bones of them, and they didn't believe in you, wouldn't you be angry?'

'Even if that's true it's too late.'

The dam had burst and Jem was struggling to speak as she recalled Matthew's final moments in her office. 'He was so c.. cold towards me. Either he's a really great actor or he's telling the truth about his role in the sell off. But then, how could he be? I've seen the report with my own eyes? And yes, perhaps I am willing to concede that the rumours about him and Kate are just that, but there's *something* there. He's shared more with Kate these past weeks than he has with me. What message do I take from that? That in his eyes I'm just some lightweight who doesn't understand the serious stuff?'

Helena pursed her lips as if considering this but said nothing.

'I can't equate the man I've been falling in love with these last few weeks with the things he's done. I just don't understand any of it.'

'So what's stopping you going to talk to him now?' Helena asked gently.

Jem shook her head slowly as another wave of tears hit. 'We can't come back from today Helena. The things that were said… It was too awful. Matthew said he's done with me, that I'm incapable of love.'

Helena sighed and shook her head sadly. 'Look, Matthew was clearly speaking out of anger today. If you're this upset about it, it's not worth throwing everything away without first trying to get some clarity. Why don't you just go to him? Tell him things got out of hand – it's hardly surprising given everything that happened – ask him for his side of the story?'

Jem drained her glass. 'Believe me, if you had seen the way he looked at me, heard the things he said,' she shook her head, 'you'd know that it's over for him as certainly as I do. Besides, before I go speaking to anyone I've got some things to consider.' Jem paused and then said quietly, 'Nick asked me if now, knowing everything, would I consider giving him another shot.'

Internally Helena winced but she tried not to show her true feelings to her friend. She took a deep breath, 'Jem, this all boils down to one thing. Who is it you're in love with? Is it Matthew or is it Nick?'

'I don't know,' Jem whispered.

Helena wanted to shake her. She couldn't contain her opinion any longer, but she tried to speak gently, 'Are you seriously thinking about throwing aside what you have with Matthew for a man who ran out on you, *on your wedding day*, twelve years ago?'

'Well that's sort of the point isn't it? What do I actually *have* with Matthew? Is there even anything to 'throw away' ? I don't know what's real and what's…' she tailed off. 'And anyway,' Jem reached for the bottle of Merlot, 'even if I did want to go speak to him, he's probably half way down the M6 by now.'

Helena shifted in her seat but remained silent.

'He's not half way down the M6?' It was a question but Jem's tone remained flat.

Helena made a face. 'Jem you may not want to hear this'.

She paused with the wine bottle in mid-air. 'Don't tell me, he's with Kate Parker?'

Helena nodded reluctantly, 'Well, at least that's where his camper was parked when I drove past on the way here.'

Jem stiffened. 'Well then I guess I have my answer.' She emptied the contents of the bottle into her glass.

CHAPTER SEVENTEEN
29th November

Matthew

'You ready to do this?' Kate asked the next morning as she and Matthew walked along the sea front to the The Barnacle Hotel.

'No. But we're doing it anyway.' Matthew walked briskly with his hands in his pocket and his face partially buried in the woollen scarf that was wrapped around his neck.

The special festive touches which had been added throughout the town were all around them as they hurried along the shore. Every street lamp had been decked with a hand made Christmas wreath of sweet smelling eucalyptus, holly and fir and large red and white spotted bows. Old fashioned filament light bulbs had been strung between each lamp and the front porch rails of the harbour facing buildings were decked with garlands of ivy.

Yes, the town was certainly brimming with Christmas cheer, but Matthew refused to notice any of it. He wasn't looking forward to what he and Kate were about to do, but it was necessary, to draw a line under everything, before he left Pine Tree for good.

The town hadn't yet fully woken up and the sound of their heavy footsteps on the fallen snow was like a muffled drum intruding on the heavy silence. As they traipsed through the wintry scene, nebulous wisps of breath hung in their wake and somewhere, far out across the sea, the warning blare of a distant foghorn cut through the early morning mist. Kate pulled her woolly hat firmly down over her ears as they approached the hotel and instructed Matthew to hang back for a moment. She stood on her tiptoes to peek through the bay fronted window then ran back over to Matthew. 'We're in luck, she's on breakfast duty.'

'What's her name again?'

'Sherry,' said Kate turning from the window. 'Blimey she must run to three jobs. They work hard in this town.'

'Yeah, just as well it's full of generous tourists and the tips are good,' muttered Matthew.

Kate turned to face him. 'Now, are you absolutely sure you want to do this?'

Matthew nodded, the set of his jaw was firm. 'One hundred percent.'

'Well stop looking so bloody miserable then.'

And despite the dead weight that was lodged in his chest, he genuinely laughed as they walked through the door together.

Isla

'I'm telling you - they both walked in as bold as brass, laughing their heads off and then... Well, they were *all over* each other!'

As soon as Sherry Crombie had finished her shift at The Barnacle Hotel she'd hurried along to the cafe with as much speed as the icy conditions would allow her six inch heels to muster. It would have been a terrible thing indeed for her to break her neck before imparting the hottest gossip to hit Pine Tree in several years. She now stood at the counter, breathless, relaying a blow-by-blow account of Kate and Matthew's breakfast shenanigans.

Isla, knowing that Sherry was prone to exaggeration and painfully aware that Jem was in the kitchen area just behind her, cautioned Sherry, just for once, not to embellish the truth.

'What do you mean they were 'all over each other'? Were they even kissing?' Isla asked irritably.

'Not exactly. But they looked like they were about to. Or like they had been doing much more all night!' Sherry said with something that resembled a cross between a leer and a jeer.

'What exactly *were* they doing then?' Isla asked, clearly exasperated. She needed facts. More to the point Jem, stood not ten paces behind her and likely catching every word of this, needed facts.

'Well,' Sherry pouted, looking slightly chastened and clearly put out because Isla had never been so insistent on *facts* before. 'For starters they were holding hands across the table. And they let go really quickly when they saw me coming with their food, like they were trying to hide the fact that they were together, as a couple I mean.'

'Ok, and apart from them holding hands briefly, what else?' asked Isla, praying that there wouldn't actually be anything else.

'Well, she asked him if he really had to go back to London today, couldn't they have a few more days *together*? And then *he* said there was nothing to keep him here any longer – *except for Kate perhaps*.' Sherry's eyes were growing wider with every revelation. 'Then she said "OK then *I'll* come with you" all dreamy like, and he said "No you've paid your rent on the cottage-"'

'OK, ok.' Isla held her hand up. 'I think we get the drift. Enough with the whole "he said, she said" routine!'

'Well, you said to be *precise*!' Sherry started to pout again. 'I don't know Isla Baxter, this is the last time I come to you with news hot off the press.'

'Oh stop sulking.' Isla berated her friend, but she softened the sting by smiling and patting Sherry's arm. 'Come on, just give us the gist ok? There'll be a queue a mile long in a minute and I won't be able to chat then.'

'Well the gist of it is. He's going back today, she would have liked a few more days together but he says he'll see her back in London *for Christmas*!'

'And they were holding hands across the table?' Isla, feeling despondent on Jem's behalf, finished for her.

'And they were holding hands across the table.' Sherry nodded in agreement. 'I have to say though. From what I heard, I don't think it's been going on for long. Although I did wonder why Kate Parker has been coming to the spa for treatments ever since she got here? I mean, who's she been making herself nice for if not this Matthew?'

'Some women get spa treatments just for themselves you know Sherry,' said Isla. Adding under her breath, 'Probably most of them in fact.' For most of the men in Pine Tree Bay, the only real criteria for choosing a woman was that she could cook and she had a pulse. Then Isla remembered to ask, 'What makes you say that you don't think it's been going on for long?'

Sherry cast her eyes to the ceiling as she recalled the exact conversation. 'As I was serving the people at the next table, Kate said that whatever happens they were friends *first* and she hoped this *new turn of events* wouldn't change that.'

'And what did he say?' Isla was all ears now.

'He said *nothing could ever change that* and then he smiled at her all gooey like. I'm telling you, they've totally done it. You don't look at someone like that if you haven't done it!'

Isla didn't even want to think how much of all this Jem might have heard from the kitchen. She knew what this town was like. Soon enough the talk would be that the notoriously frosty Jem had cooled it with Matthew and that he had rebounded straight into the arms of the very tasty blonde at Coastguard's. And that had to hurt. No matter what the truth of the matter was – the circulated version of events wouldn't bear much resemblance to it. She needed to get Sherry out of here and fast.

'Well just keep all this to yourself for now eh Sherry?' Isla inclined her head toward the kitchen and widened her eyes slightly.

'Oh aye of course I will.' Sherry nodded emphatically. But as she walked out the door she was already on the phone to one of the girls who worked at the spa, leaving Isla to wonder why she'd wasted her breath.

*

Behind Isla, hidden by the kitchen partition, Jem washed her hands and shouted over to Jamie that she was going to do some work in her study. But instead of going to her office she made her way to the store room, where she collected rubber gloves, bleach and a whole host of other cleaning paraphernalia. It was high time that life went back to normal around here and she would start by cleaning the garden flat. By the time she was finished it would all be just as if there had never been anyone there.

CHAPTER EIGHTEEN
30th November

Beryl

Beryl Clutterbuck generally took life as it came – when you were in the business of fate there wasn't much alternative - but today she had the very strong sense that something unpleasant was coming her way; and this had put her on her guard.

Beryl wasn't a woman to waste time trying to predict her own future. This was mainly because she was a shrewd business woman who saved her gift for paying clients. But she'd also learned, over the years, that there was little point; she rarely got premonitions of a personal nature. Only twice in her life had the cards given her an urgent message. The first time had been for Billy – and oh how she wished she'd paid attention to that one. The second of course was here in Pine Tree, for Jem – though she suspected there had been a bit of unfinished business from the other side that prompted that one. When it came to her own future however, she was stumbling around in the darkness just like everybody else.

Today however, something was different. She had woken that morning around six a.m. and immediately been filled with a sense of dread. She had lain in the darkness for a moment – listening to the waves roll on to the sand outside in perfect time with Billy's snoring – and taken a moment to examine the feeling.

First there was the physical sensation. A heavy weight in her chest and the impression that her stomach had somehow plummeted a few inches over night. Then there was the niggling at the back of her mind, a sense that she was standing in a supermarket trying to recall the list of groceries she had left at home. It was the same sensation that, during a reading, told her there was something she was missing in the cards. Was it telling her that there was something she wasn't seeing now, in her own life?

She had mentally run through her current situation and the people in her life. Somehow, if she landed on the right person or scenario in her head, she might receive a sign as to where she needed to focus her attention.

Beryl had met many many people over the years. She was part of a scattered community that travelled the world and kept in touch by whatever means they each had the technical nouse (*and* wifi access) to communicate through. None of these people were what Beryl would call *close*. They were off grid converts, like her, who had chosen the carefree nomadic life of the road. And whilst she knew that she could call on them, at any time, safe in the knowledge they would hitch up whatever they were currently calling home and come to her aid if she needed them, they were essentially bound by the pact of the rover and not much else. Besides, this tough group were all, by the very nature of their chosen lifestyle, as hard as the granite rock that sat out there in the harbour; it was very unlikely that this current sense of foreboding involved a warning for any of *them*.

So she turned her thoughts closer to home. Her *current* home. And her thoughts went straight to Jem. As soon as that lass had stepped into her motorhome for a reading, back at the beginning of October, Beryl had instinctively realised that Jem was on the brink of something. She'd conducted thousands of readings in her time but it was only in about ten percent of cases that she experienced what she had come to refer to as *the chills*.

It was a sensation that started out as an icy trickle in her veins but one which culminated in a painful tingling in her fingers and toes which felt what she could only imagine was akin to frostbite. This was the reason why Beryl had had to bring Jem's reading to such an abrupt close – because in these instances the sensation became unbearable. But this current sense of foreboding was not related to Jem. If it was, it would have started yesterday, when Matthew left town.

Beryl knew in her heart Matthew was a good man. You didn't need to be psychic to see that. When he had stopped in to say goodbye to Billy and Beryl yesterday morning he'd had dark circles under his eyes and sunken cheeks. And no matter that the gossip throughout Pine Tree might be – Beryl knew it wasn't from a night spent frolicking with that Kate Parker lass. The pain that had radiated invisibly from his soul to hers, told her all she needed to know.

Of course Beryl had sought Jem out. After Matthew had said his goodbyes, she had bundled herself into her coat, hat and scarf and made her way along the shore to the Small House Book & Brew. She'd found her friend, not in the cafe but in the garden flat, on her hands and knees, scrubbing as if her life depended on it. When she placed a gentle hand on Jem's shoulder the younger woman had nearly jumped out of her skin.

'Beryl! You gave me such a fright!' she had clutched her hand to her heart but she didn't laugh in the way that Beryl might have come to expect.

'Ooh I *am* sorry love.' Beryl said jovially. 'I thought you heard me come in.'

Jem rose up to her knees but she didn't stand. Beryl sensed she was keen to resume her vigorous cleaning binge and had no mind to engage in idle chit chat, but she pressed on nevertheless.

'Look have you got five minutes?'

Jem looked reluctant. She held up the scrubbing brush that she'd been using to pummel the already spotless floors. 'I'm a bit snowed under as you can see. Can it wait?'

Beryl pursed her lips, she could see she would need to wade straight in. 'I saw Matthew this morning. He came to say goodbye – to Billy and me.'

Jem's back stiffened and she rose to her feet. Her mouth became a thin grey line. 'Well that was nice of him but it's nothing to do with me anymore.' She said, not quite meeting Beryl's eye.

'I know it's not any of my business lovey, but I wouldn't feel right if I didn't say something.' Jem remained head down and silent, tapping her foot impatiently, so Beryl decided she'd best just get on with it. 'If you've finished things with Matthew because this Nick fellah is back on the scene… All as I'll say is… I think you're making a very big mistake.'

'You're right,' Jem said. 'It *is* none of your business.'

Beryl had been thrown at first, by the sharp delivery, but she could make allowances. Matthew was not the only one in pain. She tried again, 'I'm just saying Jem, that all my *senses* are urging me to remind you-'

'Beryl!' Jem cut the old woman off abruptly. 'Please don't say you're about to remind me about *what the cards said* because if you do I might just scream. To be completely honest I am up to here with what your *senses* might or might not be telling you. This isn't some bit of *fun* for the festival.' Jem, swiped a stray curl from her eyes and shook her head irritably. 'This is my *life*. My *real* life. Matthew is *not* the knight in shining armour you want him to be and no amount of tarot cards or spirit guides or *senses* you might have are going to convince me of that!' Jem's shrill voice bounced off the walls in the vaulted studio.

Beryl said nothing for a moment. She had come to think of Jem as a friend over the last few months and though she understood the younger woman was reeling, she couldn't help but feel hurt by the scathing tone with which this had all been delivered.

She gave it one last shot. 'But I wouldn't be doing right by you if I didn't remind you of the *warning* in your reading,' she said plaintively. 'Remember the Five of-.'

'Beryl! Have you not listened to a word I've said? Jem leaned forward and pointed to her mouth. Read. My. Lips. I don't *believe* any of it. I'm sorry, I really am, but I think it's all just… Nonsense… Bull… Baloney… You said so yourself remember – right at the beginning you said that I didn't believe a word of it? Well, guess what? You were right and what's happened in the last two months has certainly done nothing to change that. Quite the opposite in fact!'

The older woman inhaled sharply. 'I can see I was wrong to come love,' she said quietly and made her way to the door. 'I'll leave you to your cleaning now.' And she'd taken herself back along the shore, feeling more than a little shaken by the younger woman's words. Billy, waiting in the motorhome, had tried to calm her with a brew and, taking the cup and saucer from him she'd said, 'See, the thing is Billy, she doesn't remember the Five of Pentacles'.

Billy swallowed a large gulp of scalding tea. 'Eh?' He looked at Beryl as if she was speaking Swahili.

'In Jem's reading. When she first came to see me. There was a warning card. The Five of Pentacles. It warns against turning your back on warmth, safety, security – not seeing your salvation when it's right in front of you – but she's forgotten it.' Beryl shook her head sadly.

'Well, that's as may be Beryl, but you know as well as I do, if the lass doesn't want to listen there's nowt nobody can do about it.'

Now, as she thought back over the last twenty four hours, Beryl realised that Billy was right. She was just going to have to leave well alone where Jemima Small was concerned. But none of that answered the question that was still going round in her head; why had she woken up with this feeling of dread? What was coming at her that she couldn't see?

Then she had a brainwave. Reaching for an old pack of Lapsang Souchong that had been languishing at the back of her cupboard, Beryl decided she was going to do what her mother would have done; consult the tea-leaves.

She brewed up the pot and left it to steep for a few minutes. Then, pouring herself a small cup she sipped slowly and mindfully thinking all the while of the question she wanted to ask. When the cup was almost empty, leaving only a small amount of liquid in the bottom, she swirled what was left in it three times clockwise, touched the edge of the cup with the saucer, closed her eyes briefly to make a wish, then immediately inverted the cup above the saucer.

Before she could turn the cup upright and examine its contents, however, Billy burst back through the door. 'Chuffin Nora! It's a bit parky out there this morning!' he said carrying a bottle of milk and waving a white envelope at Beryl.

'What's that?' she asked suspiciously. One of the major benefits of living on the road was that the admin overhead was low; Beryl was frightened of anything resembling post.

'Some hoity-toity lass came into the shop and asked me to give it to you. Passed it to me from the outer reaches of her extended arm as if I was going to give her a disease she did.' He imitated the woman's accent, '"Would you mind awfully passing this on to Beryl for me?"'

'"And who shall I say sent it?" says I.'

'"You'll see when you open it," she says all posh like.'

Beryl suddenly realised who Billy was talking about it. 'Madeleine Beaver,' she said slowly turning the envelope over in her hands.

'Sounds about right. Anyway shall we open it and see what it's about?' Billy rubbed his hands together to warm himself up.

Beryl knew that anything Madeleine Beaver wanted to say in writing could not be good but she did as she was asked. She was startled to see however that the letter was not *from* Madeleine but from Gerry Monroe. The letter requested that she and 'her guest' attend a discussion being held at the community centre that afternoon about the future of motorhomes in Pine Tree Bay. The way the letter was worded suggested that Gerry was interested in considering the ways in which motorhomes could be further accommodated in the resort and wanted the community council to use Beryl as a case study.

'Well that sounds all right eh love?' Billy said cheerily. 'Bound to be a cuppa and a few biccies in it for us I should think.' Then he pulled a tin of Heinz tomato soup out of each pocket. 'What do you say to an early lunch?'

'Aye sounds good love,' she nodded distractedly, still looking at the letter. Without thinking she turned the teacup upright and took a peek inside.

Beryl felt a shiver run down her spine as the clear outline of a cloud and a snake stared up at her from the bottom of the cup.

Finn

Finn turned the key on his shop front door in a counter clockwise motion and without bothering to check that it was locked, he sprinted down the road as fast as the heavy Timberland boots he was wearing would allow.

He'd just received a text from Rab. Madeleine had called an urgent community council meeting on Gerry's behalf, something about camper vans and motorhomes in Pine Tree Bay. Finn hadn't thought it was worth closing the shop to attend. Thankfully however, Rab had smelled a rat and, leaving his team to look after The Smugglers, had come to see what Madeleine was up to. Shortly after he'd sent Finn a text.

Kangaroo court in session! Get yourself here now!!!

Just as Finn rounded the corner he collided with someone – a woman – and sent her sprawling backwards on to the floor. All he caught sight of was a long blonde pony tail and a pair of walking boots.

'Kate! I am so so sorry…' he said helping her up and, in the midst of this current crisis, totally forgetting to be cool with her. A winded Kate got to her feet and looked as if she were about to tell him to watch where he was going next time but Finn wasn't hanging about.

Quickly looking her up and down he said, 'Looks like you'll live. Sorry I've got to run, Beryl's up against some kind of lynch mob at the community centre,' then sprinted off. Out of breath he finally reached the building and pushed on the swing door. Madeleine Beaver's imperious voice boomed out from the hall and down the corridor to greet him.

'It is the right of this town to be made aware of the unsavoury characters in our midst.' Madeleine's voice boomed out around the hall. She sounded like Margaret Thatcher on steroids. 'If only to protect the vulnerable amongst us. This is a community of *families*. Think of the *children*. Think of the *elderly*! It is our duty to safeguard those who look to us for protection.'

As Finn pushed his way through the large crowd – a few of the council appointees but mainly members of the public who Madeleine had no doubt drummed up for this horrendous spectacle – he could have cried. Sitting at a table which had been placed centre stage on the raised platform of the community hall, a terrified Beryl – all dressed up for the occasion in her best woollen coat, lopsided hair and bright red lipstick – was trembling in fear; her huge eyes widening with every word that emerged from Madeleine's mouth.

Finn had only met Billy a couple of times but on each occasion the elderly man had seemed like a gentle, affable character who clearly loved

Beryl to bits. Confusion and anger now clouded his big round rosy cheeked face which was becoming redder with every word that Madeleine spoke. Finn immediately strode to the front of the hall and was only just beaten to the stage by Rab who had climbed up onto the side of the platform where Madeleine stood at a lectern. In his sternest Scottish brogue Rab shouted, 'That is enough now Madeleine!'

'No! I will *not* be silenced on this matter Robert.'

Madeleine – drunk on power and completely forgetting that she was supposed to be making all this look like someone else's idea – grabbed the microphone possessively, like a child with a toy daring anyone to wrestle it from her grasp. She stalked to the other side of the stage. 'I warned you all – *all* the council members – of the danger of these *travelling types* but would anyone listen to me? No-o-o.' Madeleine squared her shoulders, now hopelessly lost inside her own performance and pointing her finger toward the crowd. 'The people of this town are entitled to know the dubious decisions that are made by the members of their council and that starts here, *today*!' She paused for a few seconds, to build the tension, then pointed theatrically at Billy. 'This man is a convicted murderer!'

A murmur of alarm went through the audience.

'Yes, yes that's right,' Madeleine nodded, spurred on by the consternation she was causing she now resumed prowling the stage. 'And this woman,' she pointed again at the terrified couple, 'is his accomplice!'

Finn could not allow this to go on – he leapt on the stage and summoned his most commanding tone. 'Now that is enough Madeleine! This is slanderous.' He addressed the crowd, 'Of course Billy here is not a convicted murderer-' he began but Billy silenced him by slowly rising to his feet.

'Actually I am,' he said simply, drawing himself up to his full height. 'To be accurate, I was convicted for manslaughter.'

Finn's mouth hung open in mid sentence as the older man walked over to where Madeleine was eyeing him as if he might pull a knife on her at any moment. She flinched as Billy raised his hand to gently take the microphone from her clutches. Billy then continued in his soft, yet frank, Yorkshire accent, 'Ladies and gentleman I have no pleasure in telling you that Mrs Beaver here is indeed correct.' He wore a grave expression and his voice was deep and full of emotion. 'Fifty years ago I killed a man and I went to prison for manslaughter.'

Nobody made a sound. Unlike Madeleine, Billy had the uncanny knack of being able to hold a crowd without any theatrics. He returned slowly to Beryl's side and took his time before speaking again. Beryl went to protest but he laid a hand gently on her trembling shoulder before continuing.

'On the night it happened, I saw Beryl here being viciously assaulted and, in defending her, I threw her attacker through a plate glass door... and I killed him. I didn't plan it. It wasn't intentional. But it happened.' He looked directly at the crowd remorseful but unashamed. 'And, in that moment I lost many years of my life.' The whole room was now completely in Billy's thrall, waiting for the next words to come out of his mouth. 'But I also saved the woman I loved – the woman I've *continued* to love for all my life – from being beaten to death. And that is why, ladies and gentlemen, I would do it all again in a heartbeat.' Billy turned to look at Beryl, a deep tender expression on his face as if they were the only two people in the room.

The hall was deathly quiet until, suddenly, a young woman's voice deep in the crowd broke the silence. 'Marry me Billy!' she shouted and the charming heckle broke the ice, causing a ripple of nervous laughter to break like a wave across the crowd.

Billy had the good grace to smile. 'Well, that's a very kind offer but I'm kind of hoping I'm promised to someone else.' When Beryl's face lit up and Billy bent down to plant a kiss on her forehead, people in the crowd started to shout.

'Sounds like they guy had it coming!'

'You've done your time Billy!'

'You should never've gone down by the sounds of it!'

Suddenly the room was alive with calls of support for the man who, only moments ago, they had all been convinced was about to murder them in their beds.

*

As Finn and Rab helped the older couple down from the stage and into a congratulatory crowd, nobody noticed Madeleine Beaver walk unsteadily toward the door. Not even Kate who was standing at the back of the hall where she had been ever since arriving moments after Finn. Now her eyes followed him as he gently shepherded Billy and Beryl around the crowd with a protective hand. And, as Kate watched, she realised with some degree of surprise, that she was finding it almost impossible to look anywhere else.

CHAPTER NINETEEN
9th December

Jem

During the weeks leading up to Christmas, news of Matthew's recommendation to sell off the resort was all anyone in Pine Tree could talk about. Finn had dutifully informed the members of the Pine Tree Bay Community Council what was ahead and of course the information had then filtered down through the rest of the town as quickly as water through a colander.

When Gerry subsequently confirmed he would be 'dropping in' to The Smugglers on Christmas Eve to make an important announcement, a collective groan went through the town. Everyone had been hoping to get through Christmas and into the New Year without having to face the juggernaut that was hurtling toward them.

It was now almost two weeks since Matthew had left Pine Tree and Jem was focusing firmly on community matters in a bid to put the last few months behind her. As much as Nick's presence in the town would allow at least. Despite zero encouragement from Jem, Nick had, decided to hang around in Pine Tree Bay and Jem was starting to wonder if she would ever get used to seeing him around the place.

The media coup that had erupted on the day that Nick first reappeared had fizzled out as fast as it had flared. The papers had tried to sensationalise the painter's identity into a big story. Dragging up the small news item which had made it into *The Metro* when he first disappeared, they had portrayed Nick as a struggling artist who had forsaken his 'one true love' to dedicate his life to art before finally realising he couldn't live without her (details of Zara and Sophia being conveniently glossed over).

But, once it was apparent that Jem wasn't going to play ball – wasn't going to agree to the interviews that the press wanted – the story had died. The newspapers wanted a fairy tale and Jem was never going to give them that.

Besides, Nick's work was little known in the UK. His painting mostly sold in South America and even there it wasn't as if he was a household name. So thanks to the niche demand for his work and Jem's refusal to provide the journalists with the happy ever after they wanted, the media interest faded. And Jem, and Pine Tree Bay, were spared any further press intrusion.

But in the couple of weeks since he'd shown up, Nick had taken to dropping into the café on a daily basis. Jem had finally had to admit to herself that keeping up a frosty front with him was both exhausting and unprofessional. She'd eventually settled for a breezy efficiency in his presence and asked Isla or Jamie that they serve him wherever possible.

Isla of course had managed to find out practically everything about Nick, bar his inside leg measurement. She had, naturally, relayed much of it to Jem – how inspired he claimed to be with the area; his plans to find both a house and studio to rent near Pine Tree for the foreseeable future. Jem had rolled her eyes but when both Isla and Jamie had remarked upon her calm acceptance of Nick into the community, she remained tight lipped. 'He can choose to live where he likes, makes no odds to me,' was all she should say publicly on the matter of Nick Townsend

In private she acknowledged that things were more complicated however. Firstly, there was the horrible truth that Matthew had decided to pursue a relationship with Kate. After days of telling anyone who asked that she couldn't care less and nights of crying herself to sleep, she had been forced to admit that it hurt like hell.

'I can't believe he would just take up with her so publicly like that,' she had ranted to Helena a few days after Matthew left town. 'The very *night* it ended between us. To think I fell for his bullshit. I should have listened to what everyone was telling me. I should never have trusted him.' She had paced around the White Pebble Gallery giving full vent to her anger whilst her friend looked on.

'To be fair Jem, that happened on the same evening you were considering taking Nick back,' Helena had pointed out evenly.

'That's never going to happen.'

'No?' Helena didn't sound convinced.

'No.' Jem was emphatic. 'My head was all over the place that first night. I was just thrown by the sight of him. I spent twelve years wondering where he was and then he shows up out of nowhere? It took me a day or two to realise I didn't want *him* – I just wanted to know what happened to him. Turns out Nick Townsend was not the great love of my life at all, he was just the great *mystery* of my life.'

'So who *is* the great love of your life?' Helena asked.

'Doesn't matter now does it?' Jem had mumbled before stomping out and heading back to the cafe. All she wanted was for life to go back to the way it was – *before*. Before the return of Matthew or Nick; before the Tarot reading that started it all.

And that was another thing; every time Jem thought about anything connected with Beryl, she was overcome with a deep sense of shame. After the community hall meeting, Finn and Rab had reported the whole sorry affair to Jem and Helena. Jem bitterly regretted that she hadn't been there to support her new friend. She flushed every time she remembered her last conversation with Beryl. There was no excuse for the horrid things she'd said. The moment she'd learned of the horrors that Madeleine had tried to inflict, she had dashed along the shore, but the space where Beryl's motorhome had sat for the last two months was empty.

Desperately hoping that Beryl and Billy had simply taken off for a spot of Christmas shopping, Jem looked out for her friends' return every day, but there had been no sign of the couple for almost ten days now. Madeleine had got her way after all. Beryl and Billy had driven off into the night and it looked like they wouldn't be coming back any time soon. For days after, all anyone had been able to talk of was Billy's heartfelt confession and all of the town regulars coming into Small House kept asking Jem if there was any news of her new friends. She felt like such a fraud.

As she moped around the cafe in the aftermath, Isla and Jamie had tried to cheer her up, pointing out that Beryl would understand that Jem had been out of sorts at the time of their last exchange. But Jem couldn't shake the sense that she had let the lovely old woman – who she had come to be so fond of – down very badly indeed.

Isla and Jamie were right on one score however; Jem *had* decided to accepted the new status quo where Nick was concerned. Not because she was unaffected by him – his appearance still physically jolted her whenever their paths crossed. Or because she forgave him – that would, quite simply, never happen. But because regaining her equilibrium was central to one thing; the continuing success of the seaside community she called home. In other words, she was saving whatever fight there was left in her for the coming battle with Gerry Monroe.

To this end, on a Monday in early December, Jem walked up the road towards Finn's shop. It was time to set the ball rolling on project Frank. Swearing Finn to secrecy, she told him the whole story of what she had found out from Joe Kintyre. When she had finished, Finn sat back in his chair with a mixture of astonishment and excitement at this new piece of information.

Despite the enormity of the situation, Jem laughed at Finn's expression. 'I know!' she said. 'It's huge. We need a direct audience with him. How can it be so hard to contact someone in this day and age?'

'Believe me I've tried,' said Finn. 'He's too closely managed for us to get to him directly and the few friendly contacts I have at his office are all under strict orders from Gerry that Frank is not to be disturbed by anyone.' Finn worried away at a paperclip as he spoke. 'I've even thought about putting something on social media to try and get his attention, but any bad publicity for the resort damages us all, possibly even more than what Gerry's got planned. I'm also guessing you'd like to discuss this new information privately with him first.' He gave her a wry smile.

'I don't want anyone in Pine Tree Bay knowing, not until I've cleared it with Frank. The thing is – Joe Kintyre says that Frank knows and that he *is* happy about it. That Marcia is the real reason he came back and built the resort. What I don't understand is – why the secrecy? If he's happy about me being his granddaughter why has he never wanted to let me know?'

'I can think of one *very good* reason,' Finn mused.

'Ok?'

'I think Frank is trying to protect you. If Gerry Monroe was to find out there was a rival for his inheritance of Frank's stake in a billion dollar global empire, who knows what kind of trouble he could cause for that person.'

'Jesus Finn, as if I'd be interested in any of that. I wouldn't know where to start.' Jem baulked at the notion.

'Doesn't matter. You still pose a threat. My guess is that Frank has plans for you, watertight ones that make sure *you're* provided for once he's gone.'

Jem looked doubtful. 'I couldn't handle some corporate millstone around my neck. I just want to run my own business, the one I have *now*, and pay my bills! Same as I have for the last ten years.' Jem took a deep breath and spoke more evenly, 'Besides, if all this is true, and I've no reason to believe it isn't, Frank Monroe is the only family I have left. I'm not ready for him to go *anywhere* before I've had chance to get to know him a bit better... and, well.... to hell with Gerry, I think maybe Frank would like to get to know me too.'

Finn nodded and looked thoughtful for a moment. 'You know, we *could* try force Gerry's hand. Tell him we'll go public even though *we* know we won't. Gerry might just be rattled enough to avoid a media storm and grant you an audience with the old man.'

Jem snorted. 'You know as well as I do it's much more likely to make him redouble his efforts. Plus without Frank's name on the birth certificate there's no actual proof, other than Joe Kintyre's testimony.

Finn frowned. 'Did you ask Joe to write his story down?'

'Finn!' Jem was shocked at the suggestion. 'Of course not! He told me the story honestly – and that Frank knew – that's all I was interested in.'

'Still, it might be an idea to ask him to document things – especially as he's the only person who knows the truth. If anything should happen to Frank there would be no way of proving things without written evidence.'

'If anything should happen to Frank there would be *no need* to prove anything. I'm not interested in the man's fortune Finn.' Jem shook her head, exasperated at the focus Finn was putting on the legacy angle.

'But it does give me an idea,' said Finn, seemingly oblivious to the irritation in her voice. 'If Frank and Joe Kintyre have this connection, maybe Joe could be our very own Trojan Horse.'

'How do you mean?'

'Gerry is going to be looking out for any contact that comes from *us* but it's unlikely that Joe Kintyre is on his radar. We could ask Joe to try and contact him.'

'It's worth a shot I guess.' Jem looked dubious but she grabbed her coat and followed Finn to the door. He flipped the sign to *Closed* as they headed out to Jem's car.

CHAPTER TWENTY
22nd December

Finn

But two weeks later, with Christmas Eve looming, and neither sight nor sound of Joe Kintyre within that time, Jem and Finn were forced to admit defeat.

When they had rushed over to Joe's house, there had been a faint glimmer of hope that he might be the key to getting a message to Frank but there was no sign of the man and and a few discreet enquiries around the town revealed that he was staying with his daughter in Norfolk – for the whole of December and January. Nobody they approached had a number for the daughter and anyway, how would they have explained what they needed to Joe's relatives. *'Oh we just need your father to write a coded message to Frank Monroe for us?'*

Ultimately they had had to accept that it was not going to be possible to put their plan into action. There had been slim chance of getting it to work anyway; word had reached them that Gerry was running a military tight operation where his father was concerned – it was impossible for anyone to get through.

On the final Sunday before Christmas, the old gang – Finn, Helena, Rab and Jem – had agreed to meet at The Smugglers to finalise arrangements for the Christmas Eve party in two day's time. Rab had already done much of the hard work, decking out the pub in a North Pole themed display. If Santa stopped off at The Smugglers for a swift half after his rounds on Christmas Eve, he might well think he'd taken a short cut home.

A huge sleigh that customers could reserve for the evening dominated the dining room area, complete with several similarly huge reindeer. Icicle fairy lights hung from the bar canopy and every glazed surface in the place had been covered with a drift of fake snow. Rab had even hired a special machine for the area behind the bar which kept up a steady stream of falling snow flakes. The novelty of this had worn off quickly once the staff all realised that whenever they opened their mouths they inhaled a flurry of white confetti. Rab's solution was to take their minds off it by insisting they all dress up as elves.

The residents of Pine Tree Bay, having just given thanks to God that the daily assault of 'Mwah-Ha-Ha-Ha' had ceased to blight their lives, were now rolling their eyes as an echoey 'HoHoHo' reverberated along the shore every hour of the day. Rab himself was doing a fine impression of the campest Santa the town had ever seen; the fancy dress shop had clearly offloaded a wig and a beard on to the unsuspecting landlord that was really part of a Bee Gees outfit. The locals all privately thought he looked like Diana Dors with a facial hair problem, but Rab himself seemed so pleased that none of them had the heart to put him straight.

Despite the pall that had been cast over the town by the impending announcement from Gerry Monroe, everyone was doing their best to remain upbeat and festive. Pine Tree Bay was hosting a record number of Christmas and New Year's visitors thanks to the winter marketing campaign and it was important that each one of them return home wildly enthusiastic about their holiday with intentions to return. As usual, the success of the town was the galvanising factor that ensured everyone made the effort to be positive in the face of what was likely to be some pretty devastating news.

As the gang sat together on the Sunday evening before the big day, Rab poured each of them a drink and fed a handful of meaty biscuits to an eagerly waiting Bear. They clinked their glasses together and wished each other a premature Merry Christmas as they always did at this, their private Christmas shindig before the mass celebrations started. This year was different though, the optimism was manufactured, and Finn had learned something the previous night that had left him with a heavy heart. Something about Jem, that Kate Parker had told him when she unexpectedly knocked on his door.

Contrary to what most people may have thought, Finn had not been in love with Jem. He had guarded against that from the off, but he was not too proud to admit that he *had* wanted to open himself up to that opportunity. He knew all too well that in this quiet part of the world it was hard to find someone you felt you could really go the distance with and when it seemed as if that chance had come along, well, there was no shame in wanting to grab it with both hands. All his instincts had told him to take it softly. There were points when he thought their relationship may have deepened – such as when Gerry Monroe had taken things too far with Jem and Finn had stepped in – but it hadn't, and he could see now that it never would have either.

For Jem, Finn had only ever been a friend with benefits and that was the long and the short of it. One glimpse of the way she looked at Matthew Albright had been enough to tell him everything he'd needed to know. What had finally confirmed it for him however, was Jem's reaction to Nick. Here was the man who had jilted her. The mysterious disappearing man who had loomed so large in Jem's personal folklore; of all the ways that Finn had imagined Jem might react to Nick's return, indifference had certainly not been on the list.

It had become abundantly clear over the past few weeks that Nick *hadn't* been the great love of Jem's life as they had all thought – that title had gone to his friend. Hell bent on self preservation as she was though, he doubted Jem had even admitted that much to herself. Perhaps even now. Whether she had or she hadn't, her obvious feelings for him were probably the reason that no one had even heard of Matthew Albright before the day he turned up in Pine Tree Bay. Finn could only guess at the inner turmoil the current rumours about Matthew and Kate must be causing her.

When Kate had knocked on Finn's door the previous evening, he couldn't for the life of him think why she might be coming to see him. She had asked to come in, sworn him to secrecy and given him the information that had the possibility to change all their lives. Now he had a choice to make, did he break Kate's confidence, tell Jem, and possibly put what was at stake for all of them at risk. Or did he keep Kate's information to himself and let Jem, believing what she did about Matthew, turn her back on the chance for happiness.

Jem's voice brought him back to the present. 'What?' she was asking him, with a quizzical look.

Finn laughed lightly. 'What do you mean *what?*'

'You're looking at me with a strange expression on your face.'

'I'm not,' Finn said, hurriedly recovering his features.

'You bloody well were!'

'I was just miles away that's all.'

She reached for her glass with a look that said she didn't believe him. Rab and Helena were deep in conversation about some artwork for an event Rab was running in the New Year.

'You know,' Jem said, a smile spreading across her face, 'the word on the street is that you're a bit of hero on the quiet.'

'Just a bit of one? I'm outraged.' Finn feigned indignation.

Jem giggled. 'I overheard Kate Parker telling Isla how you *rescued* Billy and Beryl at the meeting.'

Finn was puzzled. He hadn't thought Kate was even at the meeting. She hadn't mentioned it last night. 'Nah, Billy was more than able to stand up against the Mad Beaver without my help. He out-manoeuvred her with his superpowers of grace and humility. It was quite something to witness.'

'Powers we would all do well to develop.' Jem took a deep breath and continued more quietly, 'I don't think I showed much of either during these last few months. I never even bothered to tell you how sorry I was about the way things ended between us.'

Finn took a moment to respond. 'I think you're being a bit hard on yourself, there's never an easy way to end things.' He took a gulp of his pint, grimaced slightly as it went down. 'But hey, look at us now. Sitting and having a drink together, no irreparable damage done. That's a pretty good break up in my book.'

'You're being kind.'

'Well I'm a bit of hero like that.' He laughed.

Jem punched him playfully on the arm. 'I'm trying to be serious.

Thank you.'

'I'm the one who should be thanking you,' he said. 'I've done a lot of thinking and I realise I really do *want* a relationship.' He laughed to soften his next remark. 'One that's actually *going somewhere*. It was time for me to acknowledge that and move on.'

'Well, I'm sincerely glad to hear that.' Jem clinked her glass against his.

'What about you?' he asked. 'What's your next move in the game of love?'

'Ah, well I've also done a lot of thinking and in that particular game I am no longer at the table, in fact, I'm refusing to even enter the room.' She laughed.

Sensing it was too soon to mention Matthew, Finn asked, 'So what's the deal with Nick then? Hanging around in Pine Tree for so long?'

Jem's face clouded over as she pondered Finn's question. 'Honestly? Your guess is as good as mine.'

CHAPTER TWENTY-ONE
23rd December

Kate

The following morning at The Barnacle Spa pool, Kate was on her fiftieth length, cutting through the water with little effort. Having perfected her front crawl technique at a triathlon training camp three years earlier, she swam with speed, grace and poise – it was just a shame she'd had little chance to put any of it into practise. A few triathlon events two years back had been enough to make her realise that, in order to place amongst the fastest finishers, she would have to devote serious time to the training; something her work schedule couldn't accommodate.

Now as she swam just for the sheer joy of it, she wondered why she hadn't just competed all the same? Had it really been so necessary to be solely focused on the results? What about that early morning, nervous excitement of heading into the open water with the rest of the competitors? The mad scramble at transition with everyone wrestling out of their wetsuits and onto their bikes, not to mention the elation of crossing the finish line? Couldn't she just have enjoyed all that and simply be glad she'd competed?

She made a pact with herself there and then that, whatever the following year had in store, she would get back into the open water – and take to the road for long cycle rides – as soon as the weather allowed. She would also book a few triathlon events into the diary. Such positive action would help to invigorate her mind and body – not to mention shedding the few winter pounds she'd gained since coming to Pine Tree Bay.

If she bought the new house, it would be an ideal base for triathlon training. There were no end of lochs and safe sea coves in the county where open water swimming would be a joy. And there were so few cars on the roads around Dumfries and Galloway that cycling would be the safest she had ever known. After the carbon monoxide greenhouse of London, she would relish taking to the open, empty roads to breathe in the pure air and power up her legs before competing in summer events.

Mind you, if she *were* to set in motion her plan to run a bed and breakfast at the villa, summer triathlons might be something of a luxury. Running tourist accommodation was not a lifestyle that came with free weekends, quite the opposite. She needed to bear in mind that she would be tied to the place all year round – at least in the beginning until it started throwing off some cash and she could pay someone else to mind it for her.

Which brought her back to the reason she was banging out lengths in the first place; all the possible versions of life were competing for supremacy, because today was the day that she had to make her decision on Gerry's villa. She had made an offer on the property which had been accepted and today was the final turning point. The last moment that she could pull out of the agreement without financial penalty. Unless she stepped in and stopped the deal, the solicitors would 'exchange missives' as it was called in Scotland. Gerry had made it a stipulation of the deal that the exchange must occur *before* Christmas Eve – tomorrow.

Of course Kate knew why Gerry had made this stipulation. He was planning to make an announcement that would affect the market price of the house and he wanted to close the deal before Kate could get wind of any information that might force her to renegotiate. Kate's solicitor had done as she requested and kept her name out of the deal thus far, so Gerry was still in the dark about who he was selling to. To him she was just some London business woman looking for a bolthole.

The breakfast at The Barnacle Hotel two weeks ago had done its job. The entire town, or at least the people who kept abreast of such trivia, now believed that Matthew and Kate had become an item immediately before Matthew left. And that meant that Gerry Monroe believed that too.

It hadn't taken much deduction on Kate and Matthew's part to work out that Sherry Crombie, amongst others, was feeding information to Gerry, but they had been able to use this to their advantage. It was essential to their plan for Gerry to believe Matthew had moved on – away from Jem, with no further interest in the welfare of Pine Tree Bay. The rumours that were circulating about Matthew and Kate had certainly achieved that – you'd be hard pressed to find anyone in Pine Tree who had a good word to say about either of them.

And whilst she fervently hoped that that would all change over the next forty eight hours, there were still, as yet, no guarantees that it *would*. This left Kate in an impossible position. Did she take the risk of investing her life savings in a property on the edge of a small community where she was currently something of a pariah? Or did she pull out all together?

Kate had known it wouldn't be easy to stay in a town where many people were labouring under the false impression that she'd somehow played a role in their downfall. Or, at the very least cosied up to the man who had. But she'd had no doubt that she was tough enough to bear it, temporarily at least. And she *had* been. Right up until the day she saw Finn helping Beryl and Billy in the community centre.

Ever since that day, what Finn might think about her had suddenly started to matter. The misapprehension he was under had begun to gnaw away at her, until finally she couldn't bear it any longer. She decided to tell him the truth. To tell him the events that she and Matthew had set in motion. She had sworn Finn to secrecy and thankfully, he seemed to have understood that this was necessary. She knew she was putting everything that she and Matthew had worked toward in jeopardy. If their plan got back to Gerry, it would be dead in the water. But she knew instinctively that she could trust Finn, and the look she had seen in his eyes once she'd completed her story, had been totally worth the risk.

Unfortunately, however, the timing stank. Allocott Investments had requested a personal meeting with Kate *tomorrow* – on Christmas Eve of all days – to discuss the findings of the investigation into her alleged misconduct. They too wanted to 'close things out' before Christmas. But it wasn't going to be the one way conversation they were expecting, thanks to Idella.

Idella had given Kate enough information to make her own demands. Kate had also explicitly requested that Tom attend the meeting. After what Idella had uncovered she was going to enjoy turning the tables on the slimy bastard.

Kate finished her lengths and rested, breathless, with her head against the pool side. Today she had to decide about the house and tomorrow she had to decide about her job. Kate was holding all the cards and all she had to do now was decide precisely how to play them.

There was just one problem. Despite dedicating the last few months to figuring out what she wanted from life, with only hours to go – and no guarantees that the people of Pine Tree Bay would ever accept her – she still couldn't figure out exactly what that was.

Jem

Jem dried her hands on a tea-towel and reluctantly made her way from the kitchen into the back of the bookshop where Nick was tucked away in one of the coffee nooks. He'd sent word, through Isla that he would like a quick chat when it was convenient. Jem decided it was best to get it over and done with.

She slid into the booth and gave him the briefest of smiles, 'Nick.'

He cleared his throat as if preparing for a speech. 'Jem, I just wanted to let you know that I'm leaving for Gloucestershire today. I want to be near Sophia for Christmas so that we can spend some time together and I've managed to rent a cottage there for a couple of weeks. Zara has agreed that it would be good for Sophia to have me near, so hopefully that bodes well for future access arrangements.'

He smiled but there was something bleak about it. It suddenly occurred to Jem that Nick was going through his own personal trauma too. She had been so wrapped up in her quiet outrage at what he'd done to her, she hadn't stopped to think about what *he* had lost in all this. And so with a compassion that she would never have believed she was capable of, she reached her hand across the table and covered his. 'You'd do anything for your little girl wouldn't you?'

A strange mixture of relief at Jem's gesture, and pain at the thought of his daughter, flooded Nick's face. 'More than anything else in the world, being apart from her is killing me.' He bowed his head for a moment then suddenly raised his watery eyes to hers. 'I wanted to say I'm sorry about the baby too. Our baby.'

Jem withdrew her hand and sat up straight. Good God this was the last thing she wanted. Nick hadn't earned the right to share in that grief which, suddenly she felt strangely possessive of. 'Helena was with me at the time. She got me through it,' Jem said firmly, bringing the subject to a close.

Talk of Helena reminded Jem of a question that she had wanted to ask him and, desperate to change the subject, she latched on to it.

'Nick, why did you suddenly send me that postcard? Was it simply to mess with my head? Like the blog posts?'

Nick looked momentarily confused. 'Postcard?' He shook his head. 'I added the comments to your blog, like I told you the night I arrived, but I don't know anything about a postcard?'

Jem went to her office to retrieve the evidence and showed it to Nick.

Nick studied the painting on the front. 'This *is* my work,' he said. 'I suppose I became a bit obsessed with paintings of the cathedral for a while after. That and the *Surf Girl* series. Trying to atone through my work is what a good therapist would probably suggest.' He focused on the card in his hand. 'But I'm not sure how this came about? Perry, that's my agent, he's really careful about how he allows my work to be reproduced.' He turned the card over. 'This has no title or anything. It looks like a DIY job from an image on the internet to be honest.'

'Someone sent it to me anonymously,' said Jem. 'I just assumed that you must have found my blog and then sent the postcard to the cafe.'

'No, I've never seen it before. I only found your blog after Frank Monroe requested the commission.'

Now it was Jem's turn to look puzzled. 'Frank commissioned a painting from you?'

'That's how this all started. One of Frank's team contacted my agent. He was offering seriously big money for me to produce a piece for The White Pebble Gallery, but he wanted me to deliver it personally and do all the media around it. Perry said it was a big publicity stunt, you know, Frank would have the scoop on the anonymous painter.' Nick snorted cynically. 'Bet he's glad he didn't pay a hundred and fifty thousand for that non-event now!'

Jem took a moment. Her mind was racing.

'But Frank is ill. Too ill to deal with what's going on in the resort. Why would he suddenly commission a painting?'

Nick shrugged. 'Beats me. But he was prepared to offer a lot of cash for it.'

Jem chewed this information over in her mind for a moment.

'Look Jem,' Nick said, deciding this was his window. 'I realise now that coming back here was selfish, and yes there was a small part of me –' he held his hand up in admission, 'admittedly the fantastical part that doesn't really live in the real world – that thought you and I might have a shot at being together once I explained everything about Zara.'

Seeing that Jem was about to protest he rushed on, 'And I realise now that was pure folly, but will you please just do me this one thing? Will you let me say this once and for all. I came here, to Pine Tree Bay, to tell you that I am so utterly, completely and downright, from the bottom of my heart, sorry for what I did to you on the day of our wedding. For not giving you warning. For letting you turn up at the church. The reason I let it go all the way to wire was because I kept convincing myself that there was a way out of the mess. That I would find it in time to make it to the ceremony. I've beaten myself up so many times for the way I handled it.'

When Jem finally spoke her tone was more resigned than angry, 'And so you should Nick. But listen, something that these last few weeks have taught me is that, although I didn't quite realise it at the time, I didn't spend the last twelve years grieving for our marriage. I simply wondered where you were. That *wondering*, it…' she searched for the right word, '*preoccupied* me, but it didn't consume me. I ended up right where I was supposed to be. Believe it or not I'm actually *glad* that you didn't turn up that day because I don't think I would have done any of the things I have if you and I had got married. And, if nothing else, if it wasn't for you, I would never have met the love of my life here.' She reached down to the faithful dog at her side and scratched his jowls. Bear yawned in thanks, then slumped back down with a huge sigh, resting his head on Jem's feet.

'And what about the other love of your life?' Nick asked, looking fondly at Bear, as if wondering what it might have been like to know the puppy he had brought home all those years ago.

Jem refused to be drawn.

When she didn't answer, Nick pressed on. 'Look, I know that I'm probably the last person you want to talk to about Matthew, but despite the twelve year gap, I'm the only person around here who actually *knows* him. I've known Matthew longer than *you even*, and certainly longer than all the people who are telling you what you should think about him, despite the fact that they've probably spent all of five minutes in his company.'

Jem continued to say nothing.

'And this is what I really wanted to say before I leave. Matthew *is* a good man. A good man who's been in love with you since the day he first found you, because that's the way it happened Jem, he was the one that rushed to call the ambulance and I just happened to be holding you when you came around. Matthew was the one who spotted you, but I was so sick of the way every girl we met always made a beeline for him, I purposely steamed in ahead. I didn't give him chance to make his move. I decided there and then to sweep you off your feet before Matthew got a look in. And I don't think he ever forgave me for it.'

Jem's eyes widened. 'What are you saying Nick, that I was just some kind of trophy you won in a competition?'

'God no! That's not what I'm saying at all. You and me... it was the real thing Jem.' He tried to reach for her hand but she pulled it away.

'Shit, I'm making a real mess of this.' He put his finger to the bridge of his nose in that old gesture that told her he was stressed. 'Look, all I'm trying to do here is explain what's important *right now*... explain Matthew's point of view. I can see it so clearly now. For him, you were *the one*. I think I always suspected but I just thought he'd get over it in time. But seeing him with you – the day I turned up – well he's never going to manage it is he?'

Nick reached for her hands across the table and covered them both with his own. He shook them, lightly, trying to gently drum his point home. 'Twenty years on from the day we all met and he *still* can't get over you? And by the look of you these last few weeks, I don't think you're ever going to get over him either.' Jem bent her head and Nick gently placed a finger under her chin and drew it upwards.

'Jem look at me.'

She did as she was asked.

'I know you say there are incriminating emails and that people around here are pairing him up with Kate. I know that he took the sonogram from your house. But I don't care what any of it *looks* like; Matthew would never do anything underhand to damage this community, and he certainly wouldn't do it if it meant hurting *you*. No amount of money or contacts could persuade him to do that.'

Jem wanted so much to believe what Nick was saying.

'When I contacted Zara about access to Sophia, she told me that Matthew had been to see her sister Rebecca, in London – on the same day that I showed up here. At first Matthew tried to pretend that he knew about me and Zara but, when it became clear I was on my way back to UK, he had to come clean. He was only there to get closure for you. Even at the risk of his own happiness, he wanted to find out where I was so that *you* could make a decision about your relationship with *him* knowing all the facts. That's how much he loves you Jem, he would forego his own happiness for yours and he would never let you know so that you didn't feel bad about it.'

The worst of it was, Jem thought to herself, she knew that Nick was right. She'd known it ever since Matthew had walked out of her office, and out of her life.

'And if you still doubt him after everything I've said then, just ask yourself this… what does your gut tell you? Not this,' Nick tapped the side of his head, 'the part of you that always overthinks everything Jem, but inside here.' He raised his hand to his chest.

Jem buried her face in her hands then raised her head slowly to face Nick. 'I've made the most terrible mistake haven't I?'

Nick pressed his lips together firmly but said nothing.

'But it's too late, Matthew's with Kate now,' said Jem.

'Have you actually heard that, for definite, not from the gossips in the town but from either of *them*?'

'But even if you're right, you saw the way he looked at me, you heard the things he said,' argued Jem. 'How could we possibly come back from that? The things I was so ready to believe. I… I didn't show any faith in him Nick. How could he forgive all that?'

He smiled and his eyes twinkled darkly in some vague facsimile of the Nick she first met. 'Well, as the guy's been crazy about you for twenty years, I'm guessing he's going to be at least willing to hear you out.'

London

Gerry

With the preliminary paperwork all signed, Gerry Monroe and Phillip Cressfield were on their way to celebrate their deal with a game of squash at the Hurlingham Club in Fulham.

All that remained now was some final rubber-stamping before Phillip's venture capitalist company were announced as the new owners of the Pine Tree Bay Resort at the town's Christmas Eve party tomorrow. A press release would go live at the same time and Gerry would be able to wash his hands of the whole place forever.

Of course he could have done all this remotely, there was no real need for the big announcement. But that would have deprived him of seeing the expressions on the faces of Jemima Small and Finn McDeer and, he couldn't pass up on that. After all, that's what these past few months had been about.

Just like Tasha Carmine – who'd thought she could renege on their deal without consequence and now suddenly found herself facing charges for illegal procurement activities – Jem and Finn were about to find out what happened when you crossed Gerry Monroe.

There was something else to celebrate too – a new owner for the villa. Which meant that Gerry was able to sever all ties with Pine Tree Bay in one clean swing of the axe. The London financier who was buying the house was business savvy. She would quickly realise that any uncertainty about the resort could help to drive the price of the villa down. Gerry wasn't going to allow some corporate skirt to get one over on him; the contracts would be exchanged today ahead of the announcement tomorrow evening.

The town car cruised past Hyde Park Corner and on towards Knightsbridge. Gerry glanced over at Phillip Cressfield. The man had been sitting with his phone glued to his ear ever since they climbed into the vehicle. Gerry had been tempted to scare up a phone call – he didn't like to be outdone in the 'busy and in demand' stakes – but for once he decided to just sit back and enjoy the ride. The hard work was over and it had all come together beautifully. He relaxed deeper into the cream leather seats of the Lexus, stretched out his legs and watched idly as the car sped past the consumer bastions of Harvey Nichols, Harrods and the fashionable boutiques of Sloane Square. Whoever said that money couldn't buy you happiness had clearly never spent an afternoon on the Kings Road.

The money that Monroe Holdings was about to make on the resort sale was certainly enough to make Gerry happy. He would have let it go for less if he'd been pushed; not that he'd have given it away – you couldn't let your eagerness to be shot of something taint your reputation as hard negotiator. But in the end he'd generated enough interest in the sale to let the deal find its own level amongst the companies who were interested.

Those bozos in Pine Tree wouldn't even think to question the speed at which this deal had evolved when he announced it tomorrow. Whilst Gerry had been lining up prospective buyers for the last six months and sending them to the resort under the guise of tourists, the locals had been completely oblivious. He smiled to himself at the thought; according to the feedback he was receiving from one or two well placed informants, the people of Pine Tree Bay really did think that Matthew Albright was behind the sell-off. Well of course they did – because that's what they were *meant* to think.

Once the papers were countersigned by both sets of lawyers tomorrow afternoon, the deal would be final. Frank would go ballistic. But there would be squat he could do about it. Gerry was only disappointed that he wouldn't be able to witness that reaction in person. Maybe that was the niggle with this one? The thing he couldn't put his finger on. He swept the feeling aside.

Gerry had never been one for self-analysis. Preferring to pore over deals, negotiations, business performance. In these matters, the art of being reflective – thinking about what hadn't gone exactly to plan and how it could be improved – was something that came natural, but he rarely wasted time trying to understand his own personal motivations. Business was only successful when conducted without emotion. In that context feelings were irrelevant. If this deal felt somehow *different*, less satisfying than he had expected, he wasn't about to examine that. Not at the eleventh hour.

Phillip Cressfield's voice penetrated his thoughts, 'What are you smiling away to yourself about?'

Gerry didn't have friends, but if he did Phillip Cressfield would be near the top of the list. Ruthless at the board table and hilarious at the dinner table, he was one of the few men with whom Gerry could stand to spend a social hour or two. But the deal with Phillip was not final yet, and Gerry wasn't about to share his mirth at the amount of people it was going to piss off, not to mention the strong signal it would send about Frank's faltering grip on his empire. He would keep all that entirely for his own amusement. Once the ink was dry. Then, it would come – the rush of closing the deal – *this* deal – then it would come.

'I was just thinking about kicking your ass on the squash court.' Gerry didn't miss a beat as the car motored along through the greenery of Hurlingham Park and past the club tennis courts.

'Oh so you *were* dreaming then – I did wonder if you'd dropped off.' Phillip was equally as competitive as Gerry in all aspects.

Gerry had already decided that, after a couple of tight games, Phillip would win the match; keep the man in high spirits for just a few days more. They drew up outside the club and the two business men, each with the lives and livelihoods of thousands of people in their hands, exited the car for a very pleasant afternoon of squash.

Jem
Scotland

It was slowly dawning on Jem that Kate Parker had returned to London. Of course that made complete sense. Don't leave it too late and have to battle the congested motorways on Christmas Eve – be sensible and set off in good time. But none of this prudent foresight was any good to Jem - she needed to speak to her *now*!

And it wasn't a conversation you could have on the phone. 'Hello, is that Kate? I wonder if you could just do me the small favour of confirming whether you are, or not, shagging the man who I now believe to be, quite possibly, the love of my life?'

Jem looked through the front window of Coastguard's Cottage whilst Bear snuffled in the bushes at her side and her fears were confirmed. Everything was extremely neat and tidy and none of the Christmas lights were on. As she was standing there, with her nose pressed up against the window like a bad burglar, Patty from the cottage next door stuck her head out of the door. 'If you're looking for Kate there, she's away back down to London m'dear.'

'Thank you,' said Jem, not wanting to get into conversation. This Patty was known to corner you for a good half hour if you'd let her.

'I think she's gone off to be with that-'

Jem scooted, leaving the nosey woman talking to mid air.

'Well that's charming isn't it?' she heard her mutter as she hurried away.

There was nothing else for it. Jem stomped along the shore road trying to keep warm, she was going to have to call Matthew. Her plan had been to talk to Kate first and suss out the lay of the land so that when she spoke to Matthew she'd know what footing she was on – now she was going to have to go in blind.

But even in her current state of anxiety, Jem's spirits couldn't fail to be lifted by the sight that lay in front of her as she turned to head back the way she had come. The harbour, with its backdrop of snow topped pine trees and twinkling white lights, curved away into a bright festive smile that filled her heart with Christmas cheer. She reminded herself that no matter what Gerry had in store for them tomorrow, she would always be glad to call this place home.

By the time she got back to the Café it was one p.m. and she knew she really should help with the lunch time rush. It was hard to believe how busy they were this Christmas. In all previous years this had been a time to catch their breath, turn inwards and return to simply being a community, as opposed to a holiday resort. But this year had brought

Christmas visitors in the same droves as the summer months. It was good news on one hand but brought with it the sense of being permanently on a treadmill with no respite in sight. January and February were always quiet months, Jem reminded herself, they would all get a bit of respite in the new year.

Feeling guilty, but unable to put it off any longer, she immediately made her way into the back of the shop without looking left or right at the many customers who were trying to get her attention. To be sure of a decent phone signal for this important call, she sat down in front of her office landline – and took a deep, galvanising breath. It was now or never. She located Matthew's contact details from her mobile and dialled his number.

Matthew

London

Matthew stood in the queue ready to board the British Airways afternoon flight to Vancouver.

The day before Christmas Eve was not the day to fly anywhere. Matthew would be sure to remember this in future. He could only hope that none of the sixteen children currently singing *Rudolph the Red Nose Reindeer* on repeat at the top of their lungs had boarding cards for Business Class. Thankfully, a contact of Idella's at the airport had managed to secure him an upgrade. Currently unemployed, his own budget was firmly restricted to economy.

Idella Achike. What an operator. There was surely nobody on this planet that the woman couldn't get access to. Kate had been right – she was something else – and better still, she knew how to stay well under everyone's radar.

Matthew's phone vibrated in his pocket, he checked the display and saw an unknown number was trying to contact him. He decided not to answer – let the caller leave a message first. He would check once in his seat and call back before take-off if there was anything urgent.

He let the number go to voicemail and then, scrolling through his contacts to Barbara Hoskins details he checked for the third time that day that he definitely had the number of Frank's assistant in his phone for when he landed in Vancouver. Firing off a quick text to let her know that his flight was departing on time he then checked his incoming messages. Seeing that the unknown number had not left a voicemail he switched the phone off. He had a long twenty-four hours ahead of him, and he planned to spend as much of this flight as he possibly could, asleep.

Jem

Scotland

Back in Pine Tree, Jem listened as the phone rang out followed by Matthew's voice asking her to leave a message. It caught her off guard. For one, she hadn't prepared what she was going to say if he didn't answer. And secondly, the sound of his voice, the reassuring timbre, made her ache to tell him how much she missed him. She put the phone down hastily.

She needed to think about what she wanted to say. Should she say she was sorry? Sorry that she had doubted him? But what if he *was* with Kate? She didn't want to pour her heart out if there was even a slim chance that they were, like everyone was saying, an item.

It sounded childish but she had to have some pride left didn't she?

She would just leave a message asking him to call her. She dialled his number again and this time it went straight to voicemail with a speed that told her that Matthew's phone had been switched off. Jesus! Had he seen a call come in from her and reached immediately for the off button? Maybe because he and Kate were spending Christmas together?

Suddenly uncertain about her decision she heard the beep ready for her to leave her message and she opened her mouth to speak. Then clamped it firmly shut again. She hurriedly pressed the end call button on her landline. Bloody hell this was worse than being a teenager! She slammed the receiver into its cradle and resisted the urge to cry.

CHAPTER TWENTY-TWO
Christmas Eve

Jem

Christmas Eve and the weather Gods were smiling down on South West Scotland. Pine Tree Bay had awoken to a silver white hoar frost that had coated every bare branch and painted the conifers with diamonds. When the sun rose and brightened the world, the whole town looked like an elaborate ice sculpture sparkling beneath a bright blue sky.

It was set to be another busy day in the café and so, for Jem and her team, it was all hands to the pump. Feeling that she had been so busy with one preoccupation or another lately that she hadn't given the team her full support, Jem was doing her best to cover as much of the work as she could. She wanted the staff to enjoy a day of high jinx getting into the party spirit for later.

Gerry's impending visit had cast a pall over the upcoming festivities but the people of Pine Tree were resolute in their quest for a good time. There was going to be a party tonight whether that bully liked it or not, and if he expected to swan in and take over the whole evening, he had another thought coming. That being said Finn, Jem, Helena and Rab were praying that the announcement would come early in the evening. Leave it too late and people would be drunk then who knows what might get thrown if everyone was half cut when Gerry Monroe stood up to deliver the awful news.

There was no getting away from it – things were going to be tense. But first Jem had today to get through. She had tossed and turned last night wondering what she should do about Matthew until, tired of thinking about it, she'd decided she was going to have a good Christmas come or hell or high water and she simply wasn't going to think about him until Boxing Day. The plan was going well – she was down to only thinking about him once every five minutes.

Jamie shouted out an order that was ready to be taken to table five and Jem scooted off to deliver it. When she returned to the kitchen she found Jamie deep in thought whilst an omelette begged to be turned over on the hob. Before it could smoke any further, Jem stepped in and flipped it, breaking Jamie from his trance.

'Sorry boss, I was miles away.'

'I can see,' Jem laughed and carried on minding the omelette. 'What's up?'

'Lorna's just sent me a text to tell me she's coming to the party tonight.'

Ever since Lorna and Jamie had split, Lorna had kept her distance but she continued to send just enough text messages to keep Jamie dangling. Jem couldn't all together blame her, Jamie had been the most outrageous flirt and Lorna was right to make him sweat, but annoyingly, it left Jem with a confused and mopey chef every time Lorna messaged him at work. Almost three months after their split, the fact that Jamie hadn't jumped at any of the (many) offers that had come his way should surely provide the reassurance the girl needed? Lorna still didn't seem to be so sure.

One thing *was* for certain, Jem thought selfishly, if Jamie was going to be of any use to her in the café for the rest of the day, she needed to spin this in the right way and get him into a positive frame of mind.

'Jamie this is *it*!' Jem said excitedly. 'Your opportunity to get back together. I have a really good feeling about this. You turn up tonight looking gorgeous – that's not going to be hard now is it? And she'll be back in your arms by midnight.' She slapped him on the back. 'Merry Christmas chef!'

Jamie straightened himself up slightly and raised his eyebrows. 'You reckon?'

'I'm sure of it.' Jem beamed, praying to God she was right.

Jem

Later, when Jem and Bear closed up the cafe and set out for The Smugglers, a few tentative flakes had started to fall, but in the twenty minutes it took to walk along the sea front, a white blanket of snow covered everything. Nevertheless the shore road was busy with party goers; the weather was not about to stop anyone's plans to enjoy the festivities.

As she and Bear hurried along in a bid to arrive at the pub without the snow having soaked them both through to the skin, Jem couldn't help but glance over at the empty lay-by where Beryl had parked her motorhome for the previous two months. Jem had been holding on to the slim hope that Beryl and Billy might come back to Pine Tree Bay for Christmas and now her heart sank, as it did every time she passed and saw that the couple hadn't returned.

Her mind drifted back to the night of Halloween, when the air had been thick with the fug of a hundred pumpkin lanterns as she and Matthew had walked along this same path. When all the customers had been queuing for Beryl along the quayside. For what seemed like the thousandth time that week, Jem swallowed down the lump in her throat that threatened to overwhelm her. How could so much have changed in such a short time?

Running into a few early revellers who were looking everywhere except the direction they were headed, she was brought back to the present with a bump. Effusive apologies and scratches for Bear ensued and Jem laughed good-naturedly, wishing the group a Merry Christmas before carrying along on her way.

Christmas was different in Pine Tree Bay this year. The number of people on the streets was not typical, even on Christmas Eve. This year, the business community had put their heads together and come up with the Pine Tree Pub Crawl. The route had been drawn up on a map of the town which took drinkers from one venue to another, in a route that culminated at The Smugglers. Quite a few venues had signed up; The Barnacle, The Bistro, even the White Pebble Gallery, were all part of the itinerary. It was clearly a roaring success if the army of giggling tourists zig-zagging their way through the town was anything to go by.

There was an unspoken agreement amongst the locals that The Smugglers would be their main watering hole for the evening. Nobody knew what time Gerry was going to make his announcement and some were still clinging on to the vague hope of a final reprieve. They all intended to be there, whatever it was he had to say.

When Jem arrived at the pub, it was already heaving; she wondered briefly whether they might have made a mistake in their design of the pub crawl. Corralling everyone into The Smugglers might be nigh on impossible come the end of the evening! Mind you, it was likely that, after Gerry's announcement, quite a few of the locals would start to drift home, especially if he *was* going to tell them the news they were all dreading.

Sadly it seemed they had all guessed correctly on that score. Gerry Monroe was at the far side of the bar looking far too pleased with himself to be delivering anything but bad news. He was holding court with several of the more wealthy businessmen who for most of the year lived elsewhere, but came to spend Christmas at their holiday homes in and around Pine Tree. Jem had nothing against the part timers, they generally spent a lot of money renovating and maintaining their homes meaning trades were always employed, and many houses were let out in the summer, bringing tourists to the area. But she hated to see the way that several of the men in particular fawned over Gerry. What a feather in their caps it must be to be able to boast about drinking with the great Gerry Monroe when they returned to the city.

To make matters worse, Lorna had joined Gerry and his clique for a drink. There was nothing unusual in this – Lorna often carried out administration work for Gerry when she was in town which meant she was on friendlier terms with him than most – but the scene made Jem uncomfortable. Tonight Gerry kept draping his arm proprietorially around Lorna's shoulders, exhibiting her like a trophy to his hangers-on. Just as Jem was thinking this, Lorna threw her head back and roared with laughter at something one of the men had said. It wasn't entirely uncharacteristic but, to Jem's eye, it seemed a little forced.

Jem rolled her eyes and ordered a drink at the bar then, sensing potential trouble afoot, searched the room looking for Jamie. He was standing at the opposite side of the room near the window. He was as far away from Lorna and Gerry's group as it was possible to be – seemingly enthralled by whatever his friends were discussing – but he wasn't fooling Jem. The way his eyes darted over to the far side of the bar every few seconds told her he'd clocked the situation. And the grim set of his jaw said even more.

She was just about to attract his attention with a wave when Helena came through the door and fell upon her, clutching her friend's arm dramatically. 'For the love of God Jem, do *not* ask me to join in with this blasted pub crawl hoo-hah next year! I've spent all day setting up the bar only to realise that the 'experienced' waiters the agency sent me didn't know a Manhattan from a Mojito! I've been teaching them how to make cocktails-sh all day.' She finished with a large hiccup and drew her hand to her mouth in shock.

'And you've sampled a few of them yourself have you?' Jem's eyes twinkled.

'One or two... Just to check the recipe obvioush-ly.' She had trouble with the word. This was shaping up to be a interesting evening; Jamie half mad with jealousy and Helena half cut on cocktails. What could possibly go wrong?

When Helena leaned over the bar towards Rab (who was currently taking money from the till and therefore had his back to them) and grabbed him by the large leather belt that was holding up his Santa suit, Jem's eyes widened further. Rab turned round in shock but Helena didn't falter. She planted a huge smacker on his lips that was so forceful, it knocked his freshly coiffured Bee Gee hair onto the floor. Speechless, in just a hairnet, a beard and couple of spots of rouge, he looked at Helena as if she had lost her mind.

Helena pointed drunkenly to the Christmas greenery which hung above the bar and winked, 'Sh'allright... Mistletoe.'

Jem found her voice, 'Er, perhaps just a tonic water to start with for Helena eh Rab?'

Rab raised his eyebrows. 'Coming right up.' Then, whilst Helena rooted in her bag for cash he mouthed silently to Jem, '*Look after her!*'

An hour later, Jem was starting to exhale. The tonic water was doing the trick and Helena was gradually starting to sound more sober. Finn had arrived fresh from his stint as the infant school Santa and was entertaining them all with tales of children who had peed their pants in the combined excitement and trauma of meeting Father Christmas. But in all the hilarity, nobody noticed that Jamie had finally lost his patience with the Gerry and Lorna situation until it was too late.

At the sound of raised voices in Gerry's corner, Jem silently broke away from the rest of the group and made her way through the crowded bar to where Jamie's voice was becoming louder and more belligerent.

'Yes, Lorna, that *is* what I'm trying to tell you! If the man has designs on you I think you've got a right to know – Gerry's got a bit of form where his assistants are concerned.' Jamie was not being the least bit subtle about discussing Gerry's sex life in front of his cronies – every one in the group including Gerry, was frowning in confusion as to whether they could have possibly heard Jamie correctly.

Gerry stepped in. 'I don't know what you think you're trying to pull here son, but the lady-'

Lorna, slightly drunk, and thinking she was being helpful, decided to interpret for Gerry. Laying a hand on his chest she slurred, 'No, it's ok Gerry, Jamie here thinks you've been sleeping with Marcus, but I've just been explaining – you're not gay!'

Oh no! Jem's hand flew to her mouth as she thought back to the day in the bookshop with Matthew. If there was one thing that Gerry Monroe prided himself on, it was his image as the virile lady-killer. Jem would bet all her worldly possessions that his views on same sex relationships were about as unenlightened as they came. Poor Jamie would have no comprehension of the insult his suggestion was to a man like Gerry Monroe, because, with all the good sense of his generation, Jamie would not imagine it to be an issue for anyone.

Gerry went pale as a barely concealed snigger rippled around his group of hangers-on. But before he could speak Jamie interrupted loudly. 'No I'm not suggesting he's *gay*, Lorna.' He looked around the assembled group, who had all paused with their drinks mid way to their mouths, eager to hear what was about to come out of the young man's mouth next. 'I'm not one for labels myself, but I'm saying he's *bisexual*.'

When Gerry finally spoke through his perfectly straight and very white gritted teeth, his rage was evident. 'Now get this straight sonny, I am neither gay nor bisexual-'

'Look pal,' Jamie cut in. 'It does'nae matter to me. You can bed whoever you want. You can *love* whoever you want. I dinnae care. But if Lorna here is just the next in a long line of the assistants you're shagging, well, in my view, the lassie has a right to know. If you've been sleeping with Marcus-.'

Jamie never saw the punch coming. In a split second he was on the floor. Gerry Monroe towered above him. 'For the last time boy! I am no fucking faggot!' he roared – loud enough for the people half a mile up the road in The Barnacle to hear.

The room went silent and all eyes turned to Gerry Monroe.

Lorna flew to Jamie's side. 'What the...? For Christ sake's Gerry!'

Jamie groaned, laying prostrate on the floor, he had gone down hard and was visibly dazed from Gerry's punch. Jem ran over to check that Jamie was ok. She was about to give Gerry Monroe a piece of her mind but a tall man, who had been drinking with Gerry all evening, slowly got to his feet. He drew himself up to his full height and spoke in a loud, booming American accent that echoed throughout the deathly quiet bar. 'Jesus Gerry, it's like the Goddamn Wild West around here!'

'I'm sorry you had to see that Phillip.' Gerry, still breathless from the exertion of his sucker punch to Jamie's jaw, was shaking his head. 'But the boy needed teaching a lesson, thinking he can call me a-'

Phillip Cressfield's eyes narrowed as something clicked in Gerry's brain, forcing him to cut his sentence short.

'A *what* Gerry?' the American prompted. 'You seem to be forgetting the wedding you attended between my son and his husband last year. I gotta tell you, I'm not one bit interested in doing business with a homophobe. Monroe or not. As far as I'm concerned, this deal is off.'

Gerry, who hadn't yet recovered his equilibrium, shook his head vigorously and twisted his mouth into an ugly sneer. 'Oh no you don't Phillip. It's too late to pull out now. The documents are all signed and the deal is done.' Still out of breath from the fight with Jamie and all pretence of the benevolent statesman gone, he addressed the crowd. 'Everyone! Say hello to the new owner of Pine Tree Bay Resort.' He held his whiskey glass aloft and downed it in one, 'And good riddance to the whole damn lot of you!'

A low disgruntled hum went round the room until a voice rang out from just inside the door.

'I should think the feeling's mutual son.'

All heads swivelled to the steel haired man who stood in the doorway of The Smugglers. Jem did a double take – Matthew was standing right behind him.

If the people of Pine Tree Bay had been the type to let out a cheer, this would have been the moment. As it was, incredulous mutterings of, 'Well I'll be buggered!' and 'Christ it's the auld yin himself!' floated around the crowd.

Gerry, looking as if he might throw up, faced off against his father with a grimly set jaw but Frank ignored his son and spoke directly to Phillip Cressfield. 'Phillip, you are free to leave. You're right. The deal *is* off. In fact, there never was any deal in the first place. You'll be happy to know you are not the new owner of Pine Tree Bay Resort because Pine Tree Bay Resort is not for sale.'

Gerry interrupted. 'That's where you're wrong *dad*.' He drew out the word bitterly. 'Whether the two of you like it or not, Phillip's company is the new owner of the resort and and I have all the paperwork to prove it. There's not a thing that you or anyone else can do about it. If you think I'm going to be saddled with this horse-shit whilst you end your days drooling into your wheelchair, you can think again.'

Frank Monroe continued to ignore Gerry. 'Phillip, the paperwork is meaningless. You have no legal obligations here.'

Gerry interrupted. 'In case you've forgotten*, I* am currently the acting head of Monroe Holdings with legal authority to sign any deal I see fit. You have absolutely no authority to overturn any of my decisions. The legals are all executed. The deal stands.'

Phillip Cressfield, his face as dark as thunder, took his suit jacket from the back of his bar stool and put it on. 'I don't know what kind of shit show you've been trying to run in your father's absence Gerry, but trying to put one over on me? That's your first and last mistake. Because once I'm finished, this little stunt of yours is going to be everywhere. Good luck doing international business after that.'

Phillip walked over to Frank and shook his hand warmly. 'Glad to see you're feeling better sir. Now if you'll excuse me I'm going to see if I can get a flight out tonight that will get me back to Boston for the morning. I can't believe I nearly missed Christmas with my family for this fiasco.'

Frank nodded. 'I'm sorry you were inconvenienced in this way Phillip. Merry Christmas.' They shook hands again and Frank turned back to the silent crowd as the younger man left. Though his contempt for his son was palpable, he was doing his best to conduct himself with the dignity worthy of his position and his years. And he was doing what he always did, putting the people of Pine Tree Bay before the business.

'Ladies and gentlemen…' Frank paused then corrected himself. '*Friends*, I'm truly sorry you've had to witness this ugly scene – on this evening of all evenings.' He paused again to cast his eyes around the crowd. 'Christmas Eve is not a time for business. It's a time for community, for family. I came here tonight because I wanted to introduce you all to a member of *my* family.' His eyes went to Jem. 'Jem, would you come over here please?'

Jem, slowly made her way through the crowd to where Frank stood. She exchanged a long questioning look with Matthew, who gave her the briefest of nods and an encouraging smile.

'As I was saying,' Frank continued. 'I came here tonight because I wanted to introduce you all to someone.' He placed an arm around Jem's shoulders. 'The darnedest thing is, you all know her better than I do. She's the person you go to when you want to get things done around here. When you want to organise an event that will bring people together. When you want to attract more visitors so you can make sure your businesses thrive. When you're having a crisis of confidence and you need someone to tell you how and why it's gonna be ok.' He looked at Jem then back at the crowd. 'And for the visitors who're here tonight, well, *you* go to Jem when you want to keep in touch with this beautiful place once you're back home.' Frank smiled down at her with great affection.

'But whilst you all know Jem and you know all of *that*, what you don't know, is that Jem is my granddaughter.' As Frank said this his smile grew wider.

More profanities floated around the crowd to register the general surprise at this news and Frank folded Jem into what was an emotional embrace for both of them. When Jem and Frank drew apart, the older man continued to address the audience with misty eyes but a steady voice.

'But that's also the reason why this town can't possibly be for sale.' He cast a long look at Gerry then turned his head back toward the crowd. 'When I first created Pine Tree Bay Resort, I made it a strict condition, that any sale of the business needed to be agreed and countersigned by Jem's grandmother, Marcia. When Marcia died, that legal responsibility was passed down to Jem.' It was Jem's turn to look shocked.

'Gerry,' Frank turned to where his son stood, livid with unconcealed rage, 'your legal team have not done their due diligence; without Jem's signature, your paperwork is worth nothing.' Frank held Gerry's gaze for a moment before turning back to the crowd with a benevolent look on his face. 'Now, given that we've sorted that out and I've had a very long flight,' he rubbed his hands together to signal that the business part of the evening was concluded, 'what's the chances of getting a drink around here?'

Everyone sprang into action at once. Rab grabbed a Bourbon glass and started to pour a shot. Gerry opened his mouth to protest. Jem turned to search for Matthew. Their eyes met and whilst everyone around then seemed to be in motion, they simply looked across at each other and smiled. Jem began to walk slowly over to where Matthew was waiting for her. She had to be the one to make the first move. She knew that. He never took his eyes from her as she pushed her way through the crowd. A few steps further and she would be there.

Then, just as she reached out for him, the doors to The Smugglers sprang forward on their hinges and Marcus burst into the bar.

'For God's sake...' Matthew groaned as he rolled around on the floor. 'What is it with me and this sodding door?' Jem rolled her lips to stop from laughing and went to help him up.

Meanwhile a sweaty looking Marcus addressed the bar. 'STOP! Stop the announcement!' he shouted breathlessly and the crowd fell silent. Marcus bent double trying to catch his breath. 'Jemima Small needs to countersign the deal!'

Frank raised his glass to a beaten looking Gerry. 'Congratulations son, looks like your lawyers did their job after all.'

After the high drama of Frank's announcement, the mood in the pub was jubilant. Something of a raucous party ensued with Frank as guest of honour. Thankfully, Gerry – the spectre at the wake – had left quickly after Marcus had arrived, bundling him out the door. Jem felt sorry for Marcus; he was likely to bear the brunt of what had unfolded this evening. But Jamie couldn't resist smirking as they watched the two men leave, 'What did I tell yees all?'

At one in the morning, when most of the crowd had drifted home, leaving just a few stalwarts at the bar, Jem looked down at a very tired Bear, who, having enjoyed a constant stream of gravy bones from his drunken fan club for the majority of the evening, now lay snoring at her feet. Realising that the poor dog had not been out for over four hours, she turned to Frank and Matthew.

'Well, I hate to be the one to break up the party but I best get this boy along home. He'll be desperate if I leave it much longer!'

'Frank and Matthew, who'd been deep in conversation, stopped to smile at her and she was suddenly overwhelmed by the feeling of warmth coming from the two of them. For her yes – but also, she detected, for each other. The two men had hit it off remarkably well.

Not wanting to curtail the budding bromance she said, 'Look, I'll head off along the road with Bear. Matthew, how about you see that Frank gets back to The Barnacle then catch me up later.'

'No chance Jem. Can't have you walking back at this time of night alone,' said Frank. 'We'll both come with you.'

Jem laid a hand on Frank's arm. 'You're not walking anywhere. You're still recovering for goodness sake. And this is *Pine Tree,* remember? I walk everywhere on my own at all hours. You honestly don't need to worry.'

Frank chuckled, conceding that Jem had a point. 'Well, if you're sure. There's one or two things I'd like to discuss with Matthew here before we shut up shop for the night.'

Matthew leaned toward Jem. 'I think Frank's trying to work out whether my intentions towards his granddaughter are honourable,' he whispered.

Jem gave him a long look. 'Always,' she murmured, trying desperately to convey what she'd had no time to tell him all evening; that she now knew she'd got it so completely and utterly wrong before he left – and perhaps for the twenty years before that. But that, if he would let her, she was going to spend the next twenty making it up to him.

She said her goodbyes and told Frank she would see him tomorrow for Christmas lunch, adding quietly to Matthew, 'Don't be too long yeah?'

'I'll be right behind you.' He met her gaze, clearly torn between showing respect for Jem's grandfather and dropping everything to follow her out the door immediately.

After bidding farewell to Rab, Helena and Finn, Jem made her way rather unsteadily along the shore road and back towards Withershins, stopping every now and then so that Bear could leave his details at a few lamp posts along the way.

When she arrived at the house it was cold, dark and unwelcoming. She'd been out since early that morning so there were no friendly lamps to greet her and the heating had gone off hours ago. Thankfully the kitchen was at least warmed by the Aga. She might want to sober up a bit for the talk she needed to have with Matthew, so she spooned several heaped dessert spoons of ground Arabica into the coffee pot and sat it on the stove. Then, leaving the back door unlocked for him, she moved through the downstairs switching on lamps and singing softly to herself in warm expectation of the night and, hopefully, the months and years to come.

The sense of gloom she had woken with that morning was gone. *It had miraculously all worked out. Just as Beryl promised it would.*

Bear's warning bark told her that Matthew had arrived so she hurried back through to the kitchen, a thrill of excitement rippling through her as she relished the thought that finally, they were getting this moment to themselves.

But the shock of what greeted her turned the excitement to dread. Gerry Monroe stood in the middle of her kitchen with Bear at his side. He spoke softly to the dog, telling him what a good boy he was, scratching his ears, and in that soft, creepy tone she remembered so well asked him, 'Now then boy, where is she?'

Beryl

'Bleedin' 'ell Beryl slow down – you'll have the whole thing over on its side!' Billy grasped the strap which sat above the passenger door and held on for dear life as Beryl rounded a corner at speed. Something in the back of the motorhome crashed to the floor.

Beryl didn't take her foot off the accelerator. The feeling she'd been unable to shake all day had, in the last hour, become so overpowering that the tell tale ache in her hands was now unbearable. Her chest felt fluttery yet constricted, as if a panicked bird was battering its way out from the inside. She knew she should let Billy drive – but she also knew he wouldn't go fast enough.

When Beryl had woken up that morning to a bright blue Loch Ness sky, she'd had the strongest instinct that she and Billy needed to return to Pine Tree Bay. At first it had been a gentle, homing inclination. She missed her new friends. But the feeling, having gnawed away at her all day, culminated in a flash of blinding clarity when, at five in the afternoon, she put down her mug of tea and said to Billy, 'We have to go back to Pine Tree Bay – right this minute.' She didn't know why – but one thing was certain – they needed to go immediately.

There had barely been time to secure the van before Beryl put the motorhome into drive and headed south from Loch Ness. It was a seven hour drive at the very least and despite Billy's misgivings at the dark, snowy conditions, he held his tongue saying nothing of the madness of tackling such a journey in a blizzard. Cautioning Beryl to slow down every once in a while was as far as he dared interfere.

Now, as they rattled through the minor roads just a few miles out of Pine Tree Bay, he placed a steadying hand on Beryl's left arm which was swaying violently back and forth as she manoeuvred around the potholes on the undulating roads. 'Just a bit slower love,' he cautioned. 'We'll make it in time. We *will* make it.'

Billy trusted Beryl's gift implicitly and the way this premonition was affecting her made one thing plain – whatever awaited them in Pine Tree Bay, they *had* to get there in one piece.

Jem

'I thought I made it clear last time you were here Gerry, you're not welcome in my house.' Jem spoke with more authority than she felt, desperate not to give herself away. She couldn't afford for either Gerry *or* Bear to scent the fear that gripped her throat and threatened to close around it like a fist.

Every fibre within her body urged her to rush to her boy. Her heart hammered in her chest as she watched his trusting eyes stare into Gerry's face, panting a wide smile for the man who stood over him with a soothing tone and a mean mouth. The proprietary way that Gerry had let himself into the house told her everything she needed to know. Any pretence of playing by the rules was now behind them.

Gerry's eyes slid across the room to Jem, all the while continuing to scratch the dog's ears and talk to him in a weird sing-song voice. He was drunk, Jem noted with growing unease, slurring his words. After leaving The Smugglers, he must have spent the remainder of the evening drowning his sorrows.

She took it all in; the crumpled jacket, the tie loose around his half open shirt, the white marks that edged his brogues where he had clearly staggered through the snow all the way from The Barnacle. He looks, she thought, like someone who'd been in the middle of undressing before suddenly deciding to take a walk.

'Take a seat,' he said, fixing her with a black eyed stare.

They were alone. He was drunk. He was stronger than she. *He had his hands on her dog.* The caustic response died on her tongue. All she needed was time. Matthew was on his way. Jem licked her lips, swallowed. 'Gerry, look,' she tried to reason, 'I understand tonight was a bit of a shock-'

'SIT THE FUCK DOWN!' Gerry roared and Bear flinched and backed away. Thankfully Gerry, now focused solely on Jem, didn't seem to notice.

Jem felt a wave of rising panic. An ice cold rivulet of fear slithered down her back as the full realisation took hold – Finn had been right all along. What was being acted out in front of her was much more than wounded pride. Demonstrating all the hallmarks of the unhinged obsession that Finn had suspected, Gerry had crossed some kind of invisible line. He had been trying to teach her a lesson for the way she had rejected him, but it had backfired. And now, she suddenly realised, he wanted *her* to pay for that.

Gerry staggered towards her and dragged a chair out from beneath the table. He grabbed her by the arm and shoved her roughly towards it. 'For once just do what I say Goddammit!'

She did as she was told reminding herself that she just needed to play for time. Just a few minutes more and Matthew would be there. Everything was going to be ok.

Gerry started to pace the room, as if unsure what to do next. And, as Bear hid under the table, Jem tried to tune in to the half formed sentences which were spewing from his mouth. The drunken ramblings of a megalomaniac.

Slowly, she began to piece it together; the way this simmering anger being played out in front of her had fuelled everything: taunting her with the anonymous postcard; the seeking out and hiring of Matthew; the offer of the commission that drove Nick back into their lives and, of course, his attempt to sell off the resort and make that look like Matthew's doing. All this just to mess with her. Mess with Finn. And to get back at his father. *Three* birds with one stone – Gerry always had to go one better.

All that effort for what? Because Finn had thrown him out of her kitchen. Because she'd turned him down? Had no woman really ever said *no* to him before? Taking in his dishevelled state, his slicked back hair and his hard black eyes, she found that very hard to believe.

His pacing and ranting suddenly stopped and her stomach lurched. Leaning against the kitchen counter in a drunken slouch, he cocked his head to one side. 'So now you know.' He closed one eye and squinted at her though the other, like someone using the sight on a gun. 'It was all for your benefit.'

She would not show him she was frightened. She would not give the bastard that satisfaction.

'Sure, having to fly up here every few months for the latest jamboree you hokeys had managed to scare up was a fucking pain in the arse.' He laughed at his own joke. 'But really, I could have put up with that for the good press it afforded. No, what these past months have all been about is teaching you a very valuable lesson.'

Gerry's black eyes narrowed and his voice grew softer, more menacing. 'But all along you had this little nugget up your sleeve didn't you? I bet you you had a good laugh with them all at my expense huh?'

'Gerry, I didn't even know-'

'You and Finn... and then Matthew. What a hoot it must have been for you all. Thought you had one over on me yeah? No wonder my advances were *so* distasteful to you, now I see why,' he laughed bitterly, as if this suddenly explained why someone in her position could ever refuse his attentions. 'But if you think your little plan is going to work...'

'What plan?' she asked weakly, keeping one eye on Bear who was still looking warily at Gerry from under the table.

'Oh don't play the innocent. Holding all this information in reserve? To outmanoeuvre me. Cosying up to Frank so you could move in and inherit the family fortune? Don't get me wrong – it's a smart play. You're cleverer than I gave you credit for. But,' he leaned in, bringing his face closer to hers, 'when he's *gone*. When the old man dies. What happens then? Have you thought about that?'

He walked around the chair to stand behind her and started to speak quietly into her ear. 'Think about it for a minute. I found out everything about you just because you pissed me off. What do you think I do to the people who really get in my way?'

The hairs were standing up on the back of Jem's neck but she willed herself not to move. Not to show fear. Instinctively knowing it was what he wanted.

'You're just saying all this to frighten me Gerry.' She said it calmly, but the slight tremble in her voice betrayed her.

A low rumbling laugh close to her ear. 'Smart girl. But I'd say it's working, wouldn't you?'

From the corner of her eye she saw Bear pad quietly to where the kitchen door stood ajar. He nosed it open before trotting off quietly down the garden path. Jem sent up a silent prayer for her dog to ignore all the years of training she had drilled into him and run free, out of the front gate.

Matthew

It had been one hell of a twenty four hours. Matthew marvelled at how, for once in his life, everything had gone so beautifully to plan. Since stepping off the flight at Vancouver and meeting the indomitable, not to mention loyal, Barbara Hoskins, Matthew had just known that things were going to work out.

Frank's right hand woman had that air of calm reassurance that was the hallmark of all good executive assistants and, even better, she was suspicious enough of Gerry to listen earnestly to everything that Matthew had to say.

Matthew had known that if he could just get an audience with Frank it would be his chance to put everything right as far as the sell-off was concerned. But to have Frank confirm that he was *Jem*'s grandfather and that *she* was the legal stranglehold to any divestment of the town, was more than he could have hoped for.

Their conversation in the pub tonight had been promising too. Frank had expressed a desire to work with Matthew in the future; always on the look out for people he could trust. When Matthew had explained that he was hoping to be in Pine Tree Bay for the foreseeable future, Frank had clapped him on the back and said that he was sure they could work something out.

Now, walking along the shore toward Jem's house in the early hours of Christmas morning, Matthew's heart swelled with the prospect of what lay ahead for them both. Finally, the path ahead was truly clear of obstacles and although they hadn't had chance to speak properly as yet, he now knew that Jem had tried to call him yesterday – and he could already guess at what she had been going to say. They had the whole night ahead to talk about their plans for the future and once they were tired of talking, there were one or two other things he could think of to fill the remaining hours.

With this thought still causing a smile to play across his lips, Matthew was brought up short by the sight of Bear running along the road toward him. He frowned. The crafty pup must have sneaked out whilst Jem's back was turned. Crouching down to give the dog a fuss he greeted Bear warmly, 'Hey Boy, what are you doing out on the road all alone? Come on let's get you home.'

Standing up, Matthew was suddenly filled with a sense of unease. He brought his hand towards his nose. All at once he was transported back to the last day of September, at the top of the Oxo Tower restaurant, with a cloying, overpowering scent invading his senses. Why was Bear out on the street alone, smelling of Gerry Monroe's sickly cologne?

Matthew started to run.

Jem

'You know, for the whole day, I've been troubled.' Gerry hands gripped Jem's shoulders, still leaning over her, speaking close to her ear. 'I couldn't put my finger on just what was bugging me about this deal.'

The stench of whiskey and cigars fused with the overpowering cologne he always wore was causing her to gag. But she couldn't move, couldn't think, paralysed by fear. Her mind was having trouble reconciling this slobbering predator with the sleek, smooth, sharp businessman that Gerry presented to the world. Until ten minutes ago it was the way that Jem had seen him too; ruthless, cutthroat but essentially sane. And she wondered now, how long had Gerry Monroe held such a tenuous grasp on that sanity? And why choose tonight as the time to finally let go?

Then Phillip Cressfield's words from earlier in the evening pushed urgently through the jumbled mess of her terrified mind. Hadn't Phillip promised to ruin Gerry's reputation? The memory caused her blood to run even colder. Was that it? After tonight, did Gerry think he had nothing left to lose?

Her eyes travelled around the kitchen, seeking some way out. The coffee that she had put on earlier was now bubbling and spitting angrily on the stove. How quickly could she make it to the door? If she could only create some distance, get just a few feet away from him, she might be able to make a run for it.

But Gerry now came to stand in front of her and resumed his unhinged ramblings. 'All day it's been niggling away at me. What was it about this deal? Why wasn't it bringing me closure? The sense of satisfaction I expected to feel? And then tonight I realised what it was.'

He took her jaw in his hand and brought his face down close to hers, so drunk he was struggling to focus. 'Thing is. Even though I'd be shot of Pine Tree. Even though I would royally piss off my father. Even though I'd torn you and Finn apart and let Matthew take the rap for the whole scheme. I still wouldn't have the thing that I really wanted all along would I?' His grip strengthened around her face forcing her to look him in the eye. 'And after tonight, that's even more impossible than it was before. So I have to ask myself, if I can't have you...?'

'You can,' she managed to whisper.

The shock of her words loosened his grip and, as if he couldn't believe what he was hearing, Gerry stepped back in astonishment regarding her with a puzzled expression.

This was her one chance.

With lightening speed her hand shot out to the steaming coffee pot. Grasping the wooden handle she summoned all her strength and screamed as she swung it violently into the side of Gerry's head. 'You can have *this*!'

She started to run for the door, but even with all the force she had brought to bear, it wasn't hard enough to knock him out. Buckling to his knees at the blow, he recovered almost immediately. Getting to his feet he grabbed for her and slammed her back onto the table. As she felt his hands close around her throat, Jem knew she was out of options.

Everything was just starting to blur when Matthew came crashing through the door. He was across the room in a single stride. Grabbing Gerry by the shirt collar, the rage within him erupting as he knocked the man out cold with one clean punch.

The trouble was, Matthew couldn't seem to stop at just the one.

CHAPTER TWENTY-THREE
New Year's Eve

Jem

A lot could happen in a week. This particular New Years Eve would probably go down in Jem's history as the quietest that she had ever known. But she couldn't face a large party. Counting down from ten with an excited crowd. Kissing relative strangers when the clock struck midnight. Party poppers going off everywhere.

No, she thought, as she stared into the fire and stroked Bear's shiny coat. For this year, and who knows, maybe every year from here on in, this would do. A night in with Billy and Beryl, catching up on the *Strictly Come Dancing* final they had all missed in the drama of the weeks before. Yes, this was much more preferable to jostling the crowds in The Smugglers.

Safely ensconced in the lounge at Withershins she had been instructed not to move from the sofa as Beryl fussed around preparing light bites and nibbles and Billy took up the mantle of cocktail waiter. Jem loved them for their kindness... she couldn't remember ever being so spoiled in her life. And tonight, after everything that had happened, she thanked God for the love and support of this great couple.

'Ok!' she shouted through to the kitchen from her perch on the sofa. 'There's a pile of food, buckets of the fizzy stuff and a warm seat but the fire. The only thing I don't have is my fellow *Strictly* obsessives to help me eat it all whilst I drool over Kelvin Fletcher's pecs.'

'Er... Excuse me! If there's going to be any drooling over pecs it had better be for these babies!'

Jem almost choked on her Prosecco as Matthew sashayed into the room looking like he was about to perform the Cha Cha Cha dressed in a frilly satin shirt which was open to the waist and tucked into a pair of bottom hugging trousers – for extra authenticity he was carrying a pair of Maracas.

'Can someone alert Rab please! There's a new fancy dress king in town!' Jem cried through howls of laughter.

'What's your bet that he asks me if he can borrow it?' Matthew asked, treating her to a small twitch of his castanets.

Jem was undone. Beryl and Billy came in from the kitchen to see what all the hilarity was about and Jem dried her eyes then ordered the older couple to stop fussing around and sit down. Having spent the last five days with Frank in Canada, whilst Bear stayed home with Billy and Beryl, Jem and Matthew were eager for all the latest town news.

'Poor Frank,' said Beryl settling down with a snifter of Harvey's Bristol Cream. 'With Gerry being under arrest he's going to have his hands full.' She shook her head sadly. 'And him just recovered from that illness too.'

'I should think that's the least of his problems now,' Billy chimed in knowledgeably. 'The Monroe Holdings share-price has nose dived since all those girls have been coming forward to the press with stories about Gerry. Listening to some of them Jem…' Billy took a swig of pale ale and swallowed it with a gulp. 'Well, let's just say, I'm glad Matthew arrived when he did.'

'Thank God *you* both arrived when you did,' said Matthew looking gratefully at Billy. 'Otherwise there might not have been anyone left alive for those girls to press charges against. And God knows what charges *I* would have been facing.'

'You'd have stopped yourself Matthew.' Beryl patted his arm.

But they all knew that without the older couple's timely intervention, that might not have been the case. Jem closed her eyes momentarily to rid herself of the image of the deranged face of Gerry Monroe. It would take a while, she knew, but she was determined not to be permanently scarred by the psycho. There weren't bogeyman around every corner. Gerry was just one bad man and he wasn't going to be coming near her ever again. She could rest easy on that score. She decided they needed a change of subject.

'Frank was just fine when we left him Beryl.' Jem smiled grateful for the older woman's concern. 'And hark at you Billy! Discussing share prices. Whatever next? A subscription to the Financial Times?'

Billy laughed. 'Aye lass, you never know.' He shifted slightly in his armchair. 'Any road up, aside from the obvious, the major talking point is why Matthew was at your house late on Christmas Eve and not with his 'girlfriend' Kate?'

Beryl shot a warning look at Billy but he placed a hand on hers. 'It's ok love, I'm putting em all straight on what's what.'

Matthew shook his head, 'Has word still not filtered through? Surely people now realise I needed Gerry to think I'd moved on so he wouldn't suspect me of trying to get to Frank?'

'Don't worry lad, I'm getting the story out there as quick as I can.' Billy puffed up his chest self importantly. Since his performance at the community meeting with Madeleine Beaver, he was something of a celebrity in the town and had been welcomed back to Pine Tree Bay like a long lost national treasure. Beryl rolled her eyes at Jem in a gesture which spoke volumes, but Jem knew Beryl wouldn't be without Billy now she had found him again – despite her grumblings that he cluttered up the motorhome something shocking.

'Has anyone actually seen Kate?' Beryl asked.

'She came to see us when we got back last night.' Jem nodded, munching on an olive. 'Said she wanted to explain everything to me first hand. I felt a bit bad when I thought back to some of the things I said to her.'

Matthew chuckled, 'It's only natural, I mean, the thought of losing all this?' He waved a hand over his torso and gave Billy a comedy wink.

Jem threw him a withering look and gestured towards the TV. 'That's just the type of thing Craig Revel Horwood would say – which is why people love to boo him.'

Beryl smiled to herself.

'Anyway,' Matthew continued, 'Kate's completed the sale on the villa so any connection that Gerry had with the town is well and truly severed, especially now he's been sacked from Monroe Holdings too.'

'The other good news for her,' said Jem, 'is that she's been offered a corporate payout from her employers. She's thinking about offering bed and breakfast up at the villa.'

Beryl looked up sharply. 'Now that's strange… The minute you said that Jem, I got a strong image of an open book.'

Matthew grinned, knowing better than to doubt Beryl's abilities ever again… 'Well that's pretty spooky, because she did say she might call it the Book Lover's Bed and Breakfast.'

CHAPTER TWENTY-FOUR
New Year's Day

Kate

With a heavy woollen shawl wrapped around her shoulders, Kate nursed her steaming mug of coffee as she leant out over the rail of her new verandah. She stood, deep in thought, staring down at the bright green sea that glistened in the bay below.

It was New Year's Day and as she ushered out the old and turned her face to the new, she found herself in contemplative mood. It was hardly surprising; a lot had happened in the final quarter of last year. If someone had told her three months ago that by New Year's Day she would be the owner and a villa on the coast of Scotland she would have asked them if they were on drugs. Yet here she was – and it was by *choice*. Astonishing! To cap it all, it was the very incident that had exiled her to here in the first place, that was going to pay for the new house in the long run; fate certainly had a sense of irony.

When Kate had walked into the Allocott offices on Christmas Eve, she had felt it – that frisson of excitement that was always there whenever she was about to close a deal. The leaden swish of the revolving doors when she entered the building, the smell of the foyer with its polished floors – all achingly familiar yet now, somehow hostile too. She squared her shoulders as she approached the front desk and announced, 'Kate Parker and lawyer. We have a meeting with Bill Cranfield.'

The security guard who was manning the front desk that morning – a man with three children and a wife back home in Thailand whom Kate had religiously sent Christmas presents to for the past five years – greeted her formally. When she had asked after his family he had looked uncomfortable. He handed her a visitor's badge and asked her to wait in the lobby area, never quite meeting her eye. Of all the things that had happened to her over the past three months, it was this one act that caused a scratch in her throat and a prickling sensation at the back of her eyes.

But once in the meeting room, there had been no room for sentiment. It had all unfolded just as Idella had predicted. The Allocott chairman outlined the situation; he was preparing to serve her with termination papers and refer the matter to the Competition and Markets Authority. Kate had enjoyed letting him ramble through his prepared speech. The Human Resources director sitting to his left ensuring that everything was read verbatim from the script they were both holding.

To the other side of the chairman sat Tom. Her former boss. Her former lover. He fiddled agitatedly with a paperclip and as she watched him she realised that the thought of those hands anywhere near her body now made her skin crawl. On the other hand she *had* enjoyed watching him put on the performance of a lifetime. The hurt, searching look when she had first walked into the office. His expression just the right combination of sympathy and sorrow as the chairman read out the scripted message.

When everyone had finished speaking – the look of relief on all their faces obvious now that the most uncomfortable part of their day was almost over – the chairman pushed the termination papers towards Kate. Throughout their speech she had remained expressionless and allowed all the charges against her to be read out.

'*Evidence of collusion with other companies that Allocott are in competition with.*'

'*The sharing of privileged information that is contrary to regulations.*'

She listened to everything they had to say. Allowed all the evidence – amounting to one missive from her business e-mail to the private mail account of a competitor – to be produced and then she cleared her throat.

'In circumstances such as these I believe I'm allowed the right to reply am I not?' she asked.

'Yes, of course, but really Kate…' the Human Resources director looked across at her sympathetically, 'you don't want to make this any more painful than it needs to be.'

Kate reached into her bag and brought out the printed material that Idella had furnished her with. She handed over ream after ream of emails sent from Tom's private account to the same addressee on the mail that had, just a moment ago, been used to incriminate Kate.

She presented them line after line of mobile phone records showing calls to the same number more than four or five times a day. 'I think you'll find that number belongs to the same man listed on the emails,' she said confidently.

As the extent of the evidence that Kate had uncovered began to dawn on Tom, he tried to interrupt her flow. 'This is outrageous,' he spluttered, waving a dismissive hand that collided with the papers which Kate had laid neatly on the table and sent them flying across the room. 'This has clearly all been fabricated! It's deflection. Look, Bill, the truth is, Kate and I have been seeing each other this past few years and you have to believe me – this is all a case of sour grapes because I won't leave my wife, because I haven't defended her during the suspension.'

Kate listened to him digging his own grave.

The chairman, an unflappable man whom Kate had always respected, looked at Tom for a long moment before saying calmly, 'Well that's as may be Tom. But, as Kate said earlier, and as her *lawyer* here will attest, she does have the right to mount a defence against the evidence presented, and we have a duty to hear her out. So let's do just that shall we?'

'Thank you Bill.' Kate nodded. 'Now, don't you think it's strange that you haven't found one single further record in any of my data that a communication has passed between me and this contact?' She pointed to the email – the single piece of evidence they had presented against her.

'I can prove, using my own CCTV records, that Tom was in my flat on the night of this email. The digital audit data from that evening will also corroborate that that's where my laptop was logged on when this email was sent. If you haven't conducted one already, a check of all my personal phone and email records will show that I have had no contact with this addressee, whereas Tom however....' her eyes went to the mountain of paperwork now strewn across the desk.

She played her final card. 'If you decide to take this further, with the mounting evidence in my favour, I *will* push it all the way. Wrongful dismissal, harassment, sexual discrimination… And I'll make sure the case gets as much media coverage as I can.'

The chairman who had been listening to everything that Kate had said with his chin resting in his hand now interrupted, 'I'm sure that won't be necessary Kate.' He turned to face Tom. 'I think you, I and Austin here,' he inclined his head in the direction of the HR director, 'need to have a conversation don't you Tom? I'll just see Kate out first.'

As Kate threw Tom one last look she almost felt sorry for him. All the colour had drained from his face and he looked frightened. It occurred to her that Idella had been right – Tom had sent that one email as a decoy. A way of explaining how information might have passed between Allocott and the company he had been feeding it to, should his illegal bid rigging activities ever be suspected.

What he hadn't banked on was Allocott's own pro-active audit processes flagging the email for investigation. And he certainly hadn't thought it possible that anyone would uncover his own part in the anti-regulatory activity – least of all Kate. Now, the idiot was looking at certain dismissal. He would never get a job in finance again and he might even go to prison. With a family to support why oh why had he risked it?

As Kate, her lawyer and the Chairman rode down in the elevator, Bill turned to her and said gravely, 'I want you to know that we will investigate everything you have brought to us thoroughly and we will be in touch.' Then, as they exited the elevator and strode across the foyer he rested his hand on Kate's arm and said quietly, 'I can't tell you how sorry I am about all this. We *will* sort it all out Kate. You'll be back in the office in no time.'

'I'm not coming back Bill.'

He paused for a moment as if he was about to try and persuade her otherwise and then thought better of it. 'I'm sorry to hear that but I can't, in all honesty, say I blame you.' He shook his head at the whole sorry mess that was now his responsibility to clean up. 'What *do* you want?' he asked.

'A financial settlement.'

Bill nodded regretfully. 'Ok let's get this investigation out of the way and then we'll talk.'

Out on the street Kate turned to Idella. 'Thanks for being my 'lawyer' for the morning,' she said, feeling the weight that had been bearing down on her like a ton of bricks for the last three months suddenly vanish.

'It was a pleasure,' Idella said with a warm smile. 'If only to see the look on that lying shit's face when you pulled out all the evidence against him.' Kate couldn't bring herself to smile about that just yet, even though it was no less than Tom deserved.

Idella laid a hand on her friend's arm. 'They know you're telling the truth Kate,' she said gently. 'Even without the look on Tom's face that confirmed it for them. I could see it dawning on Bill Cranfield, the reason why this whole situation has made no sense to him these past months I've left more for them to find too.'

'Funny they never asked how we got hold of it? All that information on Tom?'

'Yeah funny that,' Idella said mysteriously. 'You might even be forgiven for thinking that Bill and I had worked together before.' Her eyes twinkled.

'He knows you?' Kate asked incredulously.

'I'm saying nothing more. You were great in there by the way.' Idella started to laugh. 'Have you ever thought of joining the legal profession?'

'Christ! Talk about out of the frying pan!'

Right come on then, it's Christmas Eve and you and I are most certainly in need of a glass of Champagne to celebrate a job well done. The hard work's over – it's time to have some fun!'

And they *had*. Kate smiled at the memory. Now, with all the upheaval behind her, Kate felt lighter, more free and had absolutely no clue as to what she was going to do next.

She had the germ of an idea. To offer bed and breakfast holidays with a book club theme. Remembering how she'd enjoyed reconnecting with books when she first arrived in Pine Tree Bay, she had the notion of offering guests the opportunity to read, discuss and enjoy literature for weeks at a time. She didn't know if it was possible or if people would be attracted to that type of holiday… but it was a thought… something to look into.

Not today however. Today Finn was taking her on a hike. Showing her the new wild camp sites he had staked out for the coming year's backwoods retreat. He had asked her over a drink in The Smugglers the previous evening. Would she mind casting a fresh eye over the sites he had chosen? She didn't mind one bit. In fact time was moving on – she'd best get into her hiking gear – Finn was picking her up in half and hour.

As she walked through the villa on her way to her bedroom, she heard her own footsteps echoing across the empty rooms. The house wasn't lacking much... except the furniture she'd ordered and perhaps another heartbeat. Maybe she should think about the pitter patter of tiny canine feet?

The life that three months ago had seemed parochial and boring suddenly seemed filled with endless possibilities. She had woken up to a new year, in her new house, in a new town... and she urged herself to savour this moment standing, as she was, on the brink of a new *life*.

She was just pulling on her hiking socks when a knock on the door told her that Finn was early. When she didn't answer, he called through the letterbox, 'Kate? Are you ready?'

She bounded down the stairs. *Yes!* She was more than ready.

Jem

Madeleine Beaver had returned to Pine Tree Bay back on Boxing Day, having spent the whole of December at her chateau in the South of France. Whilst there, she had been forced to face some home truths. No one from Pine Tree had tried to contact her, or called to wish her a Merry Christmas. It had been too much trouble, it seemed, to even lick a stamp – not one Christmas card from the town made it to France whilst Madeleine was off playing chatelain.

And so, following the embarrassment of the failed community centre coup, she had to concede the message was coming through loud and clear; Pine Tree had had enough of Madeleine Beaver for the time being. And, as Jem had listened to Madeleine relay all this, over video call, just before Christmas, she had neither agreed nor disagreed.

But never one to give in easily, Madeleine had come up with a *brainwave*; she was going to throw a New Year's Party. Not just a tepid evening of drinks and canapés, but a stonking huge carnival with lights and stalls and rides. As she had outlined the plan to Jem through the wizardry of FaceTime, Madeleine had looked wistfully into the distance. It would be the grand Beaver gesture – a gift to the community. It would cement her in the hearts of the community for all time.

Jem privately mused that a cement heart might be a fitting tribute to Madeleine, given the way she had treated Billy and Beryl, but she diplomatically avoided saying so. Instead she nodded enthusiastically and agreed that it was a great idea; she wasn't about to deprive Pine Tree Bay of a knees up, even if she did itch to tell the obnoxious woman exactly what she thought of her.

Tonight, however, on the evening of New Year's Day standing there on the lawns of Magnolia Mansions with Matthew, Jem was doubly glad that she had held her tongue. The scene was nothing short of breathtaking. Madeleine had gone all out. It *was* the grand gesture to end all grand gestures and this spectacle must surely have cost the earth.

From the meadow below, a sea of flashing lights dazzled their eyes. In the centre of the action, the lake was one long riot of colour, reflecting the carnival that was taking place around it. Fairground rides, stalls, festival marquees even a *stage* – where a rock band were currently blasting out their back catalogue – had been set up around the lake.

Hordes of people were snaking in and out of the throng whilst elaborately dressed stilt walkers carrying flaming torches floated through the crowd like neon, fire-breathing, monsters. Music and laughter and whoops of excitement floated up to the terraced gardens and it seemed that the whole of Pine Tree and the surrounding towns had braved the frosty conditions to join in with the festivities.

As they headed down the terraced steps to thread their way through the exuberant crowd, Matthew let out a low whistle. 'Now *this* is a party!'

'It's not a party. It's a bloody festival,' shrieked Jem. 'Madeleine said it was going to be the night to end all nights but,' Jem looked around her in disbelief, 'this is one hell of a PR exercise.'

'It's like a miniature Glastonbury,' said Matthew spying what looked like a silent disco full of people shuffling around with headphones at the opposite end of the meadow.

'Knowing Madeleine, she probably pulled in a favour from the team who *organise* Glastonbury!' Jem snorted.

Strolling around arm in arm they were both aware that their presence together was attracting more than a few second glances but it was the hostess herself who, with her usual measure of tact and diplomacy, swooped in to congratulate them on their restored coupledom. 'Jem, Matthew, how wonderful to see you both here, *together*.' Madeleine raised her eyebrows and nodded as she spoke and as usual there was no need for either of them to respond. Madeleine was quite capable of holding an entire conversation in mono. 'I for one, never believed the rumours,' she shook her head sagely and closed her eyes. 'I could tell from the moment I first saw you together that there was something special. Some indefinable *chemistry* between the two of you.'

Madeleine, oblivious to the fact that Matthew and Jem were looking more uncomfortable with every word that tumbled from her mouth, rattled on without pausing for breath. She raised her voice so that everyone in ear shot might tune in. 'Even when my housekeeper called me in France to tell me that you Matthew, had taken up with that Kate girl, I said, "Sheila, I don't believe it for a second!" And, of course,' she swept her hand over the two of them as if she were the magician who had repaired their severed relationship. '*Voila!* I was right.'

Neither Jem nor Matthew could think of what to say in response to this elaborate monologue and so an awkward silence ensued.

Undeterred Madeleine laid a hand on Jem's arm. 'Well now, you two enjoy the festivities. You've earned it. I am so pleased to hear that Frank has recovered and to think that you both joined him – in Canada for Christmas week – well, wasn't that thoughtful of you?' She looked from Jem to Matthew with a manufactured sincerity so transparent you could have wrapped a sandwich in it, before swiftly returning to her favourite topic of conversation. '*I* shall need a good long rest myself after all this I can tell you. I am completely and utterly exhausted!' Madeleine rolled her eyes and wiped an imaginary bead of sweat from her brow as if she had personally constructed all the attractions with her own bare hands.

Jem was just trying to think of something to bring the interminable conversation to a close, when the walkie-talkie that Madeleine had been so firmly clutching to her breast crackled into life.

'Madeleine darling.' Bernard's stately tones hissed and whined over the airways. 'We have something of a problem.'

Irritated at being dragged away from her audience Madeleine scowled at the radio. 'Well *what is it* Bernard?' she asked sharply. 'Spit it out for heaven sake!'

'You know the giant waterbed you ordered?'

'Ye-e-es.' Madeleine began to look worried.

'The one that you said would be a "cool chill out zone" for people resting in between attractions.'

'Yes Bernard, for goodness sake *do* get on with it!'

'Well it seems to have sprung a leak and we now have a sort of… *moat* forming around the perimeter.'

Madeleine shrieked and scurried off in the direction of the leaky bed, continuing to bark orders into the walkie-talkie as she bustled through the crowd. As they watched her retreating figure, Matthew and Jem turned slowly to face each other - both wondering which one of them was going to crack up first.

'You know,' Jem said once her laughter had subsided, 'I think that's the first conversation I've had with that woman where she didn't issue *me* with an order.'

'Ah well, you know why that is,' Matthew said with a knowing smile.

Jem gave him a puzzled look. 'Why?'

'You're Frank's granddaughter now. Or, to put it another way, you're the granddaughter of a rich, influential, captain of industry. You've just climbed the ranks from 'minion' to 'useful connection' in one swift move. Madeleine Beaver is about to become your best friend.'

Jem threw her head back and pretended to cry, 'Oh God help me.'

But Matthew had spotted his favourite ride of any at the funfair and he placed his hands on Jem shoulders to gently angle her towards it. 'Look!' He pointed.

'No way!'

'Yes, way.'

'I hate them.'

'That's because you never went on one with me.'

'You think?' Jem raised an unconvinced eyebrow. 'Anyway, we've got to go and meet up with Helena and the others.'

Matthew checked his watch. 'That's not for another half hour.'

'Well,' Jem cast around for another stalling technique. 'I want candy-floss.'

'Ok, you get candy-floss, I'll get in line.'

He wasn't giving up. Jem sighed reluctantly. 'Ok deal.'

But when she returned, clutching two sticks of the bright pink floss,

Matthew was nowhere to be seen. She was sure she had the right queue but her tall, broad shouldered boyfriend with his dark blonde hair was definitely not in it. Surely he *had* meant the Ghost Train and not some other ride? She frowned, scanning the crowd.

'Jem… Jem!' She suddenly heard Matthew shouting her name. 'Come on!' He was standing inside one of the cars waving madly at her to get on the ride before it disappeared into the tunnel.

Jem scrambled into action. Pushing her way past the patiently waiting crowd and rushing up the stairs to where the cars were lined up ready for the ride to begin, she already knew it was going to be too late. The one that Matthew was riding in was setting off. She wasn't going to make it.

Suddenly Matthew leapt out of the car and held it fast so it couldn't move on the rail. A voice came over the loud speaker. 'Sir! Get back in the car and do not hold up the ride!'

Matthew signalled to the man in the booth, pointing vigorously to Jem who was desperately scrambling toward him clutching the two candy-floss.

The man in the booth sighed and shook his head but powered down long enough for Jem to clamber into the car.

As they both took their seats Jem turned to Matthew. 'You made him wait for me!' she said breathlessly, handing him his stick of floss. Feeling inexplicably choked, her eyes glistened.

'Of course I did.' Matthew kissed her gently. 'You didn't think I'd set off without you?'

It was the point of no return; a stuttering jerk forward that almost gave them both whiplash. And, as the little car manoeuvred through the swing doors, into the dark and deeply scary unknown that lay beyond, Jem heard herself scream with delight.

If you enjoyed this book please rate and review the title on Amazon – this helps other readers of romantic fiction to find it. Thank you.

Acknowledgements

Thank you to Jade Jenkinson and Christine Hogg for their tireless efforts to shape-up this little world of Pine Tree Bay. Thanks to Joanna Penn, Rachael Herron, Mark Stay and Mark Desvaux for their encouragement and commitment to helping indie writers and publishers. Thanks to Michael for the support and the *time*. And of course, the hairy duo for always letting me know when it's time for a tea break.

About the Author

Gilly M Rose is originally from Yorkshire and lived and worked in London for fifteen years. After years of binge watching back to back episodes of *Escape To The Country*, she and her husband were finally able to achieve their long held dream of moving to South West Scotland where they now run a hospitality business by the sea. Gilly has a BA Hons. in Humanities and an MSc in Business Design. She spends her days preparing for guests and writing (though not necessarily in that order) and stomping around the beautiful forests of Dumfries and Galloway with her gorgeous Labrador boys.

Printed in Great Britain
by Amazon